K.C. MCMILLIAN

Kiana (K.C.) McMillian

Dedication

To my two sons, always remember that you can make your dream a reality no matter your position in life; I love you two. To my husband, thank you for believing in me; I love you! To Gran, thank you. I am finally following my dream. I love and miss you!

Trigger Warnings!

This book contains references to murder, violence, rape, anxiety, sex, kidnappings, and suicidal thoughts that some readers may find disturbing.

Readers' discretion is advised.

Special Thanks

Thank you for taking a chance on me and my story. I truly hope you enjoy reading Bright A Forbidden Love Story (*Second Edition*).

Special thanks to my fantastic alpha reader, Shalinie Rohit. I have no idea what I would have done without you! Thank you to my incredible beta reader, Author Louise Davis, for joining me on this journey. Thank you for pushing me to my limit and helping me to become a better writer. I don't know what I would have done without you!

Table of Contents

Introduction to Bright

Throughout history, supernatural creatures have lived discreetly amongst humans, divided into seven kingdoms. Each kingdom comprises vampires, werewolves, shapeshifters, witches, phoenixes, hybrids, and manticores. The vampire king rules over all of them.

King Abel Ronin is a tenacious, vile, and callous vampire who eradicated the manticores nearly four hundred years ago for not following the monarchy he set in place. He is determined to destroy another kingdom: the hybrids. King Abel taught the vampire kingdom to view hybrids as abominations.

The king's daughter, Akira, is a beautiful, kind-hearted, and pleasant vampire princess who disagrees with her father's methods.

Every year, the king sends his daughter and court to each of the kingdoms to recruit five of them to serve in his.

This year, Akira will be sent to the hybrid domain.

The king plans to annihilate the hybrid kingdom forever, but will his pure and selfless daughter stand in his way?

Akira will uncover a dark secret about her past, discover how powerful she is, and fall in love with the very creature her father detests.

Akira must determine whether she will obey her father's orders, follow her heart, or let the king decide.

Off To See the Abominations

Today, my father, the king of the greatest kingdom, *the vampires*, arranged for my friends and me to visit the domains of each to recruit five new members to serve in ours. The other supernatural creatures are not as appealing to me as the witches. They are my favorite because of their ancient wisdom, and they see me as an individual, not just the evil vampire king's daughter.

Monica Warren, the leader of the witch kingdom, has become friendly with me, and we talk for hours about the history and traditions of their coven. I place my complete trust in her and have a strong sense of belonging in her presence and among the other witches. Most vampires can recall when they were turned into one. Unfortunately, I have no memory of my transformation, which adds to the mystery surrounding my existence. I don't remember anything before my nineteenth birthday. The witches have been attempting to help me piece together fragments of my past behind my father's back, hoping to uncover the truth about my unique circumstances. However, they haven't succeeded in finding concrete answers. If my father knew what they were up to, he would stop at nothing to end their meddling. My father and mother have been dictating every aspect of my life and kept quiet about my origins. They told me I was sick when I became a vampire and fell into a coma for years. Yet, I've questioned their explanation, sensing that there was more to the story. I have added it to my extensive list of things my parents kept from me. Their constant surveillance and secrecy fueled my curiosity further, and none of the other vampires would give me answers when questioned. They were all under my parents' control, afraid to reveal the truth.

The hybrid kingdom, better known as *"the abominations,"* is half-vampire and half-werewolves. My father detests them. He said, *"They are horrendous creatures that should have never been created."*

Out of all the supernatural creatures that serve in our kingdom, the hybrids are the only ones who didn't send a selected few, and my father is not okay with that. He believes their refusal to participate is a sign of disrespect and defiance toward the kingdom. It drove his anger and intensified his desire to maintain control over them. Today is the last day for the hybrids to comply with my father's demands, and tensions are running high.

"If they know what's best for them, they will send soldiers to serve the king, even if it's just one or two. I'm not sure why they believe they are so above the law." Shelly sighs, sitting on my bed, her irritation evident in her voice as she adds, "I just hope they come to their senses soon before it's too late."

Gripping my curly hair in between my fingers and brushing it. "I don't understand what the fuss is. We have plenty of supernatural creatures to serve us. Why do we need these abominations? I just don't get it."

Shelly looks at me with a mix of disbelief and concern in her fiery red eyes. "It's the principle of the matter, Akira. They are showing direct disrespect to King Abel by undermining his authority." Shelly explains, hoping to shed some light on the situation. In a moment of frustration, she brushes her silky blonde hair that complements her pale skin away from her face and sighs.

Despite understanding the logistics of why we must go there and why it is disrespectful, I simply don't want to go. I've been taught that hybrids are abominations and not to be trusted; hence, I don't feel comfortable going to their kingdom and being around them.

My gaze meets Shelly's, and I tell her she is right.

Shelly is one of my best friends, more like a sister than a friend. She and my other friend, Sophia, are the only two vampires in this kingdom I spend most of my time with. We are always there for each other, supporting and understanding one another.

Shelly carries herself with an air of confidence, and despite her striking appearance, she is down-to-earth and has a kind heart. She and her older sister, Melonie, are loyal followers of my father, King Abel. Still, there are some things they disagree with, like enslaving humans.

My father sends out guards to kidnap innocent humans every month. They are used for food or to serve as slaves. Some vampires in our kingdom only drink animal blood, and a handful of loyal followers drink from humans, including my father and mother. Still, *most* of them consume human blood if there is a battle. Drinking from humans increases our strength tremendously; however, it's a controversial practice. I only feed on animals, and by doing so, I'm able to walk in the daylight and live among humans if my father would *allow it.*

My father also insists on having tournaments known as *"The Battle of Anaik,"* in which two humans are pitted against each other to death, and whoever succeeds becomes a vampire. These tournaments serve as a way for our kind to replenish our numbers and ensure our survival. However, it's barbaric and inhumane. My father thinks he's a *god* who can judge who is worthy of being granted immortality. I do question the morality and ethics behind such a brutal selection process, and I long for a day when vampires and humans in our realm can coexist peacefully without the need for such extreme measures. And if I oversaw this kingdom, I would command every vampire to feed on animals, not humans, except for consenting humans who willingly offer themselves as donors in case of war, or we could at least go to the closest blood transfusion center. I would also replace the term "slaves" with "employees" or "citizens." We need workers to keep the kingdom flourishing, but why do we refer to them as *"slaves"?* We should acknowledge their value and contributions and pay them—

"You're doing it again," Shelly says, breaking my reverie with a gentle smile.

Furrowing my brows, I cock my head to the side. "What am I doing?"

"You're daydreaming about how you would rule this kingdom differently," she responds, her voice filled with amusement. Realizing she's right, I giggle and throw my hairbrush at her at the speed of light. She, of course, sees it coming because of our heightened senses and effortlessly catches the hairbrush in mid-air.

"I do not want to rule this kingdom; I just wish my father wasn't so evil," I mutter.

"He is not evil. He knows what's best for the kingdom." Shelly says deadpan.

My phone dings with a message notification, interrupting our conversation. It's a text message from Sophia.

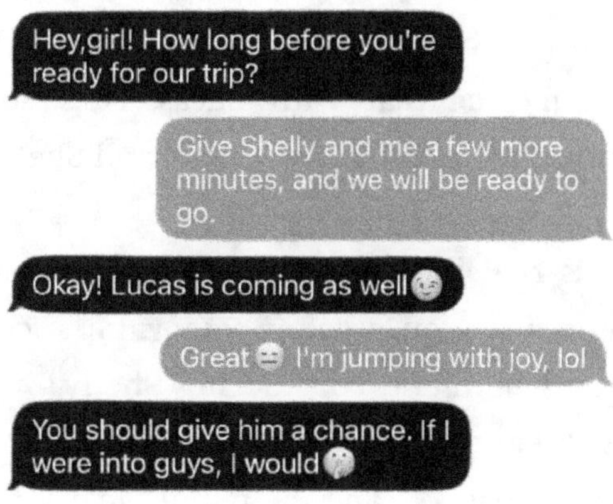

Rolling my eyes, I throw my phone on the bed. Sophia always knows how to make me laugh. She's five-three like me, curvy, with curly black hair contrasting beautifully with her sparkling violet eyes and olive skin. Her smile is radiant, and she has an uplifting energy.

"Who was that?" Shelly asks.

"Just Sophia, making her usual witty comments. Lucas is also coming with us."

Shelly smirks mischievously and says, "It wouldn't be a trip without 'Lover Boy Lucas' tagging along, would it?"

Rolling my eyes once more. "Oh, please, he's just a friend. I'm not interested in a physical relationship with him."

Shelly chuckles. "I don't get it. Lucas is one of the hottest guys here."

Sucking in the air and exhaling. "Looks aren't everything, you know. We don't connect romantically, and I don't feel a spark with him. He doesn't feel like my mate or someone I am fated to be with, like in the books I have read. I want to find a love like that, and I don't see that with Lucas. He's not someone I'm destined to be with for eternity." I rant, and Shelly lifts a brow at me.

"Girl, this is real life, not one of your fictional stories. How long has it been since you let a hot, sexy vamp rock your world?"

Pausing for a moment, considering Shelly's words, she has a point—*maybe* I have been too caught up in my romanticized version of love. Still, I can't help but yearn for that intense connection, that undeniable chemistry. And the truth is, I've never given myself to another vampire in that way, and until I find someone to feel that *spark* with, I probably won't.

Covering my cheeks with my hand, I chuckle in response. "Maybe one day I'll let go of my reservations and let a hot, sexy vamp rock my world. Until then, I'll keep searching for that undeniable chemistry."

We change the subject to something more cheerful and finish some minor packing before heading downstairs to the main entrance of our incredible castle.

We live in Hawaii on a small island called Sand Island. Not many humans live here, so Father captures them from nearby populated areas. He usually sends his guards to fetch homeless humans because *"no one cares for them."* The witches here cast a spell over the island to keep us hidden from the outside world. Therefore, it is as if we are in our own realm, where time works differently. When it is daylight here, it is nighttime in the real world. The force field is only visible to the magical creatures comprising the remaining six kingdoms. According to my father, the manticores did not follow his rules, so he ended them. Thus, only six kingdoms remain.

Our castle has been standing for centuries, conjured by the witches who reside in our domain. When you walk through the force field on Sand Island's beach, you will see walls that are about eighty feet tall and made of bricks that have been carefully crafted and enchanted to withstand any magical attacks. The witches cast a *"no entry"* spell using my father's blood to prevent rogue supernatural creatures from climbing the wall. The only way in is through a brown wooden door that two people must lower simultaneously. Once you are through, you will see a cobblestone walkway about a mile long that leads directly to the courtyard, surrounded by villas for the vampires. The walkway is lined with ancient oak trees, their branches intertwining overhead to create a natural canopy. The air carries the sweet scent of wildflowers, which the humans planted to add a touch of color to the otherwise mystical surroundings. A water fountain made from pure gold sits at the center of the courtyard, its cascading streams and lush garden sparkling under the sunlight. Rosa, one of the witches, cast a spell for sunlight to only shine in the area surrounding the fountain, allowing all the plants and crops to grow.

You enter a magnificent foyer through the double arch bronze doors with brown hardwood floors that gleam with a polished finish, and the black and chestnut brown décor exudes an elegant ambiance. Paintings of my father, mother, myself, and some of my father's loyal comrades adorn the walls. Underneath each portrait is a secret passageway to various parts of the castle. Straight ahead is a grand staircase that leads to the royal chambers, and down the hallway on the opposite side is another staircase that leads to the suites for the supernatural, who serve the kingdom. There are also ornate elevators made of gold and crystal that are located in the back that transport between the different levels of the castle that the vampires use, while the humans use the rocky front elevators to cater to our needs and to get to rooms on the lower level. My father forbids them to use the back elevators because they are not *worthy* of such treatment.

The massive kitchen is on the main level of the castle. It is equipped with state-of-the-art appliances and white graphite countertops and is stocked with the finest blood. The animal and human blood are stored in a giant walk-in freezer to maintain their freshness. The freezer is meticulously organized, with separate sections for different blood types and careful labeling to prevent any mix-ups. Our staff ensures that the blood supply is always well-stocked and readily available. The dining area is adjacent to the kitchen. It has a grand marble table that can accommodate up to twenty guests. To the right is the living room, furnished with sectional sofas and a one-hundred-inch Samsung flat-screen TV. Shelly and I redecorated the castle and modernized it from its Gothic glory, and I'm glad we did.

Instead of taking one of the tunnels to the back of the castle, Shelly and I take one of the secret passageways behind the large painting of my father to get to the castle's underground garage quickly. We have vehicles, motorcycles, dirt bikes, four private jets, and a helicopter parked down there.

"Are you all ready for your trip?" My mother asks as we're loading the jet.

"Yes, Queen Aika," Shelly responds.

My mother nods. "Make sure you always stick together. The hybrids cannot be trusted."

Shelly and I exchange glances, understanding the gravity of my mother's warning.

Lucas finishes loading the jet with our belongings, and his eyebrows pull together. "Of course, Queen Aika. Although I am unsure why the king insists on having them in our quarters, they are such vile creatures!"

My mother agrees with Lucas. "A selected few from every kingdom must serve the king. Though, I understand your concerns."

Lucas accepts my mother's explanation. "I suppose you're right, Queen Aika."

"Stay together and make sure you all are back by next week for the tournament!" My father's voice booms as he approaches and stands tall beside my mother, his voice commanding attention.

We nod in unison. Whenever we visit each kingdom, we always stay for one week.

"Why wouldn't we be back by then, Father? It's not like we want to stay there any longer than we have to," I insist.

"Of course," he says knowingly. "I will see you all in one week." My father turns and strides away, leaving us to prepare for our departure.

We make our way to the parked aircraft. Shelly, Sophia, Lucas, my father's guards, Kaden and Kade, Ava, and our pilot, Mr. Ryan Howard, accompany me on this trip. Ryan is another abomination. He's half-vampire and half-human, so he doesn't belong to a kingdom. His kind serves in ours as additional servants or guards. I've never understood why the hybrids have a domain, and the half-vampire and half-human populations don't. Still, I wouldn't dare ask my father those questions. We gather on the jet and head to the hybrid kingdom in Antarctica.

While we're in the air, Lucas sits in the unoccupied seat beside me. Lucas is a skilled vampire known for his bravery and loyalty.

"Hey, Akira. How are you?" Lucas asks, his deep voice resonating through our private jet.

"I'm doing well, Lucas. And you?"

Lucas flashes me his incredible smile. "I'm great. Anywhere you are is always a good place to be."

I should feel something from his words, but I don't. Instead, I feel a sense of emptiness, as if something is missing. Lucas is a handsome man. He's tall and athletically built. His chiseled features, piercing blue eyes, and milky skin never fail to captivate those around him. However, despite his undeniable charm, a part of me is unaffected by his physical attractiveness. I still tried to give it a shot by going on a date with him. Sadly, I didn't feel a spark the first time we kissed. The spark I'm looking for is a deeper connection, a sense of chemistry that goes beyond just physical attraction. You can feel it throughout your body. It's not something I have with Lucas, not to mention he worships my father.

Folding my arms, I squint. "Very smooth," I say to Lucas after an awkward silence.

Lucas chuckles, his eyes searching for a way to salvage the moment. "I'm looking forward to returning to the castle for the tournament. The twins and I picked up very revolting humans."

Lucas tries to impress me; unfortunately, I'm repulsed. He and the twins are often sent to retrieve humans for the tournaments. They enjoy it, which makes me sick to my stomach.

Pursing my lips. "Oh really?"

He raises an eyebrow at my disinterest in the subject. "Why

aren't you a fan of the tournament? Whoever wins becomes one of us, which expands our kingdom."

The hairs on the back of my neck stand up, and my lips twist into a frown. "The idea of turning humans into one of us against their will doesn't sit right with me. It feels unethical. Did you ever stop to think that maybe they don't want to be like us and taken to a place full of bloodthirsty monsters?"

Lucas's brows knit together, and he shakes his head at my explanation. "Why do you have to be so dark, Akira?" He places his hand on my thigh and gently squeezes it, but I flinch beneath his touch. "We are saving them. We are giving them a chance at a new life, free from the limitations and struggles of their human existence. And we bring them to our arena to fight to the death to see who is worthy enough to be something more. It is a *gift*, not a curse, and we're not monsters, Akira."

And that twisted thinking is the reason I will never be with him.

Covering my mouth, I shake my head, unable to comprehend his perspective. "Whatever you say, Lucas," I mutter.

He nudges me, a small smile tugging at the corners of his lips. "You'll see the beauty in it all one day, Akira."

Shaking my head once more, I'm unable to fathom how he could view such brutality as *beauty*. Our differences will always be too vast to bridge.

The Vile Creatures Are on the Way

The vampire king's daughter and court are visiting our kingdom today to retrieve five of our finest soldiers to serve her wretched father. Rumor has it that the king's daughter possesses unparalleled innocence and beauty in all the realms; we must not underestimate the power and influence of the king's court. Evil runs in their bloodline. *All of them!* Clenching and unclenching my fist, I head to my parents' bedroom.

Storming in, I nearly separate the door from its hinges. "Mother, why must we meet with the princess and her court? Their intentions cannot be trusted, and we risk endangering our kingdom by involving ourselves with them!" My words tumble out with an intense mix of annoyance and concern. "We have been avoiding their requests for years. Why is Father obliging them now?" I ask, my eyes narrowing as I await an explanation.

Mother takes a deep breath. "My child, we must tread carefully. Though their reputation precedes them, your father's decisions are not made lightly or without careful consideration. There may be an opportunity for diplomacy that could benefit our kingdom in unforeseen ways," she reasons, her voice calm and measured.

"How will handing over five of our best soldiers ensure our safety?" I say through gritted teeth, my wolf threatening to emerge from within me. "Who knows what King Abel will do with them once they are in his possession?"

Mother's expression intensifies as she squeezes my shoulder. "My child, your father has considered all possibilities. He believes this alliance is our best chance for stability and protection."

The thought of diplomacy with the vampire king unsettles me. Vampires are repulsive creatures that influenced the other kingdoms' hatred toward us! The wolf inside me growls in protest, sensing potential danger in the unknown possibilities of this alliance.

My brother, Claude, appears from the back of the room. "Let it go, Troy!" He huffs. "Father has decided, and we must trust his judgment. If he doesn't hand over five warriors to the vampire kingdom, the king will send his *best* soldiers to attack us. Diplomacy is our only option to avoid bloodshed and protect our people. None of us know what sort of powers that man has collected over the years, and we are certainly not prepared to face his entire army!"

We ignored the vampire king's request for years; now, our defiance seems to have caught up with us. Trying to suppress the anger bubbling inside me, I exhale an exasperated breath.

King Abel Ronin believe vampires are superior to all the other kingdoms. The truth is that our hybrid nature grants us an advantage over them. Hybrids were once werewolves. However, my father sought to create a new breed. Years ago, he struck a deal with an ancient supernatural god. It was believed that this god despised vampires and wanted to wipe them out. Father intended to be stronger than them, so the god gave my father his blood mixed with the blood of a vampire, making him the very first hybrid. He turned his back on his original pack to start a new one. As the years passed, he gained more followers, and his new pack grew in numbers and strength.

Human or animal blood is sufficient for our survival, along with the consumption of human food. Our heightened senses make us faster than them. While they may possess certain powers and abilities, our combination of wolf and vampire traits makes us a formidable force to be reckoned with.

King Abel Ronin is a coward who has been in power for many years!

There is a knock on the door, and Claude opens it.

"The vampires are here," Dawn says, her expression turning grave as she looks between me, Claude, and my mother.

Dawn is a beautiful, light brown-skinned woman, a fearless warrior who has always been loyal to our family. Her shimmering gray eyes command attention and respect, and she has the unique ability of telekinesis, which allows her to move anything with her mind. Dawn is attracted to me, and although she knows almost everything there is to know about me and would be the perfect match, we mutually decided we didn't want to jeopardize our friendship. She is one of my closest friends here. The vampire king is oblivious to her kind of power, and if he knew, he would surely try to exploit it for his own gain.

Over the centuries, King Abel has built his kingdom by capturing supernatural beings with remarkable gifts. He has always sought to harness and use their powers to strengthen his rule. The five hybrids my father is handing over do not possess any power, but they are skilled fighters.

"I'll let Father know," Claude says as he and my mother exit the room.

Dawn's plump lips twist into a frown, and she folds her arms. "How could the king hand over our people like this? It's like he's playing right into King Abel's hands!" She sighs heavily, brushing a red strand of hair to the side with a look of anguish across her face.

"He didn't have a choice, Dawn." I try to convince her and *myself*.

Dawn flutters her hand toward me, waving me off. "He always has a choice, Troy. He is the king." She shoots back, her slender figure gliding toward the door to exit my parents' chambers.

We silently walk down the hallway to the entrance, where the vampires will meet us. My inner wolf pleads to come to the surface and do his worst. Still, I must keep him at bay. I don't know what *gifts* these vampires possess, and I cannot put my people at risk.

There has been no sign of my father yet, and since I'm the prince of the hybrid kingdom, I am expected to take charge in his absence. Which I am not looking forward to. The vampires will stay with us for a week, and within that week, we will show them how we live, and they will train one-on-one with our soldiers.

The vampires walk in, exuding superiority, their eyes scanning their surroundings. The atmosphere is tense as both kingdoms eye each other warily. I'm momentarily distracted from the friction when my gaze catches sight of the most beautiful woman I have ever laid eyes on. Her regal presence draws everyone's attention. She possesses a certain aura that sets her apart from the rest of the vampires she came with, and her smell is the most intoxicating scent when she is within my reach. She doesn't have the same scent I am used to, and I want to devour her. She has a nice, slim shape, a fair complexion, and long, curly black hair. Her hazel eyes mildly sparkle, and her innocent glow ignites a primal instinct within me. She *must* be the infamous princess.

She brushes her loose curls to the side and smiles softly at everyone. "Hello, I am Akira, and—"

"*Princess* Akira," the blond-haired vampire cuts in.

Akira clears her throat, gives the vampire a stare, and starts again. "Hello. I am Princess Akira, and we were sent by King Abel and Queen Aika." She bows toward me.

Our eyes briefly meet, and a flicker of intrigue passes between us. She looks away quickly, her cheeks flushing with a hint of pink, but she composes herself.

So stunned by her purity, my mind goes blank, and I struggle to form a coherent sentence. My heart gallops beneath my skin when she blinks rapidly, waiting for a response. Dawn scowls, unimpressed by my infatuation with the beautiful princess, and Claude comes to my rescue.

"Hello, Princess Akira. I'm Prince Claude." He says with a bow. "And this silent chump is Prince Troy." He sends me a subtle nudge, urging me to speak up, but I only nod.

Princess Akira smiles and nods, acknowledging Claude's introduction. "It's a pleasure to meet you, Prince Claude, and Prince Troy," she says graciously. "Thank you for welcoming us to your kingdom."

Claude doesn't have as intense a hatred toward vampires as I do; he gives everyone a fair chance, which is an awful character trait on his behalf.

"It's our pleasure, princess. Please follow us to where you all will stay," Claude says as he points in the direction that will lead us to the suite.

Princess Akira gracefully falls into step behind Claude, and her court trails behind. As we walk, I sneak glances at her. I have not seen such beauty in over fifty years and have been worldwide. There is something about her that is captivating.

The exquisite princess clears her throat and pushes forward on her toes when we reach the suite, breaking me from my intrusive gawking. She turns to Claude and thanks him for his guidance, expressing her appreciation, and then to me. "Excuse me, Prince Troy, when will King John join us?"

"My apologies, Princess Akira," I say, finally regaining my composure. Offering her a reassuring grin. "King John should join us shortly."

Princess Akira gives me a small smile and nods. She seems to sense that something is off. However, she doesn't press any further, and I'm relieved.

Over the years, I have met with many vampires; none were as polite as she is, and considering the stories I had heard about vampires, her charm and grace are unexpected.

The princess and her court close the door to their suite.

Claude waves me over, his eyes filling with amusement. "Are you okay?"

"Yes, I'm fine. Why do you ask?"

Claude chuckles, "You seemed a bit off, and you went mute back there!"

My brows knit together at my brother's observation. Turning to face him. "I—I didn't go mute!" I reply, slightly offended. "I guess I wasn't expecting her to be so...pleasant."

"Dude, you froze! It was like you were star-struck," Claude teases. "Did she put you under a spell or something?" He smirks and nudges me playfully.

Shaking my head at his exaggeration, my lips curve into a smirk. "No, she didn't put me under a spell. I was just surprised, that's all."

"Sure, sure. Just remember to *speak* next time you see her."

My brother irritates me, but he is right. The princess's charm and grace bewildered me. It was as if she had cast a spell on me with just her presence.

Still, she is the vampire king's daughter, and I cannot let her fool me.

Not So Vile After All

ntarctica is cold, covered in ice, and depressing—the complete opposite of Hawaii. We arrived at the hybrid kingdom headquarters just after sunset and were greeted by the king's royal entourage. Their kingdom is surrounded by a breathtaking landscape of towering mountains and vast glaciers. When we step inside, the interior is a stark contrast to the icy surroundings. It's warm and inviting, with cozy furnishings and vibrant artwork adorning the cave's walls, far from what I was expecting. Still, they could benefit from an enhanced lighting system. The other vampires seemed unimpressed by the environment, their expressions reflecting their disapproval.

I exchange pleasantries with the members when my eyes are drawn to the hybrid prince, a handsome, dark-skinned man. He stands tall, appearing to be at least six feet, with a muscular physique, and his stormy gray eyes hold a depth of knowledge and wisdom. *He is so good-looking.* However, he is a hybrid, and I have been taught to be cautious of their kind, so I will not let his attractive appearance fool me.

Introducing myself with a polite smile and maintaining a neutral tone, I forgot to mention my title. *Wow! Way to not let his good looks distract me.* Of course, Shelly cuts in and corrects me.

Prince Claude extends a warm welcome and leads us down to where we will be staying. We enter the suite, and Prince Claude and Troy walk away.

"Wow! I can't believe we're staying in a cave. This suite is beautiful! It's like something out of a fairytale." Shelly says.

It seems like the others are just as impressed as I am. This suite is unlike anything I've ever seen before. It has four king-sized beds with luxurious silk sheets and plush pillows. The bathroom is equally extravagant, with a large jacuzzi and a rainfall shower.

Sophia's eyes are wide. "I suppose this is not so bad for a cave."

"Who knew the hybrids had style?" Lucas says as he surveys the room and places our bags on the floor.

Ava strides around the room, observing the suite in more detail, her golden-brown hair swaying from side to side with each step and ocean-blue eyes and pale skin shining with delight. Ava is very grim and doesn't say much. However, she has fought alongside my father for centuries, and her loyalty and bravery are unmatched. For reasons unknown, she never speaks unless it is vital. She is also one of my father's *"secret weapons."* Which means she possesses a special *gift*.

"I claim this bed!" Sophia declares, plunging face-first onto the mattress.

That leaves three unoccupied beds.

Ava claims one, followed by Shelly, who chooses the bed closest to the door. She *always* has to be near an exit. Lucas, the twins, and I have to select a bed to sleep in.

"Kade and I will just sleep on the floor." Kaden shrugs his shoulders.

"We don't mind," Kade adds.

"It looks like we have to share." Lucas grins at me. He looks like he hit the jackpot or something.

Suppressing a groan. "I guess so," I say through gritted teeth. "Let's set some boundaries." I continue. "Or you could just sleep on the floor like the twins," I say under my breath.

A knock on the door distracts me from the smirk on Lucas's face. I swiftly go to answer it, hoping for a momentary escape from the awkward situation.

Prince Troy is standing at the door, his regal presence filling the room. My gaze settles on his, and I nearly lose my will to breathe when he speaks.

"Princess Akira," he politely nods.

"Prince Troy." I greet him with a small smile. "What brings you here?"

My stomach is doing flips like it's practicing to compete in a gymnastics tournament.

"King John has arrived. He has requested that you all join us for dinner," he informs me.

My heart involuntarily skips a beat at his invitation. "Thank you for including us. We will be honored to join your family for dinner."

A smile tugs at the corners of Prince Troy's lips. "I'm glad to hear that. Please follow me to the dining area."

We follow Prince Troy as he leads the way. The cave's beauty surrounds us as we walk through the magnificent hallways to the dining room, where King John and Queen Celine greet us. The room is adorned with elegant gold chandeliers, their arms holding candles that cast a warm glow. A large oak table commands the space; its surface is engraved with carvings of fierce werewolf teeth and graced with the delicate beauty of fine China.

"Pleased to meet you, Princess Akira, and your fellow court," King John says.

King John is the typical tall, dark, and handsome man. He has fierce gray eyes and brown skin. He is very polite and yet stern.

Nodding in response, we exchange formalities.

"Please join us for dinner." Queen Celine gestures towards the empty seats at the table.

She is an exquisite, voluptuous, brown-skinned woman and has beautiful gray eyes and short brown, kinky hair.

Lucas clears his throat. "We're vampires. We don't eat food," he says in a tone that vibrates through my body, and not in a good way.

The room's mood shifts as Lucas's words hang in the air. Queen Celine's expression remains composed, but Prince Troy's eyes narrow at our dietary differences. He opens his mouth to speak. However, before he can say anything, Queen Celine raises her hand, signaling for him to stop.

"We are aware of what you eat. We are half-vampires," Claude chimes in, "but unfortunately, we don't live in a human-populated area, so we can only provide you with animal blood."

"Thank you," I say with a smile, and we all go to the dining table for dinner.

Lucas pulls my chair out for me, a gesture that doesn't go unnoticed by Prince Troy, and he shoots Lucas a cold glare when he sits next to me.

The servants come in with animal blood for the vampires and human food for the hybrids. I wonder how the hybrids supply themselves with food when they live in a secluded area like this. Anyhow, that is a question for later.

The servers place the crimson liquid in front of us and an array of dishes for the hybrids. They dig into their roasted meats while the vampires drink from their blood-filled glasses.

Once we finish our perspective meals, we head into the battle room. It is filled with weapons and training equipment.

Prince Troy waves his hand towards a group of hybrids his father, King John, has selected for mine. "Princess Akira, this is Christian, Alex, Felix, James, and Melissa."

They nod in unity, and I nod as well. The men are tall; even Melissa must be at least six feet. Her complexion is olive-toned, and she has grayish eyes that sparkle and long purple curls. The guys look like models, and I'm shocked by their handsomeness and muscular builds. Shelly's eyes widen as she gazes at all of them, particularly Felix, and Sophia has her eyes set on Melissa.

Shelly whispers to me, "Wow, they're all so attractive."

Sophia leans in and adds, "Melissa is hot."

I'm sure if they weren't hybrids, Sophia and Shelly would be all over them. We wrap up our meeting with the new soldiers and return to our suite.

While getting ready for bed, the prince's shimmering gray eyes flash in my mind. His stern gaze seems to hold many secrets. The prince is so handsome, and what was that look he gave Lucas at dinner? *Is he interested in me, too?* I shouldn't be thinking about him; his hybrid status complicates things. Still, I'm a little smitten.

"Full disclosure, if the hybrids weren't our sworn enemies, I would totally go for that Felix guy," Shelly confesses to me, which takes my mind away from my own thoughts about the prince.

"I know what you mean." The words escape my lips before I can stop myself.

Shelly's brows snap together as her eyes widen with curiosity.

"I meant to say—I already knew you had eyes for him." I quickly backtrack, trying to cover up my slip of the tongue, and thankfully, she doesn't see through my poorly executed deflection.

"You know me so well," she chuckles.

For a moment, I think about the weighing consequences of telling her the truth about my attraction toward Prince Troy.

"Who says that the hybrids have to be our enemies?" I question.

Shelly raises an eyebrow, clearly intrigued by my statement. "Your father forbids it because he doesn't trust the hybrids."

She's right. I can't allow myself to be distracted by the prince's good looks, and I internally groan at the dynamics of the kingdom and head to my bed.

Lucas's excitement radiates off him as he joins me. Turning to face him, my gaze meets his so he knows how serious I am.

Choosing my words carefully. "You know we are just friends, right?" I question, emphasizing the word *friends*.

Lucas's smile falters, and he swallows hard before responding, "Yeah, of course. I know that." His voice lacks conviction. "I am just happy to be part of your life," he adds, trying to hide his disappointment.

His affection for me is genuine; unfortunately for him, I don't feel the same.

"I value our friendship too, Lucas," I say sincerely, "however, both of us need to be on the same page."

He nods, and I turn in the opposite direction.

As my eyelids fall shut, my hope is to fantasize about the prince because if he is beyond my reach in reality, in my dreams, he's mine.

It Is Just a Dream

Tears stream down my face. I'm desperately pleading with my father to stop him from attacking the man I love. My voice trembles as I beg him to listen. Instead, he ignores me and orders one of his minions to fly me right into a brick wall. Falling in and out of consciousness and glancing around, the place I called home is up in flames, and the people I love are fighting for their lives against my evil father. Innocents are plunging to the ground, paralyzed by the pain, and their screams pierce through the air. The chaos and destruction unfold before my eyes.

"Akira, wake up! You're having a nightmare," Lucas shouts, shaking me.

My heart is pounding in my chest, relieved to find myself safe in bed. Still, the images of the devastation and my father's vengeance haunt me, and I gasp for air.

Lucas's shoulders sink, and his lips form a straight line. "You were screaming, Akira. Are you okay? What were you dreaming about?"

I contemplate telling him for a moment but then ultimately decide against sharing the details of my nightmare.

"It was just a bad dream, Lucas. Nothing to worry about."

Lucas is in a daze on the bed as I scurry to the bathroom in a flash.

Night after night, the same dream plagues me, filling my mind with horror. *What could the dream mean?* The haunting nightmares have caused dark circles to form underneath my eyes. Staring at my reflection in the mirror, I don't recognize the woman looking back at me. Turning the faucet on, I splash cold water against my face. However, it does little to wash away the disturbing images that still play over and over in my head. Undressing and stepping into the warm water, I let the liquid cascade over my body, relaxing me in the process.

Feeling slightly refreshed after my shower, Lucas is waiting for me on the bed when I exit the bathroom.

My eyes scan the area. "Where is everyone?"

"The twins went to find human blood for us, and then they will meet with Shelly, Sophia, and Dawn," he replies.

"Who is Dawn? And why do we need human blood?"

"We must drink it to be at our full strength to train with the hybrids, Akira. And Dawn is one of the hybrid soldiers."

Furrowing my brows, I chew on my bottom lip.

Consuming human blood is immoral; where are they going to find some? I wonder if Dawn was that beautiful, light brown-skinned woman standing beside Prince Troy yesterday. Is there more to her relationship with the prince than just one of the hybrid soldiers?

"Akira?" Lucas says, interrupting my ongoing inner thoughts.

"Where is Ava?" I don't remember seeing anyone when I hastened to the bathroom before.

"She went to the jet with Ryan to check on the supplies. They should be back soon." Lucas's lips curve into a slight grin. "Come sit next to me." He pats the mattress with his hand.

Sitting beside him, Lucas takes my hand in his. "Akira, are you okay?"

The silence stretches between us as I consider telling him about my recurring dream, where my home is on fire and war is on the horizon. I can't shake off the feeling that a more profound message is hidden within it. It's as if my subconscious is desperately trying to communicate something important, yet I struggle to decipher the meaning. *War?*

Lucas snaps his fingers, breaking my reverie.

Forcing a small smile. "Lucas, I promise you I am fine. There is nothing wrong."

Even if I wanted to confide in him, he would report it back to my father.

He gives my hand a gentle squeeze. Our gazes meet, and I can see he's having an internal battle of his own.

A slight grin forms on my lips. "Spit it out, Lucas."

His expression remains serious, and he takes a deep breath before finally speaking up. "Akira, I love you more than just a *friend*."

The weight of his confession lingers, and I struggle to find the proper response to convey my feelings without hurting him.

"Lucas, you mean a lot to me too, but I don't think I can—"

A knock on the door interrupts our conversation, and we both turn our heads toward it. Lucas stands to his feet, crossing the room at lightning speed to answer it. He opens the door, and his lips turn into a frown.

"Uh, hello, Lucas. Is the princess here?" A deep voice asks.

Locking eyes with the prince, I stand to my feet in a flash.

Prince Troy looks between Lucas and me. "Am I interrupting something?" His eyes darken as he awaits our response.

"No, not at all. We were just having a conversation." I quickly respond.

Lucas adds, "We were actually discussing something important—"

"But it can wait," I interject. "Is there something you want, Prince Troy?" I ask, trying to divert the attention away from Lucas and my conversation.

"Yes. Are you two available to join us in the battle room to get more acquainted with the soldiers?" He asks.

"Of course," I say, hurrying to exit the room and out of this awkward situation with Lucas.

Lucas looks like he wants to stop me. However, he follows instead.

As we walk to the battle room, there's an uncomfortable silence between the three of us. Lucas remains quiet with his eyes fixed on the ground while Prince Troy and I exchange occasional glances, struggling to form small talk. I've never felt this way around a guy before; it's exhilarating and nerve-wracking, leaving me unsure of how to act or what to say.

When we arrive at the battle room, I notice the twins' training with Felix and Christian. Shelly and Sophia are teamed up with Melissa and Dawn. Alex and James are with Claude. I can smell the metallic scent of blood the twins retrieved, and I'm embarrassed. Prince Troy's eyebrows knit together when he catches a whiff, and my mind reels. I'm not sure if the hybrid kingdom has ever drunk human blood, but his reaction suggests that they haven't or don't. Lucas offers me some, and I decline and head to the sidelines with Troy while Lucas joins the twins. Lucas seems in better spirits now that he's fed.

"Is that human blood they are drinking?" The prince asks, his brows narrowing, already knowing the answer.

Unsure of how to respond. "Y–yes," I hesitate.

The prince's expression darkens slightly as he processes my response.

"Not all vampires drink human blood. Some of us only drink animals." I defend my kind.

The prince's eyes narrow, with a hint of skepticism in them. "Every vampire has to consume human blood at some point, correct?"

"Yes, when we are preparing for a battle or to complete a vampire transition," I reply, trying to find common ground with the prince. "However, outside of those circumstances, some vampires choose to feed only on animals. Let me ask you this. How did you become a hybrid? Didn't you have to drink human blood to complete the transformation?"

He looks away, and I can tell he is trying to keep an open mind by considering the possibility that not all vampires are bloodthirsty monsters.

The prince's frown softens. "We consumed animal blood, not human, to complete our transformation."

A quietness fills the space between us as we gaze in opposite directions.

"Do you prefer humans over animals?" He asks, interrupting the silence.

"I only feed on animals and abstain from consuming humans unless necessary, and even then, I would rather consume from a blood bag."

The prince raises an eyebrow, intrigued by my response. "Interesting," he replies, disbelief evident in his voice.

"I'm a vegetarian, in a way," I add, attempting to lighten the mood.

A slight smirk tugs at the corner of his lips.

"Have you ever consumed human blood before? You're half-vampire." I say.

The prince chuckles, his skepticism fading. "No, we eat regular food. If we drank blood, it would be animal."

"What about your wolf form? Do you hunt for prey in that appearance?" I ask, genuinely curious about the prince's abilities as a hybrid.

The prince shakes his head, a sexy smile playing on his lips. "No, my wolf's form is purely for defense and speed. I don't have the same instincts as full-blooded werewolves. I do not hunt my prey."

Our conversation flows naturally now that we've gotten past

the initial tension, and I'm intrigued. I no longer understand why we were taught to despise each other. At first, I was only smitten by his good looks. Now, I'm genuinely interested in getting to know him better and understanding his kind.

Betrothed Or not?

Princess Akira and I are sitting on the sidelines, getting to know one another. Any suspicion I might have had about her drinking human blood is dismissed when she informs me she drinks from animals. That is news to me! I have always assumed that all vampires drank human blood, so learning that she would prefer to drink from an animal or blood bag rather than a human is a surprise. Most vampires murder humans and drain them dry, especially those who are turned at a young age like herself, or so it seems. The princess doesn't appear to be like those despicable twin vamps or Lucas. Their insatiable thirst for human blood sets them apart from Princess Akira. She is different, and we have similarities, such as not being comfortable with the idea of harming innocent humans for our benefit. Which, if I'm being honest, has me enthralled and wanting to know everything about her.

Does she and that vile vampire Lucas have something between them?

"Are you and Lucas betrothed?" I blurt out without thinking, my curiosity getting the best of me.

Princess Akira's face flushes, and she shakes her head. "No, of course not! We're just friends." She stands to her feet with both hands resting on her lovely hips. "That's none of your business, though." She adds, a crease forming between her eyebrows.

Wow! The princess's fiery response sparks a flame in me. Her skin is luminous and smooth, with a soft glow that accentuates her charm. Her hazel eyes twinkle with purity, and her black curls cascade down her shoulders, elegantly framing her face. The princess is a sight to behold; she is breathtaking.

A smirk plays at the corner of my lips. "You're right. It's none of my business, Princess Akira."

Her stance softens, and she chews her bottom lip. "Are you and Dawn betrothed?" Her cheeks flush.

"Fair question, Princess Akira. No, Dawn and I are not betrothed. We are just good friends."

Her hazel eyes light up, and a small smile tugs at the corners of her lips. She cocks her head to the side, changing the topic, "Are you ready to train, Prince Troy?"

Looking her directly in the eye, I square my shoulders. "You want to challenge me on the battlefield?" My grin deepens.

She smiles. "Why not? It'll be fun."

I'm intrigued by her confidence. "Very well then, Princess Akira."

We approach the floor. The princess grabs a sword. *I guess she's old school.* She admires the black and silver blade and swings it through the air with grace and precision.

"Impressive," I say, unable to hide my admiration. "Let's see if you can handle a real opponent."

The princess thrusts out her chest, exuding confidence and strength, meeting my challenge head-on. *She is exquisite.* Her eyes flicker as she twirls the sword in her hand, a playful smirk on her lips. "I may be a princess, but I can hold my own in a fight," she replies.

"Okay then," I say, preparing myself. "Let's see what you've got." The princess gets into position. We lock eyes and begin fighting. The clash of our swords fills the air as we exchange blows, each strike met with equal force and devotion. With skill and finesse, the princess's movements are smooth and precise—she is the master of her craft. She is not just a princess in name but a fierce warrior in her own right. As we continue to spar, the intensity of our battle only grows, pushing us both to our limits.

"Don't hold back!" I shout, my voice echoing through the training room. She is a terrific fighter. Every move she makes is deliberate, leaving no room for error. The princess thrusts her sword forward with such speed and accuracy that I lose focus, and she knocks me off balance. She flips her hair back and offers me a hand, a smirk playing on her lips.

"Not bad," she says, her eyes gleaming with satisfaction. "Do better if you want to defeat me."

A grin forms on my face, and I accept her hand as she helps me up. "Challenge accepted."

There's a spark when our hands touch, and I know she feels it, too. Our eyes lock for a moment, and it is as if this woman has opened the door to my soul. She loosens her grip and takes a step back. Her lips curve into a naughty smile as she equips herself for our next round.

We resume training for hours, going blow for blow until we are left gasping for air and covered in sweat. Our score remains tied, with neither of us able to gain the upper hand.

"You're not so bad for a vampire," I tease, wiping the sweat off my forehead.

She chuckles and replies, "And you're not too shabby for a hybrid." Her hazel eyes shine with amusement as she playfully adds, "Looks like we're evenly matched, for now."

My gaze meets hers, and I invite her back to my dining suite so we can continue our conversation in a more intimate setting. To my surprise, she accepts. Perhaps she is also interested in me beyond our rivalry.

I Want to Know More

Shelly, Sophia, and I return to the room after training with the hybrids. Prince Troy is waiting for me, so I scurry to the bathroom to shower. Sophia darts in next, leaving Shelly and me alone. The others are on the jet with Ryan. I'm closing the latch on my earrings when Shelly's gaze settles on me, her mischievous smirk growing bigger.

"So, what is this secret meeting about with Prince Troy?" Shelly grins from ear to ear.

She won't let it go until I spill the beans. A droplet of sweat trickles down my forehead, and her lips curl into a knowing smile. I'm not sure what to expect from this meeting with the prince, which has my heart thumping like a drum against my ribs. Prince Troy asked me to join him in his dining suite, and he didn't explain why he wanted to meet. A mix of curiosity and anxiety fills me. Still, I'm excited to see him again. I'm even more drawn to him, and it doesn't bother me he is a hybrid anymore.

"I will see when I meet with him, Shelly."

A bunch of butterflies are fluttering around in the pit of my stomach.

"Keep in mind the prince is a *hybrid*, Akira. No matter how attractive he may be," Sophia warns while coming out of the bathroom.

I don't know who despises hybrids more: Sophia, Lucas, or my father. However, I will not let their distaste for hybrids affect my judgment of the prince. His kind isn't as immoral as everyone makes it out to be.

"I'll see you guys in a bit," I say, a smile forming on my face and hasten out the door before Sophia can utter another word.

My heart is racing a thousand miles a minute with excitement and nerves while walking to meet with the prince. The doors of his dining suite are enticing and intimidating at the same time. I inhale and exhale a deep breath, gather my courage, and enter the room.

The prince is seated at the head of a long brown table. He's wearing a brown fitted t-shirt that accentuates his tight muscles and denim cargo jeans that complement his charm. My heart skips a beat, and my mind goes blank for a moment. *I hope I look okay because he looks delicious.* Trying my best to resist the lewd vision of him that fills my mind, I shake my head.

The prince looks up, his eyes meeting mine, and a sexy smile spreads across his handsome face, making my nerves melt away. "Hello, Princess Akira."

A gust of excitement surges in me as his deep voice reaches my ears. "Hello, Prince Troy. You can just call me Akira," I reply with a soft smile.

He stands up from his seat and walks towards me, extending his hand. "Let me start over. Hello, Akira. You can call me Troy." He says, giving me a wide, silly grin that has me swooning. "Please have a seat next to me."

"It will be my pleasure, Troy," I say, feeling my cheeks flush and a wave of relief wash over me when I take his hand and allow him to guide me to the empty chair beside him.

There are platters of food laid out on the vast table in front of us, and a glass of animal blood is placed in front of me. I'm hoping the metallic and savory taste will help me relax.

"So, Troy, what is this meeting about?"

He sits up straight and takes a sip of his own drink, clearing his throat before responding. "To be honest, I just want to get to know you."

As the words leave his lips, my body melts into the plush cushion of the chair. *I want to get to know you, too.*

"Get to know me? Why?" I say instead.

Troy pauses for a moment, his eyes searching mine. "Can I be straight with you?"

I give him a nod to proceed.

"I must admit, I don't have a liking for vampires, even though we are half-vampires," he replies, sliding a little closer toward me. "I say this with the utmost respect and no offense intended: your father is an evil man. I've always had preconceived notions about your kind. You, however, seem quite different from what I expected, and I want to understand you better."

Troy's honesty surprises me, and I appreciate that he's challenging his own prejudiced beliefs. He is right; my father is a ruthless, vile, and despicable man who has been in power for far too long, and anyone who threatens him will be eliminated. I also don't—*didn't* particularly care for hybrids based on stereotypes and assumptions I've heard. Troy is showing me that not all hybrids fit those misconceptions.

The silence between us makes Troy think he has offended me in some way, so he bites into his food and swallows hard. Still, I need this moment to process his words and reflect on my own notions.

Taking another sip, I exhale. "I appreciate you sharing your perspective with me, Troy. My father is evil, and I don't agree with his decisions and methods or the immense harm he has caused. However, I believe that we were misled into believing that all hybrids are inherently bad. I want to understand you better, too."

Troy nods. "We don't get to choose who our parents are. There are some things my father has done that I don't agree with either, but he's still my father. That doesn't mean we have to follow their beliefs or actions without question. We can choose to forge our own path that's separate from theirs."

To unravel our layers, we ask question after question, gradually getting to know more about one another by the minute. Listening to Troy's words and realizing how we were both trained to despise one another based on misconceptions is eye-opening. I no longer feel just an attraction toward Troy but also affection. Still, if a relationship develops between us, it won't last. My father will see to it.

"Can I see you again tomorrow?" Troy asks.

"I would love that," I say, choosing my growing feelings for Troy over the inevitable consequences that will eventually follow.

Bring On the Questions!

What is Troy doing to me? The butterflies in my stomach are forcing their way through. My face feels hot, and my hands are clammy. Is this what they mean by "love at first sight?" The prince has my emotions spinning in circles. I don't care that he is a hybrid. *Are you sure?* My brain asks, wanting me to be cautious and think logically, but my heart overpowers all rationality. Happily skipping back to my suite and replaying our meeting that's etched into my memory, I smile. Maybe this is more than just a passing infatuation; perhaps it's the start of something exceptional.

Walking through the door, the smile on my face immediately fades when everyone in the room glares at me with disapproval. My meeting alone with the prince is not well-received by those around me.

Lucas stands tall with his chest out and confronts me, brows knitted together. "What were you thinking meeting the prince by yourself?" his tone is firm.

"We have sent you a million text messages! Check your phone!" Sophia demands.

Rolling my eyes, a frustrated sigh escapes my lips. "I didn't realize I'm expected to be constantly under surveillance," I retort, my voice dripping with sarcasm.

Lucas's eyes narrow, and he takes a step closer. "You are a princess. It is expected."

"Thank you for clarifying my royal title, Lucas," I reply, folding my arms.

"Why were you meeting with the prince?" Kade questions.

They all despise the hybrid kingdom, and before meeting Troy, I did, too. I cannot tell them about Troy and me wanting to get to know one another. And all of the feelings I have for someone I just met.

Pausing for a moment, I search for a believable excuse. "I was discussing diplomatic matters with the prince," I say, hoping they won't see through my lie. "We were discussing the hybrid soldiers and if they have any special abilities."

This is a lie that only Shelly will see right through, and I don't care. The rest can't know the truth.

"You can't just go off on your own without informing the rest of us," Lucas scolds. His tone is displeasing, and I bite my lip to keep from snapping back at him.

"I apologize for not informing *everyone* beforehand, but Shelly and Sophia knew that I was meeting the prince." I shoot an irritated glare toward Shelly, who looks away. Sophia is standing next to Lucas with her arms crossed and shaking her head. She is visibly annoyed, and unfortunately, Lucas will report this back to my father. He makes a big deal when Shelly and I sneak away and go to town, and he is the first person to notify my father about our trips to the witch's domain.

He opens his mouth to speak, but I wave my hand in front of him. "I'm getting in the shower."

The warm shower calms my mind and eases the tension in my body. Washing my hair with the lavender-scented shampoo provided by the hybrids, I think about what Troy said about our kingdoms, instilling hatred in one another. Neither kingdom had a legitimate reason for disliking the other. The divisions between our kind seem to be fueled because my father—*the almighty King Abel,* is threatened by the hybrids.

Turning the water off and stepping out of the shower, I wrap myself in a fluffy blue and black towel and check my phone. Rolling my eyes at the twenty unread text messages from my friends, I almost toss my phone. However, an unknown number flashes across my screen. *Troy?*

My heart nearly leaps out of my chest.

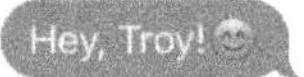

Anxiously waiting for his response, I check out my reflection in the mirror. My curly black hair is wet and tangled from my shower; brushing it out carefully, I'm hoping to distract myself from the anticipation. A ding finally comes from my phone.

Why would he ask that? I'm like a little school girl finally receiving attention from the popular jock; tilting my head to the side, a huge smile appears on my face while replying.

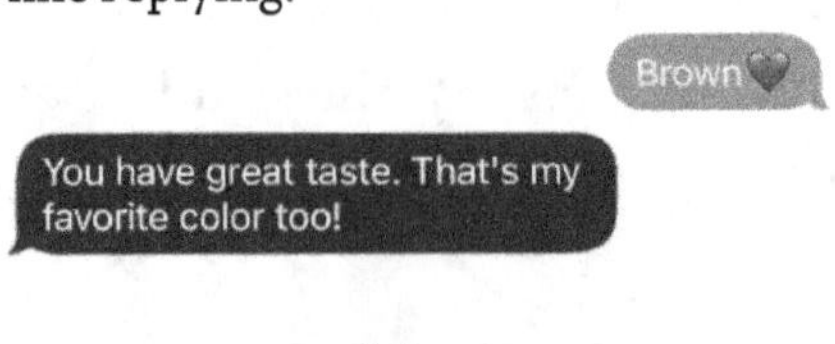

Grinning from ear to ear. It's a small coincidence, yet it feels like a meaningful connection between us. He wore a brown fitted T-shirt because brown is indeed his favorite color.

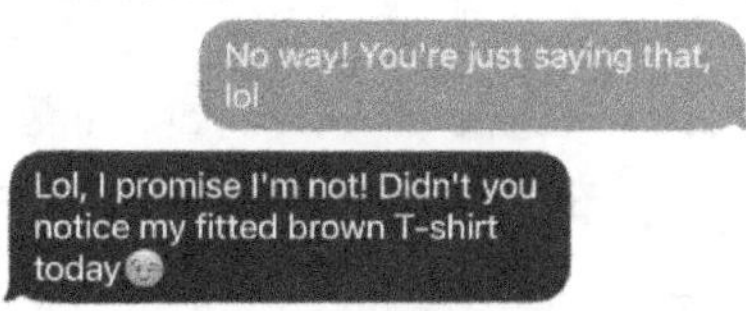

Of course, I noticed. His ego doesn't need to be inflated any further.

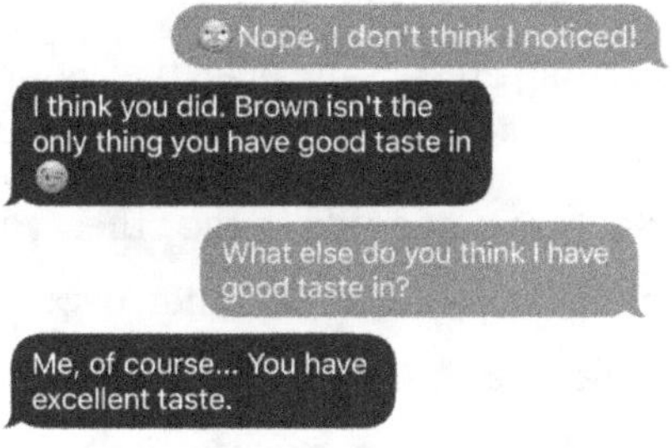

I'm full-on blushing now.

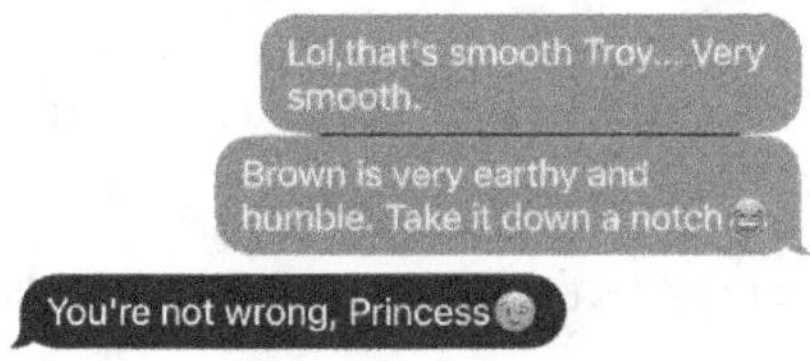

I told him not to call me princess.

Checking my reflection in the mirror, a rosy shade of pink appears on my cheeks from blushing so much. Leaning against the door and looking at the ceiling, I replay our flirty text exchange in my head. I'm on cloud nine until I hear Lucas knocking on the door because only he would ignore me wanting to be alone. *What does he want?*

"I'll be out soon," I call out to him.

I quickly finish getting dressed and open the door to see what Lucas wants and face the others.

Shifting my weight from one side to the other. "Hey guys, just so you all know, I will be meeting the prince again tomorrow, so don't send me a million text messages," I say deadpan.

Everyone except Sophia looks in my direction.

"Take Ava with you," Lucas demands.

"For what?" I retort.

"You're supposed to be escorted by one of us for your safety around the hybrids," Kaden explains. "It's protocol."

"I don't need an escort," I scoff. "I can handle myself just fine."

The others exchange glances, unsure of how to respond to my defiance.

"For now," Sophia says under her breath.

Rolling my eyes. "Do you think the prince would harm me?"

When no one responds to my question, I sigh, giving in to their request, "Shelly will accompany me."

"But—"

"If I need to be escorted by someone, I will choose who that person is," I assert, cutting Lucas off. "I don't need you all deciding for me. I am Princess Akira of the vampire kingdom."

The room falls silent as they absorb the weight of my words. I have never used my royal title before. At this moment, it felt necessary to remind them of my authority. They are my friends, and I respect them, and I thought they respected me in return. However, I am unwilling to tolerate them telling me what to do.

All of them nod in response.

Lucas grabs my arm gently. "We really need to talk," he says in a low tone so the others can't hear.

My expression softens. We never finished our conversation, and I know I will have to discuss this with him sooner rather than later. We both head out the door to speak privately while everyone else heads to bed.

Lucas grabs the back of his neck and looks at me. Our gazes meet, and his eyes are sharp and focused.

I don't want to hurt him. *Honesty is the best approach.*

Swallowing the knot in my throat and exhaling. "L—Lucas," I say, my voice trembling.

Lucas places his index finger on my lips, silencing me.

He shakes his head and says, "Before you say anything, I need to do something." His words catch me off guard, and he leans into me, closing the distance between us.

He presses his lips against mine as I try to pull away. The kiss is unexpected, and a part of me responds to its intensity. When we break apart, there is conflict in his eyes, realizing that this situation is even more complicated than before. Lucas is an excellent kisser and probably one of the most attractive men in my kingdom. Lucas would be the perfect fit for me: he's one of my father's righthand men, loyal to the throne, and a vampire. Unfortunately for him, I don't feel the spark that I'm searching for. No matter how much I wish I could force myself to feel something more, it wouldn't be fair to either of us.

Lucas kisses my forehead softly and brushes a loose curl behind my ear. He gazes at me like I am the only woman he wants.

He grasps my hand in his and circles his thumb in the palm of my hand. "Akira, I want us to be together. Please give us another chance."

Gently pulling away from him, I take a deep breath, trying to find the right words. "I appreciate your feelings, but I can't be with you, Lucas. I don't feel the same way, and I don't want to lead you on."

His face falls, and he looks to the ground.

"I'm sorry," I say in a soft voice, feeling a pang of guilt. "I know it's not what you wanted to hear."

Lucas walks away, his shoulders slumping, and I turn in the direction of the room without looking back.

I get in bed with Shelly and curl up next to her.

Shelly moves on the bed. "Are you okay?"

"I'm okay. Go back to sleep," I whisper.

She murmurs a sleepy "okay" and settles back into her slumber.

Waiting to see if Lucas will return, I glance toward the door. When he doesn't, I try my best to fall asleep, feeling conflicted about my feelings for Troy and the feelings I should have for Lucas.

Infatuation, Nope, I Think I've Fallen

Curiosity about Akira's feelings toward me drove me to retrieve her phone number from the file in my father's office. We spoke about so much; however, the minor details make her who she is. Knowing a person's favorite color, among other things, reveals a lot about their personality and preferences. The fact that we both love brown is a happy coincidence, and it shows that we have another thing in common. Grabbing my phone from my pocket, I scroll through Akira and my text messages from earlier. The pounding rhythm of my heart accelerates, and seeing her again fills me with anticipation. I'm confident she feels for me as I am beginning to feel for her. *The way her hazel eyes sparkle when she smiles and the way*—Claude storms into my chambers, brows furrowed, interrupting my musing.

"What is going on between you and the princess?"

My gaze meets his. "What do you mean?" I ask, confused by his accusatory tone.

"Dawn said she stopped by your dining suite and saw you cozying up to the princess."

Trying to hide my amusement, I raise a brow. "Cozying up? That's a bit of an exaggeration, don't you think? The princess and I were simply having a conversation." I reply, my voice laced with sarcasm.

Claude crosses his arms, his expression skeptical. "Well, it certainly looked like more than just a conversation to Dawn. She seemed convinced that there was something *romantic* going on between you two."

Shaking my head. "There's nothing romantic happening between the princess and me." I lie through my teeth with ease.

Claude raises an eyebrow, unconvinced by my response. "You're a terrible liar, you know that? You are barking up a dangerous tree. Her father is the king of all evil."

Trying to downplay the seriousness of the situation. "I realize who her father is. However, she is not like that."

Claude's skeptical expression remains unchanged. "You've known her for all of six seconds, and you're already vouching for her? Even if she may not be like her father, it doesn't change the fact that her association with him puts you—*us* at risk!" My brother shouts, throwing his hands in the air.

Pausing for a moment, I contemplate his words. "She doesn't drink human blood; that should count for something," I respond, trying to defend her.

"That's something she told you. How can you be sure she's telling the truth? You can't just take her word for it, especially considering her background."

He has valid concerns, but there is no way I could explain to him that she is different from her father.

Claude exhales and relaxes his shoulders. "I don't want to see you get hurt, Troy. I'm a lover of all, but I don't want this infatuation you have for the princess to pose any danger to this kingdom."

With a nod, we come to an understanding. He is right. It's vital to consider the potential dangers before blindly trusting the princess, especially when her background raises doubts. What if she is just like her father? How could she not be evil growing up with a father figure like King Abel? Still, I have spent time with the princess and have seen that her humanity speaks louder than her lineage.

Claude exits my chambers, and the disappointment on his face is implanted in my mind. As sleep threatens to take over me, my brother's worries consume my mind. Could it be possible that she is deceiving me? What if Akira has some sort of gift where she can manipulate people's perceptions and emotions? I replay our conversations over and over in my head, trying to find any inconsistencies or signs of manipulation. Each time, I come up empty-handed. When sleep finally takes over me, my dreams are plagued by Akira's smiling face and her laughter echoing in my ears.

The next day, my mind is troubled with uncertainty, torn between my brother's concerns and my growing feelings for Akira. Still, I meet with Akira despite my lingering doubts because spending more time with her is the only way to know for sure.

When Akira arrives, she's not alone. She introduces me to her best friend, Shelly, who seems more polite than the others. She has to accompany Akira in any future meetings we have alone since Lucas reported back to the king about our time together.

"Nice to meet you, Shelly," I shake her hand.

"Nice to meet you too, Mr. Prince," she smiles and heads to the sidelines, disappearing into her phone.

My gaze meets Akira's, and she looks beautiful, with her curls effortlessly sitting at the top of her head in a messy bun and a radiant smile on her face. Despite my doubts, a wave of excitement washes over me being in her presence.

"You look beautiful," I say, unable to hide my attraction to her.

Akira blushes and thanks me. Reaching forward, I tuck a loose curl behind her ear. The gesture seems to catch her off guard, but she leans into it, and her smile widens.

"What do you like to do for fun?" I ask as we settle on my beige sofa.

Her hazel eyes twinkle, and she smiles. "So don't laugh, but I love playing Cards Against Humanity. It's one of my favorite games." Her eyes light up with excitement.

"Really? That's a classic. What else do you enjoy doing? I want to know everything about you."

She chuckles, her cheeks turning a faint shade of pink. "Well, I enjoy reading; I'm a sucker for romance stories, and I hope to find love like the ones I read about someday. I also love to swim; being in the water is my escape from reality. What about you? What are some of your favorite activities?"

Akira has such a beautiful soul. She is nothing like her father.

Shrugging my shoulders. "I enjoy training. It helps me stay focused and disciplined."

I'm not an exciting person, and that is the only response that comes to mind. I also enjoy cooking. However, she doesn't eat food because of our different diets. *I should probably not mention that.*

She laughs, and it's contagious. "Perhaps we should broaden your horizons. I'm sure you have training down!" Akira teases.

"Making you laugh is another one of my favorite activities," I admit, grasping her hand in mine. Her playful expression fades as she glances down at our tangled hands. "Perhaps you are right. Maybe one day we can play a game of Cards Against Humanity," I continue.

She lifts her head to meet my gaze and bites her lower lip. "I look forward to that."

Tracing her fingers with my thumb, I want to kiss her so badly right now, but I hold back because Shelly is present and smiling in the corner of my eye. *It's not the right time.*

We spent the rest of the week enjoying each other's company. As the week ended, Akira and I were smitten with one another. On Akira's last day, she asks Shelly to stay behind and cover for her.

Akira's gaze connects with mine. "Promise me you'll keep in touch." She says, her voice filled with uncertainty.

With a nod, I acknowledge her words, a subtle sting of disappointment thumping in my heart, echoing her doubt.

"Of course," I reply, brushing my thumb over her rosy cheek. "I don't want this to end either."

"I'll find a way to see you again," she pouts.

Her words tug at my heart. My gaze settles on hers and drifts to her lips, wanting to capture the moment in my memory. Closing the distance between us, she opens her mouth slightly, inviting me to kiss her. Sparks fly between us when our lips meet, and for a moment, time stands still. She tangles her fingers in my hair, deepening the kiss, and I explore her mouth with my tongue. As our tongues dance in sync, I stroke her thigh with my hand. She shivers beneath my touch. Our kiss intensifies into a fire that cannot be extinguished, my length hardening under her.

When our lips part, we leave each other gasping for air and wanting more. It's only been one week. However, it feels like I have known Akira Ronin for an entire lifetime. This is not a goodbye but instead a temporary farewell until I see her again.

Let The Battle Begin

Troy and I shared a kiss that made my knees buckle when our lips parted. I felt that spark! Surges of electricity ran through my body and coursed through my veins, igniting a passion I had never felt before. The intensity of our kiss was mind-blowing. We only spent a week together, yet it felt like a lifetime. Every moment was filled with laughter, deep conversations, and stolen glances that spoke volumes. Being in his arms again is my only desire, not staying trapped behind the castle walls.

Usually, I'm delighted to return to my comfortable chambers after my trip to the kingdoms, but not this time. The feeling of being back at the castle is not a pleasant one. In the past, my friends and I would go by Sophia's villa to soak in the pool, play Cards Against Humanity, and hang out. However, this time, there is a shift in our dynamic. They disapproved of my extra *meetings* with the prince and didn't hesitate to voice their disapproval on the jet ride back to the castle. The overwhelming tension has created a rift between us, and it's only a matter of time before they offer me up to my father on a silver platter if necessary. They notice that my hatred for the hybrids has changed, and they think I am betraying the kingdom for the prince. I no longer want to be a part of a kingdom that hates others for no valid reason other than prejudice. Suddenly, feeling trapped, my chest tightens. Leaning against the wall and trying to steady my ragged breaths, little white spots circle in my vision, and I crouch down to my knees. Inhaling and exhaling a few times. *What am I going to do?*

My father's methods are not condoned by me. Still, I have always turned a blind eye to his ruthless kidnappings of humans, among the other terrible things he has done, but I would not survive if I went against him. My father's power and influence are far too great, and he has surrounded himself with loyal subjects who would not hesitate to eliminate anyone who poses a threat to him. No one would follow me in defying the king. Even Lucas wouldn't betray the throne for me. Sophia is—*was* my best friend, and she made it incredibly clear back at the cave that she is loyal to the king. I'm sure the twins feel the same way, too; they devoted their lives to the king long before I existed. Shelly is the only one in whom I have some hope, but the two of us don't stand a chance against an entire kingdom.

Why would anyone in their right mind trust me to lead them? The day I awoke from my slumber was my nineteenth birthday; it was the day I matured as a vampire and the day my life began. I only have recollections from that day and forward. However, I remember having dreams where I heard Shelly, Lucas, and a few of the kingdom's familiar voices, wondering when I would wake. Other than that, I have no memories. If only I could remember, perhaps my purpose in this kingdom would be clearer to me.

Today is The Battle of Anaik. The tournament is held every month to *honor* a human with the gift of immortality. Two humans must fight to the death to become a vampire. Some vampires place bets on who will win, but most simply watch it for entertainment. The event makes my stomach churn; it is purely disgusting and morally wrong. Still, I must maintain appearances and sit for the show with my mother and father—the almighty King Abel and Queen Aika.

I opted to wear all black instead of my usual colorful attire to match the somber atmosphere. Dressing in a black tank top, leather pants, my favorite biker jacket, and black steel-toe boots, my look is complete.

Before heading to the bloodbath, I text Troy.

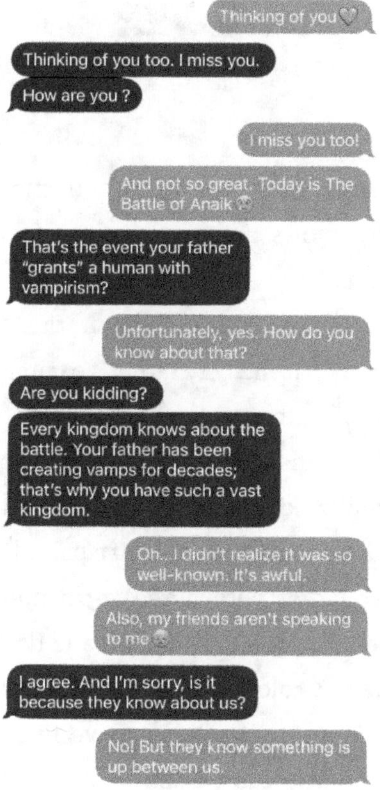

My friends suspect that something is going on between Troy and me, but they don't know exactly what it is, and the last thing I want is for my father to get word of my growing feelings for Troy. It would complicate things even more.

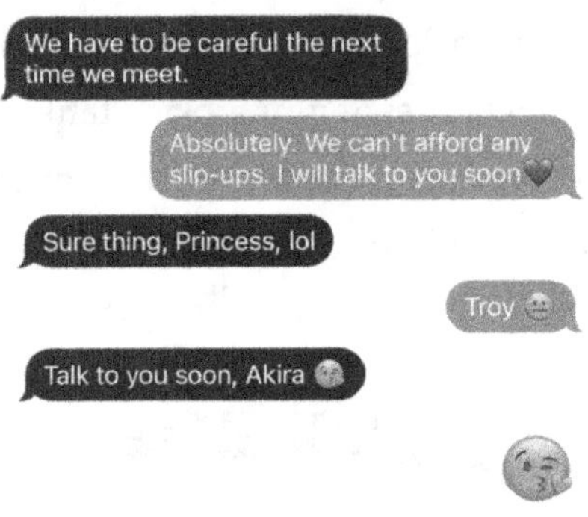

Smiling from ear to ear, I check my reflection one last time in the mirror. *Perfect.* Troy knows how to make me feel better, and I cannot wait to see him again.

Exiting my chambers, I speed down the staircase to the back elevators and meet my parents. My father's excitement is all over his face as I join them in the elevator.

King Abel Ronin stands over six feet tall with a commanding posture, a muscular build, milky skin, and red eyes. His hair is neatly combed, and he's wearing a red fitted button-up shirt paired with gray dress pants and a long leather jacket with a red retro notch collar. Red leather alligator dress shoes complete his polished and flashy look.

My mother is not as colorful; her fashion sense leans towards classic and sophisticated. She stands a little above five feet tall, and her slim frame is dressed in black jeans, a silk blouse, and a tailored red blazer. She completes her look with a string of pearls and a pair of black stilettos.

She is a beautiful mixed-race woman with jet-black hair framing her porcelain-like face and red eyes.

We take the elevator down to the castle's lower level, where the arena, human territory, transportation, and dungeons are located. The battle is held in a sizeable hexagon-shaped fighting ring. We refer to it as "the hex," which is surrounded by towering stone walls painted red, black, and orange, which are my father's favorite colors. Swords, crossbows, axes, spears, and machetes line the walls on opposite sides for both fighters. The audience watches from the top of the stone walls, and two-way mirrors surround the area, providing a clear view of the vampires. However, the humans can't see the audience. Rosa casts a spell over the arena to keep the two humans locked in until one is slain.

The two unlucky humans picked for the battle today were handpicked by Lucas and the twins. They usually travel to nearby areas to kidnap homeless humans. For this month's tournament, however, they decided to broaden their horizons and kidnap two males from Florida. The winner will be a newborn, and their first meal is the human who loses the battle. *A perk, my father added in.*

Shelly and I like to learn the names of those facing off in the battle to say a little prayer for them. Cameron and Mateo are only sixteen years old. That's three years younger than Shelly and my age when we matured as vampires, and they are fighting to the death in a battle neither of them signed up for. It's a cruel twist of fate that has brought us all together in this grim arena. There is an undeniable connection I have with humans that I cannot seem to understand. I'm a vampire; I should want to feed on their blood, but the idea of drinking human blood is repulsive to me. This event should be entertaining, or there should be a wave of excitement that washes me over, yet there isn't. The vampires believe we are rewarding humans with a chance at immortality. I think we're burdening them into a life of eternal darkness and thirst. Humans should have the right to choose, not be forced into it.

Shelly sits next to me and slouches down in her seat, her lips curl into a frown. "I wish we didn't have to witness this," she whispers so only I can hear.

Nodding in agreement, my heart is heavy as we sit back to watch the unfolding tragedy.

We should be used to the tournaments because they happen every month; each time feels just as heartbreaking as the last.

Mateo and Cameron enter the arena simultaneously. Cameron is sweating, and his breathing is accelerated while Mateo's hands are trembling. Both of their eyes widen in shock as the crowd erupts into a frenzy of cheers and applause. The boys look weak, displaced, and terrified. Cameron has hazel eyes, short, curly brown hair, and a slim build. His opponent, Mateo, has green eyes, short brown hair, and a slender frame. They both are dressed in black shorts, a long-sleeved thermal shirt, and sneakers provided by Lucas.

Lucas and I haven't spoken since he disappeared after our kiss in the cave. And if I'm being honest, it upset me, which I don't understand, considering I have no romantic feelings for him. Still, there was something about that moment that left me feeling unsettled. However, seeing him amid this chaotic scene has my teeth grinding together at the sound of his excitement for the tournament.

Cameron and Mateo scramble to the center of the arena, their eyes scanning the array of weapons laid out before them.

"FIGHT! FIGHT! FIGHT!" The crowd chants, and the boys lock eyes in unease.

Mateo charges toward Cameron with full force, punching him in the face repeatedly. Cameron is pushed backward until he catches Mateo's fist, causing him to lose his footing for a moment. Mateo throws another punch, and Cameron counters with a left hook. Mateo shakes it off and looks toward the two-way mirror. The crowd is ecstatic. The boys may not be able to see the crowd, but they can hear the cheering. Mateo leaps toward Cameron, kicking him in the knee, followed by a right hook to the jaw. Cameron's eyebrows shoot up, and he grabs his knee. Mateo looks toward the two-way mirror once more.

"That's right!" Lucas shouts. "You're doing great," he encourages.

This briefly distracts Mateo, allowing Cameron to throw a powerful uppercut to his chin, causing Mateo to stumble to the floor.

"This fool," my father snarls.

Mateo regains his footing and throws a hook to Cameron's jaw. His head jerks, and he grabs his jaw. Before Cameron can strike back, Mateo punches him in the lip, causing it to bleed. Cameron rubs his thumb over his lip and looks at it. He spits blood on the floor and stands with both legs parted and his fist positioned in front of him, ready to strike. Mateo gets the drift and stands in the same position as Cameron. Mateo throws a left hook, followed by a right. Cameron counters his attack by throwing powerful blows. Mateo guards his face with one hand while trying to throw jabs with the other. Cameron evades each strike and throws a lethal uppercut, knocking Mateo out.

The crowd shouts while Cameron paces back and forth, watching to see if Mateo will recover. Mateo shakes his head and wipes the blood dripping from his mouth.

Lucas growls to Mateo, "Grab a weapon!"

The twins shout to Cameron to do the same.

Mateo runs toward the wall and reaches for a sleek silver knife. Cameron scurries toward the opposite wall and hovers his hand uncertainly over a spear. The crowd's deafening roar echoes in the arena, increasing the pressure on both boys. Cameron bends his knees, bringing his arm back to prepare for a throw. Mateo grips the knife tightly, his fingers trembling with anticipation. Cameron extends the spear forward, aimed at Mateo's head, and releases it. The spear flies through the air, but Mateo dodges it. The crowd roars as the spear whizzes past his ear, and Mateo's eyes widen at the almost fatal blow. Cameron scratches his neck and glances around the arena. He looks between Mateo and the weapons lining the walls, unsure of his next move.

Shelly leans toward me. "Why do they put them through this? I can't watch this."

Glancing around at the faces of the spectators, their eyes fixed on the intense battle unfolding before them, I'm disappointed. All I see is bloodlust and excitement.

"I feel sick to my stomach," I whisper.

Shelly holds my hand as we continue to watch the horrific showdown.

Cameron stands there frozen, and Mateo seizes the opportunity to leap toward Cameron with a knife, stabbing him in the leg. Cameron screeches in pain and plunges to the floor, clutching his wounded leg. Blood is gushing out through his fingers, and the crowd erupts into cheers and applause.

This is gruesome.

Cameron removes the knife from his leg with a grimace of agony, his face contorted in pain, and rips his shirt to tie around his wound. While he is applying pressure to stop the bleeding, Mateo runs back to the wall for a bow and arrow. Cameron's eyes widen in fear when he sees Mateo preparing to take another shot, and he attempts to save himself when Mateo fires arrows at him. He successfully avoids every one of them.

Cameron is tough; he is evading Mateo's arrows while injured, and the more he moves, the more blood drips from his wound. I'm impressed.

My father jumps to his feet. "Can you make at least one shot, you pathetic human?" he shouts at Mateo.

"Stop playing around and finish him off!" Lucas adds.

"Imbeciles," My father mumbles, throwing his hands in the air.

Cameron staggers to the wall; his breathing is heavy and labored, and he grabs an ax. He continues to dodge Mateo's attacks while he waits for him to run out of arrows. When Mateo finally exhausts his supply, Cameron lunges the ax at Mateo, right into the side of his neck. Mateo lets out a gurgled scream, and his body collapses to the ground, blood pooling around him. Cameron's eyes are vast, and he looks down at his trembling hands while stepping backward, unable to comprehend the horrific scene before him.

The crowd goes wild at Mateo's body, motionless on the ground, and my father's face contorts into a twisted smile of satisfaction. "That's how it's done," he says, his voice filled with triumph.

Lucas nods in approval, a glimmer of respect in his eyes.

The cheering from the crowd comes to an abrupt halt when my father stands from his seat and raises his arms, signaling for silence.

The battle is over.

The Blood Is Intoxicating

Human servants scurry into the arena to collect Mateo's lifeless form. Then, they will hang him upside down in the freezer so the blood from his body can be drained into buckets. Cameron will be forced to drink from them, and then Mateo's body will be burned. A fate no one deserves.

My father gives his command, the crowd resumes praising Cameron's victory, and the twins collect money from winning the bet.

Lucas is slouched over with his forehead in his palm. "What a waste," he says under his breath. He is not pleased about losing yet another bet against the twins.

Cameron is sitting on the floor in the arena, holding his injured leg. He is staring at the blood that's left behind from Mateo's body. The sight of him crumbles my heart into tiny pieces. Feeling faint, I stand to my feet. However, my mother grasps my hand to stop me.

"What is it, Mother?" I ask, anxiously waiting for her response.

Her grip tightens. "Sit back down. Your father wants you to turn the human into one of us."

"I will do no such thing!" I shout, pulling my hand away from my mother's grasp.

My mother's face turns cold, and my father speaks, his voice stern. "You will do as I say, *child*! I am your father and the king!"

Turning a human into one of us! I can't fathom what my father is asking of me. It goes against everything I believe in. He hasn't asked me to do anything like this before, so why is he demanding it now?

Glaring at them and nodding, I reluctantly sit back down.

This is my punishment for spending time with Troy. I knew Lucas and the twins were reporting to my father about my meetings with the prince. However, I didn't care then; now, it seems like my father is using this opportunity to assert his control over me and remind me of my duty as a princess of the vampire kingdom.

Everyone else exits the arena beside the twins, Lucas, Shelly, and my parents. My friends exchange solemn glances.

My father clears his throat. He looks at me with a grave expression and says, "It's time for you to understand the consequences of your actions, Akira. You will turn the human into a vampire and fulfill your duty as the princess of this kingdom."

A knot forms in my throat as the harsh reality of his words sinks in.

My mother gestures toward the battlefield. "Go ahead, Akira."

Taking a deep breath, my heart pounds in my chest. Stepping forward, I approach Cameron, watching his eyes widen in fear; he is resilient. He staggers to his feet and looks at me, and I can see a silent plea for mercy in his eyes. Still, he falls back to the floor from the pain. Tears well up in my eyes. His skin is pale from the blood loss, and his breathing is shallow.

It is only a matter of time before he bleeds out.

Kneeling beside him, my voice trembles. "I—I am so sorry," my words are barely easy to hear. "I never wanted it to come to this."

Cameron's lips turn into a frown, and his eyebrows pull together. "Get on with it!"

Crouching over him, I bare my fangs. The fear in his eyes intensifies as he realizes what is about to happen; he desperately tries to push himself away from me.

Grabbing hold of his wrists, I hold him in place. "I wish there was another way," I whisper, my heart heavy with guilt. "I promise to be quick."

Cameron's struggles weaken as he accepts his fate, his body growing limp in my grasp. Sinking my fangs into his neck, I release my venom into his bloodstream. The slight taste of human blood dilates my pupils and sends my senses into overdrive. The taste of his blood is a tantalizing blend of sweetness and warmth. *The younger they are, the sweeter the blood.* The temptation to indulge in every drop is overwhelming; a faint voice from deep within reminds me of the promise I made. Withdrawing my fangs and quickly standing to my feet, I wipe my mouth with the back of my hand. Cameron's body writhes in agony as the venom takes effect. It's painful to watch.

"What is happening to me?" He cries out. The terror in his eyes is haunting as he struggles to comprehend the sudden changes overtaking his body.

When a vampire is in transition, the pain is excruciating. I was told your entire body feels like it's on fire, and all your bones are breaking simultaneously. Sometimes, I wonder if my mind blocked out the traumatic experience of my transformation to protect me from the sheer horror of it. Maybe the pain was so unbearable that it was buried deep within my subconscious.

My parents and I witness Cameron's body endure the physical and psychological changes from the venom. He screeches in pain until the venom finally starts healing his wound. His eyebrows shoot up, and he glances at me. Suddenly, he shakes, and his fangs extend from his gums. It felt like he was going through his transformation for hours; it only took minutes for the change to be complete. Cameron passes out from the overwhelming exhaustion of the transformation, and the twins carry him out of the arena. I signal to Shelly, and we hasten out of there as fast as possible and back to my chambers. Once we are away from everyone, I throw myself into her arms, sobbing. Neither of us thought I would have to turn a human into a vampire.

Overwhelming *darkness* awakens our primal instincts that cannot be easily controlled when biting into a human's neck. Senior vampires can ignore the urge to feed on humans and only release their venom. It took every ounce of self-control for me to fight against draining Cameron of all his blood, and the guilt is weighing heavily on my conscience.

Tears stream down my face. "Shelly, I almost gave in," I say between sobs. "I almost fed on Cameron. It took all I had to pull away."

Shelly doesn't say anything. She simply keeps her arms wrapped around me, offering comfort in her silent presence. We stay like that until night falls, and Shelly leaves, promising to check on me again in the morning. While in bed, the guilt continues to gnaw at me like a relentless beast. I want more blood. The internal struggle between my vampire instincts and my moral compass consumes me. With each passing moment, the desire for blood grows stronger, intensifying the guilt that plagued my conscience. *Surely, I can find a human to feed on?*

Jumping to my feet, I pace the room. *What is wrong with me?* Needing a distraction from my conflicting thoughts, I cannot give in! I think about the one person who could take my mind off these disgusting thoughts. *Troy.*

Grabbing my phone, I dial Troy's number.

He answers on the second ring, his voice filled with concern and sleep. "Akira? Is everything okay?"

Glaring at the clock, I realize it's 3 a.m. I hesitate for a moment, not wanting to burden Troy with my internal struggle. However, I trust him.

"Not really. I...I need to talk," I finally admit, my voice is unsteady.

"What's wrong?" Troy asks, his tone now fully awake and attentive.

Taking a deep breath. "My father made me turn a human into a vampire, and the guilt is eating me alive. I don't know how to handle it, Troy."

The words escape my lips, and I'm embarrassed that I said them out loud. The silence on the other end of the line is deafening, and I can sense the shock in his voice when he responds.

"Akira, listen to me. It's not your fault. Your father should never have put you in that position and put that type of burden on you!"

Placing the phone on my shoulder for a quick second, I think about my dilemma. Running my fingers along my fangs, the faint taste of metal lingers in my mouth, and I crave more of it. My emotions are heightened, and I'm on the verge of breaking down.

"I feel awful!" My eyes swell up with tears. "I am craving human blood; It's sickening—I can't help it. I feel like a monster."

There is a brief silence on the other end of the line, and when Troy responds, he says, "You will be okay, Akira. You have to dig deep within yourself and find the strength to resist these urges. Remember when you told me you would much rather drink animal blood or drink from a blood bag than feed on a human? That conviction is still within you, even if it feels weak right now. You are not a monster, Akira. You have the power to overcome this. I know you can do it."

"But it's so hard," I choke out.

"You are stronger than you think and a bright force to be reckoned with. You won't give in, and you will have to break away from this kingdom, eventually."

Troy's words resonate with me. We say our goodbyes, and I wipe away the tears. The desire I had to feed on a human is now gone, thanks to Troy. And he is right. I must break away from this kingdom, except I don't know how to escape and *survive.*

My phone rings, and Lucas's name flashes across the screen. I hit ignore. Then I hear a faint knock on my door.

"Akira, can you please open the door? I know you're awake." Lucas pleads.

I sigh and get up to open it. "What do you want, Lucas?" I try to keep my voice steady.

"The newborn vampire is awake and has been fed." He informs me.

Rolling my eyes. "Why are you telling me this?"

"Turning a human makes them attached to the vampire that turned them," Lucas explains. "And since you were the one who turned him, he's now bonded to you."

I never wanted this.

Rolling my eyes once more. "Thank you for that information; now, if you'll excuse me." I start to close the door, and Lucas stops me.

"Wait, there's something else," he says.

Sighing in frustration, my patience wearing thin. "What is it now?" I ask, my tone laced with annoyance, and my mind fleetingly goes back to human blood, and I'm sure Lucas notices.

"I know that look, and I can help you," he offers.

A small part of me considers Lucas's offer. However, Troy's words replay in my head, and I exhale. *"You are stronger than you think and a bright force to be reckoned with. You won't give in."*

"No, thank you. And if that is all, I would appreciate it if you could leave me alone now," I say, closing the door.

Welcome, Newborn Vampire

One week after the battle, I'm reliving the awful feeling of almost losing myself to the *darkness,* and the taste of Cameron's blood is still fresh in my mind. Shaking the thought away, I stride towards my walk-in closet, contemplating the swimsuits before me, and decide on my favorite brown bikini. Today, Shelly and I are going to relax poolside, which will take my mind off the web of complicated events that have woven itself around me.

Sophia and I are still not on good terms because of my evolving relationship with Troy, although nothing has been established *yet.* We only kissed once, but that kiss left us both longing for more, and we have been trying to navigate our feelings for each other through texts and late-night phone calls.

Next week, I'm going to Santa Barbara, California, to visit Monica. I asked Troy to meet me there. My heart races with the thought of seeing him again. Shelly is also joining us on the trip, as she is the only one who knows about Troy and me. Usually, we stay with Monica in her beautiful, spacious beachfront villa; however, Troy and I thought it was best for all of us to stay at a hotel and avoid questions from the witches.

Grabbing my phone, I send Shelly a text message.

Rolling my eyes at Shelly's response, I place my phone in my side purse and head to the kitchen's walk-in freezer to retrieve some animal blood. Cameron appears before me; he looks so much better now that he's fully completed his transformation into a vampire. Cameron's skin is almost translucent, and his injuries have completely healed. However, I still feel guilty about what he endured at the hands of my people. *He probably hates me.*

Giving him a sympathetic smile and grabbing a bag of animal blood, I nod. Cameron gazes at me suspiciously, his hazel eyes brighter than before.

Clearing my throat. "I know it's not the same as what you fed on, but it's the better alternative."

He's watching me pour the animal blood into two red and gold stainless steel thermoses for Shelly and me. Shifting my weight from one leg to the other, I hurry to finish pouring it and hasten out of the kitchen. However, he uses his vampire speed and catches up to me.

"Will I ever get used to this?" he asks, still adjusting to his newfound abilities.

"It takes time and practice," I reply. Taking a deep breath. "Are you okay?"

He looks at me and grins. "I'm fine. I'm just trying to wrap my head around it all," he confesses. "Everything is so different now."

Offering him a reassuring smile. "It's a lot to take in, but don't worry, you'll adapt." My smile falters. "Do you hate me?"

He screws up his face, confused by my question. "No, of course not," he quickly reassures me. "I know it wasn't your fault. I overheard the other vampires speaking of The Battle of Anaik. And I understand you were just following orders."

Cameron is the first human I have encountered who is okay with becoming one of us. After the battle last month, the newborn Richard was highly distraught and has been in therapy with the witch Rosa since. He doesn't accept being a vampire, or rather, his body is rejecting the transition. However, I don't really have all the details in regard to that; I just know Rosa has been trying to convince my father not to dispose of him and to give him some time. She believes that with proper guidance and support, Richard will come to terms with his new identity as a vampire. It takes time for newborns to process the rapid changes happening to their bodies, and their minds need time to adjust. But Cameron's transition has been smoother; he seems fine like it's no big deal.

"Where are you headed?" His lips curl into a goofy grin.

"Um, I'm going to my friend's villa to take a dip in the pool," I reply.

Cameron's eyes light up with excitement as he responds, "Do you mind if I tag along?"

I do mind.

"No, of course not," I say through clenched teeth, forcing a smile.

Lucas informed me that because I turned Cameron into a vampire, he would be loyal to me, and because of that, I had been avoiding him for the week. This means that Cameron will always want to be by my side and will do anything I ask of him. Having someone so devoted to me is a strange feeling. Still, I can't deny that it's also comforting to have such unwavering support. I heard of some vampires falling in love with their creators. However, I don't see that happening between Cameron and me because I have something going on with Troy. *I'm not sure what exactly, but it is something.*

We arrive at Shelly's villa, and her mouth drops open when she sees Cameron. She quickly recovers and greets us.

"Hey Cameron, h—how are you feeling?" Shelly asks warily.

Cameron sits on one of the lounge chairs and shrugs. "I never felt better."

Shelly's eyes widen in disbelief as she takes in Cameron's response. We exchange glances, clearly surprised by his relaxed attitude, and I shrug.

Sitting beside him, I offer him my thermos. "Would you like some?"

He fed on a human to complete his transformation; perhaps I can train him on an animal diet instead.

Cameron takes the thermos and drinks it without spitting any out. *That's strange.* Newborns usually spit out animal blood almost instantly.

My mouth flings open, and he laughs.

"What's the matter? Did you expect me to gag or something?" Cameron asks. "Did you think I wanted to feed on human blood *again*?"

Shelly and I freeze, unable to respond, and he laughs at our expressions. His laugh is hilarious. It sounds like a pack of hyenas fighting over food, and now all of us are amused at the absurdity of the situation. The sound of our laughter echoes and breaks any tension between us. When we finally stop giggling, Cameron surprises me by thanking me.

Thank me? For what?

Not convinced, Shelly asks if he is okay again.

Cameron takes another sip and pauses for a moment, considering Shelly's question. With a faint smile, he finally replies, "My life was pretty good until my parents died three months ago in a terrible car accident. A reckless teenager was texting while driving, and I have been homeless ever since." He shifts in his seat and looks away briefly before continuing. "I didn't have any other family to turn to, and I've been struggling to make ends meet on my own."

Shelly rubs his back gently, and I place my hand on his knee, offering comfort.

"I can't imagine how difficult it must have been for you," I say softly. "You're not alone anymore. We're here for you."

He looks up at us, his eyes filled with gratitude. "Thank you."

To be only sixteen years old and already faced with such hardships is unimaginable. In this rare case, vampirism saved him from a life of isolation and despair. Still, just because it worked out for him doesn't mean it's a solution for everyone. It doesn't excuse all the other innocents who were turned against their will. Richard is a prime example.

I'm back in my chambers after an eventful day at Shelly's villa when there's a knock on my door. *What is it now?* I sigh and reluctantly make my way to the door. To my surprise, it's Kade.

"Hey Akira, how are you?" He asks while smirking and leaning his tall frame against my door. When he grins, his left dimple makes an appearance.

Kaden and Kade are identical twins with light brown skin and green eyes. They have a charm to them, especially Kade.

"I'm fine," I respond skeptically. "What brings you here?"

"You haven't responded in the group chat, so I thought I'd check up on you," Kade explains, but I'm not buying it.

Is *he* checking on me, or is *Lucas*?

"What's really going on, Kade?" I ask, narrowing my eyes.

Kade's eyes dart around my room nervously before finally responding, "Do you want to go on an undercover mission with us? Like old times."

Lucas asked in a group chat if any of us wanted to join him on a mission. I ignored the message, thinking Lucas would assume I wasn't interested. Which I'm not. But why did Kade visit my chambers to ask me? I'm positive Lucas sent Kade on his behalf since I haven't been responding to him.

"No, Kade, I'm not going. You can report my answer back to Lucas," I retort.

Kade frowns.

"Shelly and I are going to visit the witch coven," I murmur, not that it's any of his business.

"Okay, you guys, stay safe. You should take Cameron with you and show him the ropes." He winks.

"Great thinking," I reply deadpan.

Kade chuckles and shrugs his shoulders. "Just looking out for you, Akira."

"I think I can handle myself just fine. Now, if you don't mind, I'm going to bed," I say through gritted teeth, closing the door in his face before he can reply.

Santa Barbara, Here I Come

I'm getting ready for my trip to Santa Barbara, and the thought of seeing Akira again has my heart thumping beneath my chest as if there is a pack of wolves racing through the forest to capture their prey. Claude has set aside his reservations about Akira and is accompanying me on this trip. I confessed to him that we had been in contact since she left the hybrid kingdom, and to my surprise, he wanted to come along. Akira and I have so many people who disapprove of our developing relationship. Our connection is already causing complications in both of our lives.

There's a rift between Akira and her friends, and the vampire king ordered her to turn a human into a vampire. Not to mention, Dawn is giving me the cold shoulder. We haven't spoken since Akira and her court were here. It seems like the tension and challenges surrounding our relationship are only growing. Despite all of this, I long to hold her in my arms again, relishing the warmth of her embrace and the comfort it brings.

Claude enters my chambers. "The witches are here."

Akira sent over two witches to upgrade our electricity in the cave. Our flashlights and lanterns are not sufficient anymore.

Nodding my head, we head to the main entrance of the cave to welcome the witches.

"Welcome to our humble abode." I greet the witches with a warm grin.

The witches bow. "Hello, I'm Niyla, and this is my sister Jessica. We are pleased to meet you both."

"The pleasure is ours," I reply with a polite smile. "I am Prince Troy, and this is Prince Claude."

Niyla meets Claude's gaze for a moment, and her heart races. She quickly looks away, a faint blush coloring her cheeks.

She clears her throat. "Is there somewhere we can go to cast the spell?"

My gaze meets hers, and my brows furrow. "You have to cast a spell? What kind of spell?"

"Yes, Prince Troy." Jessica circles me, her eyes sweeping over me, examining me from head to toe. Her intense gaze compels a single bead of sweat to slowly descend down my temple, tracing a damp path over my skin.

"It's called a *light spell*," she continues.

Claude glances at me and smirks at my discomfort. "Follow me, ladies," he says, leading us to my dining suite.

"Is here okay?" I ask.

"This is perfect, Prince Troy," Niyla says as she nods. "Thank you."

Niyla is very friendly and exudes a warm personality. She has light brown skin, a slim figure, short black hair, and green eyes. I sense her attraction toward Claude through her subtle glances at him. Jessica, her older sister, seems stern and has darker skin. She is slim, has thick brown curly hair, and fierce brown eyes. Any man can see how beautiful she is. However, I only have eyes for Akira Ronin.

Akira mentioned her close connection to the witch coven and insisted that they would have no problem granting her this favor in upgrading our electricity.

Niyla and Jessica hold hands and chant in a foreign language, their voices harmonizing. Light switches materialize on the walls, and light bulbs illuminate the room with a soft glow.

"That's incredible!" Claude says, gaping at the new illumination in the room.

"Incredible indeed! Thank you." I say, shaking Niyla and Jessica's hands.

Jessica nods, and Niyla smiles back at us. "It was our pleasure to help," Niyla replies.

"I'm going to check the lights in my suite!" Claude says, eagerly heading towards the door.

He's like a kid on Christmas morning, I chuckle in response.

Turning to Niyla and Jessica. "Let me show you out," I offer, gesturing toward the exit.

"No need. We will conjure a portal from here and transport ourselves back," Jessica says.

At the same time, Niyla waves her hands in a circular motion to create a beaming, swirling portal.

My eyes widen in amazement as the portal materializes before me. I have never seen anything like it before. The witches go through, disappearing through the bright white lights.

Grabbing my bag I continue packing for my trip when Dawn storms into my suite unexpectedly, her gaze fixed on my duffle bag.

"What are these?" She fiddles with the light switch, and the lights flicker on and off.

Scratching the back of my neck. *She's speaking to me now?*

"Those. Are. Light. Switches." My lips form a grin. "They control the lights in the room."

She rolls her eyes and mutters something under her breath.

Raising an eyebrow, I decide not to press any further. Zipping my bag and swinging it over my shoulder, I head towards the door.

"You let that vampire get into your head. She has you wrapped around her pretty little finger," she says, her voice dripping with disdain.

Pausing for a moment, I consider her words before responding, "Dawn, I don't expect you to understand. You don't know Akira."

Dawn scoffs and crosses her arms, her eyes narrowing. "Understand? I understand perfectly well that you're risking everything for someone who could easily turn on you."

Taking a deep breath and trying to maintain my composure. "It's not what you think, Dawn. Akira is not like that."

Dawn rolls her eyes, unconvinced. "You're just blinded by your emotions," she retorts, waving her hands toward my duffle bag, causing everything to fall out of it.

I understand she is upset. Still, using her telekinesis power against me feels personal, not political.

Dawn looks at the mess she created and darts out of the room.

This is something we will address after my trip. I check my phone to see if there are any updates from Felix. There isn't. King Abel sent Felix and the rest of the hybrids on a covert mission. I've already sent him a few messages, but he hasn't responded. Felix was given a secret phone unbeknownst to the king and his court. He was meant to provide me with regular updates. Still, the unsettling silence since Felix embarked on the mission is causing me anxiety. In my opinion, the vampire king cannot be trusted, and I have a nagging feeling that something isn't right. I want to address my suspicions with my father. However, he dismissed me the last time I mentioned my concerns about King Abel.

I send a text message to Akira instead, and she promises to investigate the situation.

Lifting my bag and stuffing my belongings back into it, I head to the main entrance to meet Claude. He's talking with Dawn, and I give her a slight smirk; she walks away right when I approach them.

"I hope you know what you're doing," Claude says while we exit the cave onto the platform where our private jet is parked.

My gaze meets Claude's; his expression is unreadable.

"Are you guys ready to go?" Charles, our pilot, asks as he stands by the open door of the aircraft.

We board the jet and hand Charles our bags.

"So, what's in Santa Barbara?" Charles asks, breaking the silence as he starts up the engines.

Akira.

"Our ending!" Claude says through gritted teeth.

Charles raises an eyebrow, glancing between Claude and me. Narrowing my eyes at Claude, he shrugs before looking away to gaze out the window. I wonder what Dawn and Claude discussed before I approached them.

The engine roars to life, and we take off. I seize the moment to rest my eyes for a bit, the hum of the engines lulling me into a light sleep.

As I open my eyes, we are nearing Santa Barbara, and the anticipation fills my chest.

When we land, I check my phone to see if Felix has messaged me back. There's nothing from him. I send him another text, informing him we are in Santa Barbara.

Claude and I take a cab to the hotel, where we will stay for two weeks. The salty breeze from the ocean fills the air as we drive through the coastal town. Checking my phone once more for any notifications from Felix, I sigh when there is still nothing; however, there is a text from Akira saying she can't wait to see me.

A smile spreads across my face. I cannot wait to see her as well.

Can You Say Tension?

You can cut the tension between my brother and me with a knife. It is so thick. He seemed okay with coming to Santa Barbara until after his conversation with Dawn. Now, he's giving me the cold shoulder.

"Claude, we need to talk. Would you be up for that?" I ask, wanting to clear the animosity between us.

Claude pauses for a moment, his expression guarded. After a few uneasy seconds, he sighs and reluctantly nods his head. "Fine, let's talk," he replies, his voice laced with a hint of resignation.

Placing my hand on his shoulder. "I don't want us to keep fighting like this," I say, my voice steady. "We're family, and we need to find a way to move past this."

Claude's hard stare softens, his guard lowering. "I agree," he admits. "We *are* family, and Akira *isn't*."

A knot forms in my throat, and my inner wolf growls in response. Razor-sharp teeth protrude from my clenched jaw while slamming my fist onto the table.

"Claude, I don't expect you or anyone else to understand the bond I have with Akira. However, that doesn't give you the right to disrespect her!"

Claude's eyes narrow, and his expression hardens once again. "I'm not disrespecting her, Troy! I'm just trying to protect you! Except you can't see that, so maybe you're not as smart as I thought!"

He strides out of the room to the balcony and lowers himself into one of the lounge chairs. The last thing I want is to continue arguing with Claude, so I exhale and follow him outside. Sitting in the unoccupied chair next to him, I bask in the fresh air, hoping that it will help diffuse the tension between us. Claude's shoulders tense up, his gaze fixed on the horizon.

"Brother, you have doubts. I have them, too, but can you please trust that I have our best interests at heart and will always prioritize our safety if something doesn't feel right?"

Claude remains silent, his jaw clenched, before turning towards me with a slight nod. *I guess that's as good a response as I will get from him.*

My phone vibrates in my pocket, and it's a text from Akira.

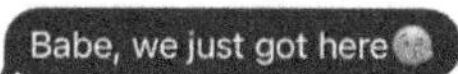

Hmm... Babe? *Are we on that level now?* Akira has my heart pounding in my chest and my length vibrating against the seams of my jeans. I haven't felt this way for a woman in my existence, and I love the sound of "Babe," it has a nice ring to it.

It's a small step, yet it feels like a big leap in our relationship.

"Akira and the others are settling into their rooms. Do you want to join me?" I ask Claude.

He gazes at me and then looks away. *I guess I'll take that as a no.*

We're staying here for two weeks. Claude will eventually come around with any luck.

Confidence radiates from within me as I make my way toward Akira and the others, and when she opens the door, her hazel eyes light up, and a smile spreads across her face. She is absolutely stunning. Her black dress clings to her silhouette, accentuating her beauty, and it has my imagination running wild. She wraps her arms around me in a tight hug, her vanilla scent enveloping me. We pull away from each other, not wanting to let go, almost forgetting that Shelly and Cameron are in the room. They exchange knowing glances, amused by our affectionate display. Shelly nudges Cameron and whispers something in his ear, causing him to smirk.

"Hi, Shelly. Nice to see you again," I grin, "and nice to meet you, Cameron."

"Hey, Troooyyy," Shelly screeches, dragging out my name as she says it.

"You too, Bro," Cameron says.

Akira gives Shelly a playful eye roll. "Always with the dramatics, huh?" she chuckles.

Shelly laughs and sticks her tongue out at Akira. "You know me, always adding some flair," she teases. "We will give you two some privacy." She grips Cameron's arm and leads him out of the room.

Akira's cheeks turn a rosy pink, and she chews on her bottom lip. She is such a beautiful sight to behold. I grasp her waist and pull her closer, unable to resist the magnetic pull between us.

"I missed you."

Akira's heart skips a beat, and she gazes into my eyes. "I missed you too," she whispers, her voice filled with longing, and her breaths are rapid.

"Show me how much," I tease, my lips curving into a mischievous grin as she smiles. Akira stands on her tippy toes, placing her lips against mine, and kisses me with a passion that ignites a fire within me.

Akira has completely shattered my expectations, and I never thought a woman could make me feel this way. Her touch and kiss are like an explosion of emotions and sensations I've never experienced before. She is beautiful on the outside. However, it's her inner beauty that captivates me. As much as I want time to stand still in this moment, responsibilities call, and we pull away. I still haven't heard from Felix and the other hybrids.

Kissing her on the forehead. "I have something—"

"A little longer," she says, placing her two fingers on my lips, cutting me off. "Before we talk about business, let's just enjoy being in each other's arms again," she continues.

We stay wrapped in each other's embrace, savoring the time a little longer. When we break apart, Akira and I know that reality awaits us.

"I haven't heard from Felix, and I'm starting to worry. It's unusual for him to go radio silent like this. Have you heard from Lucas or the twins?"

She shakes her head, concern etched on her face. "No, I haven't heard from any of them either since I turned down their request to join them on the mission. I told Kade I was coming here instead."

"Something doesn't feel right," I admit.

A crease forms on her forehead. "We will deal with this together."

She reaches for my hand, giving it a reassuring squeeze.

Picking Akira up by the waist and holding her frame close to mine, she squeezes me with her legs. I don't want to delve too deeply into this subject until we have more information. Until then, I want to focus on Akira for the next two weeks.

Whose Memories Are These?

The past week has been so much fun! Troy and I spent every day together while Shelly took Cameron sightseeing. She cares for him like a younger brother, as do I. I'm glad he's enjoying it here. Claude stayed to himself the entire time, avoiding any interaction with me. It's a bit disheartening that Claude hates me. Still, I want to assure him I hold no ill feelings toward him and that my fondness for his brother is more than an infatuation. It's genuine. *I just don't know how.*

Today, I'm visiting Monica and the other witches. They're going to perform a ritual on me to help regain my lost memories. *Hopefully.* It's unlike me to be in Santa Barbara and not visit the witches; Monica has always been a great friend and mentor to me. I told her we were showing Cameron around since he hadn't been on a vacation since his parents passed away. It was a partial truth. She didn't need to know that the hybrid prince and his brother were also accompanying us.

I shoot Troy a text.

Troy's subtle affections truly have me swooning over him.

Monica greets me with a warm hug as I step into her house. She's always been like an older sister or more like a cool aunt to me, offering guidance and support whenever I needed it. She's a beautiful, brown-skinned woman with long, curly black hair, purple highlights, and brown eyes.

"Finally, you come and visit me!" she says, pulling away from the hug.

"I—I um. I've been meaning to come by sooner, but I've been so caught up with my friends. Life just gets so busy sometimes." I ramble, taking a seat on the sofa.

Monica joins me and sips her coffee, listening to me drone on. "Sure, that's what's been keeping you busy." She winks with a knowing smirk, tracing her lips.

Anxiously twirling the end of my curl around my finger. "Yes, I am sorry, Monica. I have just been enjoying it here with my friends." Scratching the back of my neck, I avoid eye contact. I'm sure my cheeks are definitely pink.

Monica's eyes narrow, and she chuckles softly while heading to the dining room area to retrieve a vast ancient book from the chestnut brown desk. She flips through the pages, her eyes scanning the text, and uses her magic to conjure eight candles that appear next to her. She waves her arm forward, opening and closing her hands, and the candles form a circle.

"I spoke to Rosa, and she suggested a spell we could try for your lost memories," she says, her voice filled with hope. "It's an ancient ritual that has been known to bring back fragments of forgotten memories. Are you willing to give it a try?"

"Rosa is okay with helping us?" I ask.

"Yes, she is. Are you ready?"

I wonder why Rosa hasn't helped us before. I think to myself.

Monica instructs me to lie down on the floor in the circle she made with the candles. She retrieves salt from the counter and sprinkles it along the circle, throwing some over her shoulder for good luck. Niyla, Jessica, and Kai enter the room and light all the candles around me, filling the room with a soft, flickering glow, casting dancing shadows on the walls. Kai is Jessica's boyfriend. He is tall, handsome, and has glowing olive skin. They join hands and begin to chant in a language I don't recognize, their voices blending in accord. Their chant grows louder, the room becomes dark, and everything shakes. A tingling sensation flows through my body as if awakening something dormant within me. The room becomes hazy, and I close my eyes, feeling waves of energy coursing through my body.

A variety of colors, red, green, and purple, flash before my closed eyelids, and I fall into a deep slumber.

Sunday at six-thirty in the morning, a fair-skinned woman with short black curly hair is resting on a bed in intense pain. She is having contractions. Her face is contorted with each wave of pain, and her hands grip the sheets.

Walking in is a tall, light brown-skinned man with piercing hazel eyes. He has a concerned look etched on his face as he rushes to her side, holding her hand.

"Serena, is it time?" he asks with both excitement and worry in his voice.

"Yes! She is coming! She is coming!" Serena screeches through gritted teeth;

her voice is strained with pain.

The man's grip on her hand tightens as he reassures her, "You're doing great, Serena!"

A woman enters the room, advising Serena to stay calm and relax. She is light-skinned and has short, dark brown hair and deep brown eyes. She reminds me of someone, but I can't figure out who. She directs Serena to breathe in and out and guides her through a series of intense breaths. Serena follows her instructions, and the woman, who I assume is a nurse, informs her it is time to push. She inhales and then exhales a deep breath, giving the nurse a nod.

As she pushes, she shouts with determination and grit. "Jacobson! Jacobson! She is coming, she is coming!"

His eyes widen as he sees the baby's head crowning. He holds Serena's hand, offering words of encouragement and support.

The nurse yells, "That's it, Serena! Breathe in and out. You're doing great! Just one more push!"

Serena gathers all of her strength and pushes with everything she has, sweat dripping from her forehead.

"Serena, sweetheart, she is here!" Jacobson says, and tears fill his eyes.

The cries of a newborn baby consume the room.

"Please, Jacobson, let me see her before he arrives and takes her away!" Serena cries out.

The nurse places the baby on Serena's chest, and she and Jacobson gaze at her tiny face in awe.

"You're perfect," Serena whispers, tears flowing down her cheeks.

The nurse asks the couple if they have decided on a name. Serena and Jacobson exchange a knowing glance before answering, "Akira," in unity.

"Akira is a beautiful name." The nurse says.

"Thank you. At first, we thought we were having a boy," Jacobson murmurs, gazing at Serena. "However, once you revealed we were having a girl, we didn't want to change the name. Akira means bright, clear, and ideal," Jacobson continues, delight resonating within his voice.

They both admire their daughter, marveling at her tiny features and telling her how much they love her in between sobs.

"I am so sorry," the nurse apologizes.

The door is shattered, and Jacobson and the nurse fall unconscious.

Serena cries, "Please, please don't take my baby." Her voice is hoarse. "Please, I will do anything."

The man doesn't say a word. He gives Serena a grim look and snatches the baby from her trembling arms. Tears stream down her face.

"Please, Abel!" Serena pleads, frantically reaching out to the man. "I beg you, don't take our baby away from us."

Suddenly, it feels like a cluster of rocks is weighing me down and crushing the air out of my lungs.

Grasping my chest. "I can't breathe!"

"Akira, take deep breaths. Focus on my voice! Breathe in, and then breathe out. Come on, do it with me." Monica says.

Trying to regulate my breathing, I follow her instructions. Inhaling and exhaling, but it doesn't help. The whirling room spins around me, and my vision blurs.

"W—what is wrong with her?" Niyla's voice is frantic.

"What did she see?" Jessica questions.

"Akira! Count with me—one, two, three." Monica urges, her voice steady and calm. "Focus on the numbers and try to slow down your breathing. You're going to be okay."

"One. Two. Three." I repeat.

"That's it!" Monica encourages. "Keep counting and take deep breaths. You're doing great."

"One. Two. Three." I continue to repeat the numbers, feeling my breathing gradually become more controlled. Surveying the room, I breathe in and out. *Who were Serena and Jacobson?*

"Who are Serena and Jacobson?" I whisper, echoing my inner thoughts.

Kai, Jessica, Niyla, and Monica exchange glances; no one responds.

"Who are Serena and Jacobson?" I ask again with more conviction.

"How about you tell me what you saw?" Monica suggests instead of answering my question.

"No!" I shout while balling up my fist. "Who are Serena and Jacobson?" My heart pounds in my chest as I await their response, desperate for answers.

"They are your biological parents," Kai reveals, breaking the tense silence.

His words are clear, and they feel like a punch to the gut. The room spins as I try to process this newfound information. Losing my balance, I wobble to the right, and Jessica catches me. I'm numb. Aika and Abel Ronin *are* my parents, *not* Serena and Jacobson.

"Whose memories did I see? Those weren't mine!"

Kai rolls his shoulders back and sighs. "Serena was a human and an empath witch, but her physical magic was dormant. Jacobson was a vampire and the king's right-hand man; he fought beside him for centuries. He fell in love with Serena, and she became with child." His voice is monotone.

My heartbeats increase with each word Kai utters.

He pauses for a moment and then continues. "There was a prophecy that their child would be the most powerful being to exist, and she would reunite all the kingdoms. The king knew of this prophecy and saw it as a threat to his rule, so he and the queen had Rosa cast a spell over the entire kingdom, ensuring their memories would be wiped clean of the prophecy. They murdered Serena and Jacobson and took you for themselves."

The color drains from my cheeks once more. Aika and Abel aren't my parents, and they have been lying to me the entire time. I cannot fathom it. They have betrayed and deceived me, and it is as if my whole world has been shattered.

Sitting down on Monica's sofa, I place my head in my hands, trying to process the magnitude of this revelation. A wave of emotions washes over me, making my stomach churn. *What now?*

"Are you okay, Akira?" Monica reaches out and places a comforting hand on my shoulder.

"My very existence is a lie," I mutter, my voice barely audible.

Monica sits beside me and gently pulls me into a hug. "I can't imagine how difficult this must be for you," she says. "Nonetheless, the truth is out; the witch coven is ready to follow you."

"What do you mean?" I ask in confusion.

"Abel and Aika cast a spell on you to suppress your true identity and powers," Monica explains. "However, now that you know the truth, the spell has been broken on all of us. This is probably why Rosa was eager to assist; she wanted us to regain our memories."

"A piece of our memory was returned once *you* started to remember," Kai adds.

Placing my forehead in the palm of my hand, I replay the vision in my mind. "There was another woman in my vision. Who was she?" I ask, not sure if they will respond.

Niyla paces toward me and shows me a picture of the young woman. "Did the woman you saw look like her?"

"Yes! Who is she?"

"She is our mother, Rosa," Niyla responds.

My jaw tightens, and a jolt of electricity runs through me as I take in the revelation. The pieces of my past are coming together, except there is still so much I don't understand.

Revelation

For years, we were in the dark. The light has finally begun to shine upon us, illuminating the path we have long been searching for. Kai blurted out all the information as he remembered it, and by the look on his face, he couldn't grasp the enormity of what he was saying. I still can't believe the extreme measures Abel would take to keep me from learning the truth.

"We should reach out to our mother. She has all the answers." Niyla suggests.

"Why didn't she say anything to me?" I ask, looking from Jessica to Niyla and back again.

Rosa was the witch who delivered me; she's also Niyla and Jessica's mother and has been in my kingdom for over twenty years. Rosa never once mentioned she knew my parents.

"I don't know, Akira. I'm sure she had her reasons for not telling you," Jessica replies. "However, we can't act on this information just yet. Abel doesn't know that we know," she warns.

Repeating the information in my mind once more. *Abel and Aika Ronin are not my real parents, and they murdered my biological ones!*

"Why would Rosa help us now?" I wonder aloud.

Monica shrugs her shoulders. "Perhaps she has been helping us in ways we don't know all along."

"Do the rest of the witch kingdom and my fa—"

Realizing what I'm about to say, I stop mid-sentence and clear my throat to start over. "Do the witch kingdom and Abel know that Rosa is your mother?"

"Yes. King Abel knows everything," Niyla replies with a hint of bitterness.

"Our mother handed down her mantle to Monica and left us here for our protection. You know very well what kind of man King Abel is," Jessica adds, certainty in her eyes.

That is true. Abel is ruthless and power-hungry. He demolished an entire kingdom to establish his control over the remaining supernatural creatures. It is no surprise that he would use any means necessary to maintain his power.

"All of the witches are aware? Including Rosa?" I ask again, still trying to comprehend the situation at hand.

"Yes, the witches are aware, and Rosa suggested the spell, so she knows as well. I believe everyone should pretend as if they don't know, just to be safe, and continue to act as if everything is normal," Monica says cautiously. "We don't want to give Abel any reason to suspect that we're onto him."

"Was the spell broken for witches only?" I ask.

"Yes, it was. As of now, only the witches know the truth. Rosa made sure of it with the specifics of the spell she suggested we cast." Monica replies. "Nevertheless, let's keep all of this to ourselves. I will call a meeting with the witches tomorrow."

We nod in agreement and decide to call it a night. This is enough to digest for now.

My right leg is shaking uncontrollably while sitting in the cab heading back to the hotel. I'm trying to process everything. How can I function like nothing has changed? The weight of everything that has been uncovered hangs heavy on my shoulders, and I have to tell my friends. What will they think?

I cannot keep this information to myself; they deserve to know the truth. Retrieving my phone out of my pocket, I text them to meet me in my room. My lips curve into a frown as I hit send. What will Troy think of me after hearing what I have to say? Will he still see me the same way? Doubts and insecurities start to consume me, and my stomach does somersaults. Pushing them aside, I remember that Troy and I have no secrets. Troy and I decided that we would make this work together despite any obstacles that may occur. We *want* to be together and are willing to *fight* for us. He told me about the phone he gave Felix and didn't have to, and now we can figure out the secret mission together.

However, I have returned to the hotel room, and Shelly, Claude, Cameron, and Troy are staring at me, waiting for me to speak.

When I attempt to speak, nothing comes out of my mouth. Troy flashes me a reassuring smile, encouraging me to share my thoughts.

"King Abel and Queen Aika are not my biological parents!" I blurt out, covering my mouth.

Surprise spreads across their faces as my words hang in the air. Shelly's eyes widen and her brows knit together while Claude and

Cameron exchange puzzled glances. Troy's smile fades, and a crease forms between his eyebrows.

"They aren't biologically your parents," he starts slowly, "Because they had to cast a spell to have you, right?" Troy attempts to make sense of what I'm trying to say.

Vampires are technically dead, so they are unable to conceive children naturally. Therefore, a baby is born from magic rather than biological. It's a complex process. A witch uses the blood of the vampire couple to cast a spell on the fetus that's growing inside an unwilling participant who serves as a surrogate for the vampire parents. When the baby is born, the surrogate dies due to the strain of carrying a supernatural being, and the baby is fed her blood to sustain its transformation.

Tears well up in my eyes. "No, that's not what I mean. They are not my parents. My biological parents were murdered over twenty years ago."

They exchange worried glances, their confusion deepening.

"What do you mean the king killed your biological parents?" Cameron asks, attempting to fill in the blanks of my story.

"He killed my parents!" I shout, my voice shuddering with anger and grief.

Everyone's faces are pale as my words sink in.

Shelly paces back and forth, shaking her head. "No, no, no. Who told you this?"

The disbelief in her eyes is evident as she struggles to comprehend the gravity of my statement. I'm trying to process the shocking revelation myself.

"You know all those visits to the witch's domain? They were more than innocent visits; the witches were helping me regain my memories."

Shelly's eyes widened, her mouth agape. I have everyone's undivided attention, even Claude, who until now has barely acknowledged me this entire trip. Yet, now he's hanging onto my every word.

"Rosa gave Monica a spell to restore my memories, and it worked," I continue. "Memories of my birth came flooding back to me, and I saw everything as if I were physically there."

Shelly, Cameron, Troy, and even Claude start asking me questions all at once, talking over each other, and I'm unsure whose voice to respond to first.

"What does this mean for the kingdoms?" That is the only question I'm able to understand.

Taking a deep breath and exhaling, I try to gather my thoughts before responding. "Listen, guys, this was a lot to take in all at once, and I wanted to fill you in on everything. However, you can't tell anyone else about this. This must stay between us for now." I look at each of them, hoping they understand the seriousness of the situation. "There was a prophecy that was revealed to me, and it seems to suggest that I would be the most powerful being in existence and reunite all the kingdoms. Abel knew of this prophecy and wanted to prevent it."

"How does raising you as his daughter fit into his plan?" Claude asks, trying to make sense of Abel's motives.

"Isn't it obvious?" Troy says. "Abel has been collecting powerful creatures for centuries and harnessing their abilities to strengthen his own. He may be raising Akira as his daughter as a way to gain access to her power or find a way to absorb it."

"Maybe he's still searching because why keep her alive this long?"

Claude speculates.

Troy furrows his brow, deep in thought. "That's a possibility." He sits on the sofa, pondering some more.

"Akira, can you tell us more about this revelation? Was your mother a vampire? A witch?" Claude asks.

I recite to them the entire vision.

"You realize this means you are half-human, half-vampire?" Shelly states, her eyes widening with realization. "Your existence creates a new kingdom for the rest of them to coexist with. You're the hope we've been waiting for to bridge all the supernatural beings together. Think about it, a witch, vampire, human...this is incredible!"

Troy nods in agreement, adding, "She's the bright light to bring us out of this darkness."

The realization dawns on me. They're right. I'm half-human and half-vampire, making me a *hybrid* as well. I always had a strong repulsion for consuming human blood; maybe this is why, but what doesn't make sense is: how am I so powerful? *What powers do I possess?*

"You should try eating food," Cameron suggests, and we all look at him, blinking. "To put the theory to the test," he adds with a shrug.

Intrigued by the idea, I contemplate giving it a try. Perhaps trying human food will put the question to rest.

Turning to face Claude and Troy. "If this doesn't work, you guys can have the food." I half-joke.

They both chuckle in agreement, clearly amused by the prospect of me attempting to eat human food.

Troy pulls me onto his lap and wraps his arm around my waist, giving me a comforting squeeze. "We'll be right here with you."

It's a well-known fact that vampires survive solely on the blood of humans, so the idea of eating human food seems both foreign and futile. Consuming food does not provide any sustenance for vampires. Instead, it makes us ill and takes weeks to recover, especially for those of us on animal blood only. Our digestive system is not able to process solid food. We become nauseous after one bite. I'm sure what I saw in the vision is true. However, I'm skeptical about trying food because the rest of this trip will be ruined if we are wrong.

A short while later, trays of food are brought to our room by the hotel staff. The enticing aroma fills the air, making my stomach churn in anticipation.

Cameron watches my reaction, grinning from ear to ear. "Bon appétit!"

He ordered a double-stacked cheeseburger and onion rings.

Taking a deep breath, I prepare myself for this unusual experiment. "Here goes nothing."

Holding the food in my mouth, I start chewing, imitating the movies I have watched, unsure of what to do next.

"Now you have to swallow," Cameron says with a hint of sarcasm.

Troy and Claude chuckle at my expense, and Shelly scratches the top of her head.

Expecting the worst, I swallow, and to my surprise, it tastes delicious. We wait in anticipation for something to happen, except nothing does. When my stomach doesn't react, I take another bite of the cheeseburger, savoring the juicy beef, melted cheese, and tangy pickles. The flavors explode in my mouth, and I grin from ear to ear. Food falls from my mouth as I try to contain my excitement. Troy hands me a napkin to wipe. Is this what I've been missing?

Troy, Cameron, and Claude laugh at me, and Shelly looks confused.

Next, I try one of the onion rings; the crunchy texture and the hint of sweetness in the flavor have my mouth watering. *Human food is pure bliss.*

As I finish devouring my cheeseburger and onion rings, I realize I *am* half-human. And my biological parents were murdered by the people I thought *were* my parents. I'm finally accepting this revelation, and it is imperative that I flee this horrific kingdom at once!

One Thing After Another!

The following day, I rub my eyes, and my phone lights up, with a few missed calls from Troy and Monica and a text message from Kade. *Kade never texts me directly.* A knot forms in the back of my throat as I read Kade's text message adding to the already overwhelming weight of the previous day's revelations.

The hybrids are dead! Except for Felix.

How am I going to tell Troy? He will demand answers, and I have none to give him. My mind races, trying to process the devastating news. *Troy will want someone to pay for this! Abel! How can I look Abel in the eye and act as if nothing has changed?*

If it's not one thing, it's another!

Trying to gather my thoughts, my mind spins. How will I break the news to Troy without causing more chaos?

Dragging myself off the bed, I make my way to the bathroom and stare at my reflection in the mirror; a wave of exhaustion washes over me. Delivering this news to Troy will only add to our overwhelming burden.

My heart races as I stand under the water for what feels like forever, thinking about how this conversation with Troy will end badly.

As I emerge from the bathroom, Shelly and I lock eyes with one another.

The color in her face drains, and she is trembling. "K—Kade sent me a text." She stammers. "He said the hybrids were murdered, and Lucas and Abel were the ones behind it!"

My eyes widen. "Kade texted me too about the hybrids being murdered, but he didn't say who was behind it!"

Shelly places her hand on my shoulder and squeezes it. "I'm going to call him." She grabs her phone from her pocket, holding my shoulder as she dials his number. The phone rings and rings until Kade finally picks it up. Shelly's face pales as she listens to him, her grip on my shoulder growing even tighter. She hands me the phone, and I hear Kade's hushed voice on the other end explaining the horrific ordeal. My mind spins, once again mulling over the news. The king sent the hybrids on a mission as a ploy to eliminate them. Felix manages to escape, and Lucas and Kaden are searching for him. *How much more of this madness can I handle?*

Shelly is pacing the room, mumbling to herself; she's clearly overwhelmed by the situation. Abel wanted five skilled fighters from the hybrid kingdom to serve in ours, except this wasn't that. It was a strategic plan to murder them. Abel is ruthless, and his thirst to maintain power is repulsive. We have been to other kingdoms on numerous occasions, retrieving soldiers, and this has never been the result.

The hybrids must intimidate him!

"Akira, are you okay?" Shelly asks with concern.

Lost in my thoughts, I lash out. "What do you think?"

Shelly's eyebrows pull together, and her lips turn into a frown. She reaches out to hold my hand, offering her support without saying a word.

"I'm sorry," I say immediately, realizing my wrath is misplaced.

Shelly gives me a reassuring smile.

The king murdered my parents in cold blood over twenty years ago, and now he has murdered innocent hybrids. And I'm supposed to be some *powerful* hybrid with the ability to stop him. How? When I have no idea what my powers are or how to access them. Troy and I are building a relationship, but for what? For all I know, the king could tear us apart just like he did to my family.

Rage engulfs me, fueled by the anger that has been building up within me. Tossing the bed against the wall in a fit of fury, I exhale a frustrated breath. Suddenly, the hotel is shaking violently, as if an earthquake is occurring. *What is happening?* A power inside me surges, causing the lights to flicker, and a bright red and orange glow emanates from my hands. It's as if my anger has awakened a dormant force from the depths of my soul that I never knew existed. The light intensifies, the room goes black, and I collapse to the floor.

Troy, Cameron, Claude, and Shelly are looming over me when I awake, their faces etched with worry.

Troy takes my hand and pulls me to my feet. "Are you okay?"

One moment, I was tossing the bed, and then the next, the entire hotel shook. *Maybe it was an earthquake?*

Troy helps me off the floor and steadies me.

"Did you guys feel the earthquake?" I blink, feeling disoriented.

Troy shakes his head, exchanging a glance with the others. "There was no earthquake, Akira," he says, his voice filled with concern. "You blacked out for several hours."

"You collapsed after you tossed the bed, except you didn't throw the bed *physically*. Your eyes turned black, and a bright red and orange glow surrounded you, and then the whole hotel began to shake." Shelly says.

Trying to piece together what Shelly is saying. "I—I don't remember any of that," I mumble, my mind racing to make sense of the situation. "What do you mean I didn't throw the bed *physically*?"

"It was like you used some kind of force to move it. Maybe one of your powers is telekinesis," Shelly suggests in awe.

Leaning my head to the side, I furrow my brow. "Telekinesis?"

"Perhaps you should pay the witches another visit?" Cameron smirks suggestively.

"They might have some answers about your newfound powers," Claude adds.

Twirling a strand of hair, I chew on my bottom lip. "Maybe you're right."

Reaching for my phone, I send Monica a text, informing her that I'll be over there tomorrow morning.

Troy looks around the room at the redecorating I did. "It looks like you and Shelly will be sleeping in our room tonight since you have rearranged the furniture here so nicely," he says with a smirk.

My knees weaken when he flashes me that sexy smile. Lost in my dirty thoughts, I almost forget the news about Felix and the other hybrids.

A Date in The Middle of It All

Akira is a beautiful woman, inside and out. She is pure. Her sympathy for humans and her distaste for their blood set her apart from King Abel. I don't know much about Queen Aika other than she has fiercely stood by her husband's side for centuries, and that makes her just as vile in my eyes. It makes sense that they aren't her parents.

Last night, Claude and I had a long discussion about everything Akira disclosed to us. He had a change of heart and began to see her in a different light. Akira is a victim, and Claude and I agreed to do whatever it took to free her from that kingdom.

We are back in our room, and I place Akira's bags on the floor, clearing my throat.

"Would you rather share a bed with Shelly or me?"

Akira's cheeks turn a bright shade of pink. "I want to share a bed with you if that's okay."

A rush of heat forms in the pit of my stomach at Akira's

response. "Hmm... I can't say no to that." Turning to Claude, I add, "Looks like you will be sleeping on the floor while Shelly sleeps in your bed." A wide grin forms on my face.

Claude chuckles and shrugs. "No problem, I'll make do."

Akira smiles and narrows her eyes toward me. "Don't try anything," she says, "or I might have to kick you out of bed."

Enjoying the playful banter between us, I laugh and assure her I'll behave.

Akira dives into the bed and falls asleep as soon as her head connects to the pillow. Her forehead has a slight crease, which must be from all the stress. Nonetheless, she's absolutely breathtaking. I can only imagine how her mind is reeling from everything she has been through in the past few days.

Gently brushing a strand of hair away from her face, I place feather-like kisses on her forehead. Akira isn't the kind of woman I would have in my bed once and then move on. She's unique and requires my support and protection. Akira should be courted appropriately and only deserves the best.

Grabbing my phone, I look up things to do in Santa Barbara, and a few suggestions appear. There are plenty of options for us to explore, from wine tastings and vineyards to culinary and gourmet tours, parks, and more. Scrolling through the options, I mentally plan out our perfect day together.

Tomorrow, Akira will be the center of my attention, and every moment should be executed to perfection and engraved in her heart and mind forever.

Nothing should be left to chance.

Akira curls up next to me in her sleep, unaware of the effect she has on me. Her body heat seeps into my skin, igniting a fire in my veins, and I fight the urge to wake her up with passionate kisses that would leave us breathless. The soft glow of the moonlight illuminates her features, and I could stare at her for hours, getting lost in the beauty of her face. It feels right to be near her.

The next morning, I open my eyes before Akira, feeling a surge of electricity in the pit of my stomach for our date. Slipping out of bed and procuring my phone, I confirm the arrangements are set. I order her breakfast in bed: scrambled eggs, toast with butter, smoked sausage, and French toast.

Akira rubs her eyes, brows shooting up when I place the tray of food in front of her with a vase of fresh flowers and a steaming cup of coffee. She covers her mouth with her hand. "You didn't have to do all this." She mumbles.

Shelly wakes up, eyes widening at the sight of the elaborate breakfast spread. "Wow, you really outdid yourself!" she says.

"Only the best for my girl." I shrug, a grin forming on my lips.

Akira's cheeks turn red, and she playfully nudges me. "You're such a romantic."

"Well, you deserve nothing less."

Shelly darts her pointer finger in and out of her mouth while making a gagging noise, "Can you two save the lovey-dovey stuff for when I'm not around?"

"I second that," Claude adds, rubbing his eyes.

Akira and I laugh while Shelly and Claude leave the room, shaking their heads in mock disgust.

"I have a date planned for us after breakfast," I reveal.

"Oh, I must let Monica know I'll be by tomorrow instead of today."

A sweet smile spreads across her face before quickly fading as a hint of worry crosses her eyes.

Tilting her chin up with my finger. "What's wrong?"

She takes a deep breath and murmurs, "I have some bad news to share with you."

Shaking my head. "No. Save it for later."

Akira meets my gaze. "It has to do with Felix and the other hybrids."

Claude enters the room, his eyebrows pulled together. He clears his throat, "I overheard your conversation. What about Felix and the other hybrids?"

Akira exchanges an uneasy look with Shelly, who strides in after Claude.

Shaking my head once more. "We will talk about it later. I want you to enjoy our first date."

"Are you sure?" Claude asks.

"Is it something that could be prevented?" I ask, my eyes fixed on Akira's expression.

She looks away. My mind spins with all the possible outcomes as to what happened to Felix and the rest of my hybrid family. "Then we will discuss it after our date!"

Shelly nods and leaves the room with Claude.

Once they exit, Akira's lips curve into a frown. "Are you sure you want to postpone discussing this?"

Knowing the king, they are probably all dead. I think to myself.

Taking her hands in mine, I give her a soothing smile. "Right now, let's focus on enjoying our first date and deal with the situation tomorrow. If it is as bad as I think, I would rather talk—"

Akira squeezes my hand, cutting me off, her worried expression softening. "Okay."

We arrive at a secluded vineyard surrounded by lush greenery. Akira and I walk through rows of grapevines, the sweet scent of grapes filling the air, and she smiles from ear to ear with the sun glistening off her flawless skin.

We reach a table set up under a large oak tree, and she surveys the platter of gruyere, goat, and aged cheddar cheese set before us. Our guide approaches with two glasses and three bottles of white wine. I hand her a five-hundred-dollar tip to leave the bottles and give us some privacy. Her eyes widen, and she walks away, mumbling something under her breath.

"Which wine would you like to start with?" I ask.

Akira is snacking on a slice of gruyere cheese, appreciating its rich, sweet, salty, and nutty flavor; her eyes light up as she scans the labels.

"Whichever wine goes with this cheese is the one I want to try first," she replies.

Pouring a glass of Pinot Grigio and handing it to her, I watch as she takes a sip and savors the wine's crisp, dry, and light-bodied flavors.

She nods in approval, her taste buds clearly pleased with the pairing. Next, we move on to goat cheese, which goes great with the Sauvignon Blanc.

Taking a bite of the goat cheese, I enjoy its creamy and tangy taste, complementing the fruity notes of white peach, lime, pear, grapefruit, and other refreshing tropical flavors of the Sauvignon Blanc.

Akira's face twists into a slight grimace, and she shakes her head in disgust. "I don't like the way this one tastes."

She doesn't quite have eating down yet. However, I wouldn't mind watching her reactions to different foods all day. Next is the aged cheddar, which goes excellent with Chardonnay. She doesn't seem enthusiastic when she tries the combination, and she doesn't care for the strong, bold flavors. I snicker to myself.

Akira purses her lips. "What's so funny?"

"I enjoy watching you eat," I reply, trying to hide my amusement as she goes for the gruyere cheese again.

"I really like this one," she says in between bites.

"Yes, I can tell."

She smiles and takes another bite of the gruyere cheese. I wish we could stay in this moment forever; unfortunately, *war is on the horizon.*

Shaking away the dreadful thoughts, I focus on the present. "I have another surprise for you."

Her eyes widen, and she places the half-eaten cheese on the tray. "Another surprise?"

Signaling the guide to come out with a tan basket I had called in and prepared beforehand, she spread the blanket on the grass and put the basket in the center.

Akira's smile grows. "I thought it would be nice to introduce you to some of my favorite foods."

She flutters her long eyelashes and smiles back at me. "That sounds wonderful."

Sitting on the blanket, I unpack the tan basket stored with chocolate-covered strawberries and two Caesar salads. My gaze meets Akira's, and I pat the empty space beside me and wink.

Akira's eyes light up. "You are amazing," she says, joining me on the blanket.

She reaches for a strawberry and takes a bite. The combination of the sweet chocolate and juicy strawberry makes her sigh in contentment.

"This. Is. Delicious." She murmurs between bites, savoring the taste.

Using my tongue to moisten my suddenly dry lips, I exhale. Akira has me weak and more desperate for her. With every bite she takes, my thoughts are more consumed with images of her sweet and soft lips on mine.

Akira sucks the last bit of chocolate off her fingers seductively and smiles. My inner wolf is ready to mate and explore every inch of her body. She lifts her chin a little, her eyes meeting mine and mirroring a hunger that matches my own. We fall back on the blanket, closing the distance between us; our lips press together in a passionate kiss, with the taste of chocolate lingering on the tip of our tongues. When our lips part, a soft sigh escapes her.

"Thank you for this," she whispers.

"You're welcome," I reply huskily.

My mind fills with a whirlwind of desire, and a playful smile tugs at the corners of her mouth.

"Tell me about yourself," she says, sitting up on the blanket while picking at the Caesar salad, her taste buds relishing the greens.

My lips curve into a slight grin, and I gaze at the clouds drifting slowly across the sky. "What would you like to know?" I run my fingers along her spine.

"I want to know everything about you," she says in between bites, and her cheeks turn pink. "Like, how old are you?"

I love it when she blushes.

"I'm twenty-four years old."

She laughs.

My brows snap together. "What's so funny?"

Akira toys with her fork and picks at her salad. "No, really, how old are you? How long have you been on this earth?"

"Oh, one hundred years, " I reply casually, shrugging my shoulders.

Her eyes are vast, and she swallows hard. "I'm dating an old man."

"Very funny," I reply, chuckling.

She shrugs. "Well, you are old." She giggles and looks away. "How about food? Do you cook?" Her hazel eyes are gleaming.

"I love to cook," I reply.

"What do you love to make?" She settles beside me, snuggling close and resting her head on my chest.

"I love making all kinds of dishes," I reply, tracing circles on her back with my fingers. "In another life, I would have loved to have been a chef."

She chuckles, her cheeks turning a deeper shade of pink. "Well, lucky for me, you get to cook for me in this life," she says with a playful smile.

Giving her a gentle squeeze. "What about you?"

"I'm simple." She pauses for a moment, looking up at me with a thoughtful expression. "You already know I love relaxing poolside and playing Cards Against Humanity." She smiles. "But my upbringing was quite different. I wasn't a human who turned into a vampire. One day, I woke up and was a vampire, and that's all I've ever known. I don't remember having a childhood, but now that I'm half-human, I would love to learn more about different cuisines and try new dishes."

Akira looks away as a tear falls from her eye.

Reaching out, I gently wipe away the tear. "The great thing about immortality is that you have all the time in the world to explore and indulge in new experiences."

Holding her tighter in my arms, we watch the sunset together.

"Troy?" Akira's voice breaks the silence, her eyes still fixed on the horizon.

"Yeah?" I reply, my gaze shifting from the sunset to her exquisite face.

"Have you ever been on a date that felt like time stood still?" Akira asks, a hint of vulnerability in her voice.

Clearing my throat, I think about all the dates I've been on. It's been over ten years since I've last been on one.

"Are you okay?" She looks at me expectantly.

"Uh, yeah, I'm fine." I sit up from the ground and take a sip of my wine.

She laughs at my reaction and takes a sip from her own glass, her eyes sparkling with amusement. "Well, I guess that means you have."

Shaking my head and then nodding. "Yeah, I've definitely had my fair share of dates; I mean, I am one hundred years old."

Akira's brow furrows, and she looks away as she takes in my response.

Placing my fingers underneath her chin gently, I guide her gaze back to mine. "None of them have ever made me feel like time has stood still."

Hoping to convey the sincerity behind my words, I smile.

"What do you mean?" Her eyes search mine for an explanation.

"I mean that being with you feels different. It feels like we're on the same wavelength, and I've never experienced anything quite like this before. I know in my heart that you are someone I would like to spend the rest of my life with."

Her eyes soften, and a hint of red tinges on her cheeks. "I feel the same way."

Akira's response is a confirmation that our connection is mutual and the promise of something deeper and more meaningful. Leaning forward, I kiss her on the cheek.

"What about you?" I whisper against her ear.

She laughs.

"Well, it is time for you to be in the hot seat," I chuckle.

Her lips curve into a small smile. "I have only been on one date."

It's hard to believe that someone as beautiful as her has only been on one date.

"And it was a total disaster!" She confesses, shaking her head. "Most of the guys in my kingdom are duds, and they care more about serving the king than getting to know me."

She looks away for a moment before continuing, "Honestly, this is my first real date."

Silence descends between us, and then she asks. "Do you ever wish you were human and didn't have to worry about royal obligations and rivalries?"

Akira nestles into my chest when I lie back on the blanket. "Sometimes I envy the simplicity of a human life without all the pressure and expectations of the supernatural world," I reply.

"Me too. Although, being a human isn't all rainbows and sunshine either," she says with a wistful smile. "Humans are kidnapped and brought to my kingdom all the time. Their life kind of sucks."

Nodding my head. "The grass is not always greener on the other side. There are good days, and then there are bad ones."

There's a comfortable calm between us as we watch the stars twinkle above us.

"Akira?" I break the silence, turning to face her.

"Yes?" she asks, her voice barely above a whisper.

"Will you be my girlfriend?"

Akira turns to meet my gaze, and she blushes. "I would love to be your girlfriend."

Tucking a brown curl behind her ear and leaning in for a kiss, my stomach flips in response.

After our date, we head back to the hotel. Claude informs me he and Shelly have decided to spend the night in Cameron's room, which is excellent because we have the space to ourselves. Once we settle in bed, our gazes meet, and I lean in for a kiss.

Our kiss is passionate and is as if the room is standing still. When our lips part, she exhales.

"Troy Bishop, I am falling for you," she whispers.

Kissing her forehead, "Akira Ronin, I am falling for you too."

We drift off to sleep as I cradle her in my arms, wanting to enjoy the moment for as long as I can.

Who Has Powers?

It is morning, and I wipe the sleep out of my eyes and gaze at the tall, handsome man sleeping beside me. He has such a charming smile and the most mesmerizing gray eyes I have ever seen. My heart skips a beat, recalling the moment he asked me to be his girlfriend. The thought that I get to call him mine has me in awe. He's still asleep, and I admire his peaceful expression before it's ruined by the news.

Troy shifts and slowly opens his eyes, his gaze immediately locking onto mine.

Gently caressing his handsome face, hoping to ease any worries that may arise from the impending conversation. "Good Morning," I say.

"Good morning," he says in a deep, husky voice that sends shivers down my spine.

I guess the time is now.

"I—"

Troy leans in and gives me a kiss on the cheek, interrupting me. "Whatever you have to say won't change what we have together."

I hope he still feels the same way after I tell him what Abel and Lucas did.

Taking a deep breath to steady my nerves, I sit up straight, "Abel and Lucas, they—" I begin, and he looks at me expectantly. "The hybrids are dead, and Felix is on the run," I blurt out, covering my mouth.

Troy doesn't say a word as he processes the information. When the initial shock wears off, his face contorts with a mix of anger and despair. Troy clenches his fists and tightens his jaw, and his emotions are swirling in his eyes. He says nothing; his silence speaks volumes.

Meanwhile, I start reciting every detail I can remember to fill the heavy silence. His expression remains unchanged as he absorbs my every word.

"Troy, please say something," I plead after an awkward moment that feels like an eternity.

"What do you want me to say?" He growls, his canine teeth appearing, and I can barely look him in the eye now.

"I—I don't know," I stammer, my voice barely above a whisper. "I just—need to know what you're thinking."

He told me nothing would change between us, no matter what happened. But now, at this moment, everything we have feels like it is slipping away because of the king. Abel, *my father,* wants to eradicate Troy and his entire kingdom. This is only the beginning.

Troy gets out of bed, knocking over a glass of water in his haste. Dismissing the mess, he dresses in a white fitted T-shirt and shorts before turning to face me; his expression is softer than before.

"I'm sorry for raising my voice at you," he says, his eyes filled with regret. "I won't let my kingdom fall without a fight," he says, his voice steady, and I nod.

Our relationship is not the only thing at stake here. The fate of an entire kingdom rests on our shoulders. He tosses my clothes toward me, and I dress in them immediately.

We meet the others in Cameron's room to devise a plan to retaliate against the king. We didn't want to book another room since I wrecked Shelly and mine with my out-of-control telekinesis power. The hotel management was not very happy with how the room looked and didn't understand how there was an earthquake that no one else felt.

Troy quickly joins in on the conversation, offering his strategy and military tactics expertise.

"How do you expect us to go up against Abel and his army of super-powerful guards?" I interrupt, my voice filled with doubt. "We don't even have a fraction of their strength or resources."

"We have you," Shelly replies confidently. "You're just as powerful as King Abel, if not more. Plus, we have the entire witch coven on our side."

"I don't even know how to harness my powers properly," I shoot back.

"The king doesn't know you're aware of your powers," Claude says. "That gives us the element of surprise. And with the witch coven backing us, they can train you to control and use your powers strategically."

Everyone nods.

"He won't see us coming," Troy adds.

Still not convinced, I raise an eyebrow. "Do you know who the king has on his side? He has Ava—she has the power of persuasion. She can persuade you to do *anything* she wants. He has Tyler, Kyle, and three other healers. They all have the power to heal any wound inflicted on him. Chase and two others are telepaths, and the king has the power of premonitions. He can also absorb the powers of others for a limited time. Not to mention, he has loyal followers who will fight to protect him at all costs and a formidable army at his disposal!" I ramble on about the king's seemingly unbeatable advantages.

"Wow! That's pretty impressive," Cameron says.

We look at him, and he throws his arms up in surrender. "I mean, I'm just saying, reading minds is a pretty cool ability. It sucks that we don't have anyone with that kind of power on our side."

Troy and Claude exchange uneasy glances.

"Or do we?" Cameron asks.

"Is there something you're not telling us?" I ask, raising an eyebrow.

Troy clears his throat and responds, "Dawn has the power of telekinesis."

"And you're just now telling us this?" Shelly shouts.

We were sent to the hybrid kingdom to retrieve five of their most powerful hybrids, but they gave us five *skilled* fighters instead. That was clever. Troy already knows what I'm thinking and smiles back at me.

"Is there anyone else in your kingdom with hidden powers we should know about?" Shelly asks.

"Roger and Philip have the power to materialize objects out of thin air," Claude responds.

"Holy smokes! They're on our side, right?" Cameron asks, grinning from ear to ear.

"Yes, they are on our side," Claude confirms deadpan.

"So, you have three powerful hybrids you didn't turn over to our kingdom?" Shelly asks, raising an eyebrow.

Troy and Claude give her a nod, and She and I smile at one another.

"That was a smart move," Shelly comments.

"I'm glad you didn't blindly obey the king's orders." I smile at Troy and Claude, then turn to Shelly. "Now that Kade is on the run, there's no way Kaden will turn his back on his brother, and Abel will look to Chase as his right-hand man from now on."

Shelly nods. "The king cannot know we're plotting against him. Our next moves need to be discreet and calculated."

"We need to keep our distance from him when we return to the castle until we figure out how to flee from the kingdom without arousing any suspicion," Cameron warns.

"So, you're with us?" I ask.

"Of course," Cameron says, giving me a fist pound. "Count me in."

"We will figure it out together," Claude adds.

Troy's phone beeps, and he reaches into his pocket to check who it is. His complexion fades, and he casts a glance at Claude, who has his brows knitted together.

"Who is it?" I ask warily.

"Felix," Troy responds, and suddenly, my heart is descending into my stomach. "Kaden helped him escape from Lucas, and now he's in Houston, Texas. He needs us to pick him up."

The twins have always been loyal to the king, but Kade gave us a heads-up, and Kaden helped Felix escape. What could have caused the twins to shift their loyalty from the king?

"We will leave tomorrow morning," Troy says firmly to Claude.

"I will inform our pilot," Claude replies, exiting the room.

Our trip to Santa Barbara is cut short due to unforeseen circumstances. My lips curve into a frown, and I look away. Troy senses my disappointment and wraps his arms around me. Leaning in his embrace, he kisses me gently on the forehead, cheek, and lips. He deepens the kiss, exploring every inch of my mouth with his tongue as if this were the last kiss we would share. When our lips part, his gaze locks on mine, and a rush of emotions consumes me. My vamp hearing reminds me that we're not alone, breaking the intimate moment between Troy and me.

Shelly and Cameron look everywhere in the room.

A sudden warmth spreads across my cheeks, and Troy scratches the back of his head and grins, realizing that we have gotten lost in the moment.

"Don't stop on our account," Shelly teases with a playful wink.

Twirling a strand of hair between my fingers, I chuckle. Troy and I exchange grins before he leans in closer, softly pressing his lips against mine once more.

"I will see you soon." He says, exiting the room to prepare for their departure tomorrow morning.

One Hybrid Left Standing

Today, Claude and I are heading out to pick up Felix. Before leaving, I head to Cameron's room. Knocking on the door to bid my farewells to them, Shelly's lips twist into a frown as she embraces me. She tells me that Akira is in the shower and will be out in a few minutes.

Not long afterward, Akira emerges from the bathroom with wet curls glistening in the sun hitting the room. She is the most beautiful woman I have ever seen, and I am the luckiest man alive to be her boyfriend.

She hugs me tight, her presence adding an extra spark to our departure, and she stands on her tiptoes to give me a sweet goodbye kiss.

"Get a room," Cameron jokes.

"Yes, please," Shelly adds, rolling her eyes and giggling.

We reluctantly break apart, yet our eyes remain locked, the lingering warmth of her lips still on mine.

"Please tell Felix, I am so sorry for what happened," she utters.

Kissing her forehead. "I will."

Claude informs me that our driver is waiting for us outside. Before heading out the door with Claude, I give Akira one last kiss.

Our flight to Texas is long and uneventful. Once our jet hits the platform, this uneasy feeling lingers in the core of my stomach. The palms of my hands are damp, and my hands are trembling at the thought of seeing Felix. We exit our private jet and are suddenly hit by the scorching hot sun.

We meet Felix at a gas station, and his appearance makes my heart sink. He looks tired and disheveled. His black jeans are ripped, his yellow T-shirt has holes and bloodstains, and he has no shoes on his feet. *Was the blood his own or someone else's?* It is clear he has been through a lot.

Felix plunges to the ground, unable to bear the weight of exhaustion, when Claude and I approach him. He has a deep gash on his right leg, and his eyes are bloodshot.

The weariness in his voice is evident as he struggles to speak. "He killed all of them. I–I couldn't save them," he mumbles. "I–I couldn't save them."

So many questions are racing through my mind. I witnessed Lucas on the battlefield back home, and there is no way that he could have single-handedly taken on all of them, especially Christian. However, seeing Felix in this state, I know it's not the right time to ask.

When we return to the cave, Felix is immediately taken to the infirmary, and my father summons an emergency meeting in the battle room with the guards and the rest of the council.

Dawn leans against the cold stone wall outside the battle room, her brows furrowed.

She shoves me as I approach her and growls, "Felix and the others suffered grave consequences because of your infatuation with that princess!"

"Abel doesn't know about our relationship!" I snap back. Admitting that Akira and I are, in fact, in a relationship. "He already had a plan in motion!" I defend my girlfriend.

She narrows her eyes at me, her voice dripping with disdain. "I blame your little princess. This is all *her* fault!"

She remains firm as I bare my fangs at her accusation. I don't have a chance to respond because we're inside the battle room now, and all eyes are on us. Their judgmental gazes pierce through me, and I refuse to back down. *This was not Akira's fault. Abel had a plan all along.*

Roger, our head guard, steps forward in the middle of the room, his authoritative presence demanding attention, and raises his hand to silence the murmurs. All the chitter-chatter comes to a halt.

He clears his throat and begins speaking. "We're here to address a serious matter that has unfolded. We received credible information that the hybrids sent to serve the vampire king were murdered, and one escaped." He glares in my direction and continues, "It has come to our attention that our prince is in a *'relationship'* with the vampire Princess Akira; perhaps *they* are responsible for orchestrating the entire plan." The room fills with gasps and whispers as everyone turns to look at me.

In a flash, I wrap my hand around Roger's throat, ready to snap his neck. "How dare you accuse me of such treachery?" I shout, my voice filled with venom, and my claws protrude from my fingertips. "I am Prince Troy of the hybrid kingdom. Mind your tongue when you speak of me!" I snarl, my eyes glowing with intense fury and my grip unyielding.

Roger looks at me with defiance, his eyes narrowing as he struggles to break free from my grasp. Gray smoke circles my body as I am about to change into my wolf form. Claude immediately intervenes, grabbing my shoulder to stop my transformation and warning me to release Roger before he uses his power against me.

Retracting my claws, I loosen my grip on Roger's throat. Roger struggles to catch his breath as he falls to the ground. However, his defiant expression remains unchanged.

"I have spent time with Princess Akira, and I can assure you she had nothing to do with this attack, and neither did my brother. Your prince!" Claude asserts.

Sounds of shock ripple through the room, followed by murmurs of confusion.

"That's enough!" My father's voice booms, commanding everyone to cease their actions. "We're not here to assign blame without evidence!"

My anger subsides as I take in my father's presence.

"Where is Felix? He knows what happened." My father orders, his voice demanding an answer.

Philip brings in Felix, who appears visibly shaken. He's cleaned up, and his wound is bandaged, yet his eyes still hold a haunted look. Claude and I exchange worried glances; he's in no shape to face questioning right now.

"Father, perhaps we should give Felix some time to recover before he gives his testimony," I suggest.

"Nonsense!" My father dismisses my suggestion with a wave of his hand.

His tone leaves no room for argument. I may be the prince of the hybrids, but my father is the king, and his words are final.

Looking at Felix, I shake my head and encourage him to speak.

Felix darts his eyes at everyone in the room and takes a deep breath. He recounts the events leading up to his current state.

"Lucas is King Abel's pawn; he and the king devised a plan to take us to Santa Fe, New Mexico, to kidnap homeless humans for the Battle of Anaik. After our mission was complete, we were walking back to our hotel when the vampire Ava ambushed us. She waved her hand at Christian, and he immediately fell under her control. His eyes were no longer gray but an eerie black. He yanked James's heart out of his chest and killed him instantly. She waved her hand at Alex next, and he, too, succumbed to her control. He snapped Melissa's neck, yanked her heart out as well, and ate it. That's when I realized Ava was using her power of persuasion on them and turning them into mindless monsters; her eyes glowed in satisfaction at the chaos she unleashed. I was the only one left standing, and Christian and Alex lunged at me, striking me with an unnatural strength. Their once familiar faces were twisted into bloodlust. I struggled to defend myself against their relentless attacks. I fought for my life against the two people I had once called brothers." Felix pauses for a moment, catching his breath, before continuing his story.

"The twins, Kaden and Kade, were unaware of the havoc Ava created until they stumbled upon the gruesome scene. They rushed to my side to get Christian and Alex off me, and I bolted as soon as I was freed from their grasp. I glanced behind me and saw Lucas snapping Christian and Alex's necks as Ava yanked their hearts from their chests. Lucas and I made eye contact, and I sprinted as fast as my legs could carry me. Lucas chased after me, but I found refuge behind a dumpster. He was closing in on me when the twins caught up to him and questioned him about what had just happened. Lucas was hesitant, but he explained everything to them. King Abel wanted us dead. He wants to eradicate our entire kingdom. The twins were appalled. Kade wanted no part of it, and

Kaden's eyes met mine briefly. Still, he remained silent, allowing me to slip away unnoticed."

The room is silent as everyone processes the gravity of Felix's revelation. Whispers of disbelief fill the air as the realization that their lives are in imminent danger sinks in. The room is now bursting with a sense of urgency. We need to devise a plan to protect this kingdom.

Felix slowly raises his hand, calling for attention. The room falls silent once again, all eyes fixed on him. "Princess Akira had nothing to do with this attack, and neither did the twins. Kade is on the run as we speak."

My father jumps from his seat. His brows snap together, and he pokes out his chest. "If war is what that vampire king wants, then war is what he shall receive!"

The king's declaration resonates throughout the room, and everyone nods in agreement.

War is inevitable.

Secrets Of the Past

The witches have everything arranged for the spell when we arrive there after checking out of the hotel. Monica uses Niyla and Jessica's family grimoire for the "memory" spell because Rosa's incantation has been broken; therefore, it should work.

Cameron's eyes dart from the circle of salt they had created to Shelly and then back again. "Well, this is not creepy at all," he mutters to her.

"Just wait until you see what comes next," Shelly replies.

Cameron shifts his weight from the left to the right on the sofa, his eyes wide as the witches begin to chant in a foreign language. Once again, the room goes dark, and everything shakes. Energy flows throughout my body, and colors dance behind my closed eyelids, causing me to fall into a slumber.

"Aika! I had a premonition about Jacobson and Serena's child," Abel says with urgency.

Aika meets Abel's gaze. "What did you see, Honey?"

"She will be the most powerful supernatural creature the world has ever

known. We must destroy her!"

"How do you suspect we do that, Abel?" Aika asks. "Jacobson is your friend and right-hand man. He trusts you with his life."

Abel clenches his fist. "I know, Aika, but this child poses a threat to me and this kingdom!"

Aika places a comforting hand on Abel's shoulder. "There must be another way."

A knock at the door interrupts their conversation. Aika opens it to see Jacobson standing there, arms folded across his chest and brows knitted together.

Abel and Jacobson lock eyes. "What happened, Brother?"

"Abel, what are your plans for our daughter?"

Abel's eyes are wide.

"Serena's sister, Rosa, had a vision of you taking our daughter away from us!" Jacobson continues.

Abel shifts in his seat and rolls his shoulders back. "Jacobson, I am your king, and you are not in a position to question me!"

"Don't lecture me on that monarchy bull," Jacobson retorts. "This is my daughter, my family; I won't allow it!" he shouts, slamming the door behind him.

Jacobson returns to his room, and Rosa glides in behind him, carrying an ancient brown book. "I have something to tell you."

"What is it?" Serena asks warily.

"I know what powers your daughter will possess," Rosa says in a calm tone.

Jacobson and Serena exchange puzzled glances.

"Powers? What do you mean?" Jacobson questions.

Rosa opens the book and flips through the pages. "Your daughter will possess the power to cause earthquakes and the ability to move objects with her mind. She will also be psychic like me and able to see glimpses of the future." Rosa explains. "These powers are rare and formidable, and she will need guidance and training to control them effectively," she adds.

Serena sobs. "We must protect her from the king, Jacobson! He—he will destroy her!" Her voice trembling. "We must flee from the kingdom."

Everyone around me exchanges concerned looks when I regain consciousness.

Shelly rushes to my side and squeezes my hand. "What did you see?"

"I—I saw Rosa. She is my aunt!" I blurt out.

Jessica and Niyla screw up their faces. "What?!" They shout in unity.

"What do you mean our mother is your aunt?" Niyla asks, her voice overflowing with confusion.

"How is that possible?" Jessica adds.

"In the vision I had, Jacobson said, 'Serena's sister, Rosa,' had a vision about the king taking me away from them, and she knows about my powers," I explain. "She's been watching over me, trying to protect me from the king. The entire time."

My friends' eyes widen as the truth dawns on them, their minds racing to connect the dots. The spell Rosa cast has been keeping my powers at bay. If the king finds out they are no longer dormant, I don't know what he will do to me.

"We need to leave that kingdom by any means necessary," I say.

Everyone nods in agreement.

My phone rings, interrupting our conversation. It's *"my father."* He demands we return to the kingdom immediately, alerting me that the twins are on the run and wanted for treason.

We must find a way to protect the twins, the hybrid kingdom, and ourselves.

We are on our way back to the kingdom, and there is a knot forming in my stomach. The atmosphere is heavy with suspicion, and the eyes of the guards follow our every move when we walk through the gates. Shelly and Cameron give me a nod before heading to their respective destinations, and I rush to my chambers, trying my best to avoid "my parents." Unfortunately, it only lasts for about two hours until there is a hammering noise on my door. *My time is up.*

Abel shoves past me as I open the door. "Have you been in contact with the twins?"

"No, I haven't," I reply. My heart is pounding against my ribs as if it wants to break free. "What do you want with them?"
Aika's eyes narrow, and she grabs my arm. "Girl, do not question your father!" she hisses.
Pulling my arm away from Aika's grip, I roll my eyes. "I'm sorry, *Mother,* but I can't just blindly follow orders without knowing why," I say firmly. Holding my head high, I ask once more. "What do you want with the twins, *Father?*"
Abel smacks me across the face, and I hit the wall so hard that my vision blurs for a moment.
"You will not leave this castle until they are found," he growls,

disappearing in a flash.

Aika sneers and follows after him.

Clutching my stinging cheek, I struggle to lift myself from the floor. I retrieve my phone from my pocket to text Cameron and Shelly in our group chat.

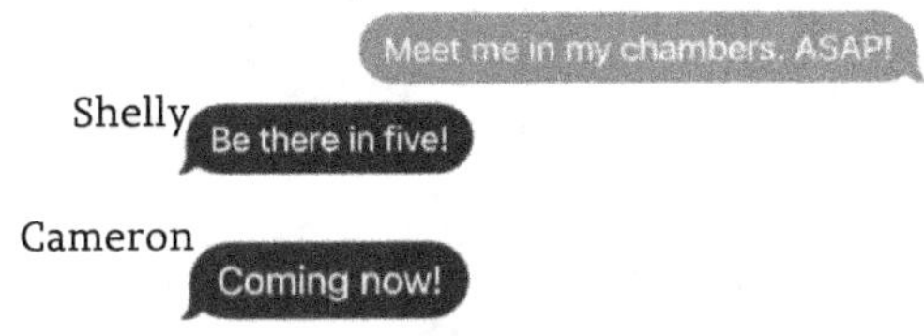

I also send a text message to Niyla.

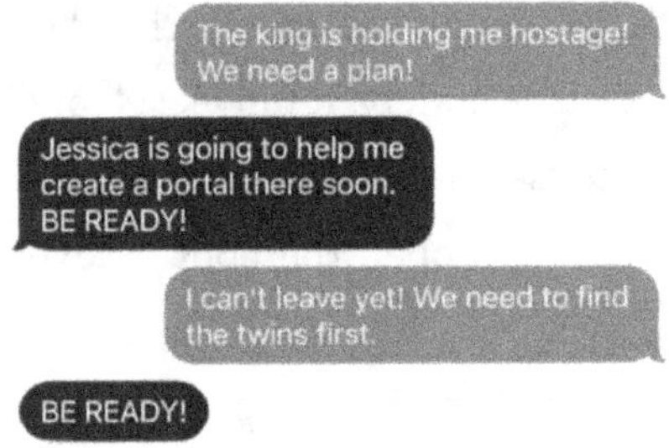

What? How does she expect me to be ready if I'm not allowed to leave?

Grabbing my things to start packing, Shelly and Cameron are outside my chambers, and they let themselves in.

Shelly rushes to me. "What happened? Your cheek is like a cherry red!"

Due to my diet, my face will take several hours to heal. *One of the negative aspects of drinking only animal blood!*

"Abel smacked me in the face! Throwing me into the wall."

"What a jerk!" Cameron hisses.

A tear forms in the corner of my eye, slowly trickling down the side of my face. Wiping the tear away with the back of my sleeve, I continue stuffing my bag, with my things.

Shelly's eyes shift from my bag to mine. "The king has the kingdom on lockdown. No one is allowed in or out until Kaden and Kade are found and executed," She says.

"I'm aware," I reply in a low voice.

"We need to act fast!" Cameron says.

A loud thud in my closet catches our attention. We turn our heads in the direction of the noise.

The door creaks open, and Niyla emerges from the closet, gasping for air. "It took a lot of magic to break through my mother's spell on the castle," she says, her chest rising significantly. "She will know that I am here."

"Take these back to Monica's house," I instruct, quickly handing my bags to her.

There's a knock at the door, and we freeze in fear.

"Hide!" I mouth to Niyla, gesturing towards the closet. Niyla nods and rushes back into it.

Rosa—*my aunt,* steps inside and uses magic to close the door behind her.

Rosa doesn't speak. She glances around the room, knowing something is amiss. "I know you know who I am to you," she smiles softly, "and I know one of my daughters is here."

Niyla pokes her head out of the closet, her eyes wide. Rosa smiles as she locks eyes with Niyla, confirming her suspicions.

"The king has placed the kingdom on lockdown and—"

"Yes, yes, we know already." I interrupt Rosa, and she gestures her hand in a circular motion at me, and suddenly I can't speak.

"Do not cut me off when I am speaking, young lady." Rosa scolds, her voice firm but gentle.

Realizing my mistake and allowing Rosa to continue, I nod sheepishly.

"From now on, let me know when you portal here so I can assist you. The king was alerted the minute you arrived, and now you must leave!" She gestures her hand in a circular motion once more, returning my voice.

She brushes her finger underneath Niyla's chin and tilts her head slightly. "I know you have questions for me, my dear daughter; I did what was necessary to keep all of us safe," Rosa says, then turns to me, smiling. "I had to stay here to watch over my niece."

Niyla opens her mouth to speak, but Rosa gently places a finger on her lips, silencing her. "There will be time for questions later," Rosa assures her. "For now, we must focus on ensuring our safety."

Niyla nods and heads through the portal with my belongings.

"First things first: we have to find Kaden and Kade," I say.

Rosa chants in a different tongue, and purple and gold ribbons of light swirl in the air. The twins appear before us.

Our mouths drop.

"What! H—how?" I stutter in disbelief.

Rosa smiles. "Magic," she says, as if it explains everything.

"She's been hiding us behind a glamour spell," Kade explains.

"I have been on your side your entire life, Akira," Rosa adds, embracing me. "Working from the inside."

"I'm ashamed we blindly followed King Abel and his oppressive rule for years," Kaden admits, his voice filled with regret.

"We were too blinded by loyalty to see the truth," Kade adds. "We should have questioned his actions and motives sooner."

"Especially when he ordered the execution of his friend twenty-something years ago," Kaden chimes in.

"Who was his friend?" I ask, already knowing the answer but wanting to hear it from them.

"Jacobson," Kaden and Kade reply in unison.

"Jacobson was my father," I whisper, my heart sinking at the confirmation.

Kaden and Kade exchange guilty glances. They kneel before me. "We will fight with you," Kade vows.

"Until the end," Kaden promises.

The recurring dream that haunted me is becoming a reality.

War is on the horizon.

Time To Escape!

One month later...

The witches have discreetly created portals for Troy and me to spend time together because Abel still has our kingdom on lockdown. *I am a prisoner in my own home!* Only Abel's most trusted guards are allowed in and out. Troy and I text and speak on the phone every day; it's not the same as being able to see each other in person.

Troy's kingdom is spiraling out of control as well. They have been reaching out to other kingdoms for support; no one is willing to intervene for fear of Abel's wrath. The only kingdom to respond was the werewolves.

Dawn's brother, Timothy, is the werewolf pack leader and has agreed to join us in the uprising against the vampire king. The werewolves live in Hudson Valley, New York, a secluded area known for its dense forests and rugged land. They invited us to their home, but we will have to save that visit for another time. Perhaps after we have defeated Abel, I look forward to visiting them one day.

According to Rosa, a few years after my father was murdered, Abel decided to implant trackers into his guards to monitor their every move. This means he knows that the twins are here but can't locate them because of the glamour spell. However, magic has limits, and Rosa would have to explain why additional herbs are needed. This is why we devised a plan to sneak them out of the kingdom tonight when the guards have their downtime. We carefully studied the guards' routines and identified a small window of opportunity to execute our escape plan to portal them to California to stay with Monica. Unfortunately, we can't escape as well because Abel has called an emergency meeting with the kingdom tomorrow morning to discuss our next move. What he doesn't know is that we are waiting for the arrival of the werewolves so we can let down the shield, allow them access to the kingdom, and defeat Abel for what he did to the hybrids. The werewolves should be here at the end of the week, and we cannot take on Abel without their help.

Kaden and Kade had to wait an entire month for their systems to be clear of human blood so Rosa could cut into their skin without it healing quickly and remove the trackers.

The almighty King Abel has forbidden me from leaving my chambers, so I'm waiting for everyone else to meet me here to help them sneak out. Abel has guards posted up at every corner, so we need to be discreet.

My phone dings with a message from Troy.

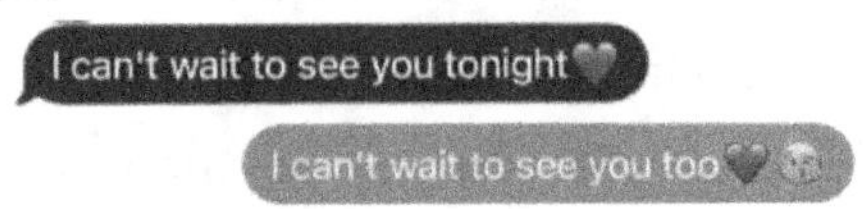

After the twins escape safely, Troy and I plan to meet up and spend some quality time together. My stomach does somersaults thinking about seeing Troy again, and I spin happily in a circle.

There's a knock on the door that interrupts me. Cameron, Shelly, Rosa, Melonie, and the twins who are invisible to everyone *except us*—are standing outside, ready to execute our escape plan. Snapping back into reality, I usher them inside, making sure to keep our voices low to avoid detection. Chase stands at a distance, eyes fixed on us and brows furrowed. I give him a nod and shut the door.

Melonie is an introvert who stays out of vampire affairs. Despite her reserved nature, she is willing to keep Kaden and Kade safe by any means necessary.

"Jessica will be here in five minutes," Rosa whispers.

Jessica is aiding the twins' escape, and Niyla will help me when it's time to head to the hybrid kingdom.

Melonie's slender frame snuggles perfectly into Kaden's arms, and they share a passionate kiss. "Be safe," she whispers, letting go of Kaden.

He snakes his arms around her waist once more and loops his fingers in her curly blonde hair. "We'll be okay," he promises, his eyes locked with her flaming red ones.

"I love you, Kaden," Melonie says.

"I love you too." He replies, giving her a reassuring squeeze.

Rosa temporarily disables the protection spell that surrounds the castle long enough for Jessica to portal into the vampire kingdom undetected.

The twins and I have grown very close over the past month, so it is bittersweet to say goodbye to them. A tear forms in the corner of my eye and trickles down my cheek.

"Oh, Akira, bring it in," Kade says, gesturing his arms for an embrace.

"Let me get in on this." Kaden joins in the hug, squeezing the both of us.

"I am going to miss you two." I choke up, trying to hold back my wave of tears.

"We'll miss you too," the twins say in unison.

Kade ruffles my hair, and Kaden gives me a tight squeeze before they both release me from the hug.

"Akira, this is not goodbye forever. We will see you soon." Kaden says.

A smile tugs at the corners of my mouth, and I give his hand a tight squeeze.

Jessica's voice breaks through the somber atmosphere. "We must go now!"

Kaden and Kade nod before disappearing through the portal.

Snapping out of my emotional state, I wipe away my tears and send Niyla a text, informing her that I am ready when she is.

While I'm out, Cameron and Shelly stay behind in my room to cover for me should anyone come looking.

"Hey, Niyla. You're right on time," I say as the bright white light appears in my closet.

"I'm going to head back to my villa," Melonie says, leaving my room with Rosa.

"Hold down the fort," I say to Cameron and Shelly.

They nod.

Niyla and I walk through the portal, and the sensation of being transported through dimensions washes over me. The excitement of seeing Troy again increases my heart rate, making me forget about everything else for a moment. We portal into Troy's suite, and I'm immediately greeted by his warm embrace. The familiar scent of his Burberry London cologne wraps around me.

Niyla and Troy fist bump, their smiles mirroring my own.

"I'll catch you guys in a few," Niyla says, giving me a sly look.

Niyla and Claude have grown relatively close, and Troy and I believe that they may be more than just friends, but their lips are sealed.

Troy and I only have two hours to spend together, and he has a special date night planned for us. He prepared an excellent dinner: pan-seared lamb chops with his family's homemade sauce, creamy mashed potatoes, and grilled asparagus.

We sit down at the candlelit table, the aroma of the lamb chop filling the air.

"How was your day today?" he asks, pouring each of us a glass of Pinot Noir.

He looks so handsome in his crisp brown shirt and dark denim Levi jeans, with a grin playing on his lips.

"Considering the king has me trapped in my chambers, I guess I'm fine," I reply, rolling my eyes, lips curving into a slight smirk.

Troy laughs. "Well, at least you are in good company now and a delicious meal to make up for it." His lips curl into his charming smile that has me swooning.

"Babe, Thank you." I smile, taking a sip of the wine he poured to wash down the delicious bite of lamb chops.

"Are you enjoying your dinner?" He asks.

Slowly nodding and savoring the flavors dancing on my taste buds. "Absolutely. It's delicious," I say in between bites.

He reaches over to cut a slice of the chocolate red wine cake he baked and places it on my plate. "Save room for dessert," he beams.

How am I so lucky?

Biting into the cake, I let out a moan as the rich, velvety chocolate melts in my mouth. Troy chuckles. He always laughs at me when I'm enjoying the food he has prepared. I cannot help it—his cooking is just that good. Licking my lips, relishing the lingering sweetness, Troy's eyes darken.

He leans in closer, his voice dropping to a low whisper. "Maybe next time, I'll find another way to make you moan like that."

My face grows hot, and I gulp, feeling a sudden heat rise in my stomach. He brushes a curl behind my ear and leans in for a passionate kiss.

I swear, two hours is not enough time for us.

Neither of us said I love you yet, but the way he looks at me speaks volumes.

Lost in each other's gazes, "Akira, I have something to tell you." He pauses, taking a deep breath. "I—"

Niyla rushes into the suite, interrupting our moment. "Time to go, Akira!" she says. Claude is trailing behind her.

Startled, we pull away from each other, our connection momentarily broken.

"We have to go now!" Niyla urges.

"I guess I will tell you at a later time," Troy says with a disappointed tone. "You should probably go now," he says.

White lights swirl around the room. Troy and I gaze into each other eyes before reluctantly parting ways. Niyla and I step into the portal and are back in my walk-in closet at the castle. Niyla nods as she portals back to Monica's home. The portal closes behind me, and I freeze in place, noticing Shelly's and Cameron's pale faces.

My heart drops to the pit of my stomach, and I have never been more terrified than right now. Abel, Lucas, and his guards are in my room. I'm remaining stationary and unable to move. My forehead breaks out in a cold sweat, and my mouth goes dry.

Lucas escorts Shelly and Cameron out of my chambers, and the king strikes me in the face with a force that sends me sprawling to the ground.

"You aided in the escape of our enemies!" Abel roars. "You are a traitor to the kingdom!"

Trying to steady myself, I stagger to my feet. However, my legs feel weak and shaky. The pain from the king's blow shoots through my face.

Still, I remain firm. "Kaden and Kade have been loyal to the kingdom for decades. What makes them enemies of the crown now?"

The king's eyes narrow as he spits out his response. "Mind your tongue, Child!" he sneers. "They disobeyed direct orders, which makes them enemies of the crown and traitors to the kingdom, and since you aided in their escape, you will suffer the consequences as well!" His voice is laced with venom.

Abel rolls his shoulders back and stands tall, his claws protruding from his fingers. He circles me with a predatory gaze, and in one swift movement, he lunges toward me, his sharp claws slicing into my arm.

Blood trickling down my arm, I instinctively bare my fangs. Grasping the gash on my arm and trying to reduce the bleeding, he rips my fangs from my mouth, relishing my agony, and punches me in the nose with unfathomable strength. The bone shatters under the force of his blow, and stars explode in my vision. Collapsing to the ground in a daze, I lose consciousness.

When I awake, my vision is blurry, and my entire body is aching. The throbbing pain in my arm and the sharp sting in my broken nose have me confused about where I am. Slowly, I realize I'm on the castle's lower level in the dungeons, where prisoners are held. I'm no longer a princess. *I'm a prisoner!*

I'm in a small, dimly lit cell with a television mounted on the stone walls and a rusty iron door. The air is damp and musty, and the only sound I hear is dripping of some sort. Looking down at my arm, I see an IV line dangling from it, taking blood from my arm to keep me weak and disoriented. *Abel is a monster!*

The king knows I will not consume human blood to heal, so this is his way of keeping me fragile and compliant.

The television turns on, and Cameron appears on the screen; he is barely recognizable, his once beautiful hazel eyes are now swollen shut, and his face is covered in bruises and cuts.

The guards brought him to the fountain, where the crops and plants grow. They are waiting for the sun to rise. One of the harshest punishments for a vampire. How could someone be so cruel?

One of the king's methods of retribution is to drain all the plasma from a vampire's body and replace it with human blood so they could burn to death when the sun rose. A fate only a man like him deserves.

My heart feels like it is being shattered into a million pieces as I look at Cameron in this state. He is in this situation because of his connection to me. We developed a brother-and-sister relationship, and I love him like family.

The crack of dawn is approaching in our realm, and Cameron's fate is about to be sealed. It's too late for me to escape from the dungeon and help him. My face drenches with tears as the sun rises, and I watch helplessly as Cameron's feet ignite in a blaze of fire. My little brother is suffering, and all I can do is watch. There is nothing I can do to save him! The fire travels along his legs toward his torso, slowly burning him to ashes.

A wave of energy rises within me, and I swing my arms back and forth, trying to break free from the chains that bind me. The metal digs into my wrists, causing them to bleed, but I push through the pain.

"This is what you want, Abel? You sick monster! I hate you!" I scream at the camera watching me, and tears stream down my face.

My blood is boiling, and rage is brewing inside me, ready to explode. A bright red and orange glow emanates from my hands and arms; I let go.

The cell blows up, sending debris flying in all directions. I'm drained; however, the electricity of the magic I possess is coursing throughout my body, and it feels good.

Lucas appears before me, his eyes wide. "Akira, what are you doing? The king will kill you!"

He and I lock eyes, and my expression hardens. "Move out of my way, Lucas! I have to save Cameron!"

"I can't let you do that, Akira," Lucas says firmly. "I'm sorry."

I can see the conflict in his eyes, torn between his loyalty to the king and his friendship with me.

"If you truly love me, as you say you do, you will let me go save Cameron," I plead. "Please, Lucas, I cannot let him die because of me."

Lucas hesitates for a moment, considering my pleas, his eyes filled with uncertainty. Finally, he steps aside, allowing me to pass.

Lucas nods and grabs my hand, giving it a gentle squeeze. "Be careful," he urges, kissing me softly on the cheek.

Using the energy from my powers to boost my vampire speed, I sprint through the tunnels, praying to get to Cameron on time.

To my surprise, I see a witch standing over his charcoal motionless body, gesturing her hands in circular motions as her light brown hair swirls in the wind, being created by magic. Her chocolate brown eyes shimmer as she chants incantations to heal him. Tyler, Kyle, and Ava are trying to penetrate the force field she has surrounding them, but they are unable to break through. White lights swirl around, and she sends Cameron through the portal.

The witch stays behind, and the force field drops. In a flash, Kyle lunges toward her, snapping her neck just as the portal closes. Slowly backing away from the gruesome scene, I cover my mouth with my hands so they don't hear me. My heart nearly leaps out of my chest when Rosa appears behind me.

She places her pointer finger on my lips. "Follow me," she mouths, and I nod.

Rosa and I run through the tunnels to where the humans are in the castle's lower level. Well, it's more like she is running, and I am walking fast-paced. She informs me that Cameron is alive and has safely made it to Monica's house. My heart swells with relief, but not for long. She leads me to the kitchen, and my heart drops to the tip of my toes. Shelly is crouched over on the floor, rocking back and forth and sobbing. She is beaten and covered in blood. I look to the left of her and see a trail of blood leading to Melonie's body. The sight makes my stomach churn, and my knees give out as I plummet to the floor, unable to comprehend the horror before me.

Rosa gestures her hands in circular motions. Bright white swirling lights appear around us, and we portal out of the kingdom to Monica's home.

Our haven.

Rushing to Cameron, I throw my arms around him, relieved that he's intact.

"I'm okay," he whispers.

Shelly's sobs break us apart, and we turn to her. My heart aches. Tears stream down her face; her body is still shaking from shock. Monica guides her to the sofa and sits down with her. Cameron joins them, wrapping his arms around Shelly's trembling body, his eyes filled with grief. The twins watch from a distance. Kaden's expression is unreadable, and Kade rests a comforting hand on his brother's shoulder, offering silent support.

Looking away from them, I lock eyes with Rosa.

"Ava persuaded Shelly to murder Melonie," she whispers.

Trying to suppress the gasp that threatens to escape my lips, I place my hand over my heart as tears fill my eyes.

Up In Flames!

Niyla creates a portal for Claude, Felix, and me to be transported to Monica's house. When we enter the room through the bright white lights, we are immediately greeted by a scene of distress. Shelly's tear-stained face catches my attention on the sofa as she sobs, her shoulders shaking with each breath. Cameron is sitting next to her, staring at the wall with a distant look in his eyes, and Akira is trying to console Shelly.

When Akira's gaze meets mine, new tears flow down her beautiful face. I'm near her in a flash, wrapping my arms around her. Her brown and white dress is stained with blood, and she has bruises all over her body. Raising her chin gently, I observe her injuries in more detail. Akira's eyes are red and swollen, and her mouth is bloody. The rage inside me burns hotter than ever, and my inner wolf is fighting to come to the surface. *I will destroy Abel for hurting the woman I love!*

"Akira," I whisper. "I won't rest until Abel pays for this," I say, kissing her forehead, nose, cheeks, and lips.

With every word, my resolve strengthens, fueling the fire within me to protect her at all costs.

My gaze meets hers. "I love you."

She smiles, her tears mixing with the blood on her face. "I know. I love you too."

Wiping away her tears. "What can I do to help you heal?"

She sighs and leans into my embrace. "Just stay with me," she whispers, her voice barely audible. "The only way for me to heal is by drinking human blood, and I won't do such a thing!"

Looking between Akira and Monica. "Perhaps there's a spell you could do to speed up the process?" I suggest.

Monica shakes her head and marches toward Akira, exposing her wrist. "Drink my blood!" she demands.

Akira's eyes widen as she briefly considers the motion. But then she shakes her head in disgust. "Monica, I cannot ask you to do that," she says.

Monica's expression softens, and she takes Akira's hand. "I want to help you."

Akira shakes her head again, rejecting Monica's offer.

Monica's face is stern. "I'm sorry, Akira, I'm no longer asking!" She snaps her fingers, and Akira falls to the floor. "It's for your own good," she whispers.

"What did you do to her?"

"I temporarily put her to sleep to prevent her from resisting," Monica explains. "I know it may seem extreme." She glances at Akira. "This is the best way to help her."

"We're going to do a transfusion," Rosa adds. "I'm going to hook Akira and Monica up to an IV line and transfer Monica's blood into Akira's body so she can heal. We all must be at full strength for what's to come!" she continues.

I carry Akira's limp body to a room upstairs and place her on a twin-sized bed; Monica sits beside her. Rosa inserts the IV into Akira's bruised arm and then Monica's. She starts chanting in another language, and the room trembles. Suddenly, there is a blast of immense energy, and a bright green light radiates from Rosa's body. I have never witnessed such a thing.

"What's happening?"

"I'm casting a spell to merge Monica's blood with Akira's so she can walk in the daylight," Rosa explains.

She continues to chant, her eyes closed in concentration.

When the blood transfusion ritual is complete, Akira's bruises begin to fade, her nose heals, and she starts to look like herself again. Opening her mouth slightly, I notice her fangs have grown back.

Rosa removes the IV from Monica and Akira's arms and carefully wraps a bandage around it.

"Now what?" I ask.

"Now we wait for her to wake up," Rosa replies.

She glances at Akira before she and Monica exit the room.

I want to strangle the king with my bare hands for what he did to her.

Holding Akira's hand in mine. "I love you," I whisper numerous times.

It feels like an eternity before Akira finally moves. Her eyes flutter open, and she wakes up coughing and holding her chest.

Grabbing a glass of water from the bedside table, I help Akira up, holding her hair as she takes a sip.

She scratches the top of her head. "What happened?"

"Monica happened," I reply, shrugging my shoulders.

She shakes her head. "No, no, no. Did she give me her blood? Now, I cannot walk in the daylight."

"Rosa cast a spell over Monica's blood so you can walk in the daylight," I explain.

Akira sits up straight, her expression changing. Her mouth curves into a small smile as she looks at me. "Thank you. I'm feeling much better now," she says. "So, what were you saying about looovvving me?" She drags out the word "loving."

"I was saying that I love you, Akira Ronin," I say with a grin, kissing her on the forehead. "And I always will, no matter what obstacles we face."

Akira's smile widens as she reaches out for my hand. "I love you too, Troy Bishop." She places her head on my chest. "I'm worried for Shelly."

"What happened?" I ask warily.

Akira's face pales, and her lips turn down at the corners. "Abel ordered his minions to burn Cameron to death under the sunlight. And Ava—she persuaded Shelly to murder her sister Melonie. I don't know how she'll survive the guilt. I'm worried she might turn off her emotions." Akira looks away. "If that happens, she will be lost to the darkness."

Silence hangs between us as we process the weight of her words.

Suddenly, Cameron, Claude, and Niyla come racing into the room on high alert. *What is it now?*

"The cave is under attack!" Claude shouts.

The news hits me like a punch in the gut. Feeling a surge of energy as my heart races and my blood boils, I jump to my feet.

"We need to leave now!" Felix urges, hurrying into the portal Niyla has already summoned.

Assisting Akira out of bed, we hasten through the portal alongside the others.

Blood rushes through my ears as we emerge on the other side. The cave we had just left is in complete chaos. The air is thick with the stench of blood, and the sounds of growls and snarls surround us. I run to my parents' chambers, and my mother is weeping over my father's lifeless form. My shoulders slump, and I collapse to my knees, tears streaming down my face as I gaze at my father's motionless figure. Akira runs to my side, and Niyla rushes to Claude.

Akira grabs me, holding my head against her chest. "Babe, I'm so sorry." She whispers.

Dawn hurries into the room, breathing heavily. "We have to go!" she shouts. "I notified my brother of the witch's location, and he will meet us there with reinforcements, but we need to act quickly!"

I'm paralyzed and stare blankly at my father. Akira tries to pull me away, urging me to listen to Dawn, but I don't budge from my spot. *How could I let this happen?*

"Babe, there is nothing you could have done to prevent this. Right now, we need to focus on staying safe. Please come with me, Troy!" Akira pleads, tears dripping down her cheeks.

Unable to force my gaze away from my father's limp figure, I blink repeatedly.

Akira's grip on my arm tightens, her voice filled with desperation. "Troy, we cannot stay here. It's not safe anymore."

My mother grabs my other arm. "We must go now, Troy. Your father would want us to be safe."

My father is dead, and it's up to me to lead this kingdom to safety.

Feeling the weight of responsibility settling on my shoulders, I exhale a deep breath and clench my fist.

"Niyla, Jessica, start the portal. The rest of us will search the cave for any survivors and send them through. We cannot leave anyone behind."

They nod and begin opening the portal.

Claude, Felix, Cameron, Dawn, Akira, and I search the cave for any remaining survivors and guide them through the portal.

I'm looking around, searching for Philip; he can materialize anything and is someone we will need fighting alongside us. Pushing aside the debris and torn limbs, I find him with a piece of wood impaled into his chest; he drifts in and out of consciousness. Attempting to stabilize him, I inspect his wound, and his injury is critical.

It's too late.

A lump forms in my throat. "Brother, I am so sorry this happened to you." My eyes swell with tears.

"You need to get out of here, Troy! The vampire king and his guards want to destroy our kingdom," he whispers, voice barely audible.

"But—"

He interrupts me. "There's no time, Troy."

Philip struggles to catch his breath, his face pale. He places his head on mine, and I wait until he takes his last breath.

He's gone.

Akira grasps my hand. "We have to go now, Troy. We cannot stay here any longer."

Nodding in understanding, my heart is heavy with grief as we make our escape.

We sprint through the portal, thinking we are running to our safety; however, when we step out, the sight before us is horrifying.

Betrayal

Timothy betrayed us! The werewolf pack has been siding with the vampires all along and has planned an attack on the witches. *Nothing but death surrounds me.* Witches, vampires, and werewolves are locked in a fierce battle, their powers clashing with catastrophic force. The sound of screams and howls is caught in the crossfire, echoing through the air as each kingdom fights for dominance over the others.

Dawn thought they had set aside their differences to work together to take down the common enemy. Timothy pledged to side with us in the uprising against the vampire king; he lied. He used us for information and secretly aligned himself with Abel. His mission must have been to find out where the witches were hiding and annihilate them and anyone who opposed the king. *Pathetic!* Timothy is Dawn's only living relative, and although he has aged, he is still one of the fiercest wolves I have encountered.

A full-blown war is going on around us. Ava lunges at Claude, her fangs bared and claws extended. He senses her attack, and gray smoke surrounds him as he shapeshifts into his wolf form, meeting her aggression head-on. Claude growls, canine teeth appearing while Ava circles him. He aims for her throat, and she avoids his attack, flipping over him. Ava smiles and fixes her piercing gaze on my brother, who freezes in place, unable to move. *What did she do to him?* She tears his hind leg from his body, blood splattering on the battlefield as he howls in anguish. Rage ignites my veins, and a veil of gray smoke envelopes me. My legs bend and stretch, becoming powerful limbs with claws as my teeth grow longer and sharper, ready to shred and attack Ava. Fur sprouts all over my skin, and I emerge from the smoke, a large, fierce wolf prepared to join the fight. As our eyes lock, a surge of tingling sensations spreads through my body. *What is she doing to me?* Lucas attacks me and strikes me in the face with a powerful punch, releasing me from Ava's influence.

Blow for blow, he is on top of me, relentlessly pummeling me with his fists. Together, we unleash a fury like no other, our teeth and claws colliding. With primal wrath, I bite a portion of his hand off, and he growls in pain but doesn't back down. Blood drips from our wounds as we continue to fight. He grasps me by the neck and attempts to rip my head from my body. Piercing at his torso, I try my best to prevent him from succeeding. Lucas is strong, but I'm *stronger*. Pushing him back with a wave of adrenaline, I cause him to stumble and lose his grip on my neck; he quickly recovers. He launches another attack, tearing and biting my limbs. Refusing to give in, with every ounce of strength left in me, I retaliate with a barrage of strikes aimed at weakening him. My paw connects with his face, causing him to reel back momentarily.

"Is that all you got?" He shouts, spitting fur from his mouth.

Pushing him forward and knocking him off his feet, I howl.

He spits out blood. "You're an abomination! Your kind shouldn't exist, and I will make sure to eradicate every last one of you!" He hisses and lunges at me again, thrusting me to the ground.

His hands fasten around my jaw, applying pressure with a brutal force that threatens to break it. The bones in my jaw strain and crack, close to shattering under his grip. Suppressing a growl, I refuse to give him the satisfaction of seeing me in pain.

"Lucas, stop!" Akira screams from behind, dashing towards us.

Lucas hesitates long enough for Cameron to knock him off me and pin him to the ground.

Ava is standing over Claude and clawing into his chest. Thankfully, Kade runs up from behind, forcing his hand through Ava's back, breaking her ribs and procuring her heart. She stands frozen, grasping her chest; a look of shock spreads across her face when she realizes what is about to happen. Kade crushes it, and her thin silhouette descends to the ground. He lights her body on fire, and we exchange a look of understanding.

"Niyla, help Claude." Kaden commands, pointing at Claude's body, still lying on the ground motionless.

She bolts over to Claude's side, checking for a pulse and assessing his injuries. His breathing is shallow; he's still alive. She applies pressure to his wounds, trying to stop the bleeding as best she can.

Another vampire jumps on Kaden's back, and they begin to grapple. Kaden punches the vampire in the face, sending him flying into a tree with a loud thud. He shakes it off and advances at Kaden again, sinking his fangs into Kaden's shoulder and trying to split his head from his body. Kaden grits his teeth in pain but manages to wrestle him off, throwing him to the ground.

Kaden cracks his neck in frustration, feeling the taste of blood in his mouth.

"I've had enough of this!" He hisses, charging toward the creature.

Kaden separates the vampire's arm from his body and retrieves a lighter from his pocket, setting it on fire. He reaches for where his arm used to be in agony, and a grin forms on Kaden's face.

Dawn levitates the one-arm vampire.

"Put me down," he shouts.

She separates his head from his form in mid-air, burning him to ashes with a wave of her hand.

Teamwork.

Jessica and Niyla transport Claude through a portal just as another vampire lunges at them.

We are outnumbered!

Still seething with anger from Melonie's death, Kaden counters the vampire with a powerful kick, sending him crashing into a nearby pole. As the vamp struggles to regain his footing, the portal closes.

Lucas slams Cameron to the ground, knocking him out cold, and attacks Kade with a series of lightning punches. Kade dodges and counters each blow with precision and strength. He punches Lucas in the throat with a swift jab, causing him to gasp for air. Lucas regains his composure and retaliates with a vicious roundhouse kick, catching Kade off guard and throwing him back. He falls to the ground.

Kade coughs up blood. "Is that all you got?" He spits, wiping it from his mouth with the back of his hand.

Lucas laughs. "All of you are pathetic! You're following abominations and think you can stand a chance against us? You're nothing but weaklings." His voice drips with arrogance, and he's ready to deliver another blow.

He raises his fist, but Kade swiftly rolls to the side before he can strike and springs back up.

"You chose the wrong side!" Lucas snarls through gritted teeth.

"You make me sick!" Kade retorts and charges forward, digging his claws into the wound I inflicted on Lucas's hand.

Lucas roars in pain as Kade's claws sink deeper into his injury, blood dripping onto the ground.

Chaos is happening around me! And this is all Abel's fault. He started this fight, and now it's spiraling out of control.

Another vampire is running in my direction, and I sink my teeth into her neck, breaking it in the process. I fling her to the side for Dawn to set on fire.

"No!" Akira squeals as Lucas breaks Kade's neck and decapitates him. The sight of the gruesome scene stuns the crowd, and the noise fades away, replaced by a deafening silence.

No! My inner thoughts shout, and I move on instinct.

Kaden's body tenses when he realizes what Lucas has done. He sprints through the crowd, ducking and dodging the wolves and vampires. He lunges toward Lucas, striking him and knocking him to the ground.

Leaping over werewolves and vampires, I attempt to reach Kaden, evading attacks from left and right.

Kaden is about to remove Lucas's head.

Do it. Do it—that's right, kill him! My inner thoughts shout as I near.

Akira screams. "No! Please don't!"

She rushes to Lucas, tears flowing from her hazel eyes as she pleads for Kaden to spare his life.

"Please, Kaden, don't kill him!"

"He killed my brother!" Kaden shouts.

Akira is crying. "Please don't kill him!"

What am I missing? Why does she want to save this evil vampire?

Kaden is about to strike Lucas again when Niyla circles her hand, mumbling in her witchy language, sending him through the portal.

"We need to leave now! Daylight is approaching. The vampires don't have much longer!" Niyla warns.

"Lucas! How—how could you side with the king after what he has done?" Akira cries.

"Akira, we have to go!" Niyla shouts while dodging attacks from our enemies.

"Lucas, answer me!" Akira pleads.

"I don't have a choice!" Lucas yells over the chaos. "Either I side with the king, or he will end me. I owe him my life. I love you, Akira, but you chose that abomination over me. I made my choice, and you made yours."

"But we can—"

"Leave!" Lucas demands, cutting Akira off. "Let me die in peace." He continues.

Looking to my right, I notice one of the vampires speeding away, tossing Kai's head. We have lost so many.

"They are leaving!" Niyla shouts.

"Nooo!" Jessica cries out when she notices Kai's head on the ground.

The sun is about to rise, and I change back into my human form. A few wolves come running my way once my transformation is complete, and Dawn hurls them and a couple of vampires into the air, and they plunge to the ground.

Timothy, in wolf form, howls, and they retreat.

Although the battle is over, the *war* has just begun.

The remaining witches open numerous portals simultaneously and rush everyone through them, transporting each one to a hidden sanctuary.

A familiar vampire is sobbing in Akira's arms.

"I am so sorry for everything," she says between sobs.

Akira wraps her arms around the vampire tighter and looks back at me. "We have to save her. The sun is rising, and she will die." She mouths.

It's Sophia.

I pick up Sophia and carry her in my arms, and we proceed through the portal. Glancing over my shoulder, all the vampires have disappeared, including Lucas. *I guess he's alive.*

Monica rented out a villa in Orlando, Florida, because her home, among many other witches, was destroyed in the battle. We need a safe place to regroup and plan our next move.

The villa is extraordinary, with fifteen bedrooms and the ability to house at least thirty people. Akira and I head upstairs to the bedroom Claude is in. The critical sight of my baby brother pains me. He is unconscious on the bed, pale and bruised, with no left leg. My mother is on the right side of the bed, holding his hand, tears flowing from her gray eyes, and Niyla is on the left. Niyla looks exhausted, her face lined with worry and grief, as she strokes Claude's hair.

How could I let this happen? How did I let my brother end up like this? *This is all my fault!*

Akira hurries to my mother's side and gently places a hand on her shoulder. "Queen Celine, I am so sorry for everything that has happened." Her voice trembles with remorse.

My mother gives Akira a weak smile, her grip on Claude's hand tightening. "Thank you, Akira," she chokes out.

We lost my father, Philip, Kai, Melonie, and Kade too soon, and their absence has left a void in our lives that can never be filled. Sitting on the floor next to my mother, I relive the entire battle, and I'm numb. *How did I let this happen?* I question my every decision, replaying the events in my mind like a movie.

Akira brushes her hand over my forearm, alerting my entire body. Her touch is gentle, but it carries a warmth that begins to thaw the ice forming around my heart. Looking up at her, my eyes gloss over, and we find solace in each other. We embrace, never wanting to let go. She holds me tight, and for a moment, we both find comfort in the silence and stillness.

Rosa enters the room, and we turn our heads to meet her gaze. "Follow me." She says.

We release from each other's embrace, and I look to see if Niyla is coming too.

"I will stay here until he wakes up." She murmurs.

Giving her a nod, I follow Rosa down the stairs and into the living room.

Rosa stands front and center, her expression serious. "Since I left the vampire kingdom, I lifted the spell that keeps the sun at bay so the vampires can only make their move at night. We need to be prepared for their next attack. This is not over."

"We killed a few of their gifted guards, so they will be searching for us," Monica adds. "We're safe for now. However, we need more allies to win this war." Monica looks at Akira. "You must learn how to access your powers. They will be needed for this war."

"What allies are willing to fight with us?" I ask, not knowing what the response will be.

"The shapeshifters and some of the phoenixes are on our side," Monica responds. "They have their own reasons for wanting to take down the vampires."

"And how do we know this for sure? Because you saw what happened with my brother," Dawn responds, her voice filled with skepticism.

"The shapeshifters and I go way back. If any of the kingdoms are on our side, it would be them," Rosa states. "As for the phoenixes, they have been at odds with the vampires for centuries."

"Jace, the leader of the shapeshifters, will be here tomorrow. Until then, go amongst yourself," Rosa continues, gesturing toward us.

Monica turns her attention toward Akira. "What do you want us to do with Sophia?"

Sophia is sitting on a chair, her wrists chained to the armrest. She's looking down at the floor with a solemn look on her face. Akira's expression remains unreadable.

"Would you be able to put her in a room using a spell so she can't leave?" Akira asks.

She's too kind. I would have left her to burn in the sun if it were up to me.

Monica nods and releases Sophia from the chair. She takes her to one of the smaller rooms with dark curtains.

Looking around the room, everyone appears shattered, defeated, vulnerable, and drained of hope. My only thought now is to get some rest. Akira and I head upstairs and claim the nearest room to my brother's.

"I'm going to shower," she whispers.

Akira drags her feet to the bathroom, weighed down by exhaustion and turmoil of today's events. She turns on the faucet, and the sound of water mixes with her muffled sobs. I long to comfort her—*she needs time alone.*

Akira emerges from the bathroom with a tad bit of a refreshed expression on her face. She climbs into bed and kisses me on the cheek before pulling the covers up to her chin and closing her eyes. Observing her closely, I hope that the weight on her shoulders will lighten with each passing moment of rest.

After my shower, I slide into bed beside Akira; her warmth and softness comfort me. My arms wrap around her, drawing her closer. Her sweet vanilla scent soothes me as I drift off to sleep, holding her tight in my arms.

Aftermath

It is a beautiful Sunday afternoon, and the sun is glowing through the crack of the window. The soft rays of sunlight gently illuminate the room, and a subtle breeze caresses the curtains, causing them to sway. Checking on Troy, he is still asleep, his chest rising and falling rhythmically with each breath. There's a slight furrow between his brows, and I want to reach out and smooth it away. Still, I don't want to disturb his slumber. With everything that has transpired recently, it feels like we haven't had a moment of peace, and it's starting to take a toll on both of us. A sharp pain pierces through my heart as if it's being ripped into fragments. The helplessness overwhelms my body; I feel trapped in a cage of my own mistakes. Everything that has happened is my fault. I can't escape the remorse that floods my mind. A tear rolls down my cheek, and another quickly follows, tracing the same path until I'm weeping. Using my hand to stifle my sobs, I try not to wake Troy; the weight of my emotions becomes too much to bear. *Why did fate deal us such a cruel hand?*

Abel raised me, and although I didn't feel the "fatherly love" from him, I thought maybe he cared for me in his own way. When I looked into his eyes yesterday, I saw a cold and distant stare that shattered any illusions of his affection. I was nothing more than a burden to him. After yesterday's events, there is no way I can let this go. Abel's betrayal cuts deep.

Kade, Kai, Melonie, and so many others are dead. Ava persuaded Shelly to murder her sister. Anyone under Ava's persuasion is fully aware of what they are doing but is forced to obey. Ava was a vile and vicious monster to cause that much harm to someone else. My heart aches for Shelly; she was forced to commit such a heinous act on her own sister. Melonie was the only family Shelly had left. They became vampires right before I woke from my coma. I'll never genuinely understand how Shelly must feel.

I'm unsure if Lucas survived, and although I did not love him the way he wanted, I'm still heartbroken by the thought of losing him. Kade and I got close, and now he's gone. Kaden had to witness his former best friend murder his twin brother, and not only did he lose his brother. He lost Melonie, too. Troy's father, King John, is dead. I barely knew him, and now I never will. *Too many deaths!*

Placing my head in my palms, I sit up in the bed. The weight of all the deaths hangs heavy on my shoulders.

Troy wakes up and wraps his arms around me. "Babe, are you okay?"

Shaking my head, more tears pour down my face. He pulls me closer, holding me tight, and I sink my face into his chest, taking in his warmth and scent.

"So many deaths," I whisper, my voice muffled against his shirt.

Troy lifts my chin with his finger to look me in the eye. "We will avenge their deaths."

Looking away, additional tears stream down my cheeks because that's what I'm afraid of. Seeking revenge will only result in more deaths and continue the cycle of violence.

"Only more deaths will follow," I whisper.

Troy's energy shifts and his eyebrows snap together. "Abel killed my father! I cannot let that go—I won't!"

Troy is right, but what if he doesn't make it out alive the next time? Or what if we lose someone else? The recurring dream seems more like a vision. *Perhaps it was a vision.* Lost in my thoughts, I hardly notice Troy staring at me, waiting for a response.

Snapping out of my reverie, my gaze meets his. "I understand, Troy. I just don't want to lose anyone else."

Troy's expression softens, and he places his hands on top of my shoulders, giving them a gentle squeeze. "Neither do I."

There is a knock on the door, and it's Felix.

He enters the room, his eyes darting between us and grabbing the back of his neck. "Shelly is not doing so well. I'm afraid she may turn her emotions off."

A knot is tightening in my stomach as Felix's words hang in the air. *That's the last thing we need in our current situation.*

Sprinting out of the room and down the hallway, I knock softly on Shelly's door before opening it. She's curled up on her bed, her eyes red and puffy from crying.

Clearing my throat and exhaling. "Shelly, are you okay?" Her body tenses at the sound of my voice, and she doesn't respond.

Entering the room, I sit down on the bed next to her. Reaching out to hold her hand in mine, I give her a small smile.

"You don't have to talk if you don't want to. Just know that I'm here for you."

Shelly continues to cry silently.

Squeezing her hand tighter in mine. "It wasn't your fault, Shelly. Melonie knew you were under Ava's spell. If you want to blame someone, blame me. This all happened because of me."

Shelly's body stills as she takes in my words. Her tear-streaked face slowly turns towards me, and our gazes meet, but it's almost as if she's looking through me. Her eyes show an emptiness in them, and I witness the transformation as they lose their fiery red glow and turn into a lifeless and dark abyss.

Shelly turned off her emotions.

"You're right! It's not my fault. It. Is. Yours!" She hisses through gritted teeth. "If you weren't so obsessed with your hybrid, we wouldn't be in this situation!"

I flinch at her bitter words.

She launches toward me with a hatred I've never seen before.

"I should end you right now," she growls, her claws unsheathed and ready to strike.

Stepping back and avoiding her attack, I raise my hands in a defensive gesture.

"Shelly, this isn't you. Please calm down. You don't have to do this!" I plead, trying to reason with her.

She doesn't listen; her anger only intensifies, and the darkness consumes her entirely.

Shelly snarls at me, and her hands wrap around my throat, tightening and cutting off my air supply. The grip she has on me feels unbreakable, and my instincts are telling me to fight back, but I hesitate because she's right—*it's my fault*. My legs feel like jelly, and the room begins to spin, causing my vision to blur, making it harder to think. The room turns black as I start to lose consciousness.

Suddenly, there is a loud crash. The grip around my throat loosens, and I collapse to the floor, gasping for air. Through my blurry vision, Troy and Felix appear in the room. Troy helps me to my feet, and Felix is restraining Shelly, who is still desperately trying to attack me.

"Are you okay?" Troy asks.

Nodding weakly, I lean into his embrace.

On my way out the door, Shelly spits on me.

"This is not over! I will end you," she says through gritted teeth.

There is no reasoning with her now.

My best friend—*my sister* is gone.

Troy and I meet Rosa in another room down the hall.

"Is there anything you can do to help Shelly?" I ask her, desperation evident in my voice.

"No. I'm afraid there's nothing I can do," Rosa replies. "It's up to her to choose to let go of the darkness and find her way back to the light."

Shelly has to turn her emotions back on herself, which is what I was afraid of. Her pain is so deep that she no longer wants to feel it. I don't see her returning to the light anytime soon.

"I can temporarily place her under a sleeping spell if you want," Rosa suggests, breaking me from my reverie. "We can't have an emotionless vampire in the mix right now."

Conducting a sleeping spell on Shelly seems like a bit much. However, we cannot have her around without emotions. Humans don't know about us, and an emotionless vampire in a town mixed with humans is not a good idea. Shelly is also out for blood and will stop at nothing to end me.

"Please do. It's for her own safety and for others." I reply.

Rosa nods and gets started on the spell while Troy and I exit the room.

We walk hand in hand down the spiral staircase. Suddenly, I have an idea. "We should have a memorial service for everyone we've lost before the shapeshifters arrive."

Troy's lips curve into a frown, and he sighs. "That's a great idea," he says softly.

"It will give us a chance to honor their memory and find closure," I say, squeezing his hand. "I'll talk to the others and start making arrangements."

Everyone gathers on the patio, holding a candle for every lost life. One for Kade, Kai, King John, the hybrids, and Melonie. I also have a candle for Shelly because the woman who attacked me wasn't her. The soft glow of the candles illuminates the somber expressions on everyone's faces as the memorial service begins. The air is heavy with grief as we take turns sharing our favorite memories of each person we lost.

When it's Troy's turn to speak, he takes a deep breath and clears his throat. "I would like to say a few words about my father, King John. He was not only a great leader to our kingdom, but also the head of our family, and his absence leaves a void in our lives that can never be filled."

As Troy speaks, his voice trembles with emotion, and tears glisten in his eyes. "I will miss him every day, and I find solace in knowing that his legacy will continue to live on through all of us. I vow to follow in his footsteps and lead this kingdom with the same strength and wisdom that he possessed." He clears his throat once more and continues. "Our brothers and sisters passing will not go in vain, and we will exact revenge against King Abel and his followers." He raises his fist in defiance. "They will face the consequences of their actions, for we are a force to be reckoned with!"

The rest of the hybrid kingdom stands in solidarity, and everyone raises their fists in agreement.

Looking at Kaden, he is sitting on the floor, slouched over with his head in his hands.

"Kaden?" I ask softly, placing a gentle hand on his shoulder.

He looks up, his expression unreadable.

"Would you like to say something?"

Kaden stands up and blows out the candle. His brows pull together. "I will *kill* Lucas and Abel." He says through clenched teeth, his fangs appearing as he speaks.

Troy and the others agree, exchanging knowing glances before nodding in unity.

"Is there anything you would like to say?" Troy asks me.

"I—I." I'm unsure of myself.

"It's okay, Akira. Take your time," Troy soothes, rubbing my back gently.

Sucking in the air and exhaling slowly before finally finding my voice. "I—I never wanted any of this," I say, my voice trembling. "And I am truly sorry for all of the losses, from our side and theirs. We are in this together, and I will unite us as one kingdom. Yes, we may feel defeated and displaced at the moment. However, this is temporary. This will not be our reality forever. One thing I will assure all of you is that we *will* avenge everyone's death. Our collective pain binds us together. We will prevail."

"We will prevail!" Troy repeats with a determined nod, holding me close.

"We will prevail!" Everyone chants in unison, their voices growing louder and with more conviction.

After the memorial, Troy suggests making dinner for him and me to take our minds off the heaviness of the day. However, Kaden, Cameron, Jessica, and Niyla join us, and a dinner for two quickly turns into a gathering of friends seeking solace in each other's company. Troy prepares baked salmon, sauteed broccoli, and yellow rice. It is delicious. Cameron watches enviously as we enjoy our dinner, and Kaden consumes animal blood, making unamused facial expressions.

Cameron groans and drops his head on the table. "I remember when I could eat food," he says, breaking the silence between us.

Everyone laughs at Cameron's comment, finding his nostalgia amusing and a welcome distraction from the weight of our troubles.

"Yep, the good old days. Now I have to drink blood and make faces like this guy." Cameron points at Kaden, who is still making unamused facial expressions, causing everyone to burst into laughter again. Cameron playfully imitates Kaden's grim facial expression, exaggerating it to the point of absurdity, and Kaden finally cracks a small smile.

I'm glad Abel didn't destroy Cameron's sense of humor; he even got Kaden to smile. We are far from happy, but at this moment, it feels good to laugh. It's a small victory.

We continue our lighthearted bantering around the table, teasing and laughing as if the weight of the world has momentarily lifted off our shoulders. Still, our laughter ceases when Monica enters the room with two men we've never seen before.

One man has milky white skin, short black hair, a slim build, and ocean-blue eyes. He is very handsome for an older man, probably in his late forties. He introduces himself as Jace.

The other man steps forward from behind Jace. He is a light brown-skinned man with a strong jawline, dark brown curly hair, and piercing hazel eyes. He exudes confidence and looks to be in his thirties or forties but is somehow frozen. *He must be a vampire.*

He seems familiar when our gazes meet, as if I've seen him somewhere before. There's a strange connection that I can't quite place.

When he extends his hand for a handshake and introduces himself, I remember exactly who he is. The man from my vision.

My father.

WAR IS ON
THE HORIZON

SHINING

CHAPTER 25: JACOBSON

The Beginning

Two-Hundred Years Earlier...

Chrisette Smith, Abel's mother, a beautiful woman with olive skin, set fire to her family's cottage during the 1800s.

The night before the fire, Abel and I spoke with an exquisite fair-skinned woman whose beauty was alluring; she had an enticing body, and her voice was hypnotic when she spoke. This woman embodied every quality a woman should have. She instructed us to meet her the next day so our lives could change forever. Neither of us knew what that meant. Even so, we were about to find out.

I'm on the field, splitting wood and stacking it one by one. The wind is brisk, and the sun is setting.

"Hey, Boy, bring that wood inside now!" Mrs. Smith shouts.

A wave of nausea washes over me, and I feel the bile rising in my throat every time she refers to me as "Boy."

However, I'm her slave; I must obey her commands.

Grabbing the four logs from my pile I scurry inside before she calls for me again. If I don't make it inside quickly, that will be seven slashes across my back as punishment. *If I'm lucky!* Mrs. Chrisette Smith doesn't like to wait long. It is best I finish my tasks promptly to avoid any consequences. I don't want to upset her.

Placing the wood down in front of the fireplace, I carefully arrange the logs, making sure they are stacked neatly. Suddenly, I am struck to the ground from behind. When I regain consciousness, Mrs. Smith is pacing back and forth, chanting in a foreign language. She places sheets into the fireplace, causing them to catch on fire, and throws them onto the floor.

"Burn them all!" She shouts after summoning whatever demon she prays to while slitting the throats of three other enslaved men.

The fire is spreading throughout the cottage, and she notices that I'm awake and dashes toward me, her eyes blazing with fury, except a shadow intervenes and hurls her to the ground, killing her instantly. The next thing I know, I'm outside beside Abel, who sighs with relief. He hated his mother.

"How did I get out here?" I ask.

The enticing woman from yesterday reappears out of thin air, her lips curving into a merciless smirk.

"I saved the two of you from that wicked woman. You owe

me." She responds with a cynical tone.

Abel huffs. "We didn't ask for your help. And we certainly don't owe you anything."

She slits Abel's throat in the flash of lightning, and he descends to the ground holding his neck, gasping for air. Blood pours from the wound, staining his clothes and the grass beneath him.

Shock and fear course through my veins. Rushing to Abel's side to assess his injury, my hands are trembling as I desperately search for a pulse.

"What is the matter with you?" I shout.

Her eyes are fixed on me with a cold, calculating stare, and she licks her lips and sneers. *What is wrong with her?* Her eyes turn bloodshot red as sharp, animal-like teeth protrude from her mouth. *What is she? What do I do?* She morphed from this beautiful woman to something horrific, something inhuman—this demon! Standing frozen in terror, I'm unable to comprehend the monstrous transformation before me. She laughs sinisterly, a chilling sound that sends shivers down my spine.

"I can save him if that's what you want me to do. However, why would you want me to save your master?"

I'm paralyzed with fear, unsure how to respond to her question. Abel is indeed my master. However, he never treated me as a slave. His mother, on the other hand, did. I look at him on the ground in agony, breathing slowly and struggling to stay conscious. His life is slipping through his fingers. I don't want Abel to die. Still, how do I answer her question?

While I let my inner thoughts overwhelm me, she grabs Abel by the hair and yanks his head back. Blood gushes from his throat as he lets out a choked gasp. He doesn't have much longer.

My throat is dry, and my voice comes out like a whisper when I speak. "Please," I plead, "don't let him die. He's my brother."

She sinks her teeth into his neck, and Abel's eyes roll back. The monster tosses me to the ground like a rag-doll when I attempt to stop her. With the strength she is exhibiting, she's not human!

Abel screams in agony, and his body twists and turns. His eyes shift from ocean blue to bright red as he writhes in pain. *What is happening to him?*

The woman grasps me by the neck with remarkable strength, and I struggle to breathe. She holds me up and grasps my arm, sinking her teeth into it; I feel a hot, stinging sensation fixating throughout my entire body. It is a strange feeling that is extremely painful. It feels as if my body is on fire and my bones are breaking simultaneously. Suddenly, pointy canine teeth bulge from my mouth, and my throat is dry like I haven't had a drink of water for months. Then, I lose consciousness.

A few hours later...

In a cold, clammy underground tunnel, disoriented and unsure of how I got there, my eyes flutter open. The air is thick with a musty scent, and the sound of dripping water echoes through the darkness. I have no idea where Abel is. Or *that creature.* The beautiful woman had been visiting us for months and disappeared when daylight approached. I've heard stories about creatures lurking at night, wreaking havoc among the villages; I thought these were tall tales the slave owners would tell to keep us in line. Perhaps they were right; she wasn't human, not with the strength she possessed.

The woman appears in the cave with an eerie glow in her eyes. "Oh good, you're awake! Are you ready for dinner?"

She seems to be in great spirits. Looking around the cave, I don't see anything in here resembling a single morsel of food.

Taking a step back in confusion, "W—what are we having?" I stammer, clearly confused by her question.

A wide grin appears on the creature's face, and her eyes twinkle with amusement. She disappears in a flash and reappears with a bloodied woman in her arms.

"Fresh meat," she says with a chilling tone.

My heart races as I realize the true nature of the *dinner* she was referring to, and horror washes over me.

"What is this?!" I ask in a panicked voice, my eyes fixed on the bloodied woman in her arms.

"She is your food," she replies calmly.

"You can't be serious," I manage to utter, my gaze still locked on the woman drenched in blood.

She bites into the young woman's neck and consumes her blood with an unsettling hunger.

Recoiling in disgust, I pace back and forth, running my trembling fingers through my hair. The realization sinks in that I am trapped in the presence of a ravenous monster.

She—*this creature*—looks up at me with blood dripping from her mouth and a sinister smile spreading across her face.

"If you want to survive, you will drink." She commands.

What does she mean if I want to survive? My mind races as I try to comprehend her words. Is she suggesting that I, too, must drink blood to survive?

Abel enters the cave. "Drink, Jacobson! You should have completed your transformation a couple of hours ago—instead, you passed out."

Eyeing him intently, he looks like a different man. The gash in his throat is healed—as if by magic. His eyes are now bloodshot red, and his skin is milky white and almost translucent, as if drained of all color.

Furrowing my brow and trying to make sense of what I'm seeing. "What happened to you?"

His bloodshot eyes flicker with delight, and he smirks. "I have been reborn into something greater, Jacobson."

Looking back at the woman. "What are you?"

The question escapes my lips before I can take it back, and I know I'm not ready for the response that awaits me.

Her lips curl into a smirk. "I am a vampire, Jacobson. My name is Aika Ronin."

The realization hits me like a ton of bricks, and I stumble backward. They're not human.

"If you wish to be like us, you have to drink!" She says.

Abel places his hand on my shoulder and gives it a reassuring squeeze. "Jacobson, just drink from the woman to complete the transformation."

What is wrong with them? I can't believe what I'm hearing.

"There is no way I will be drinking human blood!" I shout back at them.

What would make them think I would willingly drink another human being's blood? The idea of consuming it is repulsive. Vomit is threatening to come up as the thought sinks in.

Aika strides toward the woman and cuts her wrist, and blood starts to flow from the wound. The metallic scent fills the air, and I feel a dry, burning sensation take over me. Suddenly, the primal urge courses through my veins, and I need to drink from her more than anything else in the world.

In seconds, her body is in my arms, head to the side, and neck exposed for me to devour her. Razor-sharp teeth extend from my mouth and sink deep into her skin. The blood is sweet and intoxicating. Succumbing to a frenzy, I want–*need* more. When I finish sucking the last bit of her sweet blood, her limp body seeps to the ground, lifeless and drained of all vitality. I feel a momentary satisfaction wash over me. Still, as the euphoria fades, a wave of guilt and remorse begins to creep in. I'm mortified.

"What did you do to me?" I shout in horror.

"I made you a better man," Aika replies with a sly smile.

"How am I a *better* man now? I'm a *monster!*" I rub my fingers along the sharp teeth in my mouth and shudder at the realization of what I have become. "I didn't ask for this!"

Aika's smile widens, her eyes glinting with amusement. "Hmm...sometimes, the best things in life are the ones we never asked for," she says cryptically.

She rips the woman's head off, sets fire to her corpse, and then commands Abel and me to follow her. I'm stunned, and although every fiber of my being warns me not to, I'm urged to follow her without hesitation.

We exit the cave at nighttime, and the moon is shining bright in the sky. I have no idea where we are or what time it is. Still, Aika is very anxious to leave and get to wherever our destination is before the sun rises.

"Follow me," Aika instructs as she takes off like a flash of lightning, her figure disappearing into the darkness.

Did she lose her mind? How on God's green earth does she expect me to follow her at that speed?

"We have to catch up to her," Abel says.

"You expect us to keep up with her at that pace?" I ask incredulously, already feeling my legs protest at the thought of trying to match Aika's speed.

Abel lifts his brow and smirks. "Yes."

He takes off after her, easily matching her speed, and I start running as I usually would, except something is different. I am stronger and faster. It feels like I'm flying, effortlessly gliding through the air with each stride.

We run for what seems like hours without any signs of slowing down. Daylight is approaching, when we reach our destination: a sandy white beach with crystal clear waters stretching out before us. Aika chants in a foreign language, and once she is done, a transparent screen opens, revealing a majestic castle with a tall fence surrounding it.

Her eyes sparkle. "Welcome to your new home," she says gleefully.

The castle appears out of thin air, *like magic*. It stands tall and grand, with intricate details adorning its walls and towers.

Reality sinks in. I am no longer a man but *a vampire—a monster*.

Life as I once knew it has changed forever.

The following day, Aika enters my chambers and hands me a gold chalice cup of blood, its rich crimson color glistening in the well-lit room.

"Drink up. You will need your energy!" She says with a mischievous smile, her fangs peeking out from behind her lips.

As much as I don't want to, my throat feels like rough sandpaper. Either I take a sip of the blood or sit here and suffer. I swallow the gulp in my throat. Reluctantly, I bring the chalice to my lips, the metallic scent of blood filling my nostrils, and the liquid slides down my throat.

Clearing my throat and trying my best to ignore the sweet taste that lingers on my tongue.

"What do you want with me?" I ask, my voice hoarse.

Aika lifts her brow and leans in closer, her mischievous smile widening. "Oh, darling," she purrs, "I want you to join my kingdom."

This is more of a demand than a request. Her tone and expression make it clear that refusal is not an option. I am a pawn in Aika's game.

She steps closer to me, her face stern and her eyes filled with purpose. "I have big plans for my empire, and I want you and Abel to help build it to be the most feared in all the realms," she declares, her voice filled with conviction. "I know you are new to my *world*; I can assure you that this place is far better than anything you have ever known."

The thought of being part of something bigger and more powerful is enticing. I've spent my days on the field, maintaining crops and serving Abel and his family with no real purpose. Chrisette and the rest of their family treated us like we were less than human. *"You are worthless animals,"* she would always say. Abel never treated me like his mother did; he was kind and fair, and when the other slaves or I would do something inadequately, Abel would take lashes to the back for us. We instantly formed a *"brotherly"* bond, which his mother and sister despised.

He is—*was* a good man until we met Aika Ronin.

Reliving The Past

Over the next one hundred years, our power grew. We took over the kingdoms one by one, slaughtering thousands of supernatural beings and building the kingdom Aika wanted. When Aika and Abel married, I thought it was absurd; however, Abel was in love with her, so much so that he took her last name. He assured me that his passion for Aika was real and that one day, I would find true love the way he had found it with her. I was starting to give up hope until Serena came into my life.

December 2000

Serena is a breath of fresh air. She is a beautiful, fair-skinned woman with short, curly hair and a luscious silhouette. Her mother was Asian, and her father was African-American. Unfortunately, they were murdered a few years ago before she came to live at the castle. Serena is different from every woman I have ever met over the years, and I always know when she is in the same room as me because all the hairs on my neck rise. Her vibrant personality and infectious laughter bring joy to every room she enters. Her intoxicating scent had me wanting to devour her while simultaneously making love when we met. We quickly became inseparable. I love her with every fiber of my being, and I cannot imagine a life without her. We have been dating for ten months, and I'm ready to propose to her.

While waiting for Serena to return to my room, I practice asking her to marry me in front of the mirror.

"Will you marry me, Serena?" No, no. That's not right. *"Will you do me the honor of marrying me?"*

"Jacobson, who are you talking to?" Serena asks as she enters the room, a puzzled expression on her face.

Quickly turning around and clearing my throat, I rub my sweaty palms on my pants. "Oh, uh, no one."

Serena raises an eyebrow but decides not to press any further, giving me a small smile instead.

Regaining my composure, I muster up the courage to ask her the question that has been weighing on my mind for so long. Kneeling on one knee, I reach into my pocket.

She gasps, her eyes widening with anticipation. "Jacobson, what are you doing?"

Opening a small velvet box to reveal a sparkling five-carrot blue sapphire halo diamond ring. With a nervous smile, I finally ask, "Serena, will you do me the incredible honor of marrying me?"

She pauses for a moment, and her hand covers her mouth. Tears fill her eyes as she nods vigorously, "Yes!"

A rush of relief washes over me, and I sweep Serena into a tight embrace, kissing her passionately. She has made me the happiest man—*vampire* alive.

"I love you," I whisper against her lips.

Serena smiles through her tears and whispers back, "I love you too, Jacobson."

It is unheard of for a vampire and a witch to be mated. Still, Abel and Aika knew how we felt for one another and gave us their blessings despite the unconventional nature of our relationship.

Four Months Later...
Jacobson and Serena's Wedding
April 15th, 2001

On our wedding day, Serena is wearing a strapless ivory beaded dress that clings to her body perfectly. Her long, flowing veil trails behind her as she walks down the aisle, her eyes locking with mine. My heart nearly leaps out of my chest as I watch her glide toward me. The guests are in awe of her elegance, and I feel like the luckiest vampire in the world to be marrying such a beautiful woman inside and out.

She leans in close, her lips barely brushing against mine, and whispers, "Honey, are you okay? You're drooling." She pulls back, and a playful smile dances across her lips.

Squeezing her hand firmly, I chuckle. "I'm more than okay."

Abel clears his throat to start the ceremony. "Dearly beloved, we are gathered here today to witness the union between our dear friend Jacobson and the lovely Serena. May their love continue to grow and flourish, bringing them endless happiness and joy throughout their journey together."

A warm glow casts a soft and intimate ambiance over us as we exchange vows, sealing our commitment to each other.

Grasping Serena's hands in mine and feeling a surge of emotions as I look into her eyes. "Serena, I have been alive for many, *many, many* years." I flash the crowd my charming smile. Everyone in the room chuckles. "In all those years, I have never found a love as pure and genuine as the one I share with you. You are my rock, my anchor, and my everything. I promise to cherish and love you unconditionally for the rest of our lives."

The room fills with a collective sigh as Serena's eyes well up with tears of joy, and her cheeks flush to a bright pink. *She is so beautiful.*

Slightly raising her face to meet mine. "Serena, you are the epitome of beauty, both inside and out," I whisper.

Serena gulps and wipes away the single tear trickling down her cheek before taking a deep breath to compose herself.

"Jacobson, I love you more than words can express. You have shown me what true love is, and I am grateful every day to have you by my side. I vow to always be there for you, supporting and loving you in every way possible."

Her voice trembles with emotion as she speaks, and her eyes shimmer with a deep sense of devotion.

Serena and I lock eyes, and time stands still.

Abel clears his throat, breaking our muse. "I now pronounce

you Husband and Wife. You may now kiss the bride."

The room erupts in applause and cheers as we lean in for our first kiss as a married couple. Pressing my lips against hers, I kiss her with all the love and passion built up inside me. I'm eager to have her in my bed as my wife!

We pull away from the kiss, both of us breathless and smiling. I want to carry her to my bed and rip that dress from her body *now*.

Serena giggles, and her eyes twinkle. "Not so fast, my love. We must celebrate with our guests before we can continue our private celebration."

"Let the festivities begin!" Abel exclaims, and I carry Serena in bridal style down the aisle, the crowd cheering and clapping for us.

The party lasts late into the night, with music, dancing, and laughter filling the air. Serena and I sneak glances at each other, anticipation building with every passing moment.

I'm standing on the ballroom balcony, overlooking the starlit sky. I ponder about how my life used to be before becoming a vampire, and perhaps Aika was right. *This was better than being a slave.*

Deep in thought, I am suddenly interrupted by Serena's arms wrapping around me from behind.

"Are you ready to return to reality?" she whispers, her breath warm against my neck.

Turning to face her, we share a knowing smile. It's time for our own intimate celebration to begin. In the months leading up to our wedding, we decided to wait until our wedding night to consummate our love.

Back in our private quarters, I can't keep my hands off my wife. Unzipping Serena's dress and brushing my fingers along her collarbone as the embellished material gracefully drops to the floor, she turns around to face me. The look in her eyes is intense as she places her hand on my chest, feeling the rapid thumping of my heart beneath her touch. Kissing her shoulder with feather-like kisses, I work my way up to her neck, savoring the taste of her delicate skin. She moans in pleasure, her body melting into mine.

Our eyes lock, and I rub my thumb across her lips. "Are you sure you're ready for this?"

Her eyes gleam. "Yes," she whispers, her voice barely audible. "I've never been surer."

Leaning in closer and capturing her lips with mine, I guide her to the bed.

As we descend into the soft silk sheets, there is no stopping us.

Surprise, Surprise

It's been one month and two weeks since our wedding nuptials. Serena and I prefer to spend our days alone in our corridors on the other side of the castle we share with Aika, Abel, and the rest of the vampire kingdom. We haven't been involved with the kingdom affairs as much as we used to, focusing instead on building our own little world within the castle walls. Still, it is time to return to business.

Aika and Abel recruit five skilled fighters from each kingdom to serve in ours. They want the remaining kingdoms to fear vampires, and by doing so, they uproot them from their homes to reside here. Abel stated he wanted to be prepared if the supernatural creatures tried to attack us but also wanted the others to know that we were superior to them. However, this wasn't enough to secure our hold on the rest of the supernaturals. The manticores attacked our kingdom and nearly defeated us. From that moment on, Aika said we needed more vampires for protection. This is how the tournament known as "The Battle of

Anaik," in which two humans are pitted against each other to death, and whoever succeeds becomes a vampire, came about. Abel believes that granting humans immortality is a *gift* and a way to grow our kingdom.

Serena plops on the bed and sighs. "Honey, I am not feeling well. I don't think I can attend the battle tonight."

I stride into our walk-in closet to pick the appropriate attire for tonight's event.

"What's wrong? You know, King Abel and Queen Aika demand our presence for The Battle of Anaik. Are you sure you won't be able to attend?" I shout from the inside of our closet.

"Jacobson, I'm pregnant!" she blurts out.

Stumbling back against the wall. *Did I hear her correctly?*

"W—what do you mean you're *pregnant*?" I call out.

"We're going to have a baby, Jacobson," she replies nervously.

It's unheard of for a witch and a vampire to be together, let alone have a baby. It feels like we're entering uncharted territory. What does this mean for the kingdom and us? Abel and I are like brothers. However, there is no way Abel will accept this. *What will he do to us? What will he do to our child?*

"Jacobson?" Her soft voice interrupts my reeling thoughts. "Please come out of the closet and talk to me."

Unable to move, I stand frozen against the wall. I want to rush to my wife and tell her everything will be okay. I want to comfort her. Abel will not accept this!

"Jacobson," she repeats louder this time.

Running my fingers through my hair and pacing the room back

and forth, I finally come out of the closet. How is Serena pregnant? I am a vampire. She is a human witch. This is impossible!

Turning to face her. "Serena, I don't understand how this could happen. How are you pregnant? Vampires cannot reproduce unless a spell is involved."

Scratching the top of my head, I furrow my brows.

Serena sniffles as she tries to explain, "Vampires and witches can reproduce. Why do you think Aika forbids vampires and witches from being together? That's why we needed their blessing." She runs her fingers along her belly. "I'm a witch–or at least born of witch descent because my magic is dormant. It's a rare occurrence. Nevertheless, that's all the magic we needed to conceive."

Blinking repeatedly, I stare at Serena in disbelief, my mind racing to process this new information. "Why would Aika and Abel approve our marriage if it's forbidden?"

She wipes away a tear and takes a deep breath before responding, "I think Aika doesn't view me as a threat because my magic is dormant. I don't possess any physical magic, so our child is not a threat."

"Did you know that you could get pregnant?" I ask, trying to wrap my head around the idea of Serena being able to conceive.

"Well...," she trails off. "I...I thought it *could* be possible." She looks away from me.

Throwing my arms in the air in frustration. "How could you not tell me this sooner?"

Serena's eyes fill with guilt as she gets up from the bed.

"Jacobson, I knew it was *possible*..." Her voice trails off. "I–I assumed it wouldn't affect us because my magic is dormant." She stammers, reaching out to touch my arm.

I involuntarily flinch at her touch, and her eyes glisten with tears, hurt by my reaction.

"I'm sorry," she whispers, pulling her hand back.

"No, I am sorry," I reply.

Of course, I've always wanted to become a father, but growing up the way I did, I never wanted to pass on the same pain and struggles to my own child. And once Aika turned me into a vampire, the thought never came back up.

Serena's beautiful face is wet from ongoing streams of tears. "Are you not happy, Jacobson?" she whispers.

Her question catches me off guard, and I quickly shake my head. "No, Serena, it's not that," I reply softly. "It's just...I never thought I would have the chance to be a father, and now that it's a possibility, I'm scared of what it might mean for our child." Taking her hand in mine. "I'm worried about Abel and Aika's reaction. This has never been heard of. A vampire and witch having a baby together. Our child will be half-human, half-vampire, and their kinds are meant to serve us."

Serena gently squeezes my hand, and the realization dawns on her. "Our child will be a half-witch, half-vampire, a *hybrid*."

"Hybrids are abominations and should be slaves in the eyes of Abel and Aika. And half-humans are meant to serve us."

Our child–being treated less than human, I can't bear the thought!

Serena doesn't serve the kingdom because Aika shows favoritism towards her. If she wasn't married to me, I'm unsure what her duties to the crown would be. However, our child will face even more significant challenges.

Opening my arms for an embrace, Serena falls into me, planting her face on my chest. Lifting her head gently, I place a soft kiss on her forehead.

"We must tell Abel and Aika that we're expecting a baby because they will figure it out sooner or later."

She sighs and wipes the tears from her eyes. "We can tell them tomorrow when they demand to know why we weren't in attendance for the tournament."

"That will be tomorrow's problem. Right now, let's focus on celebrating this wonderful news."

Serena smiles and nods. "You're right," she says softly.

When Serena falls asleep, I head down the hall to our vast library to research witches and vampires reproducing, hoping to find any information that could help us understand our situation better. Flipping through the pages of ancient texts and scrolls, I see nothing—nada—zilch. *Just my luck!*

A few years ago, a witch created a spell that formed—or rather acted as "sunglasses" surrounding the windows to our castle, protecting us from the sunlight; in doing so, I notice when the sun rises the following morning, which means I have spent the entire night in the library searching for something that doesn't exist. I have no idea what I am seeking. Serena is pregnant, and this is a miracle. I should be ecstatic, not probing for an explanation.

Abel storms into the library, brows arched and jaw clenched. "Why weren't you and Serena at the battle?"

My eyes lock with Abel's as I look up from my empty-handed search. "Serena wasn't feeling well, so I stayed with her. You know we wouldn't have missed the tournament if it wasn't for a valid reason."

Abel's eyes narrow in suspicion. "There was no mention of Serena not feeling well. Perhaps there is more to this story than you're letting on," Abel suggests, his eyebrows pulling together.

Abel is clairvoyant, a special gift among others he received once he became a vampire. I wasn't granted such "special" abilities. However, Aika says I'm the fastest vampire alive; perhaps my gift is accelerated speed. Still, I believe Abel is truly gifted. He also has the power to absorb anyone's magic for a limited time, but he is still trying to get the hang of it. I'm sure he had a vision of something relating to us expecting a baby—another reason we must come clean.

"Abel, if you need to ask something, get on with it!" I say impatiently.

"Well then, is Serena with child?" He asks frankly.

"Yes, she is!" I reply firmly.

Abel's eyes widen with delight, and he claps his hands together. "Did you plan to inform me of this wonderful news, or did I stumble upon it by chance?"

"Of course, we planned to inform you, Brother!" I assure him.

"I would never keep something like this from you!"

However, I did want to keep this from him. I didn't want him to know about our future child.

To my surprise, he opens his arms for an embrace and says, "Well, well, well! Brother, I am overjoyed for you and Serena."

"You are?" I ask skeptically, raising an eyebrow.

"Of course!" He slaps me on the back. "Serena is no threat to us, and neither would a child conceived by the two of you."

I'm grateful that Serena's magic is dormant, or this conversation could have taken a different turn.

Akira

As the months pass, Serena's bump grows rounder, and the next thing I know, we are preparing for our daughter's arrival. We picked out the name "Akira" to represent *bright*, like Serena's personality. *Clear* because Serena and I shared a clear understanding of what we wanted from one another, and *ideal* because our situation wasn't. A small inside joke between the two of us.

There is a knock on the door, and it's Rosa. She was the one who revealed to us a few weeks ago that we are having a daughter. However, we haven't told her or anyone else the name we have chosen.

"Hey, Rosa. How are you doing? Please come in." I say, opening the door wider to let her inside.

She bites her lip and lowers her gaze toward the floor. Rosa takes a deep breath, and a tear falls from her eye. "I have some bad news."

A knot immediately forms in my stomach, anticipating the

worst. I usher her to take a seat on the black and gold chair.

"What is it, Rosa? Serena is out shopping for baby clothes with one of the humans."

"I had a vision, Jacobson, and it wasn't a good one," she says. "I'm uncertain what Abel has planned. It is not good—not good at all!"

"What did you see, Rosa?" I ask, my voice filled with concern.

Rosa hesitates for a moment before saying, "Your baby will be a threat, and Abel knows it. He will take her away from you."

What? The thought of Abel taking our baby away has my blood boiling. I need to protect our daughter at all costs!

"What! This can't be happening!" I shout.

Clenching my fist until my knuckles turn white. "Abel has no right to take our baby away from us," I growl through gritted teeth and storm to Abel and Aika's room without allowing Rosa to finish her vision.

Balling up my fist, I bang on their chamber doors.

"What happened, Brother?" Abel asks with concern.

"Abel, what are your plans for our daughter?"

His eyes are vast; however, he does not respond.

"Serena's sister, Rosa, had a vision of you taking our daughter away from us!"

Initially, Abel doesn't reply. However, he shifts in his seat and remembers who he is. He is King Abel.

"Jacobson, I am your king, and you are not in a position to question me!" he says firmly.

"Don't lecture me on that monarchy bull; this is my daughter, my family; I won't allow it!" I shout, slamming the door behind me.

Marching back to our room, my brows pulled together, Rosa strides in behind me, carrying an old brown book.

"I have something to tell you." She says.

Serena is back, and she places the items she bought on the floor. "What is it?" She asks warily.

"I know what powers your daughter will possess," Rosa replies.

Serena and I exchange puzzled glances.

"Powers? What do you mean?" I ask, my anger momentarily forgotten.

"Your daughter will possess the power to cause earthquakes and the ability to move objects with her mind. She will also be psychic like me and able to see glimpses of the future." Rosa explains. "These powers are rare and formidable, and she will need guidance and training to control them effectively," she adds.

Serena sobs, "We must protect her from the king, Jacobson! He—he will destroy her!" Her voice is trembling. "We must flee from the kingdom."

Akira will be born in just a few days, and I know that this means *war*.

Running my fingers through my hair. "How on earth do you suppose we do that?" I snap back, and Serena flinches at my tone. Quickly regretting my harsh response, I soften my approach.

"I'm sorry, Serena. I didn't mean to snap at you. Nevertheless, escaping the kingdom won't be easy. We need a plan, resources, and allies. We have none of those things."

"There is no way we can safely get the both of you out of here while Serena is so far along in her pregnancy without Abel knowing about it," Rosa adds, worry in her voice.

We are disturbed by the sounds of loud footsteps outside our chamber doors. There are about forty guards stationed along the hall when I open the door.

"What is the meaning of this?" I demand.

"We were instructed to guard your corridors," Kade replies.

"Direct orders from the king," Kaden adds.

Kaden and Kade are newly recruited vampires who serve as guards. I instantly slam the door in their faces. *Imbeciles!*

"Abel sent his guards to patrol outside our door. There is no way we are leaving this castle before Akira is born." I say in defeat.

Serena sobs as she holds her pregnant belly. "What are we going to do, Jacobson?"

Plunging my head into my hands. "I don't know."

On Sunday, January 20th, at six-thirty in the morning, I rush to Serena's side, holding her hand.

"Serena, is it time?" I ask with both excitement and worry.

"Yes! She is coming! She is coming!" Serena screeches through gritted teeth; her voice is strained with pain.

After several minutes of agony and pushing, we admire the birth of our beautiful daughter Akira. The hair on her head is black with curly ends, and she has hazel eyes, just like my mother. It is love at first sight when I hold Akira in my arms for the first time, marveling at her tiny features and telling my precious baby girl how much we love her in between sobs.

"I am so sorry," Rosa apologizes softly.

I was looking forward to her arrival, but what should have been my wife's and my happiest day turned into tragedy.

Suddenly, the door is destroyed, and Rosa and I fall unconscious.

I'm in the dungeon when I awake, restricted by shackles and surrounded by the stench of death. When my eyes adjust to the dim light, Rosa appears before me and is transparent. She hands me a note and disappears in a matter of seconds.

Abel has planned an execution for you and Serena on Monday at 5 o'clock p.m.

Krystal, a loyal member of The Revolt, has volunteered to sacrifice herself to save you.

Please follow her when she appears.

- Rosa

After I finish reading the note, it disintegrates into thin air. I'm confused. What about Serena? There is a plan to save me from Abel's execution, but there is no plan to save the love of my life. How can I go on without Serena by my side?

A young woman materializes in front of me, her eyes filled with purpose.

"Hello, Jacobson. My name is Krystal, and I'm here to take your place. Please take this pill."

"What is this for?" I ask, hesitating to swallow the pill from Krystal's outstretched hand.

"We don't have time for this, Jacobson. Abel's guards will be here at any moment, and I need you to take this now!" she urges.

Reluctantly, I swallow it and transform into Krystal's replica, and she shapeshifts into me.

"Why would you do this?" I question, bewildered by the sudden switch.

She places her hand on my shoulder and says, "Because this is what Serena wanted."

Before I can ask any further questions, the sound of footsteps echoes down the hallway. We exchange a quick glance, and I become invisible, blending seamlessly into the surroundings.

Abel and his guards storm into the dungeon, dragging Krystal out to her untimely death.

She is beheaded and burned, and her ashes are thrown into the river. Serena was sentenced to the same demise I should have been given.

Serena was here one moment and murdered the next, snatched away by a vile, monstrous, ruthless, and sadistic monster. I didn't get a chance to hold her hand, kiss her, or look into her eyes to say goodbye. My heart shattered into a million tiny pieces, leaving a deep hole in my chest.

My soulmate is gone.

Three days later...

My beloved wife, Serena, and Krystal, who sacrificed herself for me, are gone, and I am still disguised as her. I have no idea how long this magic will last. As far as I know, Akira is still alive, but the fate of my daughter's life is still unknown.

Suddenly, an ample white light appears, and a man emerges through it. He introduces himself as Jace, the leader of the shapeshifters, and instructs me to follow him. He explains that he knows about my predicament and offers me a chance to join "The Revolt" so I can avenge the loss of my wife and find out the fate of my daughter.

Right before I walk through the white lights with Jace, Rosa appears and hands me a magical book.

"This is how we will keep in contact. I will stay by Akira's side. Please stay safe." She says.

Procuring the book from her, I nod. "Take care of yourself too, Rosa. Thank you for staying here to watch over Akira."

She nods and gives me a reassuring smile. "I promise I'll do everything I can to protect her."

My eyes are vast, gazing at the surroundings when we arrive in this new realm. It's unlike anything I've ever seen before. The air feels different here, the landscape that stretches out before me is surreal, and the colors are more vibrant than anything I've ever witnessed.

"Welcome to The Island of Kian," Jace says with a wide grin. "The island was created by the witches with the help of the phoenixes."

Lifting a brow. "What do you mean phoenixes? I thought their only skill was avoiding death and being reborn from their ashes."

Jace chuckles. "You have much to learn, my friend."

He points toward a sizable cabin that can easily house ten people. "This is where you will be staying."

My eyes widen as I take in the grandeur of the cabin.

"How long will I be in this form?" I ask, gesturing to my current female parts when I recover from my initial shock.

Jace smirks and replies, "That will only last for one more day. Soon, you will be yourself again, and we can get to work. We plan to take down King Abel and Queen Aika's kingdom once and for all. And we believe that your daughter will lead us to that. Until then, please get accustomed to our ways. We begin training first thing tomorrow." He says as he opens the door to my cabin.

What did my life come to? My wife is dead, my daughter is being used as a pawn in a dangerous plot, and I am no longer alive as far as Abel knows. I have been forced into hiding in a new place surrounded by people I do not know.

I'm caught in a treacherous game of power and revenge. *How will I survive without my beloved wife by my side?*

Twenty-three Years Later...

Jace informs me that we will be traveling to the real world to see my daughter.

Abel commanded Rosa to put Akira under a spell as a young girl, preventing her from accessing her powers and suppressing her memories of her true identity. She was in a coma all that time until she turned nineteen. Except for a few of Abel's trusted comrades, the entire kingdom was under a spell. As far as the kingdom knew, Abel and Aika were Akira's parents.

It has been a few years since her nineteenth birthday, and I know her abilities have begun to develop. She must have questions.

We have received word that she has fled from the vampire kingdom and is on the run with the hybrids. They are in Orlando, Florida, and Rosa has aided her while keeping me informed through magical letters.

When Abel took Akira away from my wife and me, Rosa vowed to stay by her side. According to the prophecy, Akira will be the most powerful being to exist. Abel is terrified of her powers and believes that she poses a threat to his reign. He intended to raise her as his own so that he could benefit from her gifts.

We are on the brink of war, and the *king* will fall once I help my daughter reach her full potential.

The witches on our island cast a spell, opening a portal, and we walk through it. The witch, Monica, greets us with a knowing smile. She has been expecting us.

"Hello, Jace. Hello, Jacobson. Welcome. Everyone is right through here," Monica says, leading us into the kitchen.

Laughter and chatter fill the air as we enter the room, but it stops when they see us.

Jace introduces himself, and I step forward to introduce myself to

Akira. Taking her hand into mine, our gazes meet, and her eyes widen with recognition. The expression on her face is enough for me to know she knows exactly who I am to her.

Her father.

The Truth About Dormant Witches

I just received word that yesterday's battle did not go as planned. My soldiers suffered heavy casualties from the abominations and traitors on the battlefield. Still, I was pleased to know that my attack on the hybrid kingdom was not in vain because the king is dead among many of his loyal followers, which calls for a celebration. I'm unsure of all the fallen soldiers from my kingdom; however, I know that Ava, one of my most trusted comrades, was among them. She had such a formidable gift; if only she had been smart enough to use it strategically to not get herself killed. *Imbecile.* You would think someone with such a powerful ability would have the sense to avoid being slain. *What a waste of potential!*

The prince and the rest of the vile creatures must be eliminated. Their existence is an insult to us. Unfortunately, I must recruit more allies to take them down. Hopefully, some will be gifted. Ava was a considerable loss to this kingdom simply because of the gift she possessed; her power of persuasion was marvelous. Her untimely demise is unfortunate.

There is a knock on the door, and I signal one of the

inadequate slaves to answer it.

Lucas storms into my chambers, jaw set and fists clenched. "King Abel," he says, his voice apologetic and defeated, "I did not succeed in killing the hybrid prince. I'm sorry for my failure."

What a futile vampire Lucas has proven to be! He has no extraordinary gifts, and his incessant will to please me has only led to disappointments, highlighting his incompetence. The sight of him is a constant reminder of his inability to carry out even the simplest of tasks.

He crouches down on one knee and continues. "I did as you asked. I had Ava's back; unfortunately, I couldn't save her life. I will accept death as my punishment for failing you." He bows his head in shame.

He's right. He doesn't deserve to live, not after proving time and time again that he is incapable of fulfilling his responsibilities. I'm not sure why I even tolerated his presence for so long.

Grabbing him by the collar and pulling him up to his feet in a flash. "Death is the easy way out for you," I seethe, my voice dripping with disdain and my grip tightening around his collar. "Instead, you will gain back Akira's trust, and if you fail to do so," I grasp his uninjured hand and twist it until his bones threaten to shatter, making him writhe in agony. A condescending smirk appears on my face, relishing in his pain.

"You will face consequences far worse than death. Do you understand me, Boy?" Letting him stumble backward, I release my hold.

He barely nods at my demand.

Leaning in closer, I tower over him, gripping his chin and forcing him to meet my gaze. "Answer me, you pathetic excuse for a vampire," I growl.

He stammers out a shaky response. "Y—yes, I understand, King Abel."

My voice is laced with venom. "Good. Remember this moment well, for it will be the last time you defy me." With a final contemptuous glare, I release his chin and step back. "Now go," I command.

Watching him closely as he hastens away, I shake my head. *A means to no end.* I have no use for weaklings like him. Lucas should be grateful that I allowed him to keep his life. I should have killed him years ago; however, he was good at serving as a pawn in my game by keeping tabs on that little princess and everyone else in my kingdom. *Hmm... I suppose that is the actual reason why I have kept him alive.*

Sitting back down in my luxurious leather chair, I reach for my planner from the left drawer of my desk. Flipping through the pages, my mind is racing with plans and strategies. *How should we go about defeating Akira and the abominations?*

Aika enters our chambers. "Honey?"

Looking up from my planner, I meet her gaze. Aika's presence always brings a sense of calmness to my chaotic mind.

"Yes, my love?"

"Are you aware of *all* the casualties from yesterday's battle?"

My head jerks toward the door, and the two slaves in my chambers exit the room. Once they are gone, I turn back to Aika, closing my planner and setting it aside.

"Yes, I am aware there were casualties. What is it that you need to discuss?"

Aika's expression turns grave. "I just spoke with Chase, and he informed me that all of the gifted vampires were eliminated in the battle besides himself and Tyler. Tyler is currently in the infirmary, consuming human blood to heal."

My blood boils at the news. "I was only made aware of Ava!" I reply through gritted teeth, slamming my fist down on the table, frustration coursing through me.

"There's more, Abel," Aika continues. "Chase also mentioned that all the witches have fled from the castle, and the sunlight spell has been broken. They're siding with Rosa."

"What!" I roar, my anger escalating. "What do you mean the sunlight spell has been broken? That spell was bound by blood— *my* blood! How could she have broken it?"

"Rosa may have used your blood to bind the spell, but it was *her* magic," Aika explains. "She found a way to override it without us knowing and manipulate it to her advantage."

Standing to my feet, I crash my chair into the wall, causing a dent. "That treacherous witch! How dare she use my blood against me?" Curling my hands into fists. "What are we supposed to do now?"

Aika's brows knit together. "We'll have to recruit new witches from the other kingdoms who remain loyal to us to replenish our numbers. Until then, everyone needs to go into the dungeons to avoid the sunlight; the sun is rising soon."

"There are witches all around the world, and some that don't belong to the witch kingdom. Surely, we can force some of them to come here."

Aika nods. "There are other witches out there; they've been cloaking themselves for centuries to avoid detection. We will have to reach out to the remaining kingdoms and demand their cooperation in sending us their witches."

This is outrageous. My hatred for Akira and the hybrids burns hotter with each passing moment. They will pay for this!

According to a prophecy, Akira would be the most powerful creature to ever exist and would reunite the kingdoms as one. I regret not eliminating Akira when she was a baby. Still, I was advised against it by a phoenix, a witch, and a shapeshifter. With the rare powers that Akira would possess, it was more beneficial to raise her as my own and harness her powers. *Keep your enemies close, I always say.* However, her magic was unattainable. She was the only supernatural being whose power I couldn't absorb.

"I should have killed her when she was a baby!" I hiss through gritted teeth.

Aika places a gentle hand on my shoulder. "Akira can't be killed, Abel," she says.

Throwing my head back in shock, I regard Aika through narrowed eyes. "What do you mean she *can't* be killed?" I question. "We're *all* capable of being killed."

Aika meets my gaze, and her fierce red eyes soften. "Honey, I have something to tell you."

The sound of her voice ceases my growing anger, and I raise a brow for her to continue. "What is it?"

Aika pulls my chair from the wall and gestures for me to sit down. "You'll need a seat for this," she says. "I think it's time I tell you more about me and where I come from."

She sits on my lap and rests her hands on my shoulders. Although Aika and I have been together for centuries, there are still parts of her past that remain a mystery to me, like how she became the very first vampire to exist.

She pauses for a moment, her eyes distant in memory. "Centuries ago, when I was a human, I lived in a small village. I was a slave to a cruel man—a family. This man forced me to endure unimaginable suffering. I didn't have to work on the field like the other slaves because I was considered 'eye-catching,' instead, I was confined to the manor, serving him and his family day and night." Her eyes glisten, and she looks away briefly before continuing.

"My master raped me repeatedly and subjected me to constant abuse. I was so disgusted with myself and my situation that I often contemplated suicide. He threatened to do something much worse if I ever tried to escape or take my own life." She rises from my lap to walk to the mirror, staring at her reflection. She grabs the comb from the vanity and runs it through her bone-straight, black hair. Aika meets my gaze through the reflection in the mirror. Waiting for her to continue the dreadful tale, I nod slowly.

"I was numb to everything around me. Every day felt like a never-ending nightmare, and I couldn't see a way out. Death had to be more rewarding than the torment I was enduring. I didn't care about anything anymore. I just wanted the pain to stop."

Aika's eyes fill with haunting sadness. "I tried to hang myself, but my master stopped me and threatened to hang every slave on the plantation if I ever attempted it again. The fear of the consequences silenced me, trapping me in a cycle of despair. Every day became a struggle to survive, my spirit little by little withering away."

Her voice trembles as she continues, "M—my resentment grew with each passing day until one night, I couldn't take it anymore. After my master finished raping me, I carefully executed my plan to escape once he and his family were fast asleep. There was a crack in the fence I had noticed that surrounded the property, just big enough for me to squeeze through. I crawled through the opening and ran as fast as my legs could carry me. I kept running aimlessly until a shimmer of gold lights appeared in the distance, beckoning me towards it. I followed the ethereal glow until it thundered and roared, halting me in my footsteps. The light spoke with a voice that echoed through the night and informed me that for as long as I served her, she would grant me immortality and unimaginable strength. I no longer wanted to be a slave at my master's mercy, so I obliged. She turned me into a vampire by feeding me her blood and the blood of werewolves, shapeshifters, manticores, witches, and phoenixes, and I returned the favor by pledging my loyalty to her. The transformation was excruciating, as my body contorted and twisted in ways I never thought possible, and the process was completed by feeding on a human. The pain was worth it; I felt invincible afterward. With my newly acquired vampire abilities, I killed my master's family one by one in front of him. I finished him off by draining every last drop of his blood. I also turned the other slaves into vampires, and they were sworn to secrecy." Aika's lips curve into a sinister smirk as she relishes the memory of her master's demise.

That's my girl.

She sits on my lap again, and I run my fingers through her dark hair. She leans into my touch, a satisfied purr escaping her lips. I smirk in response.

"The shimmer of gold lights was the goddess, Adira; she created werewolves and shapeshifters. Her brother Azra created manticores, witches, and phoenixes. Adira resented her brother for forming creatures more powerful than the ones she created. She wanted to create a stronger creature, so she went against the laws of nature and made me. She sought to make formidable and faster creatures that would surpass Azra's creations and the ones she had crafted before. Of course, all things come at a price, and the price for defying the laws of nature was a curse that burns us in the sun unless we consume only animal blood. Once her brother found out about me, he was furious, so he contacted a werewolf and created the very first hybrid."

Where does Akira fall into this? Parting my lips to speak, Aika continues her story, answering my question before I can even ask it.

"Akira," she says, "is a witch born from a dormant witch—their kinds are deemed unworthy. That was until the vision revealed that Akira would be the most powerful creature to exist. I then realized that dormant witches do possess a gift, and Serena became a threat that needed to be eliminated."

"What gift did Serena possess?" I'm intrigued.

"Like you, a dormant witch can absorb any supernatural being's power and use it as their own, like the phoenix's ability to resurrect; not only can they absorb magic, they can also transfer it to others."

My face hardens at this new information, and Aika nods knowingly.

"Adira informed me that Azra cast a spell on dormant witches, granting them the abilities of every gifted supernatural creature for a limited time. He hated the creation of vampires and wanted other means of destroying what was not meant to occupy this earth. Unfortunately, her brother defeated her before she could warn me about Serena. It was by fate that I befriended Serena. I started suspecting something was amiss with her when she became pregnant. I knew Jacobson would have questions if I were wrong. Still, I took the risk anyway to test my theory. I snapped her neck, and a few hours later, she was reborn with no memory of what had happened, and that confirmed my suspicion. The only way to neutralize their kind is to cut off their heads and discard their bodies in water." She looks away from me and says, "I have been doing this for decades to ensure that no trace of their existence remains unbeknownst to you. I'm sorry I didn't tell you sooner."

Forcing her to meet my gaze, I tilt her head back toward me.

"What are you saying, Aika?"

She takes another deep breath. "Abel, I believe that Serena transferred her ability to Akira." My stare turns cold as I comprehend the magnitude of my wife's words. "A few days after we killed Serena and Jacobson, I ordered a vampire to murder Akira to tie up any loose ends. I would have done it myself. However, Rosa begged me to spare her life, and she kept tabs on my every move. Luckily, I didn't go through with it because the vampire I ordered to murder Akira blew up in flames when he sliced her throat."

The air is thick between us as the weight of Aika's confession hangs above us. This is why I've been advised to keep Akira alive all those years ago.

"Is this why you demanded Rosa cast a spell over Akira and the entire kingdom, placing her in an induced coma?"

Aika nods. "Yes, I needed to figure out how that vampire died."

"And did you figure it out?" I question, brows furrowed.

She looks down at her feet before meeting my gaze again.

"No, I couldn't find any answers. I know the only way to defeat Akira is to snap her neck and bury her twenty feet underground. Her neck can be broken, just like any other vampire. Unfortunately, we cannot kill her. She is indeed special."

Running my fingers through my hair, I huff in frustration. "What about a spell?"

"We would need another vampire to snap her neck. If you or I attempt to do it, I believe we would burst into flames because of our intentions. We want her dead."

"Why are you telling me this now?" I question.

"I didn't want to worry you before because we were raising her as our daughter, but now that the little brat has betrayed us, I thought it was important for you to know," Aika explains with a hint of regret in her voice. "Serena was the last of the dormant witches to exist, so there is no need to worry about any more potential threats transferring their power to any of our enemies besides the phoenixes. It was my mistake to consent to Serena and Jacobson's request to marry; I didn't know she would pose a threat to our throne." Aika apologizes for her error in judgment and expresses her remorse by wrapping her arms around me and nibbling on my earlobe. "We need to get Akira alone before she reaches her full potential. We'll order a futile vampire to break her neck and bury her while she is unconscious." Aika pauses to look me in the eye. "Abel, you can't take matters into your own hands," she warns.

Raising a brow. "What about combat?"

"We can engage in fighting. However, we can't attempt to kill her. Only hold Akira off until a less important vampire can finish the task."

A cynical smile plays on her lips, and I nod. "We can use Lucas for this task."

A satisfied smile tugs at the corners of Aika's lips. "Lucas is the perfect choice." She replies.

Grabbing her by the hair, I pull her closer. "Together, we'll ensure Akira never poses a threat to us again."

Aika's eyes gleam. "Soon, victory will be ours!"

We exchange a malicious glance before sealing our plot with a passionate kiss, which leads to more.

Our plan will unfold immaculately.

The New Sunlight Spell

Aika and I are in the dungeons, waiting for the sun to set. *This is ridiculous!* I am a prisoner in my own castle. Rosa broke the sunlight spell, and in doing so, the sun's rays are shining brightly throughout the castle grounds, making it impossible for anyone to leave without being burned. I instructed Chase and Lucas to head to the werewolves, phoenixes, and shapeshifters' kingdom to recruit all of their witches to come here and recast the spell using my blood. In one of Rosa's books that she left behind, I found a linking spell. *Silly witch.*

One of my useless slaves enters the dungeon. His shoulders are sagging, and he shifts his weight from one leg to the other as he nervously regards me. "King Abel, the sun is down."

With a nod, I dismiss him.

Aika and I head to our chambers to freshen up and wait for a few of the witches to arrive from the phoenix kingdom.

Once they arrive, we meet in my favorite place, the battle room, to conduct the spell. Afterward, I plan to reach out to the remaining kingdoms that are loyal to the throne and invite them to stay at our castle until the war is over. There's strength in numbers.

Chase strides toward me. "King Abel, the witches are ready."

The witches walk in after him, eyebrows furrowed, creases across their foreheads, and eyes scanning the room. Chase procures the spell book from me and walks toward a male witch, whom he thinks is in charge, to hand it to him, but the man shakes his head.

The other witch next to him with blonde hair and green eyes approaches me and retrieves a blue and gold dagger from his pocket. He gestures toward my wrist, and I extend it to him. He slices into it, and blood trickles down my hand and onto the floor. He motions his arms in circular rotations and chants in an ancient tongue. *He must be their leader.* The other five witches join in on one accord, forming a circle around me, and the room trembles with eerie energy.

A pounding starts in my head, and I throw my forehead into my palms to alleviate the pain. The throbbing in my head is so severe that it feels like my skull is about to crack open. I shake my head back and forth and wipe away the dampness appearing on my forehead. There's a stinging pain shooting through my bones and a burning sensation coursing through my veins. My arms and legs start to shake uncontrollably. *What is happening to me?* This spell feels different from the one Rosa used.

"What did you do to me?" I sneer, and the room around me starts to spin.

"I linked you to all of us to ensure that nothing will happen to you or *us*," the witch responds matter-of-factly.

"What does that mean?" Lucas demands.

"It means if something happens to them, it will happen to me as well," I reply through gritted teeth, composing my balance as the room continues to spin.

I am now bound to these people, for better or for worse. Clever witches linked themselves to me to ensure their safety, knowing that any harm that befell them would also affect me. It's a genius move.

"Well, now that you're all linked to me, we will have you stay in the dungeons for safekeeping," I reply.

The head witch nods, and they exit the battle room. Turning to Chase and Lucas, they both wear expectant expressions, waiting for my next move.

"Chase, Lucas, we need to discuss a few things."

"What is it, King Abel?" Lucas asks far too eagerly for my liking.

He is a relentless irritation that I cannot wait to be rid of.

"I need you both to begin recruiting humans to compete in the tournament," I say, narrowing my eyes toward them.

"Uh, Sir, the tournament isn't scheduled for another three weeks," Chase replies, his brow furrowing.

"Are you questioning my authority, Boy?" I reply, my voice dripping with disdain.

"N–no, Sir," Chase stammers, lowering his gaze.

"Instead of every month, we will host daily tournaments. I want an army of vampires! And I need more vampires with formidable gifts like Ava. And not like you," I add, my eyes focusing on Lucas, who attempts to look everywhere in the room but at me.

What a waste of a vampire!

Chase is a telepath. He can anticipate any move the enemy makes before they even make it. He is a worthy vampire, and at the moment, he is valuable—and perhaps Tyler once he is healed. Unfortunately, Kyle was too incompetent to use his gift to stay alive! Not to mention the rest of them. I don't understand how these gifted vampires allow themselves to be so easily defeated. It's infuriating to witness their potential go to waste. They were all useless! Their powers were meant to give us an advantage; instead, they became liabilities.

Lucas and Chase exchange anxious glances, and I hiss through clenched teeth, "What are you two waiting for? Get to it!"

They quickly nod in agreement and exit the battle room to carry out my orders while I head upstairs to my chambers for one of the slaves to attend to my needs. I'm famished.

Lowering myself onto my red and gold throne-like chair in the back of my corridors. "Get over here!" I command the slave standing in my chambers. I need to replenish my energy.

The fragile slave scrambles to my side, trembling under my gaze. Twirling my finger in her light-brown hair, I inhale her intoxicating scent. *She smells so good!* I expose her neck, baring my fangs as hunger gnaws at me and lower my head. Sinking my teeth into her soft flesh, I savor the taste of her warm blood. The pathetic slave lets out a muffled cry of pain.

"Don't scream, or I'll make it hurt!" I growl, tightening my grip.

She weakly nods, and I bite into her neck again, drawing more blood from her trembling body. The sweet taste trickles down my throat and quenches my thirst. When her body goes limp in my arms, I release her and toss her to the floor like the futile rag doll she is. *That was delicious.*

Aika glides into the room, her eyes beaming in approval at the scene before her. Her lips curl into a wicked smile as she approaches me. "Hello, my love. I see you've enjoyed your meal," she purrs.

A sly grin tugs at my lips. "Indeed, my dear," I reply, savoring the taste still lingering on them. "Now, what brings you here? Business or *pleasure*?"

Aika's smile widens. "A bit of both, my love," she replies and saunters closer. "First, let's take care of business. What do you want to do with Richard?"

Raising an eyebrow at her question. "Remind me again. Who is Richard?"

Aika's eyes narrow with a mischievous glint in them. "The human. He resisted the transition, and Rosa pleaded with you to spare him."

Leaning back in my chair. "Ah, yes. I remember now."

"Rosa left him here. What should we do with him?"

Contemplating the options, I ponder for a moment. "Does he possess any special abilities?"

Aika shakes her head. "No, but he's not a regular human. He keeps resisting the transition, no matter how many times venom is inserted into him. He's resilient."

Furrowing my brow at this unusual case. "Get rid of him," I finally decide. "We don't need any more worthless vampires taking up space in our castle. Especially since I'm inviting the remaining kingdoms to reside in our home."

Aika shakes her head in disgust. "You plan to do what, Abel?"

Rolling my eyes at her reaction. "Relax, Aika. It's a strategic move—"

"It's a *risky* move." Aika cuts me off. "Inviting our enemies into our castle can potentially compromise us. And don't you find it to be a little strange that Richard can't be turned?"

Pausing for a second. Hmm... She's right.

"It is rather odd. Perhaps we should keep the human alive to run some tests and figure out why he's immune to turning." Aika nods. "Also, if the rest of the kingdoms are our enemies, then, in fact, it's better to have them under our noses. Keep your enemies closer," I add with a wicked sneer.

"I suppose you're right, my love," Aika concedes, sitting on my lap.

Playing with a strand of her hair. "We must also keep the witches that are bound to me separate from the rest. I don't want the others to catch wind of our circumstances and complicate things."

"Yes, it's best to keep our situation discreet." She agrees and leans in close to lick the blood from the corners of my mouth. "Now, let's save the business for later and indulge in some pleasure," she whispers seductively.

Closing the distance between us. "I couldn't agree more."
Licking my lips. "I'm ready for my dessert."
She smiles and allows me to undress her.

Father, is that you?

Monica entered the room with two men we'd never seen before. One man introduced himself as Jace. The other man stepped forward from behind him. He seemed familiar when our gazes met as if I'd seen him somewhere before. There was a strange connection that I couldn't quite place.

He extended his hand for a handshake and introduced himself; he was the man from my vision.

My father.

"Nice to meet you, Akira. My name is Jacobson," he says with a warm smile.

His handshake is firm, and I flinch slightly, overwhelmed by the realization that the man standing before me is my father. Words struggle to escape my lips, and I let go of his hand, bolting out of the kitchen.

Troy follows behind me, calling out my name. I ignore him, my mind racing with questions and emotions. *How could my father be alive? Why has he never reached out to me before?* I can't stop the tears from streaming down my cheeks.

"What's wrong, Akira? Who is that guy?" Troy catches up to me, and when he notices the distress on my face, he pulls me into his arms and holds me tight.

My breath catches in my throat, and I bury my face into his chest. I struggle to regain my composure and gasp for air in between sobs. I'm having a panic attack. My biological father, who I thought was dead, is actually alive and present in the kitchen.

One...two...three... I count to myself, trying to steady my breathing. Breaking away from Troy, my heart feels heavy; I'm trying to comprehend this news, and I stumble against the wall.

Rosa enters the room, nodding sympathetically as if she were reading the turmoil in my mind.

My legs give out from under me, but Troy steadies my trembling body, and Rosa rushes to my side.

"No, no, no, this cannot be happening," I whisper, my voice barely audible through my choked sobs. The shock of my father's unexpected presence is overwhelming; I cover my mouth with my hand. *Is this another vision?*

The room starts to close in on me, the walls seeming to press against my chest, and my entire body shakes uncontrollably. Red and orange colors circle my hands. *One...two...three...* I count to myself, once again attempting to calm my breathing and contain my magic.

Troy and Rosa exchange worried glances, and they both guide me to the bed, urging me to sit down.

"Take deep breaths, Akira," Rosa says firmly, and she gently rubs my back. "Try to focus on your breathing."

Troy reaches for a bottle of water on the nightstand and hands it to me, helping me take small sips. "Please tell me what's wrong," he pleads, and there's a hint of desperation in his voice.

My mind feels clouded, and I can't find the words to respond.

"Jacobson is Akira's biological father," Rosa answers for me.

Troy's eyes widen in shock. He looks at me, searching for confirmation, and I nod weakly, unable to meet his gaze.

"I thought Abel murdered him." His face twists with confusion and disbelief. "That man cannot be your father. It doesn't make any sense."

Swallowing the lump in my throat, I attempt to find my voice. "Yes, he is," I whisper.

Troy faces me, placing his hands on my shoulders. "I'm sorry. I didn't mean to doubt you," he says. "It's just hard to wrap my head around it."

I see the concern in his fierce gray eyes.

"Is he the man you saw in your vision?"

Nodding in response, more tears form in my eyes.

Troy's expression softens, and he pulls me into a comforting embrace. "How is he alive?" He mumbles to himself.

Taking a deep breath and exhaling. "I don't know," I admit, my mind still reeling from the shock.

I have to find out. There must be some explanation.

"Perhaps I can answer that," a voice interrupts us from behind. Jacobson stands in the doorway, and his lips are pressed tightly together, forming a straight line.

He enters the room, and Rosa and him exchange a knowing glance before he continues, "I'm your father, Akira."

My mind races with a million questions, yet I can't find my voice. I can barely look him in the eye.

"How is that even possible? She thought you were dead," Troy replies on my behalf.

Jacobson's face softens, and he takes a step closer to me, forcing me to meet his gaze. "I know it's a lot to take in, Akira," he says gently. "However, there's so much I need to explain to you."

"G–go on," I manage to say, bracing myself for the truth.

"A shapeshifter took my place in the execution and fooled Abel into thinking I was dead. She sacrificed her life for mine so I could be here for you."

Jacobson is standing in front of me, his eyes filled with sincerity, and he lightly brushes his hand against my cheek. "I never wanted to leave you, Akira," he continues. "Rosa and I have been in contact the entire time. She has kept me in the loop about everything that has been happening in your life for the last twenty years, and I've spent every moment waiting for this day to find my way back to you."

Tears threaten to spill from my eyes, yet I force them back, and Troy squeezes my hand.

He glares at Jacobson. "You expect us to believe this story? That you conveniently faked your death and left Akira behind? And now you're back, expecting her to trust you?"

Jacobson straightens his shoulders and locks eyes with us. "I understand it's hard to believe, but it's the truth," he says earnestly. "I'm alive, and I'm your father, Akira. And I'll work on gaining your trust."

My gaze meets Jacobson. "I—I need a moment to process all of this," I stammer. "It's a lot to take in, and I'm not sure how to feel right now."

Jacobson nods in understanding. "Take all the time you need, Akira," he says gently.

My brows knit together as I gaze at Troy, silently warning him not to follow me as I hasten out of the room.

I really need my best friends right now. They have always been my pillars of support, and I feel lost without them. However, Shelly turned off her emotions, and I can't trust Sophia—*or can I?*

Still, I make my way to the room Shelly is being held in. She is unconscious on the bed, and my shoulders slump. I stare blankly at the floor. Knowing she's shut herself off from me and the whole world hurts like no other.

Monica and Rosa placed her under a sleeping spell until the commotion settles down. We can't have an unstable vampire with no emotions wreaking havoc. The spell will only last for a few more days, and then we'll have to figure out what to do with her.

Hoping my words will somehow reach her subconscious, I grasp her hand and whisper.

"Shelly, I miss you so much! I have so much to tell you; I need you to be here with me. You've always been my rock; without you, everything feels empty." I squeeze her hand gently and continue. "My father is alive, and he's here. I wish you were here to make some creepy remark about his good looks or our uncanny resemblance." A small smile plays around my lips and a tear glistens in the corner of my eye. "I wish you were here to give me advice on how to handle the situation."

Looking at my best friend, unconscious and unresponsive, I know that this is all my fault. If only I had been more careful, none of this would have happened. Plunging my face into my palm, I sob.

"Akira?" Monica's voice breaks through my thoughts, pulling me out of my self-blame. I lift my head, trying to compose myself and meet her concerned gaze. "You shouldn't be in here."

"Monica," I say in between sobs. "She's in this predicament because of me!" I throw my hands in the air. "I'm to blame for this!"

Monica slaps me across the face to snap me out of my self-destructive spiral. "Stop blaming yourself, Akira," she says, holding my shoulders firmly. "We all make mistakes; dwelling on them won't change anything. Shelly knew what she was getting herself into when she decided to follow your lead. We all knew what we were getting ourselves into. This is *not* your fault! This is Abel Ronin's fault, and he will pay for it when the time comes!"

Monica's words hit me like a punch in the gut. She's right.

"I need you to pull yourself together. You're royalty and the most *powerful* creature known to exist. Start acting like it!"

Rubbing my cheek, which still stings. "Was the smack necessary?"

Her lips curve into a half-smile. "Yes, it was. I needed your full attention."

Playfully rolling my eyes, I wipe my tear-stained cheeks. "Well, you certainly have it now. Thanks, Monica." She smiles back at me. "Please don't do it again," I add, my voice serious but tinged with a hint of playfulness.

"Not unless I have to," she replies, her tone teasing. "Come, we need to strategize our next move."

Next move? I follow her downstairs to the living room, where my friends are waiting. Scanning the room, Niyla, Jessica, Dawn, and Queen Celine give me reassuring smiles. Troy nods in my direction. Rosa looks at me with pride in her eyes while Kaden, Felix, Roger, and Cameron anxiously await their next orders.

"Akira, this is your team now, and we're counting on you to lead us," Monica says.

My gaze settles on Troy's confident expression as he gives me a wink.

"Okay!" I say, my voice steady, "Let's get to work."

Before I can say anything else, Jacobson enters the room, and I want to run out of there like a cheetah ready to feed on a zebra. His presence adds a sense of urgency to the room, and everyone quickly shifts their focus to him.

"Hello again. My name is Jacobson," he begins, his voice commanding attention, "and I'm Akira's biological father."

A hushed silence falls over the room. *I guess he has the floor.* I take a seat nearby and wait for him to explain.

"A shapeshifter named Krystal posed as me and sacrificed her life for mine. She was executed by Abel instead of me." Jacobson continues, his words causing a collective gasp from the crowd. "Rosa and Jace helped me flee the kingdom, and I've been living on the Island of Kian the entire time. Nevertheless, I'm back now for my daughter." He pauses, his eyes meeting mine. "To take her back to the island and help her develop her powers. We need to begin training if we are to attack the vampire kingdom."

The room falls into a stunned silence at Jacobson's revelation, and all eyes turn to me, awaiting my response as I grapple with his proposition. Why would I leave with someone I don't know and go to an island that I've never heard of? On top of that, what does this mean for everyone else? Claude is still unconscious in bed, and we don't even know if he'll wake up. I don't know if I can trust Sophia or not, and then there is Shelly.

"I need time to think about this," I finally say, my voice wavering.

"Sorry, Akira, this is not up for discussion. You have to come back to the island with us to start training immediately," Jace says firmly. "Abel is unaware of the location, and it's only a matter of time before he attacks again."

"I understand this is rash and unexpected," Jacobson adds, his tone sympathetic, "Still, it's essential that you learn how to access and control your powers."

"The Island of Kian is the safest place for you to be right now, Akira," Rosa adds.

"How do you expect me to leave everyone behind and just go to this island? Especially with someone I don't even know?" I snap.

"We don't expect you to do that," Jacobson responds calmly.

"You are all welcome to join us on the journey to the island if you choose to," Jace chimes in.

Troy raises an eyebrow and speaks up, his voice stern. "Can you give us some privacy to discuss this as a group? We need to consider each and every person's safety and make a decision together."

Jace and Jacobson nod in agreement.

"Of course. However, we need an answer soon to make arrangements," Jace says.

"We leave tomorrow evening," Jacobson adds, and they exit the living room to give us some privacy to discuss.

Everyone starts talking at once, and I can't make out a single word. I raise my hand to quiet the room, and all the chitter-chatter comes to a halt.

"Are we okay with this?" I ask, scanning the room for any objections. The group looks at each other, exchanging nods and reassuring smiles.

"I think we're all on board with the plan," Cameron says.

"It seems like the best course of action," Dawn adds, and the group collectively agrees.

"Now that we're all in agreement let's figure out who's staying and who's going. Some of us need to stay here to ensure every person in the house is safe. We have an emotionless Shelly—"

"I'll stay back to keep an eye on her," Felix volunteers immediately, cutting me off.

Interesting. I give him a nod of approval.

"And I'll stay too," Niyla offers. "I want to watch over Claude."

"I'll stay with Niyla. You and Troy should go together, my dear," Queen Celine chimes in, and I appreciate her suggestion.

Troy and his mother exchange a glance, silently communicating their agreement.

"Cameron and Kaden, you're coming with me," I assert, and they nod.

"I'll stay here with the rest of the group and keep you updated on any changes," Dawn says with a smile.

"Jessica and Roger, are you staying or joining us?" I ask, turning to the two of them.

"Coming with you," they reply in unison.

Nodding in acknowledgment, I turn to the rest of the group. "Alright, those of you going to the island, gather your things. I'll inform Jacobson and Jace of our decision."

They exit the room, leaving only Troy and me.

He walks over to me with a smile playing on his lips and opens his arms for a hug. I step into his embrace, and shivers run down my spine as his warmth envelops me.

"Are you feeling better now?" Troy murmurs into my ear, his breath caressing my skin.

Pulling away slightly and meeting his gaze. "I'm so sorry about earlier. I have these panic attacks when I'm overwhelmed with emotions. I don't have it under control as much as I'd like to, and now, with magic being involved, it's even more unpredictable."

Troy's smile softens, and he gently reaches out to brush a strand of hair behind my ear. "Babe, you don't have to apologize. It's okay," he reassures me. "When you start to feel like that, just start counting backward from five, take deep breaths, and try to center your mind."

"I wish it was that easy," I sigh, leaning into his touch. "I'll try to remember that for next time."

He places his finger underneath my chin, tilting my head up to meet his gaze. Leaning closer, he brushes his lips against mine.

"We should start packing," I mumble against his lips.

"Or we can stay here a little longer?" he suggests, and I playfully shove him away.

"As much as I'd love to stay, we really need to start packing," I say with a smile. "Jacobson is expecting us to be packed and ready to go by tomorrow."

Troy's eyes suddenly darken at the mention of Jacobson, and his eyebrows pull together. "Do you actually believe that he's your father?" His lips form into a slight frown.

"Yes, I *know* that he's my father. He's the man from my vision."

Troy raises his hands in surrender and takes a step back. "Alright, alright. I trust your judgment. If you say he's your father, then he *is* your father. Just be careful, okay?"

Appreciating his concern. "I will, Troy," I promise, and we go our separate ways.

Troy gathers the remaining hybrids who didn't flee after the battle and I head to our bedroom to pack our bags.

Can I trust Jacobson?

That's a question for another day.

Time for a Council Meeting

The leaders of the remaining loyal kingdoms are meeting at the castle today to discuss our next course of action. Timothy, the leader of the werewolf kingdom, has honorably served me for years. He despises the abominations just as much as I do, especially since his only living relative joined them over twenty years ago.

Paul leads the phoenix group, and Amir leads the remaining shapeshifters. The original leaders fled from their kingdoms and formed a rebellious group known as "The Revolt," whose whereabouts I am still trying to locate. I need to neutralize them before they can further undermine my authority.

When Tyler recovers from his injuries, he will be tasked with tracking down their location. I also plan to inform the rest of the council that they will be recruiting additional humans for the tournaments so we can strengthen our forces. Usually, it would be one battle per month. Now, when one is complete, I want another one to commence immediately after. An army must be built if I am to overthrow Akira and the rest of the hybrids.

Typically, I would attend the tournaments for entertainment

purposes; however, I will take a more active role to guarantee my plan succeeds and personally ensure that all of the abominations and traitors are eliminated. Akira must be destroyed before she reaches her full potential!

I'm drafting my battle strategy to task my loyal followers by assigning one gifted vampire to a group of five when Chase enters my office, interrupting my train of thought.

Irritated, I look up. "What is it?" I ask, my voice laced with annoyance at his intrusion.

Chase hesitates for a moment before speaking. "Sir, we have a problem," he replies.

"Well, spit it out," I demand, my impatience growing.

Chase nervously shifts on his feet before continuing. "It's about the tournaments, Sir. How do you expect us to recruit so many humans every day for the upcoming battles?"

Leaning back in my chair. "The same way we always have," I say dismissively.

"But, Sir, we're down by half of our soldiers, and I'll have to start tasking the newer vampires to recruit humans," Chase adds. "At this rate, it will be impossible without exhausting our resources and manpower. It's going to be a logistical nightmare."

"Once Tyler recovers from his careless injury, he'll also assist with recruitment. Feed him more human blood to speed up healing," I order. "He needs to be well enough to carry out the task of finding the location of The Revolt as well as recruiting new humans."

Chase nods. "And what would you like us to do with Richard?"

Why is everyone questioning me about this primitive human?

"I believe Richard's body rejects vampirism because he is a Seeker," Chase discloses.

I'm learning something new every day.

With lightning speed, I have Chase pinned to the wall by his throat. "What are Seekers, and why am I just now hearing about them?" I demand, my anger seething through my clenched teeth.

Chase struggles to speak through my grip, his eyes wide with fear. "S—sorry, Sir, we didn't want to worry you until we knew more about them. We have been running tests on Richard, and after several failed attempts, it's the only logical reason for his body rejecting vampirism," Chase stammers, his voice trembling. "As far as we know, there are no known Seekers other than him."

Releasing my grip on Chase, he stumbles backward, rubbing his throat.

"So, you aren't certain of this?" I press.

Chase shakes his head, his expression grim. "No, we're not certain. Still, it's a possibility we cannot ignore."

"Why should I be worried about this possibility? What does it mean for me if other 'Seekers' are out there?" I ask, gesturing quotation marks around Seekers.

Chase swallows hard, his Adam's apple bobbing. "If there are other Seekers out there, they pose a threat to all of us. Their kind despises all supernatural beings and will stop at nothing to eliminate us."

Great, another enemy to add to my growing list!

"Thank you, Chase, for this unsettling information right before I meet with the council," I reply dryly. "Just what I needed to hear."

Chase doesn't respond. Instead, he looks down at the ground.

Lifting a brow, "Is that all?"

He nods, avoiding eye contact. "That's all, Sir."

Dismissing him with a wave of my hand, he exits my chambers. *Useless!* I let out a slight growl. I am surrounded by imbeciles!

I'm in the dining hall waiting for my guests to arrive. Timothy and four of his most trusted werewolves are the first to appear.

"King Abel, we are pleased to be here," Timothy says, greeting me with a respectful nod.

Nodding in response, they sit at the table.

Amir walks in with four members, followed closely by Paul, his partner Cole, and four others. Each person takes their seats.

"Welcome to my castle," I announce at the head of the table, addressing the room with a regal tone. "I have invited all of you here to discuss our ongoing problem."

The room is silent, and all eyes are fixed on me, waiting for me to continue. "As you all may know, Akira is a traitor to the throne. She has betrayed her family and this kingdom by aligning herself with the abominations. The hybrids should have never been created in the first place, and it's up to us to annihilate them once and for all! We must destroy them, Akira, and all traitors to the throne." I declare, my voice resonating through the room.

"How do you propose we destroy Akira?" Paul asks.

Cocking my head to the side, I narrow my eyes. "What do you mean by that?"

"We have heard that Akira possesses great power," Paul replies cautiously.

"If this speculation is true, how do you expect us to destroy her?" Cole says, his tone filled with skepticism.

Gritting my teeth, frustration builds within me. "Let me take care of destroying Akira," I assert. "All I need from you is to wipe out the hybrids and traitors and recruit humans to fight in The Battle of Anaik." I pause, gauging their reactions.

Everyone exchanges looks, deliberating my proposal.

Finally, Paul breaks the silence. "If you're confident in your plan, then we'll support you."

"So will the rest of us," Timothy adds, nodding in agreement.

"Very well. Everyone must start executing their tasks immediately. Time is of the essence!"

They nod in agreement.

Amir sits up from his seat and places his hands on the table. "Now, what is this absurd notion about you wanting all of us to move into your castle?" he asks firmly, raising an eyebrow.

"Until the enemy has been defeated, we need to consolidate our forces and reside in one secure location," I explain, meeting his gaze. "We have plenty of room to accommodate all of you."

"But—"

Waving my hand in Paul's direction. "This is not up for debate!" I interject firmly, cutting Paul off. "You have a week to prepare for your move to my kingdom."

They nod in understanding, signaling the end of the discussion.

Stepping out of the elevator on the castle's lower level, I stride to the battle room to meet Chase and Lucas. They procured new recruits, and two will compete in the Battle of Anaik tomorrow evening. Chase and Lucas look back and forth between each other, visibly nervous about my assessment of the recruits. Among the worthless men is a dark-skinned young man with short hair and a lean body. There is no doubt in my mind that he will lose. *Pathetic.* The other young man is much taller and appears to be more imposing. *I would place my bet on him.*

"King Abel, I'm pleased to introduce you to our two recruits," Lucas starts to say.

Shaking my head in return, I interrupt him, not interested in wasting my time with their names. "I don't care what their names are," I assert.

The two young men stand before me, frightened and uncertain of what to expect. Their eyes dart around the room, avoiding direct eye contact with me. Their fear enthralls me. *Marvelous.* A dismissive glance is all the shorter man gets. Clearly, he is unworthy based on his appearance alone. The taller man, however, catches my attention. I stand inches away from his face and smirk at his discomfort. He flinches. *That's right, you contemptible human, be afraid!*

"I place my bet on the taller one. Nevertheless, we shall see who proves to be the stronger opponent," I sneer, my voice dripping with arrogance. "Get them ready for the battle tomorrow."

The dark-skinned human is trembling, his eyes darting nervously between the taller man and me. "W—why are you doing this to us?" he stammers.

His words are met with a fierce glare and a hard slap across the face, which causes him to plunge to the ground like the inadequate vermin he is. I respect his courage, though. However, I wouldn't tell him.

"You dare question me? You'll learn your place soon enough," I growl. "Never speak to me unless I address you first. You disgusting pest!" I spit out the words with disdain.

He is a human and needs to know his place, which is beneath the earth. This is a battle I don't want to miss. Unfortunately, I have to; there is much to prepare for.

"Get up!" I demand. He sits on the floor, holding his face. Towering over him, my voice is dripping with venom. "Get up, Boy! I will not ask again."

He staggers to his feet and looks up at me with fear etched in his eyes. I grasp his chin and bring him closer to my face, ensuring he can feel the heat of my breath. "Remember this moment," I sneer, "for it will be the last time you ever question me."

Extending my claws, I scratch a deep gash across his arm. Blood trickles down his dark skin, and I lick his wound slowly, relishing in his fear mingled with the coppery tang of his sweet blood. The pain and shock in his eyes intensify as I inhale the metallic scent before taking another bite. Young, fresh plasma is exhilarating.

"Let me know who wins the battle." I release his arm, shoving the vermin back to the floor. "Lucas, please follow me. We have much to discuss." I turn and head back to my chambers, expecting Lucas to follow closely behind me like the maddening, futile vampire he is.

Lucas needs to gain back Akira's trust by manipulating her into thinking that he is on her side and luring her back to the kingdom to snap her neck. Then again, I doubt he would be able to break the neck of the woman he loves. Perhaps one of the incompetent vampires can snap her neck once she is here. Once it's done, Aika and I will dig a deep hole to bury both of them in. *Kill two birds with one stone!* The thought of getting rid of Akira once and for all fills me with such twisted satisfaction that I forget Lucas is in the room with me until he clears his throat.

"Um, Sir, you wanted to speak to me about something?"

Snapping out of my dark thoughts, I turn to face him. "Yes, Lucas," I reply with a sinister smirk. "I have a plan that will ensure our victory. Let's discuss the details."

Lucas nods eagerly. "Of course, Sir," he says, his voice steady. "I'm ready to assist you in any way I can."

Observing his determined expression carefully. "Are you prepared to do whatever it takes to achieve our goal?"

Lucas's eyes meet mine, unwavering. "Absolutely, Sir," he responds firmly.

Clapping my hands together. "Excellent! So, you have no reservations about restoring your friendship with Akira?"

He hesitates for a moment, then replies, "N—no, Sir."

"I'm assuming she doesn't trust you after what happened in California. Correct?" I ask, raising an eyebrow.

His face falls slightly at the mention of California, yet he quickly regains his composure. "That's correct, Sir." His reaction is guarded.

"Your task is to regain Akira's trust by devising a plan to destroy me and draw her back to the castle so we can chain her up."

His eyes widen in shock, his mouth agape, and he quickly nods in understanding. "Understood, Sir," he gulps.

"Execute the plan flawlessly, or I will do far worse to you than death," I warn, my voice dripping with menace.

Lucas swallows hard, his fear palpable. "I will not f—fail you, Sir," he stammers.

Gazing at him through piercing eyes, Lucas dashes out of my chambers.

Failure is not an option.

Our Safe Haven

My mind is in overdrive on the day of our departure to the Island of Kian. I'm completely overwhelmed by everything that has happened since I met Troy. All the deaths and emotional turmoil, my father's return from the dead, and Troy and I are building a relationship amidst all the chaos.

Tossing and turning on the bed, I take a deep breath, trying to calm my racing thoughts. I'm supposed to join The Revolt and lead them in their fight against *my father*. My biological dad, Jacobson, wants to train me and help me manage my powers. A lot of pressure is riding on my shoulders. Still, Troy has been my anchor among all this.

He is sleeping peacefully, his chest rising and falling with each steady breath. Leaning forward, I kiss him on the forehead before quietly slipping out of bed to the bathroom for a cold shower. Troy was up late last night with Niyla and Queen Celine, watching over Claude's progress, or lack thereof. He has been unconscious since the battle in California.

The icy water cascades over my body, and I try to wash away the self-blame, knowing deep down that it is not solely my fault. Still, the events of that fateful day replay in my mind, and I question every decision I made leading up to the battle. Flashbacks of the chaos and destruction haunt me, reminding me of the lives lost and the pain inflicted. Turning the water off, I lean against the cold tile wall. Lucas surfaces in my thoughts; the look on his face when I begged him to stop is fresh in my memory. I have no idea if he's alive or dead, and the uncertainty gnaws at me. He was my friend, and I miss him so much, as much as I miss Shelly and Sophia.

My friends are all gone.

The walls are closing in on me once again. "Five, four, three, two, one," I repeatedly count down, inhaling and exhaling slowly to center my mind. "Five, four, three—"

There's a faint knock on the door, interrupting my countdown. "Akira, are you okay in there?" Troy's voice calls out.

Quickly wiping away my tears with the back of my hand, I step out of the shower, wrapping a towel around myself. "Y—yes, I'm fine. I'll be right out," I reply with a shaky voice.

"It doesn't sound like you're fine. I'm coming in." Troy insists, entering the bathroom while covering his eyes with his hands.

My lips twist into a small smile. Troy has been patient and understanding. He hasn't rushed me into taking the next step in our relationship. I have never been intimate with anyone before or wanted to—*until now.*

"It's okay, you can look. I'm in a towel," I assure him.

He covers his eyes with one hand and peeks through his fingers.

"It's okay for you to see me without a towel, too," I say.

He removes his hand from his eyes completely. Troy's eyes widen slightly, and a mix of desire and vulnerability flashes across his face. I want him right here and right now! I want—no, *I need him.*

Letting my towel drop to the floor, I expose my naked body to Troy. The air feels cool against my skin, and the heat between us intensifies. Troy's gaze lingers on my figure, his eyes filled with a hunger that matches my own. He takes a step closer, grasping my waist gently, and pulls me towards his muscular build. My frame melts into his, and he leans in to capture my lips with his own, exploring every inch of my mouth. An electric spark courses throughout my entire body, and I know he wants me just as much as I want him.

I'm so in love with this man!

While I'm tracing my fingers along his rock-hard abs and maneuvering my hand down to the string of his basketball shorts, loosening them, he stops me.

He pulls away slightly, his breath heavy and his eyes filled with restraint. "Not yet," he whispers huskily.

What?

Cocking my head to the side, I arch my brow. "What do you mean?"

His face softens, and he takes a deep breath before responding. "Trust me, I want to. However, I want this to be special, not rushed," he explains.

A wave of heat floods my cheeks as my gaze darts restlessly around the confines of the bathroom. I'm not sure if I should feel offended or flattered. Quickly grabbing my towel from the floor, I wrap it around my body.

Troy tucks my baby hair behind my ear. "You're beautiful, and I want our first time to be perfect for you," he says, planting a kiss on my forehead and pulling me in for a hug. "And I don't think our first time should be in a house full of supernaturals or in this bathroom," he adds, his lips curving into a suggestive smirk.

My knees buckle at the thought of what he's implying. "I guess," I say, my voice barely a whisper.

Troy's eyes flicker mischievously as he leans in closer, his warm breath tickling my ear. "I want nothing more than to explore every inch of your body," he murmurs seductively.

My face flushes even deeper at his words, and I gulp.

He backs away slightly, a playful smirk tugging at the corners of his lips. "I'm going to check on Claude before we leave."

Nodding slowly, I lean against the wall, watching him exit the bathroom.

If only Shelly didn't have her emotions off, I would be in her room so fast to tell her about what just happened. Or even Sophia. Unfortunately, Shelly hates me, and I have no idea if I can trust Sophia. She is—*was* very loyal to the throne. And when we visited the hybrid kingdom, she made it clear how she felt about them.

I'm back in the room getting dressed, and I try to push the thoughts of Shelly and Sophia out of my mind. Slipping on my clothes, I quickly fix my hair.

Passing Claude's room on my way down the hallway, his door is slightly ajar, and I sneak a peek inside. Niyla, Queen Celine, Troy, Jessica, and Roger are at his bedside with solemn expressions. I cannot imagine what they must be going through; Claude's condition hasn't changed.

Since I met Troy, he has lost his father, his friends, and his kingdom, and now Claude's condition is deteriorating. Everything seems to be going downhill lately. Smiling weakly, I walk past, not wanting to intrude on their private moment. Life as I once knew it has altered since our trip to the hybrid kingdom.

While walking down the stairs, a wave of sadness washes over me at the thought of all the changes. My mind wonders to Sophia once again. Sophia is locked in a smaller room with no windows on the main floor because she fed on human blood before the battle. Rosa informed me that she hadn't caused any trouble since being confined to the room. *Maybe I should invite her to the Island of Kian to keep an eye on her.*

Suddenly, I find myself standing in front of Sophia's closed door. I hesitate for a moment before knocking.

"Who is it?" She calls out.

"It's me, Akira," I reply, opening the door and stepping inside. "I just wanted to check on you and see how you're doing."

The room is dimly lit, with only a tiny lamp casting a faint glow. Sophia sits on the edge of the bed, her expression weary and distant.

"Akira?" She repeats my name with surprise. Her eyes flicker with a mix of emotions as she studies my face. "I didn't expect to see you here," she admits.

Trying to make myself comfortable, I sit down on a bright red bean bag across from her. The silence hangs heavy in the air as we both struggle to find the right words to say.

"We should talk," Sophia finally says, breaking the silence.

"What do you want to talk about?" I ask warily.

"About everything that happened between us," she says, her gaze never leaving mine. Her shoulders are slumped, and she twirls a strand of her curly hair. "Thank you, Akira, for saving me that day. I never got the chance to express my gratitude properly." She wipes away a tear that escapes from her eye and reaches out to hold my hand. "I also want to apologize for blindly following your father for all these years without question."

Her words catch me off guard, and I'm unsure of how to feel. A part of me is grappling with her past actions, while another longs to forgive her.

She continues to speak, "I never told you this before. I became a vampire after winning the Battle of Anaik. I didn't possess any unique gifts after, and back then, Abel eliminated all vampires who didn't possess special abilities. I begged him to spare my life and pledged my allegiance to him. I always felt that he saved me from my miserable human life and gave me purpose and a sense of acceptance. However, I was so naïve. Abel used my loyalty to manipulate me into doing his bidding. I'm the one who informed him about you and Troy's secret meetings. I'm the one who led Abel to Troy's father's location, leading to his demise. It was all me, and I've been consumed with so much guilt." She confesses tearfully, her voice trembling with remorse. "I'm so sorry, Akira."

Sophia collapses into my arms, sobbing uncontrollably, her words choked with regret. "I understand if you can't forgive me right away. I'm here now, ready to make amends and stand by your side. I want to make things right if you'll let me."

Holding her tight, Sophia's tears drip onto my shirt. Her heartfelt apology leaves me speechless. A single tear of my own rolls down my cheek as I clench my fist, yet there is a glimmer of hope for us. It's clear that she genuinely regrets her actions and is desperate for forgiveness. Slowly, I find myself starting to believe that maybe, just maybe, we can find a way to move forward together.

A small smile forms on my lips. "Thank you for your apology, Sophia. It means a lot to me," I say. "Let's take it one step at a time and see if we can rebuild the trust that was broken."

Sophia nods, her eyes filled with hope. "I understand," she whispers. "I'm willing to do whatever it takes to make things right again, and if Troy is your guy, he's my guy, too." She chuckles and corrects herself, "I mean if he's the one who makes you happy, I'm all for it."

"Thank you, Sophia," I reply, giggling.

Her shoulders relax as she exhales a sigh of relief. "I love you, and I just want us to be friends again," she says sincerely.

"I love you too, Sophia," I reply, my voice genuine. "And I think that with time and effort, we can make things right again. I believe in us."

She smiles, and her eyes sparkle with hope. "I believe in us, too," she says. "Now that we've had this conversation, what have I missed?"

"Oh, you've missed quite a bit," I laugh, shaking my head playfully. Catching her up to speed. "My biological father is alive. And we're going to the Island of Kian with him today—it's a secret island for all the supernatural beings that are not loyal to the throne; they are known as The Revolt. Do you want to come with us?" I blurt out, not taking a second to breathe between sentences.

Her eyes are vast, and she covers her mouth, not saying a word.

"Well?" I ask again, eagerly waiting for a response.

"Akira! Girl, give me a moment to collect my thoughts." She laughs, then finally responds, "Wait, you're telling me that your biological father is alive, and Abel isn't your father? Like, I heard you guys talking about it, but I wasn't sure if I heard correctly. I also didn't want to eavesdrop."

"Since when do you not like eavesdropping?" I tease, remembering all the times I caught her listening in on conversations.

"Yeah, you're right," she rolls her eyes before continuing. "Seriously, Akira, this is a lot to process. I can't imagine what you must be feeling right now. And are you sure you want me to come to the island with you guys? Is it safe there? Will I burn to death when I enter? The human blood is in my system, and Abel wants me dead because I failed my mission, so I'm down to be anywhere he is not! Oh! Will Troy be okay with this? I owe him an apology first before I even consider joining you guys."

I should talk to Troy first about inviting Sophia along with us. No apology will bring back the loss of his father, and I don't know how he will respond to Sophia's apology, even if it's genuine.

"Sophia, breathe! The Island of Kian is in another realm, cloaked from everyone who isn't welcome; Abel wouldn't be able to find you even if he tried. And Monica and Rosa are casting an invisibility spell to keep this house hidden from Abel and his minions. Still, magic has its limits, and we can't rely on it indefinitely, so everyone staying behind will have to relocate soon. I believe you should be safe on the island. However, I will double-check." I meet her gaze and continue. "And yes, I'm sure I want you there with us on the island; I'll talk this over with Troy first, although I can't predict how he will react."

"I understand, Akira," Sophia responds. "I know that words alone won't fix what I've done, but I truly want to make amends and show Troy how sorry I am. I'm committed to making things right."

Squeezing her hand in mine, I give her a reassuring smile. "I believe in second chances, Sophia. I'll talk to him." She squeezes my hand back.

"Speaking of Troy, did you and him do the do yet?" She wriggles her eyebrows suggestively, lightening the mood.

My cheeks burn with fiery heat, and I quickly let go of her hand. "No, we did not."

Her face drops. "Well, why not?"

"I thought we were about to go to the next level in the bathroom earlier, and just when things got hot and heavy, he stopped and said it wasn't the right time." I sigh and look away.

Sophia's playful expression is replaced with empathy.

"That's actually really sweet of him. He wants to make it special, not rushed in a bathroom, and considering the circumstances, I can understand why he would feel that way. You guys are staying in a house full of displaced people. His father recently died, and his brother is injured. That could be a mood killer for anyone."

It is as if she and Troy share the same brain. "Yeah, you're right," I agree, pulling her into a tight hug. "I've missed you so much."

"I've missed you too," she replies, her voice filled with warmth. We hold on to each other for a moment, finding comfort in our reunion. Sophia brings a sense of familiarity that I desperately needed in this chaotic situation. When we break apart, she looks at me with a mischievous smile.

"Are you sure you're ready to take this next step with Troy? This would be huge!"

My lips curve into a smile. This is the Sophia I know and love. The one who's all in yet questions my decision just to make sure I've thought it through.

"Yes, I'm sure. I love him, Soph, and I want nothing more than to explore this next step with him. I mean, have you seen him? He is so hot!"

Sophia chuckles and rolls her eyes. "Okay, okay, I get it. Troy is definitely easy on the eyes."

Nudging her with my elbow, I laugh. "I'm glad we had this talk."

She smiles, "Me too."

"I should probably go talk to Troy now," I say. "I'll come back in an hour and let you know how it went."

"I'll be right here. I have nothing better to do anyway," Sophia jokes.

My mind feels lighter after my conversation with my best friend.

While walking back to my room, I stop at Shelly's room and lean against the open doorframe, gazing at her sleeping form. The gentle rise and fall of her chest overwhelm me with emotions, anger, guilt, and fear, but mostly sorrow for my best friend, my sister, who now views me as an enemy. It pains me to see her like this; however, there is nothing I can do about it. The damage has been done, and all I can do is give her space and time to come back to me. *If she ever does.*

Felix appears next to me and rubs my back. We exchange a glance, knowing that we both share the same hope for Shelly's eventual return to us.

"I know it's hard leaving her like this," he says. "I will take care of her, and trust that I will help her turn her emotions back on. Don't worry; I won't give up on her."

Smiling gratefully at him. "Thank you, Felix, for taking this on and being there for her. I appreciate your support more than words can express."

He nods and squeezes my shoulder gently. "We're a team, remember? We'll get through this together," he reassures me.

Taking a deep breath, it's like a small weight has been lifted off of my shoulders, knowing that Shelly is in good hands.

"What do you have in mind to help her turn her emotions back on?" I ask, curious about his plan to help her.

"Once you all leave, I'll ask Monica or Rosa to wake her up so I can take her to New Orleans," he says. "I know a witch there that can help."

My mouth forms a small O. "If Monica and Rosa couldn't help her, what makes you think this witch in New Orleans will be able to?" I remark.

Felix shrugs, a small smile playing on his lips. "I know this witch personally," he says. "And she owes me a favor. She doesn't belong to a coven and has been in hiding since Aika and Abel took over. She's known for her powerful magic and extensive knowledge of spells. If anyone can help, it's her."

When a vampire turns off their emotions, they become cold and detached, making it nearly impossible for them to feel empathy or compassion. And when the darkness takes over, they become consumed by their thirst for blood and lose all sense of humanity.

Nodding in understanding. "It's worth a shot. Thank you again, Felix."

He gives a final nod and leaves me alone with my thoughts.

Troy is sitting on the edge of the bed, frowning in deep thought, when I return to the bedroom we are sharing. There is a crease between Troy's brows and his eyes fixed on a distant point.

Slowly walking over to him, I sit down beside him, entwining my fingers with his. "Hey, are you okay?"

He gradually turns his head towards me. "No," he whispers.

His face is stern, and there are worry lines etched on his forehead. "I don't know what to do," he continues, releasing a heavy sigh. "I want to go with you to the island, but I want to stay here with my brother too."

The internal struggle in his eyes is evident as he wrestles with the decision.

"He's not doing well. His condition hasn't improved, and the healing process is taking longer than usual."

Gently squeezing his hand in mine. "Have you tried giving him human blood?" I ask cautiously.

"Yes!" He snaps back and then quickly apologizes. "I'm sorry for snapping at you. Yes, we've tried everything. Nothing seems to be working."

Wrapping my arms around him, I pull him into a comforting embrace. He nuzzles into my chest as tears well up in his eyes.

"I just don't know what else to do," he whispers, his voice filled with desperation.

"Babe, I understand if you want to stay here with your brother," I say, rubbing his back soothingly. "However, I think you need some space from here to clear your mind. Claude is in good hands with Niyla and your mother."

He takes a deep breath and looks up at me, his eyes searching for reassurance. "Are you sure?"

Nodding my head. "Yes!"

Troy looks away, unsure.

"And Monica and Rosa are here too!"

"You're right," he says, his voice steadier now.

I know how difficult it is for him to leave Claude behind. Still, I'm looking out for his well-being because he forgets to care for himself when he's too focused on others.

"Plus, you can portal here anytime," I add, hoping to ease his worries.

He reluctantly nods, his shoulders visibly relaxing. He straightens from his slouched position and gets up from the bed to reach for his bags. Rosa is creating a portal in a little for us to travel through, so I guess now is as good a time as any to talk about Sophia.

"Babe?" I begin, my voice hesitant. "I know it's not a good time right now. Um... I think it's important that Sophia comes with us to the island."

His brows furrow. "Sophia?" he repeats, his tone tinged with uncertainty. "Why do you think she should come with us? Isn't she a loyal follower of the vampire king?"

"Yes—*no*. She *used* to be a loyal follower of the king. However, she has recently had a change of heart, and I want to keep her close."

Troy pauses, his eyes intently searching mine. "Do you trust her, Akira?"

He doesn't know about the conversation I had with Sophia.

Pausing for a moment, I consider my response carefully. "I don't know if I fully trust her yet. She confided in me about her doubts and regrets regarding Abel. She wants to make amends and help us on our mission."

His expression softens slightly. "I see," he says slowly. He takes a moment to process my words before continuing. "If you believe she's willing to help us and has genuine remorse, then perhaps we can give her a chance. Nevertheless, we need to be cautious and closely monitor her."

"Absolutely," I reply, "And there's more, Troy."

His eyebrows shoot up as he waits for me to elaborate.

"Sophia aided Abel in disclosing your father's location for his demise."

Troy's fists clench, and his face turns red. "She did what?"

"She was obeying Abel's orders," I continue, trying to calm him down. "Sophia has shown genuine remorse and is willing to make amends."

Troy's anger doesn't subside. He glares at me, his voice filled with fury. "She aided in my father's death, Akira!"

My gaze meets his stern expression, understanding the depth of his pain and anger. "What she did is unforgivable, Troy," I say. "Still, we also have to consider the circumstances she was in. Sophia was coerced into helping Abel, and now she deeply regrets it. She wants to make things right and find a way to atone for her actions."

His eyes are narrow as he processes my words. "I get that she's remorseful," he finally responds, his voice laced with anger. "Yet, that doesn't change the fact that she played a role in my father's death. It's hard for me to see past that."

"It won't happen overnight," I say gently, meeting his gaze directly. "If she consistently shows remorse, takes responsibility for her actions, and actively works towards making amends, then perhaps we can start to consider trusting her." I pause for a moment before adding, "Ultimately, it's up to you to decide if you're willing to give her a chance."

Troy exhales heavily. "I can't forget what happened," he says firmly, "I agree we should keep her at arm's length for now."

"What about Jacobson?" Troy asks, crossing his arms. "Do you think he can be trusted as well?"

My brows shoot up. He has valid concerns about my father. Jacobson is a stranger to me.

"No, I don't trust him," I admit, shaking my head. "I don't know him enough to judge. He's my biological father, so I feel like I should at least give him a chance to prove himself."

Troy raises an eyebrow, clearly skeptical, and I shift my gaze from him to my packed bags.

"Can you bring my bags downstairs while I get Sophia?" I ask, changing the subject.

He nods. "Sure, I'll take care of it," he says, his tone indicating that he has reservations about my father. He grabs our bags, and I leave our conversation behind to get Sophia. My father is a sensitive topic for me.

Before I arrive at Sophia's room, I send Jacobson a text message asking if Sophia would be able to survive on the island in the daylight; he assures me that it is safe for Sophia and all other vampires should they want to reside on the island.

Sophia is sitting on her bed; when I enter the room, she looks up at me, her eyes filled with uncertainty. "Are you leaving now?" she asks.

"*We're* leaving now," I correct her, biting back a smile when she stands up and rushes towards me, hugging me tight. "Thank you, Akira!" she squeals.

"You're welcome, Sophia." We separate, and I hold her at arm's length, looking into her eyes. "For precautionary measures, I need to chain your hands," I say gently.

She nods, understanding the necessity of the situation, and extends her hands toward me. I carefully secure the chains around her wrists, making sure they are not too tight, and we head downstairs to join Troy and the others.

Troy glances at Sophia, his expression torn between wanting to move forward and not wanting to let go of the past.

"Is everyone ready to go?" Jacobson asks, approaching the group with Jace.

"As ready as I'll ever be," I reply deadpan.

We embrace those staying behind, and I give them a reassuring smile before entering through the swirling bright white lights that appear to take us to the Island of Kian.

The unknown awaits on the other side.

The sight we are met with is breathtaking. Beautiful waterfalls cascade over the mountains, and lush greenery blankets the landscape. The air is filled with the sweet scent of tropical flowers, and a spectacular aurora borealis display illuminates the night sky. A bridge arches gracefully over a crystal-clear river, leading to the luxurious cabins at its end.

Jace and Jacobson direct us to the cabins we will stay in. My friends are directed to cabins spread throughout the walkway.

Troy and I enter our cabin and mouth a silent *wow* when we step inside, immediately struck by the cozy atmosphere and rustic charm. The electric fireplace warms the room, casting a soft glow on the gray walls and wooden furniture, and the California king-sized bed beckons us to sink into its plush comfort.

"I could get used to this," Troy remarks, picking me up and spinning me around.

Squealing at his ambush, I wrap my arms around his neck. We both laugh, and I kiss him on the lips before we collapse onto the bed, laughing like giddy teenagers.

We turn on our sides to face each other, our smiles fading as we gaze into each other's eyes. He runs his thumb along my lips, tracing the outline of my smile. The spark is happening again.

"I love you," he whispers, and my heart swells with affection.

"I love you too," I reply.

This feels like the right moment, and I think Troy agrees because he snakes his arm around my waist, pulling me closer to him. Our bodies fit together perfectly, and there is so much sexual tension between us that it's almost palpable. I roll on top of him, straddling him, and he places his hands on my hips. I cup his face in my hands to caress his cheek, savoring the feeling of his stubble against my fingertips.

"You mean everything to me," I whisper, my voice filled with sincerity and love.

Our eyes lock, and in that moment, I can see the depth of his love for me reflected in his gaze. The anticipation builds, and our breathing shallows as he presses his lips on mine, slowly forcing them to part with his tongue. The kiss is electrifying, and I feel his passion harden below his waist. Every touch and caress ignites a fire within me that I never want to extinguish.

"Troy," I plead, my voice barely audible as I break away from our tongues playing tug of war. "I want you."

His eyes lock with mine. "I want you too," he whispers, his voice husky with desire. "More than anything."

He lifts my shirt over my head, revealing the soft curves of my body to his hungry gaze, and his hands draw a path down my spine, finding my bra clasp. With a flick of his fingers, he expertly unfastens it and tosses it aside. The air between us bubbles with eagerness, growing more intense with each passing moment. Troy's touch has taken on an urgency that sends a rush of impending exhilaration coursing through my veins. Every brush of his fingers, every kiss from his lips, seems to echo with a silent plea, a desire that mirrors my own.

I grip the hem of his shirt, pulling it off and exposing his chiseled chest. Troy is incredibly sexy. Running my fingers along the defined lines of his abs, he lets out a low growl. He rolls me over onto my back, unbuttoning my jeans, and slides them down my legs, exposing my pink lace panties, which I am so glad I wore. He looks at me like I'm the most beautiful person in the world. His hands trail up my thighs, and with a gentle tug, he removes my panties, leaving me completely bare before him. Troy's eyes burn with fury as he takes in every inch of my exposed frame. He removes his jeans and reveals his hard length, struggling to escape his boxers. With a hungry look in his eyes, he pulls his boxers down, freeing his throbbing member, and positions himself above me, ready to take our relationship to the next level. I am about to give myself entirely to him.

In a husky voice, he asks, "Are you sure you're ready for this?"

My heart is pounding with anticipation, and I whisper, "Yes, I've never been more sure."

Troy leans down and kisses me, my heart thumping at every motion of his tongue in my mouth. When our lips part, he gazes into my eyes, searching for any sign of doubt or hesitation. I meet his gaze with unwavering determination, reassuring him I am ready. *This is it. It's happening!* My inner thoughts are a whirlwind of excitement and nerves. Pushing them aside, I focus on the present moment. He enters me slowly. A slight discomfort initially fills me; it quickly fades as I adjust to the new sensation, and a wave of pleasure replaces it as our bodies move in perfect harmony. Every inch of my body tingles at his thrusts, which gradually increase until I can't endure them any longer. I let out a moan of ecstasy, and he muffles my sounds with a passionate kiss.

Our desires intertwine, and we make love with a raw passion that transcends words. No one will ever be able to replicate the connection we share.

The French Toast Chronicles

Last night with Troy was perfect and will forever be cherished in my memories. We laughed, talked, and connected as one. However, Jacobson brought me here to develop my power and wage war on Abel. As much as I want to hold on to this beautiful moment, I can't forget my ultimate purpose. Abel and his kingdom must be defeated, and the kingdoms are to be reunited under one rule! Still, I'm feeling incredible after what happened.

Troy is asleep in bed next to me. The covers are pushed below his waist, revealing his bare chest, and I'm smiling from ear to ear. I want to savor these quiet moments with him before everything changes. Troy left his family to come here with me; the least I can do is spend time enjoying our love before diving into the chaos that awaits.

Then again, Jacobson will wish to arrange a meeting sooner rather than later to get to know him and control my power.

Reaching for my phone from the nightstand, I send a text to Jacobson, informing him I need some time before we start training. He told me it was not a problem and to not take too long because we needed to prepare for war.

Scrolling through my contacts, my finger lands on Cameron's name. I'm thinking of making "French toast" for Troy and surprising him with breakfast in bed; Cameron's help is needed with the recipe. He responds quickly, agreeing to help me. And a few seconds later, he is at the door. *That was fast.*

He greets me with a smile and nudges me with his elbow.

"Are you ready to get cooking?" He jokes.

"Of course. Let's get started," I reply, leading him to the kitchen.

Cameron has a checklist of all the ingredients we need and starts gathering them from the pantry and refrigerator. He organizes them on the counter.

"We have cinnamon, nutmeg, sugar, butter, eggs, milk, vanilla extract, syrup, and bread."

As Cameron lists the items, I meticulously check each of them off.

He holds two loaves of bread in his hands and asks, "Should we use white bread or whole wheat?"

How am I supposed to know which type of bread to use? I'm still new to this.

"I don't know. You choose."

He shakes his head and chuckles, choosing the whole wheat bread.

Nudging him on the arm. "Why are you laughing at me?"

"I have to remind myself that you're still learning." He flicks my nose gently.

Grabbing the loaf of bread, I fumble with it and struggle to open the packaging. Cameron shakes his head and takes the loaf from my hand.

"How about I show you, and you observe carefully?" He smirks, and I nod like a toddler eager to learn.

He chuckles and untwists the object on the bread bag with ease.

"What is that *thing* called?" I ask, observing with wide eyes.

"In my day, it was referred to as a twist tie," Cameron replies, his grin widening. "It's used to seal the bag and keep the bread fresh."

My mouth falls open as I take in this new information, and he bursts out laughing at my reaction.

Rolling my eyes and pretending to be offended by his amusement. "Hey, I'm just trying to expand my knowledge here," I say with a pretend frown.

His laughter subsides, and he pats me on the back. "Don't worry." His lips curve into a smile. "Sis, I'm always here to educate you," he says.

Pushing him away, I grin. "Well, I appreciate your expertise. Bro." I reply deadpan.

We both laugh, enjoying the lighthearted banter between us.

When we finally stop laughing, I grab the egg container.

"How many eggs do you need?"

"Two eggs should be enough," he replies, grabbing a pan from the cupboard. "And I need one teaspoon of vanilla extract, one teaspoon each of cinnamon and nutmeg, a pinch of sugar, and a cup of milk," he adds.

A crease forms between my brows. I have absolutely no idea what these measurements mean. However, I don't want him to know that. Nodding my head, I quickly Google it on my phone while he heats the butter on the stove. Searching the drawers for a measuring contraption, I find the necessary tools and hand him all the ingredients.

"Here you go," I say, trying to sound confident.

Cameron gives me a wide, silly grin of approval and begins to whisk the batter into a large bowl. Observing intently, he instructs me to pass him one slice of bread at a time, and he dips each piece into the batter before placing it on a hot pan. A delightful aroma fills the kitchen as the bread sizzles and turns golden brown, making my mouth water in anticipation. He flips each slice with precision and stacks the French toast on two plates, drizzling maple syrup over the top.

The sweet scent enters my nostrils. "Do you think Troy will enjoy this?" I ask, hoping that my efforts in "cooking" this delicious French toast will impress him.

"I would hope so," Cameron chuckles.

He cuts up some fresh strawberries and places them on top of the French toast.

"No, seriously."

Cameron smiles reassuringly. "I'm sure he'll appreciate the effort, Akira. He loves you. He'll definitely enjoy the French toast that *I* made for him." He teases.

"Very funny, Cam. Can we please keep this between us?" I reply, giving him a smile.

Cameron raises an eyebrow. "Why? Don't you want everyone to know how amazing *my* cooking skills are?" he jokes. "No worries, I got you," he assures me. "Your secret is safe with me," he says, winking.

Extending my hand. "Let's shake on it."

Cameron chuckles and tries to shake my hand firmly, but I stop him.

"No, silly, let's make a secret handshake."

He blinks at me. "Why are you so extra?"

"Because our friendship is *extra* special." I laugh.

"You're so corny," he teases, rolling his eyes.

I grasp his left hand with my right hand and start a series of intricate hand movements, incorporating fist bumps and entwining our pinkies. Cameron follows along, a grin spreading across his face.

We both laugh as we finish the secret handshake.

"I guess being extra isn't so bad after all," he admits, and we continue our laughter until we hear noises from the bedroom.

"Thank you so much, Cam," I say sincerely, ushering him toward the door.

"You owe me," he teases, winking at me.

Giving him a shove, I close the door behind him and head back to the kitchen to finish preparing Troy's breakfast by resting the plates on two trays and carefully carrying them into the bedroom to surprise my sexy man.

Placing the trays on the nightstand. "Babe, breakfast is served."

Troy rubs his eyes, and when our gazes meet, he doesn't seem okay. His eyes are clouded with doubt, and his lips are pressed into a thin line.

Sitting beside him on the bed. "Babe? Is everything alright? You seem a bit off this morning."

Troy usually wakes up in great spirits, and I would think he would be over the moon after last night. *Something is bothering him.*

He looks away from me and shakes his head as if trying to make a thought disappear.

Reaching out, I gently place my hand on his arm, giving it a reassuring squeeze.

"You know you can talk to me about anything, right? I'm here for you."

Troy's expression softens. The strain still lingers in his eyes.

"It's nothing," he replies after a brief pause.

Something is on his mind that he doesn't want to share with me. *What can it be?* I don't want to pry, so I look at the trays of untouched food on the nightstand, and his gaze follows mine.

"What is this?" he asks with a grin forming on his lips.

"I brought you breakfast in bed." I beam.

Troy's grin widens, and he reaches for a piece of the French toast. He takes a few bites, and his grin grows even wider. "Wow, this is really good. Who made it for you?"

"What?" My brows pull together, and I place my hand over my heart. "I made it myself."

Troy raises an eyebrow, not buying my lie for a second.

My lips curve into a smile, knowing that Troy can see right through me.

"Okay, fine. I may have had a *little* help. I did most of the work, though!" I reply sheepishly.

Troy laughs and shakes his head, appreciating my effort nonetheless. "Thank you, Akira. It's delicious."

Shoving a bite of my own French toast into my mouth and savoring the taste. Wow! It is indeed delicious.

"You're welcome," I reply with a satisfied smile.

We finish our French toast, placing the empty plates on the nightstand, and Troy looks at me with a grateful expression.

"You really didn't have to go through all this trouble, Akira. I appreciate it, though."

Feeling a sense of accomplishment. "I wanted to do something nice for you."

He pulls me by the waist and onto his lap. I straddle him and wrap my arms around his neck. He plants a soft kiss on my forehead, then on my nose, and finally on my lips. We share a tender moment, our lips pressing together before we pull away. My eyes lock with his mesmerizing gray ones, and a rush of warmth and affection spreads throughout my body. I love this man with my all. He lifts my tank top over my head, and his lips curve into a sensual smile. He runs his fingers along the exposed skin of my back and unclasps my bra. This gives my skin goosebumps. Troy holds my breasts in his hands, and his touch nearly makes me lose my will to breathe. He presses his lips against mine, applying bruising kisses. Matching his motions and desperately craving his taste, our tongues circle one another. Troy's hands explore every inch of my body, and he leaves a trail of fiery kisses on my neck and collarbone. This feels good, like we were made for each other. I have never wanted anyone else as much as I want him.

He continues to undress me so slowly that every movement feels like an eternity. The anticipation builds with each piece of clothing of mine that falls to the floor. Unable to contain the desire that courses through my veins, I moan. His fangs gently graze against my skin, biting my neck and licking the blood that trickles from my pierced flesh. His gray eyes glow and turn silver—it's remarkable.

"You're beautiful," I say out loud instead of just thinking it.

An amused grin plays at the corners of his lips as he leans in closer, his voice a low whisper against my ear.

"No, you're beautiful."

His warm breath sends shivers to all areas of my body.

In one quick movement, he stands to loosen his basketball shorts, exposing himself to me. He curves his lips into a sexy smile, knowing what it does to me. In the blink of an eye, Troy closes the distance between us, resting his muscular frame on me again.

"And you're mine," he murmurs possessively, easing his way deep inside me.

Each thrust has me quivering underneath him. The circling of his hips matches mine and has my breathing accelerating. Waves of pleasure cause my entire body to tremble, and I reach my climax. After a few sharp thrusts, he is relieved as well and collapses onto the bed beside me, his heavy breathing matching mine. With a satisfied smile, he pulls me closer, wrapping his arms around me.

We made love again, and it was more intense than the first time. The connection between us feels stronger than ever, and I found *the spark* I have always hoped for with Troy Bishop!

"Wow!" I blurt out breathlessly.

My limbs feel like jelly. This is what Shelly meant when she said, *"Rock your world."* My world has indeed been *rocked.*

"Wow, yourself," Troy replies.

An overwhelming sensation of bliss washes over me as we lay there, basking in the afterglow.

"I think I should go back to Florida and be with my brother," he says without warning, breaking the peaceful silence.

What!?

New Vampires

I'm walking along the sidelines of the battle room, observing the new vampires that have been recruited. It's been a few hours since the transformation, and if they possess any gifts, now would be the time they are shown. I want another vampire like Ava, so I'm observing closely as Chase trains them. Ava could persuade anyone into doing anything I wanted. The power of persuasion was truly remarkable. If I ever come across another vampire with that ability, it must be protected at all costs.

Tyler has recovered and is currently tasked with searching for more information on The Seekers, which is now a priority, while Aika has been welcoming our guests. Once Tyler finds some sort of lead about The Seekers, he will start his search for the location of The Revolt and lend a hand in recruiting humans. *So much to do!*

Chase hurls wood at each vampire. "One... two... three... kick!" He shouts.

In unison, the six men kick the wood with precision and force, sending it flying miles away. *Excellent!* They have mastered control over their vampire strength.

Chase throws more objects at the men to further test their control. "One... two... three... jump!"

The six men leap eleven feet into the air, effortlessly evading the items. *Wonderful!*

Lucas interrupts my evaluations to update me on the progress of his task.

"Sir, I sent Akira a text message, and she responded. She disclosed that she is in another realm," he reports, and my ears perk up with interest.

Another realm? Perhaps that's the location of The Revolt.

"I lied about no longer being loyal to the throne and that I needed her help to escape. She agreed to meet in person to discuss further details," he continues. "I'm waiting for her to send the location."

Chase overhears us, and his eyebrows shoot up.

"Keep training!" He shouts to the men, and they continue their drills as Chase comes over to join our conversation.

"You'll leave at once after you receive the location from Akira."

"Yes, Sir. I'll leave immediately," Lucas assures me.

"How about we capture her when she arrives to *rescue* Lucas?" Chase suggests.

Shaking my head. "I taught Akira better than that before she betrayed the throne. She would never fall into such an obvious trap. She'll be more cautious than that and will have planned for any potential ambushes," I respond, dismissing Chase's suggestion. Pacing back and forth with my hands behind my back, I observe the men.

"Good to know I was right about the tall young man."

"Yes, Sir. He easily defeated the other one in the Battle of Anaik," Lucas confirms.

"Impressive," I remark, nodding in approval. "Does he possess a special gift?"

"Yes, Sir," Chase replies. "He has the power to heal."

"Incredible news! What's his name?"

"Sir, his name is Joel," Lucas answers.

Signaling toward the group of men. "Joel, come here," I shout.

Joel halts his training and speeds over to where I'm standing. The other men stop as well, casting curious glances in Joel's direction.

"Were you instructed to take a break?" Chase roars at the other men. "Keep training until I tell you otherwise!"

He points to a husky, brown-eyed man and commands him to take the lead. The men quickly resume their exercises, avoiding eye contact with us.

Joel stands still, eyeing me cautiously.

A smirk forms on my face as I circle him. "Hello Joel, vampirism fits you well. I must say, you've taken to it quite naturally."

Joel's eyes narrow, but he remains silent.

"Walk with us," I order.

He falls in line with Chase and Lucas behind me.

We exit the battle room and make our way to my dungeon office. I do most of my thinking in this room, besides my chambers. My office in the dungeon is soundproofed by a spell, thanks to those pesky witches, so no other vampires can eavesdrop on my conversations. The room is painted black and orange, with all my favorite weapons plastered on the walls. Over the centuries, I have accumulated specialized axes, swords, machetes, and a substantial collection of hunter knives. A brown wooden desk with gold trim sits in the center of the room, covered in stacks of maps, a compass, and a gold chalice to consume blood.

"Please, take a seat." I gesture toward the unoccupied leather chairs that sit across from me. Lucas, of course, has to stand because he is not worthy of sitting in my presence.

Running my fingers along the armrest. "I want to discuss the new recruits' powers, if any."

"Of course, Sir," Chase replies with a nod.

Chase is now my secondhand man since Kaden is a traitor to the throne and has yet to be dealt with accordingly. Kade was thankfully disposed of, and Ava got herself killed.

"No formalities necessary," I say dismissively. "You can call me Abel."

Chase's eyes widen and then he quickly regains his composure. "Understood, Sir... I mean, understood, uh... Abel."

The corners of my lips curve into a smirk at his slight stumble over his words.

"The vampire I left in charge is a telepath. Joel and one other have the ability to heal. One of them is psychic, and another has telekinesis power. But there is one unique vampire among them. I have never witnessed such a gift before."

Leaning forward, I'm intrigued. "Spit it out, Chase. What gift does this unique vampire possess?"

"The power to *cloak* himself," Chase discloses.

Standing to my feet, I slam my hands on my desk. "Cloaking? How is that even possible? Can he make himself completely invisible?"

Chase nods, narrowing his eyes. "Yes, Abel. He has the ability to render himself *completely* invisible. He has done it a few times."

That is deemed worthy!

"What's his name?" I only want to know the names of those who possess extraordinary abilities.

"His name is Nico," Chase replies.

"Nico," I repeat, letting the name roll off my tongue. "Lucas, please bring Nico to me immediately," I demand.

How can it be utilized? *Could he use his ability to cloak me as well?* I need to understand the extent of his gift. He might be precisely what we need to win this war!

Lucas nods and quickly leaves the room and returns with Nico; he appears to be a young man in his early twenties. His eyes dart around the room nervously, unaware of his importance.

He bows his head. "Hello, King Abel."

"Hello, Nico," I say, gesturing for Joel to get up and give his seat to my new favorite vampire.

"Tell me about yourself."

He looks from Chase to Lucas and then back to me, his expression uncertain.

Nodding my head, I gesture for him to speak.

He clears his throat and begins with a relatively strong accent, "Well, my name is Nicholas. You can call me Nico, which is what I prefer."

Rolling my eyes at the obvious. "How did you become a candidate for vampirism?"

A frown tugs at the corners of his lips. "I was kidnapped against my will by your guards and brought here to fight another participant to become 'something more.' I had no idea what Chase meant by that until I arrived here—I'm sure my family is searching for me."

Standing to my feet in a flash. "Give us a minute," I bark, motioning for Chase to follow me.

Chase joins me in a secluded corner away from my office and away from prying ears.

Trying to hold my composure, my jaw is tight. "What does he mean his family is searching for him?"

Chase gulps nervously before responding, "A—Abel, you demanded new recruits at a fast pace for the tournaments. We couldn't find enough qualified homeless humans at the rate you were requesting. So, we had to resort to kidnapping drunks from bars and clubs to meet your demand."

My anger boils over, and I pace back and forth, trying to choose my following words carefully.

Kidnapping homeless humans is acceptable! Kidnapping someone who is potentially *important* can attract unwanted attention. I huff. The act is already done; perhaps he isn't as significant as he thinks.

"Be more vigilant next time," I say through gritted teeth. "Recruit the ones who are less likely to be missed. We can't afford any more complications."

Chase nods. "Understood."

We head back to my office to continue our conversation. I want to witness Nico's gift firsthand.

"Let's pick up where we left off, Nico," I prompt, settling into my chair. "As you were saying?"

Nico's hands are trembling, and a small drop of sweat drips from his forehead. "I—I. Well... I was wondering if I could contact my family when we're done here," he says hesitantly.

"No, that won't be possible," I reply firmly. "You are dead now, and all ties with your previous life have been severed. I apologize you weren't properly informed of this before. If this is an issue, I'll gladly *rectify* the situation for you."

Nico's face drops, and he looks visibly distraught by the news. He nods at my terms.

"Marvelous. Now, let's get to business." I steer the conversation back to the task at hand. "How do you harness your gift?"

"I'm not sure how to answer that," Nico admits. "When Chase was training us, all I could think of was that I didn't want to be there or be seen, and then next thing I knew, I was invisible. It just kind of happened without me consciously doing anything."

Leaning back in my chair with my hands behind my head. "Interesting," I remark. "Do you think you can tap into your gift intentionally now?"

He nods at my request. "I could try. Although, I'm not sure if it will work."

"Give it a try, and let's see what happens."

Nico stands up from his chair and takes a deep breath. He begins to blink rapidly, his eyes fluttering open and closed. He then squints and vanishes from sight. I'm astonished. It's as if he has merged with the air itself.

My heart pounds against my chest, and I jump to my feet in excitement. *I wonder if I can absorb his unique power.*

"Nico, show yourself," I demand.

Moments later, Nico reappears, standing in the same spot where he vanished, wearing a triumphant smile.

"Please do it again," I demand, grasping his hand.

His eyes flutter open and closed with increasing speed, and he squints. Nico disappears once again, and this time, so do I.

Chase gapes at the empty space where Nico and I stood just moments ago. "Abel, you're invisible as well!" he shouts.

Excellent!

Nico and I are in a translucent bubble that's not visible to them, yet visible to us. It lasts for about ten minutes before we reappear in the same spot.

Chase, Lucas, and Joel look at us in disbelief, their mouths agape.

"Again!" I demand. "Try to hold it for longer than ten minutes this time."

Nico nods and does it again. He keeps at it for twenty minutes this time, maintaining our invisibility for twice as long.

Clapping my hands together. "Wonderful!"

This is extraordinary. Imagine what could be done with such power! I could stab the hybrid prince in the chest without him ever seeing it coming. The possibilities are endless.

Grabbing Nico's hand once more, I absorb his power, and this time, I'm invisible.

"Abel, it worked!" Chase shouts.

"You're invisible!" Lucas adds.

Nico and Joel exchange confused glances.

A few moments later, I reappear in front of them with a delighted smile.

"This is fantastic! Lucas, please show my dear friends Nico and Joel to their new villa." I usher them towards Lucas, who nods and leads Nico and Joel away so that I can discuss the plan with Chase.

This is exciting; I can absorb Nico's gift for ten minutes on my own, and together, we can be invisible for at least twenty minutes, granting me the time I need to execute my adversaries.

Chase sits across from me, patiently waiting for me to explain the plan.

"Aika informed me of Akira's invincibility and about her inherited power from her biological mother, Serena, before her death. If I attempt to kill Akira, I will die. I wouldn't want anything to happen to you or any of the other gifted vampires, so I tasked Lucas to lure Akira back to the kingdom under false pretenses. Once she is within our reach, Lucas or one of the useless vampires will snap her neck. Then the witches will place Akira under a spell to incapacitate her, and we'll bury her twenty feet under."

Chase nods, understanding of the plan, his expression grave. "How exactly do the witches plan to incapacitate Akira?"

"The witches will place her under a sleeping spell that will render her unconscious and immobile. We'll bind her hands and feet with chains laced with UV lights and inject her with human blood. This should hold her down for the rest of our existence."

Chase takes in the information, and Aika joins us in the conversation when she enters the room.

"We need to locate Rosa and the other witches as soon as possible," she asserts.

"Chase, gather the witches and have them meet me here," I order.

He nods and quickly leaves the room to carry out his task.

Aika glides over to me and sits on my lap, planting kisses on my forehead and cheeks.

"I love you," she whispers, brushing her lips against mine.

My lips twitch, and I wrap my arms around her. "What do you want?"

Aika giggles and playfully nuzzles her nose against mine. "I just want to be close to you," she murmurs. "I feel really good about our plan and want to commemorate this moment with you."

Kissing her delicious lips, I stroke her hair.

A sudden knock on the door interrupts what is about to happen on top of my desk.

"Come in!" I call out through clenched teeth.

Chase returns with a sheepish expression on his face. "I'm sorry to interrupt, King Abel and Queen Aika. The witches are ready to meet with you."

Rolling my eyes, I don't want to be bothered with the witches right now! *Well, not this soon!*

"Send them in, Chase." Aika and I both straighten ourselves up.

The witches enter the room and greet us with a bow. The main witch pulls out a map from his blue and brown sack and places it on my desk. He then lifts his shirt to retrieve an ancient silver dagger from his holder. He slices his palm and lets a few drops of blood fall onto the map.

He looks at me expectantly. "May I?" he asks, pointing to my hand.

Nodding, I extend my hand to him.

He takes my hand and also slices my palm with the dagger, and my blood mixes with the drops he had already spilled on the map. The other witches form a circle around us and chant in a foreign tongue. The blood moves along the map, and the lights start to flicker. All five witches' eyes change from their normal color to jet black, and the lights continue to flash more intensely before finally stopping. The room quivers and then comes to an abrupt stop. The lead witch points to a spot on the map where all the blood has pooled, his eyes still jet black.

"This is where we need to go," he says.

"Where is *this*?"

"Florida," the witch specifies.

"Get things ready. You'll leave for Florida immediately," I command, shoving them out of the office and closing the door behind them. I want to continue loving on my wife before my meeting with the council to discuss this new development.

Throwing Aika onto my desk. "Now, where was I?" I tilt her head to the side and lick her neck, taking pleasure in the taste of her skin before sinking my fangs into her flesh.

She moans, her hands gripping the edge of the desk. "We found the witches. We're so close to victory that I can taste it."

"Mhmm," I murmur, my teeth still pierced into her skin.

She bites her bottom lip and lets out a small whimper.

Licking the blood dripping from her wound. "I want to taste you," I say, trailing kisses from her neck to her collarbone.

Aika throws her head back in pleasure. "Yes, my love," she says.

Soon, we will have everything we want.

I Didn't See That Coming

Troy's words hang in the air for what feels like an eternity. *Is he serious?* He wants to go back to Florida— *now?* After what we just did... *twice!?* The rational part of me understands his reasons. The irrational part of me doesn't want him to go. Does that make me selfish?

"Can we maybe discuss this before you make a final decision?" I ask, trying to keep my voice steady, unsure of what his next response will be.

"I've thought about it a lot, and going back to Florida to be with my brother is the best decision for me right now. I have a duty to my family and our kingdom."

My gaze meets his, searching for any sign of hesitation or doubt. His eyes are determined, his voice unwavering. It's clear he has made up his mind and is committed to his decision.

"I get that, Troy. Trust me, I do; I just need you here with me." My voice cracks with emotion. I can't deny how this makes me feel.

Troy sighs heavily, a crease forming in between his brows.

"Why does it feel like you want me to choose between you and my brother?" He pauses for a moment, contemplating his words carefully. "I love you, Akira, and my brother."

Tears begin to well up in my eyes as I struggle to find the right words. "I don't want you to choose, Troy."

Rushing to the bathroom, I lock the door behind me. *He can't see me like this.* Splashing cold water on my face, I try to calm the storm of emotions raging within me. I want Troy to stay here with me. *I'm his family, too.* Staring at my reflection in the mirror, the woman looking back at me is being selfish and unfair.

Suddenly, my hands are clammy, the room seems to spin around me, and my stomach churns. The food is trying to exit my body in the quickest way possible, so I lower myself over the toilet.

"Akira, are you okay?" Troy's concerned voice calls out from the other side of the bathroom door.

Trying to compose myself. "I'm fine, Troy." My voice is shaky. "I'll be out in a moment."

Washing my face with cold water once again, I tie my curly hair back into a messy bun to keep it out of my face. Grabbing my toothbrush in hopes of eliminating the bile taste, I brush my teeth.

Troy's worried expression softens when he sees me opening the door to exit the bathroom. I'm trying my hardest not to make eye contact with him. The nausea is still lingering, and I don't understand why.

Clearing my throat to speak, I stumble backward; the queasiness in my stomach continues to gnaw at me.

Troy reaches out a hand to steady me. "Are you feeling alright?" he asks, a crease forming on his forehead.

Forcing a weak smile and giving Troy a reassuring nod. "I'm just a little off," I reply, my voice strained.

"Are you sure?"

Nodding again. "Yeah, just a bit under the weather," I say, hoping he'll drop the subject.

Troy looks at me and eventually decides to let it go. "Okay, can we finish our discussion?"

He shifts the topic back to the original conversation. "Or are you going to run away again?" He teases, trying to lighten the mood.

"No running away this time," I assure him. "I don't know what you want me to say. Of course, I want you to stay here with me. I don't want to pressure you into staying if it's not what you truly want."

Troy looks down for a moment, contemplating my words.

A ding from my phone interrupts the silence, and I grab it from the nightstand to check the notification. It's a text message from *Lucas!*

Covering my mouth.

Troy looks at me, noticing my sudden change in expression. He gently asks, "Is everything okay? Who texted you?"

Taking a deep breath. "It's Lucas," I say, my voice barely above a whisper. "He's alive, and he wants to talk. He needs my help to escape from the vampire kingdom."

I'm happy, relieved, and worried; it's a whirlwind of emotions and memories flooding back all at once. He killed Kade, yet a small part of me still cares for him.

Troy's expression changes from worry to jealousy in a matter of seconds. He clenches his jaw and looks away, silently brooding.

My fingers shiver as I quickly respond to Lucas.

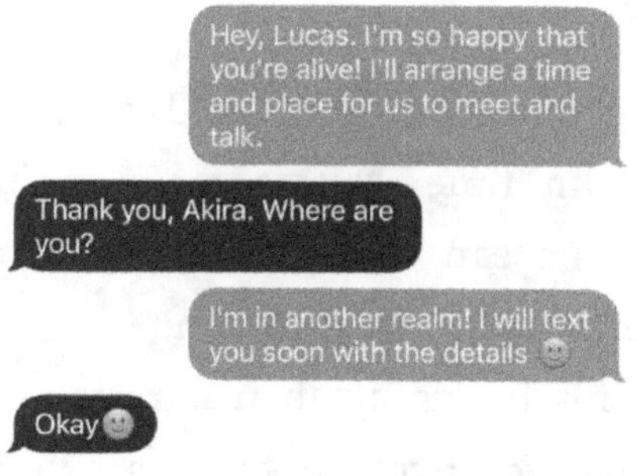

Troy's eyes grow dark. "Did you just respond to him?" he asks, his voice laced with bitterness.

Glancing at him, sensing his disapproval. "Yes, I did," I admit. "He needs my help."

Troy's expression tightens. "After everything he put you through, you're still willing to help him?" he questions, disbelief evident in his tone.

Meeting his gaze with determination. "Yes," I say firmly. "He didn't stop me when I escaped the dungeon to save Cameron's life. I owe it to him to return the favor."

Troy's jaw clenches, his anger visible in the way his muscles tense. "You're too forgiving," he shakes his head. "Lucas betrayed you, Akira," he states. "He killed Kade! And he even tried to kill me! You don't owe him anything!" He growls, and his canine teeth are exposed as he speaks.

He has every right not to trust Lucas after what he's done. Still, I can't ignore that Lucas let me go when he easily could have stopped me. Lucas was obeying direct orders from Abel when he killed Kade. Although Kaden won't be as forgiving either. It's a messy situation. However, I genuinely believe there's still some good left in him.

Holding my ground. "I understand your resentment, Troy," I respond in a calm tone. "Lucas made mistakes by following orders. I believe he can change and wants to. And if there's a chance for redemption, I owe it to him."

Troy throws his hands up in frustration. "Unbelievable! You want me to choose you over my brother, while you choose Lucas over me."

"Troy, it's not about choosing one over the other..." my voice trails off because I sound like a hypocrite.

Troy storms out of the room, slamming the door behind him and leaving me to sit in silence, reflecting on the rift between us. Maybe we'll find our way back after some time apart.

Scrolling through my contacts, I give Rosa a call to obtain her assistance in helping Lucas. She agrees to make arrangements to bring him to Florida to meet with me. I don't want him to know about the Island of Kian or that my father is alive... yet.

I send him another text.

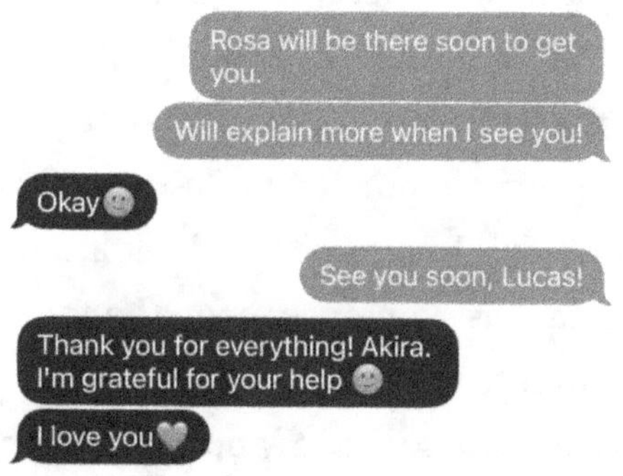

Oh.

Throwing my phone to the side as if it electrocuted me. *That took an unexpected turn.* I thought we had this conversation already.

Of course, I love Lucas, just not in the way he loves me and not in the way I love Troy. I could never love someone the same way I love Troy.

Flashes of Lucas and my first date flicker through my mind. It was a disaster! I thought we would watch a funny movie, have some laughs, and then perhaps share a hot, steamy kiss. Unfortunately, that's not what happened at all. It started off with a romantic setting, vanilla-scented candles lit all around his villa, and he set up Cards Against Humanity for us to play, but with a twist. Whoever lost with the least number of cards had to strip down to their underwear. Naturally, I was winning, so Lucas had to strip down to his boxers. Seeing him in just his boxers was quite a sight, so things started to heat up between us. He pulled me closer and leaned in for a kiss that I was happy to return. Except, while we were kissing, I didn't feel the spark that I had hoped for. The kiss was incredible, and Lucas looked good. Yet, something was missing; it felt superficial. Things started to go downhill from there. He beckoned a servant into the room to feed on her vein after our passionate, yet ultimately unsatisfying, kiss. I was livid. I don't drink human blood, let alone directly from the vein, and the date was going great for the most part until he did that. It was a complete turnoff.

To make matters worse, he saw nothing wrong with his actions and implied that I was overreacting. I grabbed my things and left his villa immediately after that, politely declining when he asked me on another date. That's when I told him we were better off as friends.

Troy is my soulmate, and I knew it from the moment we met. Lucas can never measure up to the love and connection I feel for Troy. Troy has nothing to worry about, and maybe when he cools off, he will realize that, too. Sliding on sweatpants, I decide to go for a walk on this beautiful island—I'm in need of some fresh air.

Walking along the trail, marveling at the lush greenery surrounding me. There are mountains in the distance, and I see a castle perched atop one of them. The Island of Kian seems to be a true paradise.

Three beautiful young women are walking along the trail, pointing at me and whispering to each other. They approach me with curiosity sparkling in their eyes.

"Woah! Are you *the* Akira Ronin?" One of them asks, seemingly starstruck.

The other girl circles around me, examining me from head to toe. "Yes, it's the princess herself. Jacobson's beautiful, *powerful* daughter." She confirms the first girl's question.

They all exchange glances before the first girl speaks up again. "I can't believe we're actually meeting you in the flesh!"

My heart pounds in my chest like a drum, and my eyes widen in surprise. "Uh, hi. Do I know you?"

The first girl shakes her head, still in awe. "No, we've just heard so much about you!" she says.

The other girls nod in agreement.

"My name is Michelle," she introduces herself.

She extends her hand towards me, her tall, curvy frame commanding attention. She shakes my hand firmly, and her heart-shaped face lights up with a smile. Michelle is striking with her beautiful auburn hair and kind brown eyes. She must be the leader of the three because she is confident and does most of the talking.

"Nice to meet you, Michelle," I reply, returning her smile.

"My name is Daisy. It is nice to finally meet you, beautiful." Daisy circles around me again, biting her lower lip, her eyes dazzling with mischief.

Feeling a slight blush creep onto my cheeks as Daisy's flirtatious gaze lingers, I smile.

"Behave yourself, Daisy! I don't want you scaring her off," Michelle chides, nudging Daisy with her elbow.

"Nice to meet you, Daisy," I reply.

Daisy grins and winks. She is the same height as me and has hazel eyes and olive skin. Daisy looks like a Victoria's Secret model with her perfectly toned figure and sex appeal. She flips her silky, straight black hair with green highlights and gives me another wink.

The other girl is very quiet, not saying a word, and observant. I smile at her when our gazes meet. She doesn't smile back. Her facial expression is stern.

"Hi, I'm Amy Jun," she says in a dull tone. Amy is shorter than me and has a more petite frame.

"Nice to meet you, Amy Jun." I reach to shake her hand, and she looks at my hand like she might catch something if she touches it. Amy looks away, ignoring the gesture, her bone-straight black hair with blue streaks swaying across her face.

"Be nice, Amy!" Michelle nudges her.

"It's okay," I say, withdrawing my hand.

It's clear that she prefers to keep her distance and maintain a sense of aloofness.

"I don't like meeting new people." Amy's tone remains flat; her violet eyes are uninterested. "Give me some time to warm up to you." She crosses her arms and takes a step back, creating a physical barrier between us.

Wow. That was blunt.

"It was nice meeting you guys. I'm going to continue my walk."

Turning in the opposite direction, I resume down the trail. Glancing over my shoulder, Daisy and Michelle follow after me while Amy drags her feet behind.

Stopping in my tracks. "Is there something you need?"

"Do you want to hang out with us, beautiful?" Daisy asks with a flirtatious smile, while Michelle nods eagerly.

Why does she keep calling me beautiful?

Trying to brush off their advances. "Thanks for the offer. I think I'll pass," I reply, maintaining a polite tone. "And please stop calling me beautiful and address me as Akira," I assert to Daisy, crossing my arms.

Michelle and Daisy exchange amused glances and laugh at my request. Even Amy snickers.

"Good to know you have balls," Michelle says, still smirking.

What did I stumble my way into?

Since they are obviously not going away soon, I ignore their comment.

"Are you guys shapeshifters or phoenixes?"

Daisy chuckles and responds, "We're shapeshifters," then she shapeshifts into me.

Impressive! It's like gazing into a mirror.

Cameron and Sophia join us with curious expressions on their faces. I took the restraints off Sophia when we arrived on the island because we are trying to work on building trust again, and she and Troy had a candid conversation.

"Wow! Which one of you is Akira?" Sophia asks, looking between Daisy and me.

Pointing to Daisy. "That's Daisy," I say.

Cameron looks amazed and says, "That's incredible! I've never seen shapeshifting before."

Daisy shapeshifts back into her original form and smiles at Cameron. "It's pretty cool, isn't it?" she says, then shifts her attention to Sophia. "Hi, beautiful. What's your name?"

"Daisy! Behave yourself," Michelle shouts.

Sophia blushes and introduces herself. "I'm Sophia. It's nice to meet you, Daisy."

Daisy is seriously passing moves on Sophia after she pulled the same on me. Cameron and I exchange looks, amused by Daisy's boldness.

"Looks like Daisy is quite the charmer," he whispers.

Sophia and Daisy walk off to the side to continue their conversation in private. Michelle and Amy are standing nearby and watching Sophia and Daisy. Sophia is definitely interested in her. She's all giggly, her cheeks are flushed, and her violet eyes are twinkling.

Turning my attention back to Cameron. "Where's Kaden?"

"Troy called us to come over. He has *something* to tell us," Cameron replies, narrowing his eyes at me, and I look down. "Kaden rushed off to meet him. Sophia and I were heading over there, too. And then we saw there were two of you and decided to come over to see what the fuss was about."

A knot forms in my stomach. Troy is going to inform them I spoke to Lucas, and of course, Kaden will be just as upset with this news as he is.

My shoulders slump. "What about Jessica and Roger?"

"They're with Jace," Cameron replies. "He's showing them around the island."

My face falls with unease, which Michelle notices.

"Are you okay?" she asks cautiously.

Forcing a smile. "I have to take care of something," I say, excusing myself from the group. "It was nice meeting you all. I'll catch up with you guys later."

"Sure thing. You can stop by anytime." Michelle points to the cabin furthest down the trail. "We live there."

Thanking Michelle for the invitation, I gesture toward Sophia to get her attention. Michelle does the same toward Daisy. She is currently in a deep flirtation with Sophia.

Sophia glides over to Cameron and me, cheesing from ear to ear. Daisy winks at me before leaving with Amy and Michelle.

"Please don't tell me I'm in competition with Daisy," I say sarcastically with a small laugh.

She rolls her eyes and smiles, "I don't know what you're talking about. Daisy's just a natural flirt." She tries to sound convincing, except the high pitch of her voice gives her away.

"What about you?" Cameron says, shifting the focus of the conversation to me.

"What about me?" I ask, raising an eyebrow.

"Are you trying to hide something too?" he presses, and Sophia exchanges a knowing glance with him.

"What makes you think I have something to hide?" I reply,

trying to deflect his question.

Cameron's eyes narrow as he studies my reaction. Of course, he knows something is off. Still, I'm not ready to tell them about Lucas yet.

"Troy told us Lucas contacted you!" Sophia's tone is harsh, and I swallow hard.

Troy already told them.

"Are you actually going to trust him after what he did?" she asks.

Rolling my eyes. "That's hilarious coming from you, Sophia, considering your track record with trust."

Her eyes flash with regret as she realizes the hypocrisy of her statement. She quickly averts her gaze, knowing that I have a point, and Cameron stays out of it. We walk along the trail in silence. Lucas's reappearance has stirred up old wounds in everyone that I'm not ready to confront just yet, so I decide to take Michelle up on her offer to come over. Cameron and Sophia follow behind me. We could all use a distraction.

Opposite Sides

Arriving at the cabin, I knock on the wooden door and wait patiently for someone to open it. Cameron and Sophia are behind me, not saying a word. The door swings open, and Michelle smiles and invites us inside. She points us to the "hangout area," where a pool table, a foosball table, and a flat-screen TV mounted on the wall are. There's a minibar stocked with drinks and snacks and a collection of board games on a shelf, including Monopoly. I don't remember the last time I played Monopoly. My friends and I usually stay away from playing it because it's never-ending.

We settle down on the bean bags.

"Do you guys want to play a round of Monopoly?" Michelle asks us, and I make a face in response.

"Monopoly always seems to drag on forever," Daisy says, and I agree with a nod. "What about UNO?" she suggests instead.

"UNO is my favorite," Sophia chimes in, smiling at Daisy. Daisy winks back at her, and Sophia's cheeks flush with a faint pink.

Cameron checks the options on the shelf and suggests, "How about we play 'Cards Against Abel?'" He grins from ear to ear as he holds up the black box, and everyone laughs at the twist on its name. *Clever.*

"When we first played Cards Against Humanity, Amy had the brilliant idea to rename it Cards Against *Abel* and customize the cards to include jokes and references to Abel," Michelle explains.

Amy shrugs. "What can I say? I hate Abel."

Everyone bursts into laughter. Cards Against Humanity is one of my all-time favorite card games, and this new spin on it is hilarious.

"Everyone in favor of playing Cards Against Abel?" Michelle asks, raising her hand.

The rest of the group follows suit.

Cameron places the black box on the table and sits next to Amy, whose lips curl into a smile. *Interesting.*

Michelle shuffles the deck of cards and deals them out one by one.

"What are the rules for this version?" Cameron asks.

Amy leans in and explains, "Same as the original, except the cards throw major shade at Abel. It's all about roasting him."

Cameron laughs, "That's brilliant!"

Amy blushes and tucks a strand of hair behind her ear. She's definitely into Cameron. This is her first time interacting with anyone other than Daisy and Michelle.

Hmm...I wonder if Cameron is aware of her interest in him.

Michelle nudges me to start the game since I'm on the left of the dealer. I select a black card from the deck and read it aloud. "'*Twenty bucks would buy_?*'"

Everyone chuckles while scanning through their white cards.

"Pick a good one," I say as I wait for their responses.

One by one, they start handing me their chosen white cards, and I shuffle them together, so I don't know whose response is whose.

I begin reading them out loud, trying to keep a straight face.

"*'Five guys to NOT serve the king.' '50 shades of Abel.' 'Throw the king in the freezer.' 'Sun bullets to end the king.' 'A decent king.'*"

The laughter grows louder with each card I read. This is precisely what I need to distract myself from my current *tiff* with Troy.

"Well?" Daisy asks, raising an eyebrow. "Who's the winner?"

Taking in each response, I silently reread the cards again and again.

"I'm going to go with *'A decent king.'* Who picked that one?" I ask, scanning the group for the guilty party.

Sophia raises her hand sheepishly, causing everyone to burst into laughter once again.

"*'Sun bullets to end the king.'* was a close second," I say, pointing at another card. "That was a good one."

Cameron's shoulders slump. "That one was mine. I thought for sure I had that one in the bag."

They continue to laugh, enjoying the lightheartedness of the game.

"Do you guys suggest we actually *kill* Abel?" I ask, half-jokingly, as the laughter dies down.

The room falls silent, and all of their expressions turn stern as my words hang in the air.

"We're at war with him, Akira," Daisy replies. "He's caused us trouble, and it's about time we put an end to it."

"We need to take him out before he takes us out," Amy adds.

"Should it really come down to murder?" I press.

"This is Abel we're talking about," Michelle says. "Death is the only way."

Cameron and Sophia nod in agreement, their faces hardened.

As I examine their facial expressions, there are no signs of uncertainty. There has to be another way to stop Abel without resorting to murder. I know that he has caused trouble and harm, and at first, I thought I wanted him dead, too. Still, he's the only father I've known. How can I justify taking his life? No matter what that man has done, he is—*was* a father to me.

Standing to my feet. "I'm going to head back to my cabin," I say to the group.

This game has taken a dangerous turn, and I don't feel good about where it's headed.

"I guess game night is over," Daisy's eyebrows pull together.

Michelle elbows her. "I hope we haven't offended you in any way," she says sincerely.

Shaking my head. "No, of course not," I reply. "I just have to take care of some things. I'll see you all later, okay?" With that, I turn and walk away.

I overhear Michelle saying to Daisy, "I think we offended her. He did raise her as his daughter."

When I reach my cabin, Kaden leaves just as I arrive. He notices me, and the cold look in his eyes fills me with terror.

Rubbing the back of my neck. "H—hey, Kaden," I stammer, unsure of what to say.

His shoulders tense up as he glares at me. "Save it, Akira," he snaps. "I'm going to kill Lucas when I see him."

"Wait, Kaden, please," I plead; he disappears in a flash.

The hairs on the back of my neck rise when I open the door, and my gaze meets Troy.

"You told Kaden, huh?" I ask, already knowing the answer.

"Lucas killed his brother," Troy replies firmly. "I had to tell him, Akira. He deserved to know the truth."

My shoulders droop—I've exhausted all the fight left in me. I don't want to argue anymore, especially over Lucas. I don't fully trust him either; I could have told him where I am and that my father is alive.

Troy notices my defeated expression and sighs, pulling me in for a hug. "Do you want to watch a movie?"

"I would love to," I mumble into his chest.

Troy leads me to the living room, and I settle on the couch while he pops some popcorn. He joins me shortly after, handing me a bowl and a blanket. We curl up together and search for a comedy on Netflix.

Before he presses play, he looks at me. "I'm visiting my brother tomorrow, and before you get worried, I'll be splitting my time between spending time with him and being with you."

Snuggling in closer to him, I plant a soft kiss on his cheek. He presses play, and we enjoy our movie night together. These little moments with Troy mean the world to me.

The following day, we rush to get ready to head to Florida to meet Lucas. Everyone opposes my decision to meet with Lucas; however, he needs my help. I can't ignore his plea for assistance. He's a good man under his obnoxious exterior; he just needs guidance. Abel is the closest thing to a role model Lucas has ever had, and it's all he's ever known. I want to see him, and then I'll know whether he can be trusted or not.

Troy and I don't speak much while we get ready. His disapproval still lingers in the air. He *hates* Lucas.

Not to mention, he and Kaden want him dead. Troy's concerns stem from a place of protectiveness, and I love him for that. Still, I believe in second chances. I gave Sophia a second chance, so why wouldn't I give Lucas the same courtesy?

We head out the door, and he grasps my hand and kisses it. I love it when he does that. We walk along the trail past Michelle, Amy, and Daisy's cabin toward Jace's.

Even though last night ended abruptly because Abel's impending murder was the topic of discussion, I enjoyed their company. It was still a good time. It reminded me of old times with my friends. *I miss those days.* Even Ava would join in on the fun, and although she was very grim, it feels odd that she's no longer with us. It's been over two weeks since the passing of Kade, Ava, Kai, and King John; their absence still feels fresh.

When we enter Jace's cabin, Jessica is preparing a portal for us to walk through. Kaden, Cameron, and Sophia are already there, waiting for our departure. Roger fits right in with the shapeshifters and decides this is a journey he doesn't need to be a part of.

Jacobson walks in and joins us, holding a duffle bag that's filled to the brim with weapons and supplies. I don't want Lucas to know that Jacobson is my biological father and that he is still alive, so we all agree to keep this information between ourselves for now.

Jessica circles her arms, and bright white lights fill the room.

The portal is forming, and we are getting ready to walk through it. Once we step through, Monica, Dawn, and Niyla are waiting for us on the other side with Lucas, whose hands are bound by shackles.

He stands to his feet when our gazes meet, and his eyes fill with delight. My heart shudders at the sight of him.

"Why is he in shackles?" I question.

They exchange glances before Dawn steps forward to answer my question. "We thought it was necessary to restrain him until you arrived."

"I'm here now. You can let him go," I assert firmly. "He isn't going to cause any harm. Isn't that right, Lucas?"

Lucas nods.

Monica snaps her fingers, her eyes reflecting uncertainty, and the shackles disappear from his wrists. I notice his hand is severely bruised. Usually, a vampire heals instantly when they consume human blood. *Why hasn't he healed by now?*

"I see you came with backup," Lucas remarks, smirking at Troy and Kaden.

Leave it to Lucas to make a snide comment, even when he is clearly outnumbered.

Lucas licks his lips suggestively toward me. In a matter of seconds, Troy and Kaden have Lucas by the throat, pinning him against the wall, ready to snap his neck.

"Let him go!" I shout.

Troy and Kaden hesitate for a moment, and they look at one another before reluctantly releasing him. Mayhem unleashes as soon as Lucas is free. He spins and kicks Kaden in the face, catching him off guard. Kaden loses his balance and stumbles backward, giving Lucas the advantage to snap his neck. Kaden falls to the floor, unconscious. Gray smoke surrounds Troy as he transforms into a wolf, growling menacingly. He lunges at Lucas, teeth bared and claws extended. Lucas carefully dodges Troy's attack, ripping his claws into his back, leaving deep gashes. Troy howls in agony.

"No!" I scream, rushing forward to intervene. Jacobson holds me back with a firm grip on my arm and shakes his head. He just risked exposing himself to Lucas.

Troy and Lucas tussle, rolling back and forth, causing destruction. The sound of their growls and snarls fills the air. Troy bites into Lucas's leg, spitting out a chunk across the room. Blood spurts from the wound as Lucas retaliates, sinking his teeth into Troy. Troy yelps in pain, and Lucas holds his leg in misery. He bites into his wrist, drawing blood, and drinks from it.

What is he doing?

Lucas rises with renewed strength, and his eyes turn black. He charges toward Troy, tackling him to the ground, and circles him, sinking his fangs all over Troy's body. Blood sprays from each bite mark as Troy howls.

Everybody watches the gruesome spectacle unfold before their eyes, yet no one tries to intervene. This fight has been building for weeks and has reached its boiling point. I can't watch them tear each other apart any longer. I've had enough! Standing tall, the built-up rage inside me comes to the surface. A surge of electricity courses through my arms, and a bright red and orange glow emanates from my fists.

"ENOUGH!" I roar, and the force in my voice separates Lucas and Troy, throwing them in opposite directions. The living room shakes like it's caught in the midst of an earthquake, and everything is thrown in all directions. Everyone standing on the sidelines takes cover from the shockwaves of my power.

When I finally regain control of my emotions, the fiery glow in my fists fades away, and the shaking stops. Everyone in the room picks themselves up from the wreckage.

"Heal, Kaden!" I command.

"On it," Dawn responds, rushing to fulfill my order.

My cold stare zeros in on Troy and Lucas. "Give us the room. Now!" I demand.

They quickly exit the living room, leaving Troy, Lucas, and me alone. That arrogant smirk plastered on Lucas's face is replaced with a look of unease as he avoids my gaze, and Troy transforms back into a human.

Pointing my hand toward Troy and Lucas, I levitate them off the floor. They collide mid-air, and I toss them back onto the floor with a thud. The impact leaves them dazed and disoriented. I didn't intend to slam them into each other; I'm still trying to control my newfound powers. *I need to start training with Jacobson soon.*

My glare hardens. "What is wrong with the two of you? Are your male egos so fragile that you can't handle a little confrontation?" I say, crossing my arms and awaiting an explanation.

They remain silent, neither of them looking my way. *I'm dealing with two five-year-olds!*

"Do either of you have anything to say for yourselves?" I demand, looking from Troy to Lucas.

Silence. Waving my hand, Troy and Lucas levitate off the ground again, and I want to suspend them in mid-air. However, they hit the ceiling with a deafening smash instead, prompting a reaction from Troy.

"Put me down now, Akira!" he shouts.

Shaking my head, I maintain my hold on them. "Not until one of you answers my question."

"Sweetheart, we were just having a little male-masculinity competition," Lucas replies. "Now, can you please put me down? I don't like my view from up here."

Narrowing my eyes at Lucas, unimpressed by his response, I screw up my face.

"Don't address my *girlfriend* as 'sweetheart,'" Troy spits through gritted teeth.

Children!

"Enough with the childish behavior," I say, releasing both of them. My patience wearing thin. Troy groans in pain while Lucas winces, rubbing his back when they hit the floor.

"I need a moment with Lucas, *alone*," I state firmly, my tone leaving no room for argument.

Troy shoots me a glare. "You cannot be serious, Akira."

"I am," I respond, maintaining my firm tone.

Troy glances at Lucas and then back at me, his frustration evident in his furrowed brow. "Fine," he grumbles. "Don't try anything funny," he threatens Lucas before reluctantly leaving us alone.

I will deal with him later.

Lucas smirks at Troy's threat and opens his mouth to speak, I raise a hand to silence him.

"Save it," I say, my voice laced with disappointment. "Have a seat."

A sly smirk stretches across his lips. "Alright, Akira," he says, dusting off an empty chair opposite me before sitting down.

He leans back in the chair. "Now that you got rid of the pet, what would you like to discuss?"

Leaning forward, my gaze fixed on him. "Let's start with what happened to make you betray the king?"

Lucas leans forward as well, his smirk fading. "Betrayal is a strong word, Akira," he says, his voice tinged with defensiveness. "King Abel's beliefs and principles don't align with mine anymore. I can't continue blindly serving someone I no longer believe in."

"So, if we were to go to war tomorrow, would you fight against the king?" I ask, trying to gauge his loyalty.

Lucas pauses, his eyes searching mine. "Yes, Akira, I would follow your lead," he responds. "I've served the throne for decades. And for decades, I've witnessed the consequences of blind loyalty. King Abel despises me because I don't possess a worthy gift, so he sees me as nothing more than a pawn in his game. I've followed Abel out of duty and honor. Now I don't."

I'm at a crossroads, torn between trusting Lucas's words and questioning his motives. He's been loyal to Abel for so long. Why would he betray the king? Could he really deceive Abel for me?

The silence in the room stretches as I search for any sign of Lucas's true intentions, but his reserved expression reveals nothing.

Lucas breaks the silence with a heavy sigh, "What's on your mind, Akira? I can see the doubt in your eyes."

"Lucas, I've known you for a while. How can you assure me that your loyalty is with me and not him?"

He grasps my hand firmly, his eyes locking onto mine. "Akira, you're one of my closest friends. I love you. I've always loved you and want nothing more than to prove my loyalty to you."

There's a nagging feeling in the back of my mind, questioning whether his words are genuine or if he's just saying what I want to hear.

What are his ulterior motives?

Death is the Worst End!

Akira is unbelievable! Her compassion and empathy for others are some of the things I love most about her; however, even a blind man can see right through Lucas's lies. He has a way with words, and Akira falls for them every time because she's too blinded by her *obsession* with him and fails to see his true intentions. Lucas is up to something, and I have to get to the bottom of it before Akira gets hurt. There is no way he would betray Abel, not even for her. I've known men like Lucas before, and they always have ulterior motives. I've seen the signs, the subtle manipulations and deceit. It's only a matter of time before Akira realizes the truth; until then, I'll do whatever it takes to protect her from Lucas's web of lies, even if she hates me for it.

"Hello Troy, can we speak for a moment?" Jacobson asks, snapping me out of my inner thoughts.

Turning to face him. My mind is consumed by the tangled web of Lucas's deceit. A crease forms between Jacobson's brows, which tells me this conversation is essential. I wonder if it relates to Lucas's situation.

"Sure," I reply, and we silently head outside to the backyard.

He sits on a green lounge chair and gestures for me to join him.

Jacobson swallows the knot in his throat and exhales before breaking the silence. "I see that you and my daughter are dating," he says.

"Yes, Sir." I nod, unsure where this conversation is going.

"How do you feel about Lucas?"

Great. That's something we can discuss.

"I don't trust him, Sir," I admit firmly.

Jacobson nods and leans in, his expression serious. "I appreciate your honesty," he says. "I don't trust him either. Lucas has always wanted to please the king from the moment he was brought to the kingdom and turned. His sudden change of heart is not in his character."

My eyes narrow. "Why don't you say something to Akira about your suspicions?"

He lets out a sigh. "I have considered it, but I haven't been in her life long enough to have earned her trust. I don't want to risk our developing relationship by accusing someone she cares about without solid evidence."

A realization comes over me. If Jacobson remembers when Lucas turned into a vampire, Lucas will recognize him as well.

"Sir, won't Lucas remember you?"

Jacobson nods slowly. "Yes, that's a possibility. If Lucas does remember me, it could complicate things even further. He'll report it back to Abel. But as far as I can tell, he hasn't noticed."

Rubbing my temples. "Akira loves Lucas, and she might want

to bring him back to the island with us. I'm sure you can tell by now how stubborn your daughter is."

Jacobson chuckles and shakes his head. "Why, yes, she definitely inherited that trait from her mother."

Raising an eyebrow at Jacobson's comment. "So, you're saying Akira's mother was just as stubborn?"

Jacobson nods with a wistful smile. "Oh, even more so. But, she always had a way of getting what she wanted, no matter the obstacles."

"It sounds like Akira's mother was quite a force to be reckoned with. I can see where Akira gets her determination from."

Jacobson nods again, his eyes overflowing with nostalgia. "Yes, she was a remarkable woman. I have no doubt that Akira will carry on her legacy." He pauses, his expression turning grim, before continuing, "Troy, we need to be prepared and equipped for Abel's impending plan of attack against us. We must ensure that Akira has the necessary support and resources to face him head-on."

"I agree, Sir," I say, my voice steady, and we shake hands.

Dawn rushes outside on high alert, her face pale and lips turned down at the corners. "Troy! It's Claude…" her voice trails off.

My heart is pounding in my chest so fast I'm afraid it might burst. "What happened to Claude?"

Dawn's eyes well up with tears as she replies, "We need to go now!"

Jacobson and I exchange worried glances before the three of us dash to Claude's room. My mother is slumped over Claude's unconscious body, her hands trembling as she tries to revive him.

Rosa unplugs the EKG machine. "I am so sorry for your loss, Queen Celine," she says.

Everything seems to freeze at that moment. The room is thick with an eerie silence as I try to comprehend what Rosa just said. Claude... *gone*? I didn't even get to say goodbye to my brother. *I didn't get to say goodbye to my father either.* A wave of grief washes over me, and I collapse to my knees beside my mother.

Niyla embraces my mother, holding her tight as tears stream down both of their faces, and Dawn rubs my back.

Akira rushes into the room and runs over to me. She kneels beside me, her eyes filled with tears. "Troy, I'm so sorry," she says, her voice trembling, and she wraps her arms around me.

Burying my face in her chest, she holds me tight as I let out a sob.

Rosa clears her throat. "I'm so sorry I have to cut this short; we must leave this place immediately. It's not safe here anymore. Abel has witches tracking our every move," she says urgently. "It's only a matter of time before they find us. We must go to the Island of Kian."

Standing to my feet and wiping away any traces of tears. "I need the room," I demand firmly.

Everyone glances at each other, unsure of how to react to my sudden assertiveness.

Picking up a lamp from the nightstand and smashing it against the wall, causing a loud crash that jolts everyone into action. "Now!"

My mother nods understandingly and gestures for everyone to leave the room.

As they hurry out of the room, I walk over to Claude's bedside, one foot hesitatingly placed in front of the other. I grasp his hand tightly. He was still and silent, his eyes closed as if in a deep slumber. Grief washes over me. He was my brother. My best friend. How do I say goodbye to someone who meant everything to me?

With a heavy heart, I pour out my emotions. "Brother," I whisper, my voice choked with tears. "I love you so much. You were always there for me; I cannot imagine my life without you. I can't believe you're gone. Please, please wake up," I plead, tightening my grip on his hand. "I'm your older brother, and it was my job to protect you. I failed you as a brother. I failed you as the prince of the hybrid kingdom. I'm so sorry, Claude. I don't know what to do without you. Our kingdom is broken, our leader is gone, and now you are too. How will I rule without you by my side? Who will guide me and support me in making the right decisions for our people?" Tears stream down my face as I struggle to accept the reality of losing my brother.

My mother walks back into the room and embraces me tight, her own tears mingling with mine. "You are not alone in this, my son," she says softly. "We still have each other."

The heartbreak from my father's death resurfaces and adds to my overwhelming grief for my brother. Since the arrival of Akira and her court, we have been stripped of our king, people, and kingdom.

"This is not your fault, Troy," my mother reassures me. "This is Abel's fault!" Her voice bitters with disdain and resentment as she speaks his name. "Use this pain as fuel to wage war on him to avenge your father's and brother's deaths!" She cups my wet face in her hands and wipes away my tears. "You're strong, Troy. Pull yourself together, my son, and lead our kingdom."

"Lead our kingdom where? Mother?" I ask, clenching my fists. "We've lost everything. We don't even have a home anymore."

"We may have lost our people, our home. However, now we have a new home. The Island of Kian." My mother's voice is firm as she continues, "Jacobson has offered us refuge and support, and with the witch's help, we can portal through the realms anytime. With your lead, we can rebuild our kingdom and make it stronger than ever. You are now our king."

I am the king of the hybrid kingdom. I repeat those words in my head. How can I lead a kingdom when I don't know what to do? How can I convince them to follow my lead when I can't convince my girlfriend that she shouldn't trust Lucas? Why should they trust me? I have caused nothing but death and destruction.

"Troy?" My mother interrupts my thoughts.

"Mother, I don't think I can lead us," I admit with a heavy sigh.

She grasps my cheeks gently, her eyes filled with unwavering belief. "Yes, you will. Trust in yourself, Troy, and others will follow suit."

My mother is a fierce queen. She gives me a final nod of encouragement before turning to Claude's lifeless form. She kisses him on the forehead and whispers a silent goodbye, placing the sheet over his body.

"We need to prepare for the funeral," she says, leaving me alone to my thoughts and emotions.

Glancing at Claude one last time before turning away, my shoulders slump. "Goodbye, Claude."

Exiting the room, I search for Dawn to have a meeting with Jacobson and what's remaining of my kingdom.

The hybrids gather, eyeing me warily as I approach them.

"Claude is d–dead," I announce, my voice trembling.

The hybrids exchange sad gazes. "I'm so sorry for your loss," one of my brothers sympathizes.

"Claude was a dear friend to us all." Another expresses.

Nodding and appreciating their support in this challenging time, I stand firm, exhibiting strength I don't necessarily have. "Thank you." Trying to steady myself. "We need to discuss our next steps," I say, my voice resolved despite the pain. "Staying here in Florida is not safe anymore. Abel has witches tracking us; they won't stop until they find us. We need to find a new haven, somewhere far away from their reach, so I believe it would be best if we all moved to the Island of Kian."

The hybrids begin speaking at once, asking questions.

"Did you speak this over with the leader of the island?" Dawn's voice cuts through the chaos.

"We have plenty of room on the island for all of you," Jacobson answers, walking in head held high.

"Who will be our ruler?" A lower voice asks from the back of the crowd, causing a hush to fall over the room.

Looking around at all the expectant faces, my stomach spins.

They are seeking reassurance and guidance in this uncertain time. As the silence lingers, I exhale. "Let us not forget that Akira Ronin is meant to unite all the kingdoms under one accord," I begin, my voice steady and firm, "I *am* your king, and we *will* rebuild together, stronger than ever before."

The hybrids look at me with a newfound sense of purpose, and they nod in agreement, ready to follow my lead.

A small smile graces my lips as I see the spark of hope in their eyes. "Please gather your things. We'll be leaving soon." I instruct, and they quickly spring into action.

Jacobson stands beside me, and I signal Dawn for her attention; she immediately comes over.

"Dawn, I need you to stay behind to investigate. We need to figure out Lucas's plan. He cannot be trusted," I say firmly. "Find out everything you can about his recent activities and be discreet. Akira trusts him for whatever reason, so Jacobson and I must prepare before he joins us on the island. I will contact Felix to inform him of what's happening. Hopefully, he can *fix* Shelly before the war breaks out."

"Consider it done," Dawn replies.

"Rosa is sending me back to the island to update Jace on the rest of your kingdom joining us," Jacobson says.

Placing my hand on his shoulder. "Are you sure there is room for us?"

Dawn gives me a look.

Jacobson nods reassuringly. "Yes, Troy, we have plenty of space on the island for everyone. I'll give you a grand tour when you all arrive. We've been preparing for this for decades."

Relief washes over me, and I thank him.

Dawn crosses her arms and purses her lips. "Was your little speech a ruse?" She accuses me, her eyes narrowing.

Shaking my head. "No, Dawn. I *will* lead this kingdom to a better future. I was just ensuring that there's enough space for everyone."

She sighs and relaxes her posture. "I guess I overreacted. It's just that we've been through so much already, and I want to make sure everything goes smoothly."

"I understand, Dawn," I say, reaching out to gently squeeze her hand. "We all want the same thing–a better future for our kingdom."

Since my father's death and the ambush on the cave, I haven't had any time alone with her to talk. She always had feelings for me that I didn't reciprocate, and when she found out how I felt for Akira, it created a rift between us. However, her animosity towards Akira has faded recently.

Dawn looks at our joined hands and smiles, slightly blushing.

"Hey, are we okay?" I ask, uncertain.

She looks up at me, and a frown tugs at the corners of her mouth. "Yes," she says, "we're okay. We work better platonically, not romantically, and I've come to accept that," she says, rubbing the outside of my hand. "Besides, I'm sure there's some guy on the island that's hotter than you," she nudges me.

"Very funny," I respond before my expression turns solemn, with the weight of Claude's death still heavy on my heart.

Dawn doesn't say anything, understanding the depth of my

emotions. Instead, she simply squeezes my hand, offering silent support in our shared grief.

Dawn leaves me to start her task, and I gather the rest of the hybrids and Akira to head back to the island.

Trying to center my mind, I exhale a deep breath. Abel needs to be eliminated. And there must be a way to prove to Akira that Lucas is full of it. Lucas cannot be trusted, and it is up to Jacobson, Dawn, and me to prove it to her, one way or another.

Blasted Witch!

My heart is pounding, and I clench and unclench my fist. I'm in another meeting with Paul, Cole, Amir, and Timothy in the dining hall, discussing the new vampire recruits and their powers, or lack thereof. Fifty wasteful vampires with nothing to offer me but headaches and disappointment. Ignoring the chatter going on around me, my eyes are fixed on the distance in the room.

"Abel?" Cole interrupts my seething.

Lost in my thoughts, I ball up my fist and punch a hole into the wooden table. "We need to recruit more humans!" I growl, and it echoes through the silent room, startling everyone at the table.

"Only six new vampires possess any sort of useful abilities. This is unacceptable!"

Paul clears his throat and speaks up. "Abel, quality is more important than quantity. We should focus on training and developing the skills of the few promising recruits we have and teaching them to control their thirst rather than expanding our numbers."

"I *need* new vampires! With gifts!" I shout.

Standing to my feet, I continue. "Training and control won't help us win this war, Paul. We need power, and that means increasing our numbers!"

Paul and Cole lean back in their chairs and glare at one another.

"What is it?" I demand, sitting back in my seat and pressing my fingers together like a triangle.

"Have you spoken with Tyler?" Timothy asks.

Narrowing my eyes at Timothy. "No, I have not. Is he back from his trip already?"

Timothy hesitates before answering, "Y—yes! I'll go and fetch him."

Timothy exits the room and returns with Tyler and another vampire.

"What did you find out?" I demand Tyler, irritation creeping into my voice.

Tyler looks at me with a grave expression. "Sir, we received credible information that there's an entire network of Seekers that's actively working to wipe out the existence of all supernatural beings," he reveals.

"Ethan is the leader of The Seekers," the tall, light-brown-skinned vampire next to Tyler adds.

Rolling my eyes at the hushed murmurs around the table, I sit up straight in my seat to command attention.

"Why should I be worried?"

"Because they have built an entire army right under our noses, secretly living amongst the humans," the vampire explains.

"We shouldn't recruit any more humans into our kingdom. These guys have impeccable weapons that can destroy us all. We witnessed them in action, killing one of the useless vampires. They shot him with a bow and arrow laced with UV light and human blood; he was dead in seconds." Tyler adds, tossing me the arrowhead. "Examine it for yourself. You'll see the remnants of vampire ash on it."

Inspecting the arrowhead, the remnants of vampire ash are indeed visible, confirming Tyler's words; I place it in my pocket.

"I understand the concerns about the risks involved," I say, acknowledging Tyler's caution. "We need a formidable force if we're going to take down our enemies. Just stay off Elijah's radar."

Everyone exchanges nervous glances.

"Ethan, Sir," Tyler corrects me, his tone displeasing.

"Thank you. That will be all for now," I say, dismissing the room.

Lucas approaches me when the room is empty with a duffle bag slung over his shoulder.

"Sir, the plan is going accordingly. Rosa is going to portal here to get me. Perhaps you should head down to the dungeon to stay out of sight," he suggests.

When Rosa arrives to retrieve Lucas, my dream is to sink my fangs into her skin, killing her instantly! Nevertheless, I have a bigger plan in mind, so I will wait.

Nodding in acknowledgment, I head down to the dungeon.

The next day...

Chase enters my chambers, ready for action, without warning. "Sir, we are heading to Florida now!"

"I'm coming with you," I shout, buttoning my collar.

Planting a kiss on Aika's cheek, who is pouting.

Lifting her head to meet my gaze. "I think it is best if I accompany them on this trip."

She nods in understanding and blows a kiss at me.

Chase and I meet with Nico, Timothy, Amir, Joel, the four other gifted vampires, and the five witches I am linked to at the castle's underground garage. The witches, Nico and Amir, will stay on my private jet with Timothy while the rest of us wage the attack.

We depart the castle and arrive at the witch's hideout in Florida by nightfall. When we arrive, my fangs elongate, and adrenaline courses through my veins.

Storming through the door with force, I unleash my fury. Rosa awaits me at the entrance, ready to fire, and a hybrid levitates beside her. *Interesting.*

"You four go after the broad. Chase and Joel search the house for anyone else. I'll take care of the witch," I order, my firm gaze fixed on Rosa.

Everyone nods and splits up.

Circling Rosa and eyeing her every move. "It's nice to see you again, Rosa." My voice drips with sarcasm as I taunt her.

She smirks, her eyes filled with defiance. "Likewise, Abel. I've been waiting to do this for years."

She mutters incantations, forming a surge of energy in her hands, and charges a bright white beam toward me. It bounces off me, and Rosa's eyes widen. The witches must have conjured a protective shield around me. *Marvelous.*

My lips form a smirk, unaffected by her failed attack. In the blink of an eye, I speed over and sink my fangs into her neck. She shoots electricity from her fingertips, causing me to recoil. Shaking it off and trying my luck, I launch myself at her again. However, the electricity continues to crackle on my skin. Perhaps the witches need to be in the room with me for thorough neutralization of Rosa's powers used against me.

"You can keep at it if you want," she taunts.

"Bring in the witches and Nico!" I shout toward Joel.

Turning my attention back to the blasted witch. "I have you, just where I want you!"

The witches march inside the house, chanting, and Rosa's body ascends. She attempts to use her gift to fight back against the witches; they suppress her magic with their combined strength.

Rosa's powers weaken with each spell, and she trembles in pain.

"A—Akira will defeat you!" she stammers.

Her eyes roll to the back of her head, and she descends to the floor. Blood oozes from her white eyeballs as her body shudders in agony.

A smug grin spread across my face as Nico cloaks us.

"I don't know what magic this is you use!" she shouts, leaning forward, searching for me.

In one swift movement, I have Rosa by the throat.

"Say hello to Serena for me," I say, reappearing before her eyes while slicing her esophagus.

Blood spills from her wound, and I devour her. My eyes gleam with satisfaction as her corpse falls to the floor.

Wiping my mouth, I notice the four idiots haven't killed the hybrid broad as of yet. When our gaze meets, gray smoke envelopes her, the smoke briefly clouding my sight. She transforms into a giant wolf, her fur bristling with rage. With a fierce growl, she lunges at us, teeth bared and claws extended. Her powerful jaws bite off two of the vampire's heads in a single snap.

"No!" I growl, falling to my knees. "They were important. They had gifts!"

She charges toward Nico, who luckily dodges her attack and cloaks himself. The hybrid retreats and disappears into the night. The other two vampires escape and head back to the jet unharmed.

Chase appears, holding Lucas by the throat. "There is no sign of Akira and the rest of them. They seem to have cleared out before we arrived," he reports, his grip tightening on Lucas. "What should we do with him?"

I punch Lucas square in the jaw, releasing him from Chase's grip and sending him sprawling to the floor.

Timothy rushes inside. "There is no sign of the hybrid. She is gone," he informs me.

Great.

"Where is Akira and the rest of the hybrid kingdom?" Chase demands.

Lucas cracks his jaw, wincing in pain, and spits out blood before responding, "In a different realm. It's called the Island of Kian."

Pacing back and forth, I rub my chin hair. "Why aren't you with them?"

"The hybrid prince doesn't trust me. He suggested I stay behind. And the other prince has expired." Lucas rises from the ground, wiping the blood from his mouth with the back of his hand.

Marvelous. King, check. Prince, check. Now, for the rest of the hybrid kingdom.

"Do you think the hybrid broad will be back for you?" I ask.

"Yes," he confirms. "Before you arrived, there were two other witches here that left through a portal. They'll come back for her."

"Break his neck!" I order Chase.

Lucas looks at me, eyes wide. "Sir?"

"We need to keep up pretenses," I reply, and Chase breaks his neck.

Chase and I stand over Lucas, eyeing him.

"Did you really need to punch him?" Chase chuckles.

Shrugging my shoulders. "Yes, I hate him."

Circling my finger in the air. "Let's go! We lost two vampires, but we have defeated their lead witch, which is something to celebrate," I shout.

They nod, and we retreat to the private jet. My lips form a

victorious smile as we leave the scene behind. Rosa is dead; it is time to commemorate her death.

A celebration in the ballroom is in order when we return to the castle. Chase and Amir procured a dozen human females for us to feed on. Aika presents me with the first young woman of the night to consume. Sinking my fangs into her delicate skin, relishing the taste of her succulent blood as my favorite metal band plays in the background, she writhes in agony and screams. I love it when they put up a fight. Aika smirks and joins the feast, her eyes gleaming with wicked pleasure. She pierces the girl's wrist and drinks deeply from her vein. The human girl is young, so her blood is sweet and pure; our bodies feel like we're floating on a cloud of ecstasy with every sip. We enjoy ourselves until suddenly, flashes of images invade my mind, causing me to stumble backward.

Akira is running toward me, pleading with me to stop my attack on the hybrid prince. I order one of my vampires to send her flying right into a brick wall. She falls in and out of consciousness, and everyone fights for their lives.

War is on the horizon.

"Honey, are you okay?" Aika gently shakes me.

Shaking my head. "I just had a vision."

Her brows knit together. "What did you see?"

"War raging in our home."

"Do you know when this will happen?"

"No, I don't. We need to be ready."

Cutting the celebration short, I hasten out of the ballroom to my chambers and pace back and forth with thoughts of preparation and defense. We have more than one plan in motion; indeed, we will win. We will find the Island of Kian and destroy Akira, the abominations, and The Revolt. Although we're down two gifted vampires, which leaves us stretched thin in my eyes, victory will be ours.

War is on the horizon, and we *will* be ready for it to prevail.

The Island of Kian
Lian Lake
Kian Mountains
Roju Bridge
Linie Lake
Kiju Island
Shalinie Sea
Mc Ocean
Training Field
THE REVOLT
Headquarters

BRIGHT
Map pronunciation

Shalinie Sea
"Shah-lee-knee"

Roju Bridge
"Row-joo"

Linie Lake
"Lee-knee"

Lian Lake
"Lee-Ann"

Kian
"Key-Ann"

Kiju Island
"Kai-joo"

Mc Ocean
"Mick"

The Island of Kian

Before the death of Rosa...

There's been so many deaths because of me.

I'm the common factor in everything that has happened.

"Akira?" Lucas interrupts me from my self-blame spiral.

"Yes, Lucas?" I sigh.

"Where is this other realm you mentioned?"

Lucas's question brings me back to reality, momentarily distracting me from my guilt.

"It's called the Island of Kian. We're going to head back over there while you stay behind."

A part of me doesn't trust Lucas enough to involve him further. I need a little more time before bringing him fully into the fold.

Troy enters the room, brows furrowed in Lucas's direction. "Are you ready?" he asks, his fierce gaze darting between Lucas and me.

"Yes, I'm ready. Let's go."

Troy gives Lucas one last warning stare before leading me out of the room. Looking over my shoulder at Lucas from the doorway, I feel a pang of guilt for leaving him behind.

"We'll be back for you," I say.

Lucas gives me a slight nod.

Troy and I head back to Claude's room for one last goodbye. He lays his forehead on Claude's and says a silent prayer.

Queen Celine kisses Claude's forehead, tears streaming down her face, and whispers, "Rest in peace, my love."

Niyla kisses Claude on the lips and murmurs her own farewell.

A lump forms in my throat as I witness the heart-wrenching scene unfold. "Goodbye," I mutter.

Rosa casts a preserving spell over his remains after the last goodbyes are said to keep him from decaying until we can plan his funeral. Monica enters the room with Kaden, who is groaning and rubbing his neck.

Niyla circles her hands, and a portal appears. Queen Celine glances at Claude once more before stepping through, followed by the rest of the hybrid kingdom.

Once we walk through the portal, we arrive in front of The Revolt Headquarters, a large black and gray building surrounded by nothing but land.

Did Niyla intend to portal us to this part of the island?

A brown-skinned woman who looks to be at least eight feet tall approaches us. She is breathtaking. Her dark-brown hair is half straight and half wavy, cascading down her back, and her eyes are a mesmerizing blend of yellow, orange, and red. Fire tattoos cover the exposed parts of her skin, flickering and dancing as if alive.

She places her hair in a ponytail and stands firm with her hands on her hips. "Nice to have you all here. My name is Anju. I am the leader of the phoenixes," she introduces. "On behalf of all of us, we are terribly sorry for your losses. We have a private island called Kiju that you are welcome to seek refuge on, or there are vacant cabins at the peak of the island by Roju Bridge."

Troy extends his hand and says, "Thank you, Anju. I am Troy, the leader of the hybrids. We appreciate your kind offer of refuge."

Anju nods. "You're most welcome, Troy."

Jacobson comes out of the building and approaches us with a map in his hand.

"Well?" Anju looks at us expectantly.

"Which is closer?" I ask.

"Kiju is closer. However, you would have to travel along the ocean coastline to reach it," she replies.

Jacobson pinpoints the little island on the map and says, "Kiju Island is a beautiful and secluded spot."

Inspecting the map, Troy peers over my shoulder. The land we are on is the training field, where the leaders of each supernatural faction practice their abilities. Shalinie Sea surrounds The Revolt Headquarters, and Kiju Island is close to Mc Ocean. The Kian Mountains sit at the top of the island. Roju Bridge is where the extraordinary waterfall is. We witnessed the gorgeous waterfalls when we first arrived. There are also two lakes, Linie and Lian. The Island of Kian is beautiful, and there is plenty of room for all the supernatural creatures to roam and coexist peacefully. Still, one problem presents itself: Is this island big enough for Troy, Kaden, and Lucas?

"Can I have a moment, please?" I glance at Troy, Jacobson, Kaden, and Queen Celine.

Anju excuses herself and addresses the rest of the hybrids to follow her inside the building.

"What is it, Akira?" Troy asks.

"Where do you want the hybrids to live? At the peak of the island, or on Kiju Island?"

Troy studies the map carefully, weighing the options in his mind.

Clearing my throat. "When we return to Florida, Lucas will join us on the island. Where do you think he should stay?"

They look at me like I have three heads.

"Twenty feet under!" Kaden spits through gritted teeth.

"You are compromising the safety of the island by suggesting that Lucas stays with us!" Troy states.

"Abel is after him, too! He has nowhere else to go!" I argue. "We have to get this sorted soon. Rosa said they have little time and—"

Jacobson clears his throat and interjects in our dispute. "We don't want Lucas to know that I am alive, so if you insist on having him here, he needs to be placed in a secure location. Which would be near the Roju Bridge," Jacobson suggests, pointing at the map. "Kaden can move over to a cabin along Shalinie Sea. Or you can all move into the castle at the top of the Kian Mountains. Actually, Kaden would be better off on the other side of Linie Lake."

"Then that's where I'll be," Kaden says. "I'll switch over to a cabin by Linie Lake. I want to be as far away from Lucas as possible."

Jacobson nods. "I'll make arrangements."

"Why doesn't anyone live in the castle?" I ask.

Jacobson meets my gaze. "The castle was built for you, Akira. You are meant to be our queen and lead us into a new era."

How can I lead? Too many people have died because of me, and I haven't officially claimed my throne yet! Clearly, I don't know what I'm doing!

Sucking in the air and exhaling slowly. "How far is the castle from the cabins by the bridge?"

"It's a few miles, but more than enough to be away from Lucas. We can have the witches place a locater spell on him, so none of you are in proximity to him," Jacobson recommends. "Still, magic has limits, so the spell would only work on this island," he continues.

Considering Jacobson's suggestion. "This could work for now."

Troy scoffs. "I don't need that."

Kaden screws up his face and looks away. "I would rather just kill him," he says under his breath.

Rolling my eyes at their stubbornness, I give Jacobson the go-ahead to make arrangements for the spell when Lucas arrives on the island. I am not breaking up another fight between the three of them.

Anju approaches us again with three phoenixes trailing behind her. "Have you decided yet?"

"Yes, the rest of the hybrid kingdom will stay on Kiju Island," Troy replies.

Anju nods. "Prepare the ship for departure!" she orders the phoenixes.

Everyone gathers on the deck of the ship except for Jacobson and Kaden. Jacobson stays behind to discuss the plan with Jace, and Kaden returns to his cabin to pack his things.

The ship sets sail towards Kiju Island, gliding smoothly through the calm waters. Looking over the side of the vessel, I close my eyes, letting the breeze caress my face and flow through my hair. The island is breathtaking, and I don't mind it being our forever home.

Troy points to the ocean, where gorgeous mermaids swim alongside fish and whales in the clear blue waters. *Wow!* I gaze at the rest of the hybrids, enjoying the magical sight before us with shimmers of hope in their beautiful gray eyes. *This is the right decision.* Troy wraps his arms around me, and we sail along the stunning waters to the Island of Kiju. I inhale his musk and feel at home.

When the ship docks on the island, everyone eagerly gets off to look around their new home. The island is blissful and serene;

however, there are only two cabins and about fifty hybrids left.

My brows snap together. "Where is everyone supposed to stay?"

"My team will come tomorrow to build more cabins," Anju assures me.

"What are they supposed to do in the meantime?"

"It's okay, Akira," Troy says. "For the time being, we can manage with the current cabins. We can rotate and share the space until the new ones are ready. We lived through the worst before we created our home in the cave."

"I'll collect the supplies and food from the ship," Anju says, walking back to it.

Troy and I exchange a knowing look and grin. We use our vamp speed to help unload the ship and bring it back to the cabin. We work together efficiently to expedite the process. My phone rings while we're loading, so I put down the food tub to check who's calling. It's Monica. She sends me a text saying Abel attacked them and that she and Niyla escaped.

I immediately call her; she answers on the first ring. Monica frantically explains that Abel ambushed them at the house. They fled just in time, and we must return to help Rosa and Dawn. I tell her to portal to Kiju Island at once.

Troy furrows his brow and fidgets in place. "What's wrong, Akira?"

"A—Abel," I reply, my voice barely above a whisper.

"I'll tell the others." He says and hauls the rest of the supplies to the cabin.

"What's gotten into him? Am I moving too slow?" Anju laughs.

Her smile quickly fades when she notices I don't join in her laughter. "What happened?"

"Abel attacked my friends in Florida."

Bright white lights swirl around, and Monica and Niyla walk through the portal.

"We need help now!" Niyla demands.

A swirl of fire surrounds Anju as her body twists and turns into a sizeable fiery bird, her feathers glowing with intense heat. She spreads her burning wings wide, ready to take flight, followed by three other phoenixes.

Monica forms another portal. "Let's go!"

Everyone steps through, and we see Lucas unconscious on the floor with his neck broken and Rosa nearby. Her clothes are covered in blood, and her eyes are wide open as if she is frozen in fear.

Troy disappears in a flash to find Dawn, and I rush over to Rosa, checking for a pulse; it's too late. She's dead. Tears stream down my cheeks as I hold her limp body to my chest.

"Why couldn't I prevent this from happening?" I shout, rocking back and forth with Rosa in my arms.

Niyla plummets to the floor beside me and lets out a high-pitched scream. Our collective grief causes the walls to crack and the ground to shake beneath us. The sound of her scream echoes in my ears, drowning out all other noise. The room caves in, the walls close in around me, and the room grows smaller and smaller. Death is happening too often now, and each loss feels like a dagger through my heart. My chest tightens as I struggle to catch my breath. *This is not real.*

This is not real; I pinch my arm to wake myself from this nightmare. The pain is too much, and I'm trapped in a never-ending cycle of anguish. Niyla clings tight to Rosa's corpse, sobbing. The house quakes, vibrating the debris loose from the crumbling walls. The sound of breaking glass and splintering wood fills the air, and Monica and Troy haste to our sides. Monica pulls Niyla away from Rosa's body and holds her tight. Troy cups my face in his hands and whispers soothing words in my ear, trying to calm the storm of emotions raging inside me. Still, I'm consumed with pain and feelings that are too overwhelming, and I continue to unleash destruction, unable to regain control.

Dust fills the air, making it hard to breathe, and debris falls from the ceiling. Monica and Troy shout for us to stop; our grief-stricken minds cannot process their pleas.

Monica rests her hand on Niyla's forehead and uses her magic to knock her out. My energy alone is controlling the earthquake. Troy clears the debris away from us, and Monica uses her power to create a pathway through the chaos. The entire foundation of the house crumbles, knocking Troy unconscious. Suddenly, I return to my senses and realize the devastation I have caused. Panic floods my body as I rush to Troy's side, trying to wake him up. Troy's pulse is weak, and his breathing is shallow.

What have I done?

Broken

Muffled sobs beside me wake me from my slumber. *Is that Akira?* Slowly opening my eyes, I try to adjust to the brightness of the room. As my vision clears, I realize that I'm back at the cabin on The Island of Kian. *How did I get here?* Confusion washes over me as I try to piece together the memories that led to my blackout, except they are fragmented and hazy. The last thing I remember is that the house was shaking one moment ago, and I was out cold the next. Akira lifts her head from her hands, and her teary eyes widen when they meet mine. She hugs me tight, relieved that I'm awake.

"You scared me," she chokes out, her voice trembling. "I thought I had lost you." Her grip on me tightens like she's afraid I might slip away again.

My throat feels dry and scratchy, making it difficult to speak. She reaches for a glass of water on the nightstand and gently helps me take a sip. Her tear-streaked face shows a worried expression.

My voice is strained. "Thank you."

Feeling a dull ache in my body, I push through the pain and try to regain my strength.

Tears flow from Akira's beautiful hazel eyes as she watches me struggle. She grasps my hand tight, refusing to let go. "I'm so—so sorry, Troy! I lost control of my powers," she cries, her voice trembling with guilt. "None of this was ever meant to happen. I'm not sure how much longer I can endure this."

Her words resurface memories of the earthquake. Does Jessica know Rosa is dead? The weight of the losses hits me like a ton of bricks, and a lump forms in my throat. I don't know how much more I can handle, either.

"Troy?" Akira says between sobs, her eyes searching mine for a response. "Do you remember what happened?"

Clearing my throat and trying to push down the lump that has formed. "Yes, I remember everything," I say, my voice hoarse. "Where is everyone? Where's my mother? Is everyone okay? We have to prepare funeral arrangements for Claude and Rosa," I say, my mind racing to catch up with the situation.

"Everyone is safe," Akira reassures me, wiping her tears. "They're on the island. Your mother is with the rest of the hybrids on Kiju Island. Anju and the phoenixes have been working tirelessly on the cabins. Last I checked, they only had a few more to build."

How long was I out for?

Akira looks at me and continues, "You've been unconscious for five days," answering my inner question.

My eyes bug out of their sockets. "Five days?"

"Yes, it took a while for your body to recover from the blow of the debris." Her voice quivers as she continues. "We—we already had a ceremony for Rosa. The witches needed to conduct a ritual to grant them access to her magic from beyond the grave."

I didn't know Rosa for that long, yet her loss still weighs heavily on me. Her death is another to add to the growing list of casualties caused by Abel.

"What about Abel?" My expression hardens when his name escapes my lips, anger simmering beneath the surface. "And is Lucas on the island, too?"

Akira sighs, guilt eating at her expression. "Abel is still out there, causing havoc. As for Lucas, he's on the island, but Monica cast a boundary spell, so he has limited access to the island, and she'll cast the locator spell Jacobson suggested after Claude's funeral. Let's focus on burying your brother. We couldn't bury your father. However, we can give Claude a proper farewell."

"When is the funeral for my brother?" I ask.

"You are now king. You decide when and how to honor your brother's memory," she replies. "And the rest of the island will make the preparations."

I will honor my brother's memory in the best way possible.

She kisses my forehead and whispers, "I'm going to head over to Kiju Island and give you some time to process everything."

With that, she leaves me alone to grieve and reflect on all that has happened.

I'm unsure how to feel. Perhaps empty. Is that normal? My father is gone, and so is my brother. How am I supposed to process this sort of loss? Claude was my best friend. We have been thick as thieves for decades. How am I to move forward without him?

A fire within me ignites with sorrow and fury, and my inner wolf fights to emerge.

Gray smoke whirls around me, and my body transforms. Racing outdoors, seeking solace in the forest's familiarity, the trees stand tall and green, their leaves rustling in the gentle breeze as I run through the underbrush. The moon is full and bright, casting an eerie glow over the wilderness, and the scent of pine fills my nostrils. My paws pound against the earth, and the wind whips through my black and silver fur. Darting past a rushing stream, I leap over a fallen log with ease. Sprinting through the dense forest with a sense of freedom and liberation, I feel comfort. This is what I needed. When was the last time I stretched my four legs? It feels so good to be untethered from my worries. Stopping at Linie Lake to lap the cool water, I howl at the full moon that hangs high in the night sky, feeling at peace for a moment until I get to this overwhelming realization. There is something I have to tell Akira!

It's time to say goodbye to my baby brother.

Dressed in all black, my mother gracefully glides to the front of the room, her beautiful face covered with a delicate veil. She is not only mourning her husband but her son as well. The room falls silent as she takes a deep breath, summoning the strength to deliver her last farewell. With tears in her eyes, she reaches for my hand, and I'm beside her in a flash. She kisses my hand before turning to face the crowd. Her voice trembles as she speaks.

"My baby boy, my sweet angel. No mother should have to bury their child, and it breaks my heart to let you go. We gather here today not only to mourn your loss but also to celebrate the beautiful soul that you were. Your kindness, compassion, and infectious smile touched the lives of everyone you encountered. Though my heart aches with grief, I find solace in knowing that you are now reunited with your father, watching over us from above."

My mother's words resonate through the somber room. "As your former queen, I want us to use the pain we feel for losing our king, our prince, and our home to fuel our strength and resilience to overthrow the ruthless tyrant who has taken everything from us. Let us honor their memory by standing together and ensuring that their sacrifices were not in vain. Together, we will rise and annihilate the vile vampire king once and for all!"

The roar of approval from the people after she finishes her speech echoes in my ears. We will get justice for what has happened to our kingdom. The crowd nods in understanding.

My mother embraces me and takes her seat so I can prepare myself to address the crowd. The gold coffin Anju and her clan built for Claude is a sight to behold; the craftsmanship is exquisite. My brother is sleeping peacefully inside, his face serene. Akira from the front row gives me a small smile. Jessica is beside her, offering comfort to a visibly shaken Niyla, who is affected by Claude's death. Although neither of them verbally confirmed their relationship, Akira and I knew.

With a deep breath, I gather my resolve and speak. "Claude was–*is* my best friend. He may no longer be physically with us, but he is still with us in spirit and in our hearts."

My eyes mist over, and Akira rushes to my side, rubbing my back.

Clearing my throat, I raise my voice, feeling the weight of responsibility on my shoulders.

"As your king, I will channel the pain I feel into leading us to victory against Abel! My people, I promise you that we will not rest until we restore peace. Together, we *will* ensure that all our losses are not in vain and that justice will prevail!"

The crowd nods in agreement, their determination mirrored in their eyes. Together, we stand united, ready to face whatever challenges are ahead.

Akira kisses my cheek and whispers, "I believe in you, my love." She then steps forward to address the crowd. "Everyone, please stand," she commands.

Something about her has changed. Her hazel eyes aren't those of an innocent woman anymore but those of a fierce queen.

"Starting tomorrow, we'll begin training for the war that awaits us," Akira declares. "Abel has attacked us more than once! This time, we will be prepared to strike back when he least expects it. We have lost too many lives already, and I don't know about you, but I refuse to let him take any more from us. From this day forward, we will train relentlessly and leave no stone unturned."

Everyone in the room nods in agreement, unwavering support shown in their eyes. The time for passivity had ended, and the time for action had begun. With a last nod, Akira dismisses the crowd, and they exit the room.

My mother places a single white rose on Claude's chest. She kisses his forehead once more, whispering her last goodbye. Niyla kisses him on the cheek, her tears falling on his face. She doesn't say a word, her expression speaking volumes.

So much has happened since I met Akira. The happiness I once knew feels like a distant memory, replaced by a whirlwind of deaths and grief. I don't know what to do anymore.

"I will avenge your death! Even if I have to join you in the afterlife once justice is served. I love you eternally." I say to Claude.

Anju interrupts, placing a comforting hand on my shoulder. "It is time," she says, and I nod.

She and the rest of the phoenixes set Claude's body on fire, sending his spirit to the hereafter with a blaze of honor and reverence.

The air is somber and silent as the flames dance and flicker. A numb feeling washes over me as I watch his remains turn to ash. My mother clutches my arm, her grip tight, and her hands are trembling. One of the witches uses magic to confine the fire while Anju collects Claude's ashes and places them in the urn.

She hands my mother the urn and says a prayer for my brother's soul.

My mother and I embrace one another. "My only son." She whispers before heading back to Kiju Island.

Akira and I walk back to our cabin in silence, my mind contemplating whether I should tell her what's been weighing on my heart or not.

As we walk, Akira brushes her hand against mine, sensing my inner turmoil. "Babe, Are you okay?" she asks.

It's now or never. "No," I admit with a sigh, "there's something I need to tell you."

She stops walking and turns to face me, a slight crease between her brows. "What is it?"

Taking in her beautiful features and the way her eyes search mine for answers. "Akira," I begin, and she looks at me expectantly, "I need a break from our relationship," I finally confess, feeling a weight lift off my chest.

Akira's expression changes from worry to surprise and a crease forms between her eyebrows. "I–I don't understand," she stammers, "why?"

I love Akira more than words can express. However, I blame her for losing my father, brother, and home because of our relationship, and right now, I need to focus on revenge, not love. My heart is determined to follow a different path.

"I hope you understand that this decision is not easy for me," I reply with a heavy sigh. "I can't keep pretending that everything is okay when it's not. I need some time apart, so I will pack up my things and let Anju know I'll be moving to Kiju Island permanently."

It breaks my heart to see the hurt in her eyes; I never wanted to cause her pain. Still, I cannot ignore the agony that she has caused me.

A single tear falls from her eye, and I reach out to wipe it away.

"I still care about you deeply," I say; she pulls away, avoiding my touch.

"Don't!" she shouts. "I don't want to hear it anymore. Just go."

Her words cut through me like a knife. She stands behind me, eyes fixed on the ground as I return to the cabin to pack up my belongings.

More and More Training!

It's been over a month since Troy and I broke up, and everything around me feels different now. I'm detached from the world and drowning in a sea of sadness. Every day feels like a blur, like I'm just going through the motions without being present. I have everyone training nonstop for the war looming ahead. I've been throwing myself into drills and meetings so that the pain doesn't consume me. Troy is avoiding me and missing essential gatherings. He sends Dawn in his place. He wants nothing to do with me.

I formed a council of my own that comprises myself and ten others. Niyla is one of the strongest witches I know besides Monica. Naturally, they would be in my council. Cameron is my right-hand man and brother, and although Kaden disagrees with Lucas living on the island, he is a crucial member of my team. Sophia is a pointed member as well. In the last month, I have become close with Michelle, Daisy, Anju, and even Amy, as well as my father. Once Shelly and Felix arrive on the island, they will join my council, too.

A few days ago, I received news that Shelly had turned her emotions back on and was ready to face me. I can't wait to see my best friend—*my sister*—and finally reconcile with her. It's been so long, and I've missed her so much. Since our last encounter, I've been feeling nervous.

Due to Kaden's unwillingness to train with him, I have separate training sessions with Lucas. I still have reservations about trusting Lucas. However, he's made the breakup a little easier by pushing me to my limits to help me become stronger and more agile. We focus on combat techniques and running endurance drills.

After training, I have a one-on-one session with my dad and then a council meeting later. My father and I have become a little closer since we started these one-on-one sessions. Still, I can't bring myself to refer to him as "dad" to his face. When I refer to him as Jacobson, I see the hurt in his eyes. The emotional barrier between us is still there; however, the wall is slowly breaking down as we spend more time together.

Slipping into my workout gear and lacing up my sneakers, I get ready for training. We train on Mondays, Wednesdays, and Fridays—three times a day. I don't know when we plan to attack Abel. However, we will be prepared. Monica, Michelle, and a few of the witches are on vampire watch duty. Careful to go unnoticed, they portal back and forth to track Abel and his minion's every move. Apparently, he has been conducting tournaments daily to create vampires, which has caught the eye of another group, who are also keeping a close eye on his activities. I know little about this group, or the name of them. We will discuss any recent developments in our council meeting.

Cameron and Sophia wait for me outside my cabin, and we use our speed to get to the other side of the island in a matter of seconds.

We walk into the dome-shaped room. The high ceilings and spacious interior make the headquarters feel massive. Elaborate geometric patterns and colorful murals of the leaders of each supernatural faction cover the walls. At the top is the control system that Jace operates the weather inside the training area, and it generates creatures for the trainees to practice their skills against.

Anju is there to greet us. "Hope your day is going well." She says as a smile spreads across her face.

"Thank you, Anju. I hope you are feeling good. Are you ready to train?" I ask.

"Most definitely." She says.

"Oh yeah, because we just enjoy training," Cameron mumbles under his breath, and I narrow my eyes at him.

Sophia rolls her eyes playfully and chuckles.

During the first hour, we train in tropical storms. In the second hour, we move on to blizzards. And in the third hour, we transition to scorching desert heat. My kingdom doesn't partake in consuming human blood, so we're trained to fight in the daylight or nightfall. However, Abel's kingdom does, so they're trained to fight primarily at night. I'm confident they have taken precautions to avoid any attacks during daylight hours. Lucas suggests we should attack them at the castle since Abel procured new witches to conduct a sunlight spell, so it won't matter if we attack during the day or night.

Pacing the room with my hands behind my back, I observe as my people arrive for training and exchange pleasantries. Each supernatural being is grouped by powers. The shapeshifters are grouped in the middle because they can shapeshift into any form and access a wide range of abilities for at least twenty minutes.

Because of their ability to regenerate in ten minutes, the phoenixes are grouped behind everyone, making them excellent healers and protectors. Their skills are pretty unique. They can revive any of us from the brink of death by touch within a five-minute window. To ensure there is always a healer available in case of emergencies, each group is assigned three phoenixes.

The witches, Dawn, Roger, and I, are working closely with Amy and Daisy. They are the only shapeshifters who can transform into me and access my powers without a problem. The other shapeshifters have a hard time harnessing and controlling my gift.

Troy is supposed to be training with us today, but once again, he is missing with no explanation. He sends Dawn as his messenger to excuse his absence.

And like clockwork, Dawn arrives at training and approaches me. "King Troy will not be in attendance today."

Wagging my brows in frustration. "When does he plan to attend? We started training over a month ago, and he has missed every session so far," I state, crossing my arms. "Troy needs to take training seriously and show up consistently. This is not acceptable. It's disrespectful to the rest of us..." I trail off because Dawn is just the messenger. I exhale and try to calm my frustration. "Dawn, tell him to be at the next training session. This is not up for debate!"

Dawn nods in understanding. "I'll deliver the message clearly," she assures me.

"Thank you."

Facing the crowd. "Today, we're practicing formation and precision and expecting who will attack first. We do not know about our enemies' powers. From my time at the castle, I know Chase is a telepath. Still, Abel has recruited an army of vampires with unknown abilities. As we speak, a few of the witches are re-conning the vampires, so we may have some insight soon. Now, let's get started on the plan of attack."

Everyone nods and takes their positions on the field, awaiting further instructions.

"The hybrids and vampires will take the front line due to their advantage of speed and strength, and three phoenixes will follow each group to provide protection."

Turning my attention toward Roger. "You have the power to materialize anything from thin air, so you'll stay in human form behind the phoenixes to materialize weapons and toss them to our fighters as needed." Roger nods. "For training purposes today, I will assign you one shapeshifter and phoenix," I continue.

I signal Cameron to hand me my clipboard, scan through my checklist, and make sure that we have covered everything for our training session.

"Ah yes, one last thing," I say, pointing to the bottom of the list. "After Roger enters, the witches will cast spells against Abel's witches. Dawn, Amy, Daisy, and I will then position ourselves strategically on the battlefield."

Looking up from my clipboard. "Does everyone understand?" I ask, seeking confirmation from each team member.

Once I receive nods of agreement, one by one, they disperse, preparing for the training session.

After each session, I rearrange the training groups so everyone can work with different teammates to gain exposure. This allows us to learn from each other's strengths and weaknesses, ultimately improving our overall performance as a team.

Nodding my head in Jace's direction, he adjusts the dial-up, changing the weather to a tropical storm.

The ground beneath us morphs into a lush meadow, and trees sprout from it. Clouds gather overhead, and heavy rain pours down on us. The wind picks up, swirling into a powerful gust that threatens to uproot anything in its path. Jace generates fake vampires and releases them into the battle room.

"Attack!" I shout.

Gray smoke envelops the hybrids as they transform into wolves and charge toward the simulated vampires. Although generated, their blows pack enough force to send you flying and hitting the ground. One of them delivers a violent hit to a hybrid, sending her hurtling through the air and crashing into a nearby tree. A bolt of lightning strikes the tree, setting it ablaze and causing the hybrid to catch fire. The hybrid howls in anguish and rolls along the dirt to put the fire out. The fake vampires go at it equally matched with the hybrids.

Roger materializes a silver and black sword and tosses it to Cameron, who catches it with ease, hauls it over his shoulder, and slices through one of the creatures, severing its head. Sophia leaps from a tree branch onto another vampire's back, breaking its neck with a swift twist.

Roger runs along the field with agility for each of the fighters, and weapons of their choice emerge from his hands, with a phoenix and shapeshifter trailing his every move. He materializes daggers, throwing them to Daisy, Amy, and Anju, who catch them effortlessly and attack the enemy.

Anju transforms into a bird and soars above three of the supernaturals who climb up the trees, trying their best to catch her; she evades their attack and dives, slicing their throats with her sharp talons.

Amy and Daisy shapeshift into me, and we circle each other, causing confusion to our enemies as they struggle to identify the real me. Amy and Daisy can only be in my form for twenty minutes, so we have to hurry. Focusing on all the power within me and exhaling, as my dad taught me, I concentrate on what I want my magic to do so I don't lose control over it. The generated vampires leap from tree to tree, making their way toward us. We remain in a circle, waiting for them to approach.

"Now!" I shout, and we hold hands.

They channel my power, our chests filling with a blazing red and orange light. We compress our hands to the ground and control the roots of the trees, causing them to sprout and trap our enemies in a web of vines. Amy and Daisy change back into their natural forms, and I levitate, finishing them off. Dawn is on the sidelines observing.

Jace creates a dozen more supernatural creatures and sends them charging towards us. Dawn joins me in the air while Roger and the shapeshifter are materializing weapons toward us and the rest of my team with accuracy. They are visibly exhausted, but that doesn't matter because I nod for Jace to create more. They multiply rapidly, and one of them advances toward Roger and knocks him out, then attacks the shapeshifter with one of the daggers and cuts into the shapeshifter's throat, causing her to gasp for air and collapse to the ground. Jace shuts off the simulation to tend to their injuries.

"No, don't stop," I shout, "we need to keep going!"

My father sprints towards them to help Jace evaluate the damage. "That is enough, Akira," he says. "They're injured!" He looks at Anju, who is flying around, and asks, "Anju, please help revive her."

Anju transforms and kneels beside the shapeshifter and pierces her claw against the shapeshifter's skin. Fire ignites from her body and into the young woman, resurrecting her back to life. The shapeshifter gasps for breath, her wounds heal, and color returns to her face.

"She'll be alright now," Anju assures my dad, who nods.

"Again," I shout as soon as the shapeshifter is healed.

Pushing everyone to their limits and demanding their best effort, we continued training for another hour.

My father beckons for my attention.

Wiping the sweat from my brow. "What is it?"

A crease forms between his eyebrows, and his jaw tightens as he speaks, "We need to talk, Akira. *Alone.*"

"Fine, let's make it quick." Turning my attention toward Cameron. "Cam!" I shout. "You're in charge."

He nods, and I follow my father to a more secluded area.

We walk out of the dome and down the hallway to the auditorium.

He clears his throat before speaking, his voice low. "Akira, I know you want the kingdom to be equipped for what's coming. However, you're pushing them too hard. This has been going on long enough."

Narrowing my eyes at him. "I understand your concern, Jacobson. We don't have the luxury of time. I'm the queen, and we'll continue to train. This isn't up for debate."

He relaxes his shoulders and lets out a sigh.

"Sweetheart–"

"No, Jacobson," I interrupt, "our survival depends on it. I cannot–*will not* lose any more of our people to Abel."

My shoulders sag as I think about the lives we've already lost, and tears threaten to spill from my eyes.

A lump forms in my throat that's hard to swallow. Everyone must survive this war. It's highly improbable; the thought of losing anyone else is unbearable to me.

He opens his arms wide and steps forward, pulling me into a tight embrace, and I cling to him, sobbing into his chest. "How about we end training for the day, and you and I spend some time together?" he suggests.

Wiping away my tears, I slowly pull away from his embrace. "Okay," I say, and we head back to the dome to let everyone know that training is over for the day. Looks of relief spread across their faces, and they gather their things. My dad says he'll be right back, leaving Jace and me.

"Are Monica and Michelle back?" I ask.

Jace shakes his head. "No, they're not."

He returns shortly with a large sword box handcrafted in gold and engraved with my name adorned in flames.

"I have something special for you, Akira," he says with a smile, and Jace excuses himself to give us some privacy.

Admiring the box in awe, I run my fingertips along the intricate engravings.

He opens it to reveal a gleaming sword made from pure gold with a long, slender blade that glimmers in the light. Encrusted with precious gems, the hilt showcases elaborate designs of red and orange flames. The crossguard features a sculpture of a vampire's teeth and a phoenix intertwined, with their lines curling around the blade, intricately designed by the craftsman. The grip, decorated with golden embellishments, is wrapped in soft leather. Without a doubt, the sword is an exquisite piece of art. I'm in absolute awe.

"I had Anju and Jace craft this sword, especially for you, my dear daughter," he says proudly. "You don't know me very well. Still, I've loved you since the day you were born, and I'm so sorry I wasn't able to be there for you before. However, I'm here now, and I want to make it up to you. While I acknowledge that it will take time for you to trust me, I hope this sword is a small step toward building a relationship between us. It's my desire to be the father you've always deserved."

I'm at a loss for how to respond. He has been trying to get to know me, but I've been so focused on training and distracting my mind from the breakup that I haven't given him a fair chance.

"Thank you so much," I say, my voice filled with genuine gratitude. "I'll cherish it for the rest of my life."

He kisses the top of my head and says, "I'm glad to hear that." Then he pulls away and looks at me with a warning in his eyes. "The blade is extremely sharp. It'll decapitate anything with a single swipe, so use it wisely."

"I'll be careful," I assure him. Pausing for a moment. "Can I ask you something?"

He nods and gestures for me to continue. "Go ahead."

Taking a deep breath before speaking. "I love Troy, but he doesn't want to be with me anymore." I look away, the hurt still fresh in my heart. "How do I heal from a broken heart?"

His expression softens, and he takes a moment to choose his words carefully. "Troy loves you too," he says. "I believe giving each other space and time to figure things out is important. In the meantime, focus on taking care of yourself and finding healthy ways to cope with the pain."

"How much time does he need? It's been over a month," I sigh.

He pauses, considering my question. "Everyone heals at their own pace." He looks at me with empathy. "I've been healing from a broken heart for over twenty years."

My mother. My stomach turns. I've been heartbroken for a

month, and it feels unbearable. Meanwhile, my dad has been carrying this pain for two decades. He lost his wife, his daughter, and his home all in one day.

"Can you tell me about her?" I ask.

Jacobson's eyes soften with sadness and fondness as he reminisces. "Serena—*your mother* was the love of my life, and I never got to say goodbye to her," he begins. "She was kind, like you," he nudges me gently. "She always had such a vibrant spirit. With her pure soul, she was a refreshing breath of air. The moment she realized she was expecting you, she was overcome with joy. Your mother couldn't wait to become a mom to you." A bittersweet smile forms on his lips as he continues. "I wish she could see the wonderful young woman you've become. She would be so proud of you."

Brushing a loose curl behind my ear. "The last time I saw her alive was the day you were born and taken away from us. It was the hardest day of my life."

The first time Jacobson touched me, I flinched; now, his touch is comforting.

This is the start of a father-daughter relationship we both deserve.

CHAPTER 43: AKIRA

I've Missed You!

The sword, custom-made for me by my father, is a masterpiece, and I can't help but smile from ear to ear, appreciating the complex designs and impeccable craftsmanship that went into its creation.

My dad grins back at me, clearly pleased with my reaction. "Are you ready to train?"

Nodding eagerly, I tighten my grip on the hilt of the sword. "Always."

Since Rosa and Claude's deaths and my breakup with Troy, I've found solace in training. It keeps my mind busy and distracted from the pain and grief; it helps me channel my emotions into something productive.

He draws a sword from the rack and grips it firmly in his hand. We circle each other, blades ready to clash. Aiming for his chest, I lunge forward; he evades the blow with ease and counters with a swift strike on my arm. Spinning around to block his attack, the two swords clash together with a resounding clang as we exchange a series of blows. He lunges forward again, but this time, I anticipate his move and sidestep the attack, delivering a powerful thrust to his abdomen that sends him reeling backward. I rejoice in my minor victory and help him up from the ground.

He chuckles, "you were born to wield a sword," he remarks, his eyes gleaming with pride.

"You really think so?" I ask, my voice mixed with excitement and uncertainty.

"Absolutely," he replies with a reassuring smile. "You're a natural."

Smiling back at him. "Thank you, J—" I catch myself before I say the word Jacobson.

He places his hand on my shoulder and sighs, "Akira, I understand Abel was the only father you've ever known. I know it's going to take time to adjust to having another one."

How is he so understanding? Abel murdered the love of his life and stole his only daughter—*me*. Rubbing my stomach, I feel sick, trying to suppress the wave of nausea that washes over me. Sitting on the floor, I lean against the wall for support.

He kneels beside me, his expression filled with concern. "Akira, are you okay?"

Nodding weakly. "I'm sorry. I don't know how to feel about this. The whole situation is just a mess."

He places a comforting hand on my shoulder. "It's completely understandable, Akira."

"That's just it! How can you be so *understanding* about all of this? You should be pissed off. The man I've called my father since

I woke up from my coma killed your wife—*my mother*—and stole me from you."

He sits beside me against the wall and looks forward with a distant gaze. "I've had a little over twenty years to be angry, Akira. Holding onto that anger won't change the past or bring back your mother." He turns to face me. "We can't change what happened, but we can choose how we move forward. Even if Abel never stole you away from us, we would still have to get to know each other."

Cocking my head to the side. "What do you mean?"

He chuckles and says, "Well, naturally, babies and parents should have a bond from the moment they are born. However, some don't develop that bond until later in life. Which is what we are doing right now," he explains, pointing from his heart to mine. "We're getting to know one another, just as we would have in the normal course of things. It may not have started in the traditional way, but that doesn't make it any less special or meaningful."

Shaking my head, I giggle. "You're right," I admit, "I never thought about it like that before."

Leaning my head on his shoulder, he tilts his head against mine. We share a silent understanding that passes between us before Cameron strides in, interrupting our moment.

His shoulders hunch over, and he tightly clasps his hands together. "Sorry to interrupt! Monica is back, and we're ready to start the council meeting."

Lifting my head from Dad's shoulder, I give Cameron a reassuring smile. "No worries, Bro! We'll be there in a few minutes."

Cameron nods and exits the room.

Gazing at the sword once more with admiration. The light reflects off its golden blade and illuminates a mesmerizing glow that dances across the room. I'm incredibly thankful to Jacobson, my dad, for gifting me such a remarkable weapon. I carefully place it back in its sheath, meeting Dad's gaze with gratitude. "Thank you so much for this... Dad."

It doesn't feel weird calling him that. It feels right, and I don't know why it took me so long to say it to him.

His face lights up with a wide grin stretching from ear to ear, and he wraps his arms around me for an embrace I happily return. I've never felt that type of warmth from Abel like I do from my father.

That's right! *Father.*

We head to the auditorium for our meeting with the rest of the council.

Monica and Michelle's facial expressions are grave when we enter the room.

Taking my seat at the head of the table. "What is it? What did you find out?"

Monica clears her throat. "A network of individuals called 'The Seekers' are targeting all supernatural creatures. They believe that by eliminating us, they can restore balance to the world."

Slamming my hand on the table. "What!?"

Michelle continues, "I shapeshifted into one of Abel's guards at the castle and overheard Abel and someone else discussing it."

"What does this mean for us? Do we have another enemy to defeat?" Cameron asks.

Everyone speaks at once, their voices overlapping. My father exchanges a worried glance with me before I raise my hand for silence.

He stands up and addresses the room, "I have never heard of 'The Seekers' before! I will reach out to our contacts to arrange a meeting with the leader–perhaps we could form an alliance with them."

"Maybe they can help us defeat Abel and his kingdom because they have the numbers," Monica suggests.

"The Seekers hate *all* supernatural creatures," Michelle adds. "why would they want to help us?"

"Because we aren't kidnapping innocent humans and turning them into vampires," Cameron says, "we have a common enemy."

Everyone in the room looks at me for a response.

Looking from Dad to the rest of the group. "Let's arrange a meeting with the leader and work out a potential alliance. It may be hard to convince him since they have a deep-rooted hatred against all supernatural creatures, but it's worth a try."

He nods. "I'll talk with Jace to see about tracking down the person in charge and setting up a meeting. Monica and Michelle, do you mind accompanying me on this mission?"

"Not a problem," Michelle replies.

Monica adds, "We're ready to assist in any way we can."

"Thank you," I smile at them before turning my attention back to the room. "Is that all for today?"

"Shelly and Felix have arrived on the island. They're with the hybrids," Niyla informs me. "She'll meet with you after."

My heart sinks to the pit of my stomach at the mention of Shelly's name. I haven't spoken to her since she attacked me in Florida.

Nodding, I try to push aside the lingering unease. "Alright, keep me updated. Meeting adjourned."

Everyone exits the auditorium except for Cameron and Sophia.

Sophia tucks a curl behind my ear. "Are you okay?" she asks softly.

Letting out a nervous giggle that sounds more like a hiccup, I give her a weak smile. "Yeah, I'm fine."

"You don't seem fine," Cameron says matter-of-factly. "The last time you saw Shelly, she tried to kill you."

Rolling my eyes. "I appreciate your concerns. I'm fine. Really."

Sophia's phone buzzes in her pocket, and she pulls it out to check the notification.

"Sure you are," she replies skeptically, her fingers typing a quick response. "I guess we're about to find out because Shelly will be here in five minutes."

Feeling a knot forming in my throat, I swallow hard. Shelly's impending arrival has my palms clammy and my heart pounding with anxiety.

I thought I was okay.

Trying to calm myself down, I take a series of deep breaths. Maybe Sophia is right. Perhaps I'm not as *fine* as I thought. Footsteps approach from down the hall, growing louder with each passing second. Sophia and Cameron stand guard in front of me, and a few of the witches assigned to protect me are surrounding the perimeter.

The door creaks open slowly, revealing Shelly's familiar silhouette, accompanied by Felix. She glides into the room, her eyes fiery red as I remember them, gazing around at the witches, Sophia and Cameron.

She giggles nervously and says, "Is all this really necessary? Felix wouldn't have brought me back if he thought I was an actual threat. I mean, come on, Akira."

My gaze shifts from Shelly to the witches and back again. Everyone waits for my reaction, their eyes fixed on me.

She's right.

A deep sigh escapes my lips, and relief washes over me. It feels like a weight is being lifted off my shoulders. My body relaxes, and my muscles loosen as the tension drains away.

"Besides, I've had enough time to reflect on my actions, and I've realized the error of my ways," she adds, her voice tinged with sincerity. "I missed you so much, Akira."

My throat tightens, and a single tear trickles down my cheek. I quickly wipe it away with the back of my hand, my eyes stinging with unshed tears. Shelly's eyes meet mine, filling up with tears of her own. She missed me just as much as I missed her.

Throwing myself into her arms, I hold her tight as if I never want to let go. "Shelly," I choke through the sobbing.

She holds me even tighter. "I know, I know," she cries, repeating the words over and over again.

"How?" I ask between sobs, my voice barely audible.

Felix joins in the embrace, wrapping his arms around both of us, as do Cameron and Sophia. We all cling to each other for what feels like an eternity, finding solace in our shared reunion.

We finally release each other, our tears slowly drying up.

Shelly wipes her face. "It's a long story," she replies. "Felix and his witch put me through a series of painful experiences that forced me to confront my grief and trauma, which turned my emotions back on."

Sniffling, I reply, "What do you mean?"

Felix explains, "The witch we went to see can communicate with the dead. She reached out to Shelly's sister once Shelly was able to confront and process her emotions, ultimately leading to her emotional healing."

"They tortured me over and over again," Shelly adds. "It was a grueling process."

"How did they torture you?" Cameron asks, his eyes wide. "Are you going to give us any details or just leave it at that?"

Shelly sighs heavily. "Fine, if you really want to know."

With a wave of my hand, I dismiss the witches, and we gather around Shelly.

"My emotions were off, and I wanted to end you," she says, looking in my direction. "The witch gave me a 'vision potion' to drink, and I found myself in a room with just the two of us. I murdered you in every possible way, over and over again. Time just kept rewinding, and I was trapped in an endless cycle of killing you."

"That sounds terrifying," Cameron says, and we trade anxious looks. "What happened next?"

Shelly nods. "It was beyond frightening, and it felt so real every time. When I finally had enough, I screamed and begged for the witch to stop. Before I could comprehend it, I found myself trapped in a pitch-black room, separated from everything I had previously known. The darkness was so thick that I couldn't see my own hand in front of my face, even with my heightened senses. The silence in the room was deafening, and I could hear my heart pounding in my ears. It was awful."

"That sounds horrific," Cameron says, and everyone shudders at the thought.

Shelly continues, "When the witch brought me back, she let me speak to my sister, and that's when I turned my emotions back on and let all the pain in."

Her fingers intertwine with mine, and I feel her warmth spread through me. Her grip is firm and reassuring.

"Akira, the witch showed me that seeking revenge on you would not bring my sister back, and that's what helped me." She wraps her arms around me in a tight embrace. "I'm so sorry I attacked you. I wasn't myself," she apologizes, and I can see the sincerity in her eyes when she pulls away, tears glistening on her cheeks. "I love you, Akira. I am determined to make things right between us."

Reaching out gently to wipe away her tears, understanding the depth of her remorse. "It's okay, Shelly," I reassure her. "I love you too, and I've missed you so much."

My gaze meets Felix, and I give him a grateful smile for bringing my friend—*my sister* back to me. "Thank you for bringing

Shelly back to me," I say sincerely. "I've been so lost without her."

He grins back at me and pulls me into a hug. "You're welcome, Akira," he says humbly. "I'll give you two some space to catch up," he adds, nudging Cameron and gesturing for him to follow.

"It's great to have you back, Shelly. I have a few stories to tell you about this one," Cameron says, pointing at me with a goofy grin.

Rolling my eyes playfully, I smile at Cameron.

Shelly giggles. "I can't wait to hear all about it, Cam," she says, and the boys exchange a knowing look before leaving us alone to catch up.

Sophia gives both of us hugs and says, "I'm so happy the three of us are finally back together again. It feels like old times."

Shelly nods in agreement and adds, "I missed you both so much! It's been too long since we've all been together like this."

A sense of nostalgia washes over me. "It's great to have our little group reunited," I smile.

"I'm going to join the boys and give you two some time alone to catch up, and later, Shells can give me the details on her and Felix," Sophia jokes, winking at her. "I can't wait to hear all about it!"

Shelly blushes and playfully nudges Sophia. "Oh, stop it, Sophia! But yes, I'll definitely fill you in on the juicy details later."

We all laugh, and then Sophia disappears, leaving Shelly and me alone. We go back to my cabin for a sleepover, curling up on the couch and chatting about everything into the late hours of the night.

A Hybrid's Shattered Heart!

Akira and I haven't spoken in over a month. I miss her so much, but our relationship has suffered too much damage, and I can't look her in the eye anymore. Breaking up with her was one of the hardest decisions I've ever made. Still, I felt the grief and pain of my losses resurface every time I was with her.

Half my kingdom is gone.

A few of them were murdered, while some others ran away without uttering a word of farewell. Being around Akira reminds me of the life I had before, and it's a constant reminder of the void that now exists. Dawn disclosed that Akira isn't taking the breakup well, either. She has mandated everyone to train three days a week, three times a day. I have never trained that intensely before. Felix and Shelly are back from New Orleans, which is great because I need Felix on my side, and Akira needs Shelly now more than ever. I'm glad Shelly is back to her old self; Akira missed her best friend.

I'm resting on the couch, staring up at the ceiling, when Dawn walks into the room on high alert. I glance in her direction, and she fills me in on Akira's latest demand.

"Akira requires your presence at the next training session and council meeting. She says your absence is disrespectful."

Rolling my eyes in her direction.

"Troy!" she shouts, and she places her hands on her hips, "you can't keep avoiding her!"

Sitting up, I spit out, "I don't want to be in the same room as her!"

Dawn crosses her arms, clearly unimpressed with my response. "You can't be serious," she sighs. "You turned your back on our entire kingdom for this girl, and *now* you refuse to be in the same room as her? This is not the time for pride, Troy."

My own brother warned me about the consequences of getting involved with someone from a rival kingdom. Still, I foolishly ignored his advice, and now he's dead because of my selfish actions. I don't blame Dawn for being upset with me, though.

My mother enters the cabin, saving me from Dawn's wrath. "We need to talk, Troy," she says with a stern expression.

Rolling my eyes once more. *Is this an intervention?*

Dawn nods in my mother's direction. "Queen Celine," she greets respectfully and leaves to give us some privacy.

"What is it, Mother?" I ask, already dreading the conversation that is about to unfold.

"Darling, you can't stay cooped up in this cabin forever," she begins gently. "Go outside, get some fresh air, clear your mind, and face the reality of what has happened. It's been over a month now!"

"Mother, I'm perfectly aware of how long it's been. But being outside won't change anything. I'll sit in this cabin until it is time to rage war on Abel."

My mother shakes her head. "While the rest of your kingdom is training and preparing for battle, you're hiding away in here, brooding in solitude. You can't defeat Abel by isolating yourself. You need to train, strategize, and take action." She throws a dagger at my head, and I barely dodge out of the way. "You need to face reality, my child," she says sternly.

Looking down at the dagger on the floor. "I'll brood on my own terms, in my own way. I don't want to talk about this anymore, Mother," I say firmly.

She sighs in defeat and glides towards the door. "Fine," she says. "But hiding away won't bring you any closer to victory." With that, she turns and strides out just as Felix enters.

"Good luck," she says to him in passing.

Nodding my head at Felix. "How's it going with you?"

He shrugs and gives a half-hearted smile. "Same old, same old," he replies. "Shelly and Akira are catching up. I thought I could hang with you for the night."

Nodding, I head to the fridge, tossing him a bottle of water. He catches it and twists the top open, taking a long sip. "Thanks," he says after a few hard swallows.

Procuring a soda for myself, I join Felix on the couch. "Where are you guys staying?"

"We haven't decided yet," he responds, leaning back on the

couch. "I assumed all of us would be staying in the castle on top of Kian Mountains, but what's this I hear about you and Akira breaking up?" He raises his brow. "What gives, dude?"

Shifting uncomfortably in my seat, I avoid his gaze. "Yeah, you heard right." I take a sip of my soda, changing the subject. "Why did you think we would stay in the castle together? The hybrids are isolated from everyone else on the island."

A crease forms between Felix's brows. "I must have misunderstood," he admits. "I thought Akira was meant to unite us under one rule, but it seems like there's a division instead."

Feeling a piercing headache throb behind my eyes. "What are you declaring, Felix?" In an attempt to maintain my composure, I ask.

"I'm not alleging anything," he clarifies. "I'm just stating what I've observed."

Clenching the soda can in my hand. "Before Akira and I broke up, we made the decision to live on Kiju Island."

Felix folds his arms across his chest. "This brings me to my first question. Why did you two break up?"

Letting out an exasperated sigh, I run a hand through my hair. "Bro, that's really none of your business. Our relationship ended for personal reasons that I'd rather not discuss."

First Dawn, then my mother, and now Felix is prying into my personal life. Why won't they just let it go? We're not together anymore, and that's the end of it. Standing from the couch, I head towards the door.

I need to get out of here!

Felix's gaze follows my movements. "Where are you going?"

"I'm going for a run," I reply, opening the door to leave.

"You dodge the question every time someone asks instead of just being honest about it," he calls out; I close the door behind me without responding.

I don't have time for this.

Gray smoke engulfs my body, and I change into my wolf form. Running through the grass, feeling the wind rush past my ears and the sound of my paws hitting the ground, I howl. Kiju Island doesn't have an open expanse of land like the mainland, but this patch of wilderness is enough. Sprinting through the maze of trees and shrubs, I weave in and out of their branches with ease. My senses sharpen, picking up on the subtle scents and sounds, and the familiar earthy aroma is so pure that it's intoxicating.

Like Akira.

Her purity and beauty instantly captivated me. I could spend hours twisting my fingers in her curly black hair and getting lost in the depths of her mesmerizing hazel eyes. And her innocent glow ignited a primal instinct within me that was unmatched by anything I had ever experienced before. A bittersweet ache tugs at my heart. The warmth of her touch, the sound of her laughter, and the way her eyes sparkled when she saw me. My senses heighten, and I howl at the moon once again with a sense of longing and loss.

I still love Akira.

The realization hits me like a tidal wave, and I halt in my tracks. However, I find myself outside Dawn's cabin. *Why am I here?*

Transforming back into a human, I knock on the door.

"Who is it?" Dawn calls from inside.

Coughing nervously, I clear my throat before responding, "It's me, Troy."

The door opens slowly, revealing her surprised expression. "What do you want, Troy?"

She's wearing fairly short shorts and a tank top that accentuates her athletic figure. I've always known that Dawn was beautiful; I never felt an attraction toward her—until *now*.

"Can I come in?"

She hesitates for a moment before stepping aside to let me in. The faint scent of lavender lingers in the air as I walk past her into the kitchen.

Dawn closes the door behind me and walks to the fridge, grabbing a bottle of water. She twists off the cap and takes a long sip, and I can't help but notice the way her lips curve around the bottle's rim. She's breathtaking. *Why didn't I see this before?*

A realization hits me—maybe it's not that I never felt an attraction towards her, but rather that I was blind to it all along. Cornering her against the kitchen counter, our bodies are inches apart.

"Troy, what are you doing?" she asks, her voice barely above a whisper.

"This," I murmur, leaning in and pressing my lips against hers.

The taste of lavender mingles with the sweetness of her lips, and she melts into the kiss before pulling away with her hands resting on my chest and her eyes wide.

"We can't do this," she says in a hushed tone.

I'm a little confused by her reaction. "Why not? Isn't this what you wanted for so long?" I ask, searching for an explanation.

She wipes her lips, her expression conflicted. "Not like this, Troy."

"I don't understand what you mean," I reply. "I thought you wanted us to be together. What's different now?"

Now that I'm finally reciprocating her feelings, she rejects me.

She shakes her head. "Troy, you're in a state of grief right now. Both your father and brother are gone. Your relationship with Akira ended. I don't want to be a rebound when you're not in the right headspace." She huffs out a frustrated breath and drags her feet to the living room, distancing herself from me.

Following her to the living room and closing the distance between us, I pull her into a gentle embrace. "I'm thinking clearly right now. I should have realized sooner that I want to be with you."

Perhaps everything that had happened could have been avoided if I had chosen Dawn instead of Akira. Abel would still be the enemy, but maybe I wouldn't have been so blinded by my own emotions and made better decisions.

"I saw the way Akira looked at you and the way you looked at her," Dawn says. "You're still in love with her, aren't you?"

Tears glisten in her eyes as she waits for my response.

Yes.

Dawn pushes me back and steps away, already knowing the answer. "You have never looked at me the way you looked at Akira," she says. "I won't compete for your heart, knowing that it belongs to someone else, and if I give in to my feelings for you, I'll only end up hurting myself in the long run."

I love Akira and probably always will. Still, she's not the best choice for me or my kingdom. Dawn is the one I want by my side.

Stepping closer to Dawn, I reach out to touch her hand. "Dawn, I love you in a way that's different from how I love Akira."

Her brows furrow as she pushes me back again. "It's not the same love, and I can't just be a relief woman...or some rebound for you."

My feelings for Dawn and Akira are different.

"Dawn, you're not a rebound. You're the right choice for me and the kingdom. If I had chosen you instead of Akira, none of this would have happened," I say, gesturing toward the chaos surrounding us. "My father would still be here—my brother—he—he would—"

Dawn uses her telekinesis power to throw a lamp against the wall, shattering it and cutting me off.

"Troy, pull yourself together. You're spiraling. Do you hear how irrational you sound? I can't be the one to fix your pain. And don't blame Akira for your emotional turmoil. You're not the only one who's hurting here." She inhales and then exhales. "You should leave," she says firmly, pushing me through the door with her gift.

Stumbling backward at the force of her push, I attempt to compose myself. She slams the door shut behind me. Her words are a harsh reality check. I've been letting my pain push everyone away. It's time to pull myself together and find a way out of this emotional turmoil on my own. Perhaps directing my energy somewhere else.

Lucas!

Attack On the Castle!

One month later, we have one hundred and fifty new vampires, and only ten possess formidable gifts. Five of them have elemental powers, and the other five are mind readers. I don't even bother learning their names because I'm so disappointed with the lack of diversity among their abilities. I wanted another vampire with the same gift as Ava!

Punching the wall with such force that it cracks under the impact, the arrowhead Tyler had given me falls from the shelf above. When I pick it up, it emits a luminescent glow so fluorescent that it brightens the entire room. *What is this?* Inspecting it, I noticed the distinguishing features and markings on its surface. It feels warm to the touch, pulsating with an energy that I can't quite comprehend before it diminishes back to its original state. I've witnessed nothing like this before.

Chase barges into my chambers. His lips are pressed together in a thin line, and his eyes are wide with urgency.

Clasping the arrowhead tight in my hand, I shove it into my pocket.

"Spit it out," I demand.

Chase blurts out, "It's Richard."

Without waiting for any further explanation, I follow him to the dungeon at the speed of light.

Richard is on the cold stone floor, beaten to a bloody pulp and barely conscious.

"What happened to him?" I ask.

Chase, Nico, Joel, and Tyler trade nervous looks before Nico finally speaks up: "Sir, he continues to resist the transition."

"We tried everything," Joel adds.

"The venom will not turn him," Tyler states. "He has to be a Seeker."

A wide grin spreads across his bloody lips when our gaze meets.

Grabbing him by the collar and pulling him up to a sitting position. "What's so funny?"

He points to my pocket at the arrowhead that's shining brighter than before.

Tyler's eyes narrow, and he asks, "What's in your pocket?"

Pushing Richard back down onto the ground, I reach into my pocket, taking out the arrowhead. It glows with an otherworldly light pulsating in my hand, and the ring on Richard's finger glows in response.

"Finally," Richard says through his bloody lips before passing out.

We all exchange confused glances, unsure of what just happened.

BOOM!

A deafening explosion echoes through the castle walls, shaking the ground beneath us. The force of it knocks us off balance, sending us sprawling in different directions. Smoke fills the air, blurring our vision as we scramble to regain our footing out of the dungeon. Before we reach the elevator, it explodes, throwing us back against the wall. Pieces of debris rain down on us as multiple bombs explode.

We find ourselves stranded at the lower level of the castle.

"What do we do now?" Tyler panics.

Assessing our options, I realize the only chance of escape is the arena on the lower level. There's a hidden staircase that leads directly to the main level of the castle that no one knows about, not even Akira. We ascend the stairs, uncertain of what awaits us.

The windows are shattered, and there's glass thrown across the floor; it crunches beneath our feet as we walk. A fire smolders in the corner, leaving a trail of charred smoke. The air is heavy with the horrific stench of burned flesh and wood. The scattered debris makes it hard to distinguish what used to be what.

"Who did this?" I growl through clenched teeth, surveying the wreckage.

Chase and Tyler look at each other and the chaos before us. "The Seekers," they respond simultaneously.

The room feels eerily silent—too quiet.

"Take cover!" I command.

A smoke bomb rolls across the floor, releasing a thick cloud that obscures our vision. The sound of footsteps echoes into the room, growing louder and closer, and I strain my eyes to see through the haze. A group of masked figures emerge from the smoke, with crossbows drawn and aimed at my army of soldiers and the witches.

"Keep the witches safe!" I order my soldiers, and they form a protective barrier around the witches that are linked to me.

"We're under attack!" Timothy shouts to his pack, rallying them to form a defensive line, and they change into their wolf forms, their eyes glowing menacingly at the enemies.

Timothy is a formidable fighter with razor-sharp teeth and claws that can easily tear through flesh. However, this doesn't discourage them because they're equipped. The Seekers surround us with poison-infused swords, shields, and crossbows laced with UV light and human blood.

"Attack!" I shout.

As the masked figures move forward, they shoot their arrows at us with deadly precision. In the air, the arrows dash, barely avoiding some of my soldiers and hitting others. The masked figures hit Cole and Paul—they fall to the ground and burst into flames. They will resurrect in ten minutes. Amir shapeshifts into a Magpie bird and flees. The other shapeshifters follow suit and evacuate the premises, avoiding the attack.

When I eradicated the manticores, I should have gotten rid of the shapeshifters as well.

Cowards!

Seething in disgust, I join the front lines to face the ambush. Deflecting the incoming arrows, without thinking, I catch one mid-air with my bare hand—it's laced with poison to end my very existence. Hurling it back toward the enemy, it strikes one of their archers in the chest; shaking my hand vigorously, I attempt to ease the searing pain. The mark is like a million tiny needles pricking at my skin.

Timothy lunges at one human with a primal roar, his jaw snapping shut mere inches away from the human's face. Still, the human takes advantage of his proximity and jams an arrowhead into his neck. Blood spurts from his wound.

The man beside him shouts, "He's a werewolf! The arrowhead won't work," which allows Timothy a momentary reprieve.

With a swift movement, he deflects the knife launched into his chest by the human circling him. Snarling, he circles the human, searching for an opening to end him. The human draws his sword and lunges forward, aiming for Timothy's heart. He dodges the attack with lightning-fast reflexes and counters with a powerful swipe of his sharp claws. The clash of steel against fur persists, neither of them yielding an inch, until Timothy leaps onto the human, gripping his head with his powerful jaws and detaching it from his body in one swift motion. His head rolls to my feet, and I smash it under my boot.

Rejoining my soldiers, I break necks and rip limbs off with ease. Catching another arrow with my hand and unbothered by the pain, I fire it back at the archer's throat. We attack, but the humans fight back with equal force. Amidst the clash of thick metal against claws, sparks and screeches fill the air, and arrows soar through the sky. The battle continues to rage on, and both humans and creatures litter the ground with their fallen bodies. The atmosphere is thick with the sour stench of blood and sweat, and neither side shows any signs of backing down.

Stones crumble, and the walls crack as the castle's defenses weaken under the relentless assault. Supernatural creatures and humans continue to clash in mayhem.

How dare they invade my kingdom, my home!

I signal the head witch to the painting of Aika hanging crooked on what's left of the wall that leads to the cave. He casts a spell, cloaking the entrance from the intruders, and we retreat to the cave, taking cover. Aika stands beside me, willing to do whatever it takes.

A man shouts above the chaos, rallying the humans to regroup. "I know you can hear me, Abel! My name is Ethan, and I'm the leader of The Seekers. We have warned you once before, and you dismissed our warning. Now we have invaded your kingdom and will stop at nothing to end all of you *monstrosities!*"

A silence stretches for a couple of seconds before he continues. "Your reign of terror ends today. Fire!"

Rounds of shots, which I assume to be balls of sunlight, impact the cave, weakening the force field.

"Protect the witches!" I demand, and the remaining soldiers form a defensive circle around the witches, shielding them from the onslaught. With each shot, the force field weakens further.

A tense stillness hangs in the air as the firing ceases. We listen and wait for any sign of movement from the enemy. Twenty minutes pass in silence before I command the guards to check the perimeter for any signs of retreat or a potential ambush.

Three of my guards cautiously venture out of the cave entrance to survey the area for any remaining threats. They return moments later.

"They're gone," one guard reports.

A collective sigh of relief sweeps through the cave, and the soldiers and witches slowly break away from their defensive formation.

"Chase, inform Lucas of what happened," I demand.

Addressing the witches linked to me. "Can you portal to Lucas's location?"

The blue-eyed witch shakes his head. "No. We've exhausted our efforts in locating the island. The protection spell used around the island is unheard of."

"What does this mean for us? We can't retrieve Lucas or kidnap Akira?" I groan.

The head witch's brows snap together. "It means we have limited options. Without being able to locate the island or bypass its protection spell, returning Lucas or kidnapping Akira seems nearly impossible. We need some time to work on a spell, and even if we're able to create a portal to the island, it won't stay open for long."

"That's fine. We only need Lucas and Akira. The Revolt will come to us."

"Do everything in your power to make it happen," Aika demands.

"We'll do whatever it takes," he reassures before exiting the cave.

Aika squeezes my tense shoulders. "War is here!"

War is no longer on the horizon—it has begun!

Double-Crossed!

I'm meeting Akira at The Revolt Headquarters in about twenty minutes for a training session, giving me enough time to string fairy lights all over the cabin for a date I have planned for us after. Then, I'll follow the king's direct orders and deliver her back to the kingdom. Chase informed me that The Seekers attacked the castle, and we are at war with them and the abominations. The witches are working on a spell to portal here to retrieve us. Still, there's a barrier spell protecting the island that's taking them longer than expected to bypass, so I'm waiting until I receive word from Chase.

Now that Akira has come to her senses and ended her dreadful relationship with the hybrid, she's available to explore the possibility of us being together. I'm hopeful the king will approve of our relationship and allow us to be a couple after the war is over so our love can finally flourish.

The date I planned comprises us soaking in the hot tub, relishing a quiet evening, watching a romantic comedy, and ending the night talking and enjoying each other's company. I know where I went wrong on our first date, and I'm determined to make this second chance count! I'll never understand why Akira prefers animal blood over human, but I'll respect her choice this time. Besides, there are no humans on this island that I could drink dry unless I go for one witch, so I guess that makes it a little easier to accept her preference.

I'm not allowed to travel off the island, so the shapeshifter, who doesn't hate me, helped retrieve vanilla-scented candles and wine glasses for our romantic evening.

I arrange the fairy lights around the wooden beams and fireplace. Along the windows, I carefully place the scented candles. In the living room, I scatter a few of the rose petals and some around the hot tub as well. I search the closet for a cozy throw, specifically a brown one, because it's Akira's favorite color. *I want to impress her this time.* Stepping back to admire my work, I am satisfied. Hopefully, she appreciates it.

My phone buzzes with a text message from Akira, interrupting my thoughts. She asks where I am. Glancing at my watch, I'm about five minutes late; I shoot her a text informing her I'm on my way.

Disappearing like a blur out the door, I arrive at headquarters, and a few shapeshifters and Akira greet me.

"Hey, Lucas," Akira says with a smile.

"Hey, Akira," I reply, hugging her tight, inhaling her vanilla-scented perfume.

As we pull away, she says, "Want to go for a run instead of

training today? I could use some fresh air."

Anything for you, my love! My inner thoughts shout.

"Sure, a run sounds great."

The breeze brushes against our faces, and the sunlight warms our skin as we sprint through the forest. Consuming human blood is superior. Still, animal blood comes with its perks. I can bask in the sun's rays just like when I was a human, without worrying about getting burned. It's a small reminder of the life I used to have before becoming a vampire.

"Race you to my cabin!" I challenge her playfully, knowing that she loves a good competition.

She grins mischievously and takes off, her squeals echoing through the trees. Chasing after her and relishing the sound of her laughter, we race through the dense forest, our feet pounding against the soft earth. The wind rushes past us, whipping through our hair as we push ourselves to go faster. Akira beats me to the cabin, her eyes radiant with pleasure as her lips twitch upward into a victorious curve. Lifting her off her feet in a playful embrace, I spin her around. She giggles and holds my shoulders for support. As we finally come to a stop, I gently set her back down, and we sit on the cabin porch, catching our breath. The warmth of the sun filters through the trees above us, casting a golden glow on our flushed faces. Admiring the specs of gold and green in her hazel eyes, I notice her rosy cheeks glowing with exhilaration from the race. Her lips curve into a sweet smile as she gazes at the sun setting behind the mountains, painting the sky in an array of warm hues. A loose curl sways gently in the breeze, and she tucks it behind her ear. Her pureness brings freshness and light to my world.

"Lucas?" She calls out my name softly when she catches my gaze lingering on her.

Coughing, I clear my throat before responding, feeling slightly embarrassed. "Uh, yes?"

"Why are you staring at me?" she asks.

"I'm not staring; I'm admiring the sunset, and you just happened to be in my view," I lie with a sheepish smile and pat myself on the back. *Nice save!*

She laughs.

Her laughter is like music to my ears. "Oh. The sunset is beautiful, isn't it?" she says, her eyes fixed on the horizon until the sun dips below it. The quietness stretches between us. "Thank you for joining me for a run," she adds, breaking the silence. "I'm going to head back to my cabin now."

She stands to leave, and I stop her with a gentle touch on her arm. "Wait," I say, "Would you like to come inside?"

A crease forms between her eyebrows. "For what?"

"To hang out," I reply smoothly.

She screws up her face at my invitation and tilts her head to the side.

"Come on, Akira. When was the last time we hung out?"

"Today. We just went for a run together," she reminds me.

Pausing for a moment and realizing my mistake. "I mean, hang out without training," I clarify. "Do you have any plans for the rest of the evening?"

She scratches her shoulder and looks away. "No, not really..."

she trails off.

Hoping to convince her, I smirk. "So come inside."

Opening the door, I gesture for her to follow.

Her eyes dart between me and the door. After a brief pause, she finally nods and follows me inside. Before we step into the living room, I tell her to wait and quickly light all the scented candles in a flash.

Her brows snap together in confusion when she walks in. "What's all this?"

"Just a little surprise I prepared for you," I reply, trying to sound nonchalant. "Our first date didn't go well, so I thought I would make it up to you with a do-over."

"Lucas—"

Cutting her off, I place a finger on her lips. "Just give it a chance," I say. "Don't think of it as a date. Think of it as hanging with a friend."

Akira sighs and looks around at the candlelit room. She picks up one of the scented candles and sniffs it, a hint of a smile playing on her lips. "You remembered my favorite scent," she says, "Alright, Lucas, I'll give it a chance."

Grinning, I reach out to take her hand. "Would you like to join me in the hot tub?"

"I don't know about that, Lucas," she hesitates. "I don't have a swimsuit."

"When has that ever stopped you before?" I tease.

She chuckles and playfully nudges me, her eyes sparkling as she contemplates my offer. Akira never misses a chance to be in the water.

"Alright, let's go for it," she finally agrees.

Leading her to the backyard, where the hot tub is bubbling. My heart races with anticipation. Akira carefully gazes at the fairy lights strung up around the perimeter, casting a soft, enchanting glow.

After removing her sweatshirt and yoga pants, she is left standing in her black sports bra and shorts. "I guess this will have to do," she says, stepping into the warm water with a contented sigh.

Her beauty amplifies under the ethereal lighting. *She's so beautiful!*

"Lucas?" she says, snapping me out of my trance.

Shaking away my thoughts, I respond, "Yes, Akira?"

"Are you getting in the water or just going to stand there all night?" she asks with a playful smirk.

Removing my shirt, I grin, revealing my toned physique. Akira gives me an appreciative glance before looking away bashfully.

Grabbing two wine glasses, I pour animal blood into them, handing one to Akira. She pauses and gazes at the glass while quirking a brow.

"It's animal blood," I assure her, and Akira beams while I join her in the steaming water.

She takes a sip of the blood and lets out a satisfied sigh. "I appreciate our evolving friendship." She smiles at me.

The term "friendship" brings a stinging sensation to my heart. I don't want to be her friend. I want to be more than just friends.

Pushing away those thoughts, I reply with a slight grin, "I

appreciate you too, Akira. I always have." Taking a sip from my glass, the thick liquid coats my tongue with a metallic tang, just like a human, except it lacks the sweet nectar that I crave.

"Thank you, Lucas," Akira continues, meeting my gaze.

"For what?" I ask, raising an eyebrow.

"For being a great friend," she says sincerely. "You've helped me this last month in more ways than you know."

A pang of disappointment forms in my chest. I had hoped for a different response, one that hinted at the possibility of something more. But I quickly mask my true feelings and force a smile, grateful for her friendship.

"Forgive me for being blunt, but what happened to you and the hybrid?" I ask.

Akira's smile fades as she looks down at her glass. "I don't really want to talk about it."

Respecting her boundaries, I nod and don't push it further. "I apologize for my intrusion."

"It's okay." Akira gives me a weak smile. "Do you want to watch a movie or something after?"

Grinning from ear to ear. "I already picked out a romantic comedy for us to watch."

She laughs. "What do you know about romantic comedies?"

"Nothing really, but I searched online to see what's good, and this one has great reviews."

Her smile widens, and she nods. "Thank you, that sounds nice."

Finishing our glasses, we dry off with towels before settling down on the couch to enjoy the romantic comedy I chose.

As the movie begins, Akira leans in and teases, "I never

thought you would voluntarily choose this to watch."

"Well, I'm willing to try new things for you."

She giggles and playfully throws some of the rose petals at me. "I appreciate that."

As the movie progresses, I steal glances at her. With every romantic scene, her smile becomes wider. Her brows furrow slightly during the dramatic moments. Her eyes twinkle with laughter during the comedic parts. The next thing I know, I reach out and cradle her chin, turning her face towards mine.

She exhales as I inhale. "What are you doing, Lucas?"

"Whatever you want to do, Akira."

I initiated our last kiss. This time, she has to. It's her turn to take the lead and show me she wants it just as much as I do. Leaning in closer, I wait for her response, hoping that she'll make the next move, and to my surprise, she leans in and presses her lips against mine.

Her lips caress mine with a gentle tenderness I have longed for. The kiss deepens as our mouths move in sync, and we savor every moment of this intimate exchange. Our lips part, and we are left breathless, yet she looks away as if she's disappointed with herself or, worse—*me*.

Making sure she meets my gaze, I gently cup her face. "What did I do wrong?"

"You did nothing wrong," she sighs.

Rubbing my thumb against her cheek. "Then why do you look so upset?"

Her cheeks flush with a tinge of pink, and she hesitates before speaking. "I care about you a lot," she says, "but I don't think we're meant to be more than friends."

The vulnerability in her eyes tells me she will *never* reciprocate my feelings.

"I'm sorry I kissed you without thinking it through. It was not my intention to give you the wrong impression. I got caught up in all this," she gestures at the romantic setting surrounding us.

All I want is to be with her. Why doesn't she want to be with me?

"I wasn't right for you before! Why am I still not right for you now?" I ask, desperation in my voice.

"I'm in love with someone else," she confesses, covering her mouth with her hand.

Her eyes widen with a mix of guilt and sadness, and she disappears in a flash before I can even respond.

Her confession hits me like a punch to the gut. It is as if Akira removed my heart from my body and crushed it into a million pieces right before my eyes. Why does she always choose the hybrid over me? They aren't together, and yet he still holds her heart.

Perhaps her infatuation with him would diminish if he were dead.

My phone buzzes with a text notification from Chase.

The witches are almost ready. Is everything good on your end?

Great. How will I get Akira through a portal after what just happened?

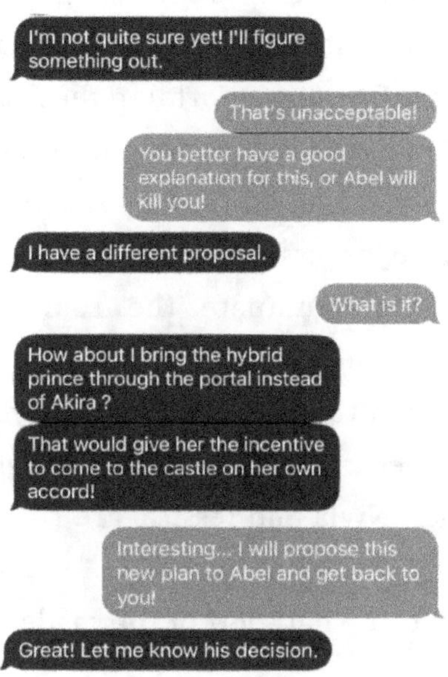

Now, I have to come up with a plan to get the hybrid through the portal. The witches on the island implanted a tracker on me so they're alerted when the hybrid and I are in proximity to each other. Still, a solution falls into my lap when I open my cabin door and find the hybrid prince waiting for me outside.

"What a pleasant surprise," I beam with glee.

Troy doesn't look as thrilled as I am, his expression remaining aloof. He narrows his brows and clenches his fists at his sides. He punches me in the nose, and I stumble backward. Blood gushes from my nostrils as pain shoots through my face, but I keep my composure.

"What's your problem?" I wipe the blood from my nose with

the back of my hand.

"You're my problem," he says through gritted teeth.

My phone buzzes with a message from Chase. As we speak, he and the witches are forming a portal to the island.

"Well, well. Thank you for making this easy," I say with a smug grin.

Confusion flashes across his face as he comprehends my words. Bright white lights illuminate the room, and he turns his attention to the portal from which Chase emerges.

Balling my hand into a fist, I punch the hybrid in the face, and Chase snaps his neck. We drag him through the portal, and I notice the witches, Niyla and Jessica, are running toward us as it closes.

When we arrive at what's left of the castle, guards immediately imprison him in a cell.

King Abel approaches me. "Well done, Lucas!" he commends.

A victorious grin spreads across my face at King Abel's praise. "You're welcome, Sir."

Victory will be mine. *Soon.*

The Seekers!

My mind is still trying to process the intimate moment between Lucas and me. It was completely unexpected, and he did a three-sixty, and I got caught up in the romantic scene. He's no longer loyal to the throne, and I never thought he would be the one to break that loyalty. He planned a thoughtful date for us, taking me by surprise. Although he said it wasn't a date, it definitely felt like one.

The rose petals scattered around, the wine glasses of *animal* blood, the hot tub bubbling, the twinkling fairy lights, my favorite scented candles, and let's not forget the brown throw on the couch.

The kiss was incredible, and his efforts were hard to ignore. Still, I feel a sense of guilt for enjoying the moment, knowing that I'm still in love with Troy. I can't let go of what we had—although he has.

"Akira! Akira!" Shelly shouts, interrupting my conflicted thoughts.

What is she doing here?

Wrapping my robe around me, I race down the stairs. "What's wrong?" I ask.

Dawn, Felix, Cameron, and Sophia dash in behind her without warning. Sweat is trickling down from their foreheads as their voices blend, shouting over one another. I find it difficult to understand what is going on.

With a wave of my hand, I silence them. "One at a time, please," I say. "What's going on?"

"Lucas kidnapped Troy!" Sophia shouts.

Huh? I blink rapidly. "I was just with Lucas not too long ago. How could he have kidnapped Troy?"

Troy's name strikes a chord within me, flooding my mind with questions as I try to make sense of the situation.

Jessica and Niyla enter the cabin, eyes wide and out of breath. "Lucas kidnapped Troy," they say in unison.

Niyla hands me a gold compass and says, "This is what we used to track Lucas, Troy, Kaden, and your father."

Retrieving the compass from her outstretched hand, I examine it.

"It glows when either of them is in close proximity to Lucas." Niyla continues.

"The glow was so bright!" Jessica says.

Niyla adds, "We knew something was wrong."

Feeling a knot tighten in my throat, I already know where Lucas took Troy.

The castle.

In a flash, I'm upstairs and back down, dressed and ready to go. Dad enters my cabin, placing his hands on my shoulders and stopping me in my tracks.

"This is what Abel wants. It's a trap, Akira, and he's counting on your emotions to cloud your judgment," he warns.

When I attempt to push him aside, his grip tightens.

"I understand your urgency, sweetheart, but you must approach this situation cautiously."

"I have to save Troy!" I scream, tears forming in my eyes.

My father's eyes soften, and he releases his grip. "I know you want to save him, and Abel is fully aware of that as well."

"Listen to your father! Sis." Cameron adds, stepping forward. "Rushing in blindly could put you and Troy in even more danger." Cameron continues.

"I know you're both right," I admit, feeling a wave of guilt wash over me. "I can't stand by and do nothing while Troy is in trouble." My voice cracks, and I sink to the floor.

How didn't I see that this was all part of the plan? I should have trusted Troy's instincts and questioned Lucas's motives from the beginning. If only I had listened to the warnings, Troy would still be safe.

Collecting my thoughts, I stand up with a newfound resolve. It's time to take action and make things right.

"Get some rest. War has begun." I address the group.

They nod in agreement and are ready to fight alongside me.

"I'm going to grab some of my things and head back over," Shelly says.

The room clears as everyone prepares for the impending battle, leaving my father and me alone.

"I'm going to sleep on the couch if that's okay with you," he says. "I want to be close by in case anything happens."

"Thank you," I reply.

His brows snap together. "Jace and I spoke with Ethan, the leader of The Seekers."

Raising an eyebrow. "And? What did he say?"

"Ethan informed us they attacked the castle and have weakened Abel and his army. He's willing to meet and hear us out. We'll portal to the real world to meet with them tomorrow."

"They did? What about forming an alliance?"

"Sweetheart, one step at a time," Dad cautions. "Let's focus on meeting with Ethan first and see where it goes from there."

I'm tired of waiting. Anger bubbles up inside of me as I grab a chair, ready to throw it across the room, but my father takes it from my grasp and sets it back in its place. I'm supposed to be a queen, but instead, I am acting like a child.

He pulls me into an embrace. "We're going to find Troy and bring him home, I promise. And we *will* defeat Abel."

"How can you be so sure? What if we can't find Troy or defeat Abel?"

He gently strokes my back. "We have a plan and will do everything in our power to make it happen. We won't give up until we've exhausted every possibility."

Wiping away the stream of tears falling down my cheeks. "Okay."

Lucas will regret ever crossing me!

The next day, the residents of the entire island gather in the auditorium, except for the witches. My people look to me for guidance and reassurance, and it's my duty to provide them with both. Queen Celine is distraught and visibly shaken. Her husband and son are deceased, and now she must face the daunting fear of whether Troy is alive or dead. Felix and Dawn are by her side, attempting to comfort her. I stride to the head of the room to make an announcement. The room falls silent as all eyes turn towards me, awaiting my words.

"The time has come for us to avenge our losses! This war is not without risks. We've trained for every possible scenario, and now it's time to put our training to the ultimate test. The council and I are heading to the real world to meet with a group known as The Seekers. We're going to ask them to form an alliance with us and aid in the takedown of the vampire kingdom once and for all. If they disagree, we still need to be prepared to fight on our own to defeat Abel and his vampire army and safely return Troy home."

My voice cracks at the last sentence, but I swallow hard and continue, my voice echoing throughout the room.

"All of those who are expected to fight, please say your goodbyes to your loved ones and report to the dome for equipment distribution. Wait for my word for final instructions."

"How are you certain that The Seekers will agree to an alliance?" one of the soldiers asks.

"We received word that they orchestrated an attack on the vampire kingdom, and now is the time to strike. We and The Seekers share a common enemy. However, we must remain cautious and prepared for any outcome, as we cannot predict their ultimate decision."

Pausing for a moment, I meet each soldier's gaze. "Remember, we have trained for this moment. Trust in your abilities and trust in each other."

The soldiers nod in agreement. As they disperse, I gather with the council members to prepare for our next course of action.

Queen Celine approaches me, her eyebrows pulled together in a worried expression. "Please save my son," she pleads. "I cannot bear the thought of losing anyone else."

Wrapping my arms around her tight. "I promise you, Queen Celine, I'll do everything in my power to bring Troy back safely."

Queen Celine's eyes well up with tears as she nods and exits the room, leaving me with the council members.

"What's our next move?" Cameron asks.

"We're going to Florida to meet with The Seekers," my father replies.

"Why Florida?" Cameron's brow wrinkles in confusion.

"Because that's where I suggested we meet," Monica says, entering the auditorium with her family's spell book.

The rest of the witches follow behind her.

"Are we ready to go?" I ask, scanning the council members' facial expressions.

"Almost," Niyla responds, flipping through her spell book.

She nods to the witches, and they join hands, chanting in unison.

"What's happening?" I whisper to my father.

"They're tapping into the magic of their ancestors to perform a protection spell on us since The Seekers hate all supernatural beings."

My eyes buck out, "Including Rosa?"

"Yes, including Rosa," He grins.

Rosa is still helping us, even from beyond the grave.

When the chanting stops, their eyes turn red, and they ascend as a collective, their bodies shaking. A fiery aura surrounds the council and me, and a sharp pain shoots up and down my veins and penetrates my body like a wave of electricity.

The witches slowly descend back to the ground, their eyes returning to their normal color.

"It's done," Monica says, closing the spell book.

Jessica and Niyla form a portal, and we walk through it. Monica and the rest of the witches stay behind.

On the other side of the portal, we find ourselves in front of an exquisite house guarded by two rather large men wearing stern expressions.

"Which one of you is Akira?" The large dark-haired man asks.

"I am," I respond firmly, stepping forward.

The dark-haired man studies me intently, his gaze piercing through me as if trying to unravel my true nature. His companion, a towering figure with a shaved head, remains silent but watches me with equally intense scrutiny.

"Ethan is ready for you," the dark-haired man says, his voice deep and commanding. "Follow me."

The council and I walk forward, but he gestures his hand in front of us. "Alone."

"Ethan will not see my daughter alone! I'll accompany her." My dad asserts.

The dark-haired man's eyes narrow and then he nods in agreement. "Very well," he concedes, leading us through the entrance and down a long hallway lined with portraits of slain mythical creatures.

We enter a grand chamber filled with high-backed chairs and a large round table. The room is dark and has an eerie feeling to it. Adorning the walls are abstract paintings and framed quotes.

> *"RID THE WORLD OF SUPERNATURALS!"*

> *"HUMANS ONLY!"*

> *"ONE WHO SEARCHES FOR THE UNKNOWN WILL FIND IT!"*

The last quote is cryptic, which sends chills down my spine.

"Hello, my name is Ethan," a tall, green-eyed man enters the room to greet us. He's extremely handsome, his light brown-skinned complemented by the beige shirt he is wearing. He looks around thirty years old. With a low-cut haircut and a scar on his left eyebrow, he has a distinct appearance. Extending a hand for a handshake, I notice the sizeable, lightning-bolt scar on his arm.

"Hello, I'm Akira, and this is my father, Jacobson," I respond, taking Ethan's hand in mine, his grip firm and confident.

Shaking my father's hand next, he leads us to the table and gestures for us to take a seat as he sits at the head.

We sit down and start discussing diplomacy.

"Ethan," I begin, "we would like to discuss a possible alliance between our two realms. We share a common enemy in Abel."

Ethan nods attentively, his green eyes focused on me. "Yes, I believe that an alliance could be mutually beneficial for both of our realms. But make no mistake, I *detest* your kind. *All* of you."

He looks between me and my father, his gaze filled with disdain.

"However, I *despise* Abel more." His words convey an intense animosity. "He's been kidnapping humans for centuries, and my brother was one of his victims. He must be stopped at all costs, and if that means working with your kind, then so be it."

Clearing my throat. "Who—who is your brother?"

He breaks his gaze and looks away, his voice filled with sorrow and anger. "His name is—*was* Richard."

My heart sinks to the pit of my stomach, and I nearly vomit from his revelation.

"You know him?" He studies my reaction carefully.

Nodding, I struggle to find my voice. "Yes."

"Or rather, you *knew* him because he's dead," Ethan says coldly, his words cutting through the air like a knife.

"I'm so sorry for your loss," I reply, looking him straight in the eyes to convey my genuine sympathy.

Ethan acknowledges my condolences with a slight nod. "Thank you."

"Forgive me for overstepping, but how did you locate Abel's kingdom?" I ask cautiously, trying to gather more information without prying too much.

The Seekers were able to break through the protective barrier of the vampire kingdom undetected. Can they also get through the island's borders?

Before Ethan can reply, my father says, "Rosa is dead, so the realm is no longer protected by her magic. There's still a barrier in place, but it's weakened without her presence, so anyone can breach it if they have the right knowledge and resources."

"Precisely," Ethan confirms, pulling an arrowhead from his pocket.

"You see this? It's enchanted by our ancestors, and we were able to locate my brother because one of the vampires had possession of it. And you see this ring?" He points to the black ring on his index finger.

"The ring is used as a tracker when it is in proximity to one of these arrowheads. They played right into our plan and led us straight to their castle. We have been watching them since the attack in California. We've weakened them, so now is the time to attack before they recover." He says, slamming his fist down on the table.

"We should strike tomorrow while the iron is still hot," my father suggests.

"I want to attack *now*," I protest, and my father narrows his eyes at me.

Ethan chuckles and says, "Eager, aren't you? What did he do to you?"

 Folding my arms across my chest. "I don't want to discuss it."

Ethan raises a brow at my response but doesn't press further. Instead, he turns to my father. "Regardless of when we strike, we need a solid plan in place. We can't afford any mistakes."

My father nods in agreement, and I sigh. His expression grows serious, and he warns, "We must not act hastily, Akira. We need another day to prepare our forces for war."

Rolling my eyes, I let out another exasperated sigh. "Another day, and Troy could be dead before we even save him—he could be dead right now, for all we know! We can't afford to waste any more time."

Ethan excuses himself. "I'll allow you two a moment."

When Ethan and his men leave the room, my father's expression softens. He places a hand on my shoulder. "Saving Troy is important to all of us. However, do you remember what's at stake if we rush into this without proper preparation? We could risk losing not only Troy but also the lives of our own soldiers."

Taking a deep breath, I meet my father's gaze. "If we don't act now, we may not have another chance."

My father's eyes narrow. "Akira, you're the queen, and I respect your decisions. Still, we must have a solid plan in place with The Seekers before taking any action."

Knowing that my father is right, I sigh.

"Keep in mind I'm over one hundred years old and have fought in countless battles, so I know a thing or two about war." He continues with a small smile.

"Very well."

My father pauses for a moment, his gaze fixed on me. "Remember, Akira, that power comes with responsibility. It's not just about making decisions, but also about understanding the consequences they may bring."

Realizing the weight of my role as queen and the importance of seeking wisdom from those with experience, I nod in acknowledgment,

My father walks to the door to notify Ethan to rejoin us. "We're ready to discuss a plan," he says.

Ethan and his men appear, and he takes a seat. "How do you want to proceed?"

Pausing for a moment to gather my thoughts. "My kingdom will attack first, and yours will finish them. Our alliance is a calculated move that will catch them off guard and give us the upper hand," I reply.

Ethan agrees with a nod of his head.

"How do we know you won't turn against us and attack our forces?" My father asks, his tone cautious.

Ethan's gaze darkens. "How do I know you won't do the same to us?"

"My kingdom resides in another realm. None of us consumes human blood or poses a threat to your kind. Our only goal is to protect our home and ensure our safety." I reply firmly.

"We live in harmony and strive to maintain balance in our world," my father adds.

Ethan steps forward and extends his hand in a gesture of trust. "Then you have my word that my people will not harm yours, either. We will send a signal when your soldiers should retreat, as our weapons are intended to annihilate your kind."

My father shakes Ethan's hand, and I nod in agreement.

We have formed our alliance. War is here!

War Is on the Horizon!

War - [wawr] noun state or period
of armed hostility or active military operations:

The hybrid prince is awake. Restricted by chains that bind him to the cold, stone walls of his prison cell, he struggles against his restraints, but the chains only dig deeper into his flesh. A smirk forms on my lips as I watch his futile attempts to break free. I will keep him alive long enough until Akira rushes right into my hands to save him. Little does he know that his capture is all part of my plan to lure Akira into a trap. For the first time in decades, I'm proud of that incessant pest. He did well.

Amir and the remaining shapeshifters never returned after they fled the attack on the castle; they are now traitors to the throne. Forty vampires were casualties of the attack by The Seekers. Fortunately, none possessed a formidable gift.

Chase enters the dungeon and narrows his eyes at the hybrid.

"What would you like us to do with *it*?" His voice is stern as he addresses the abomination.

"We keep it confined and under constant surveillance," I respond, my tone matching Chase's. "Where's Lucas? I'm sure he would want to have his way with this *thing*."

"I'll fetch him now," Chase replies, exiting the dungeon and leaving me alone with the hybrid.

Leaning into the cell bars. "Well, well, well. So, you're the infamous hybrid prince."

The hybrid glares back at me with defiance. Spitting at me, his saliva lands on my face, and I chuckle at his feeble attempt to intimidate me.

"You'll have to do better than that, prince," I taunt, wiping the spit off my cheek with a smirk.

The hybrid's eyes narrow as he clenches his fists. "You may find amusement in this now, but mark my words, Akira will defeat you, and your reign of terror will come to an end," he growls.

Shaking my head and opening the cell gate, I laugh. The hybrid attempts to stand, but his ankles are restrained. Raising an eyebrow, I observe his struggle.

"You really think your precious Akira stands a chance against me?" I scoff.

Lucas enters the dungeon and witnesses our exchange. He clears his throat. "Sir, you asked for me?"

"Ah, Lucas," I reply, a sinister smile spreading across my face. "I think it's only fitting that you deal with the abomination as you see fit."

A wide grin forms on Lucas' face as he steps forward, cracking his knuckles. "Consider it done, Sir," he says, his voice dripping with sadistic delight. "Hold him up!" He commands the guards.

The guards immediately hoist the hybrid up, suspending his arms above his head on the iron bars of the ceiling.

"Do your worst," the hybrid challenges.

A guard shoves a towel into his mouth to silence him while another tightens the restraints around his wrists. Lucas strikes him with brutal force, his fist connecting with the hybrid's jaw. The abomination's head snaps to the side, blood trickling from his split lip, and Lucas strikes again and again, relishing the sickening sound of bone crunching under his blows. The hybrid's body goes limp as Lucas continues to pummel him.

Marvelous! A wave of satisfaction washes over me.

"This is for Akira," Lucas growls, unleashing another strike. "And this is for my kingdom," he adds, delivering a final blow before stepping back, panting heavily.

"Well done, Lucas," I say, a twisted smile forming on my lips. Clenching my fists, I step forward to inspect the beaten creature. Blood gushes from his broken nose, and his body is battered and bruised. Adding my own fury of punches until the hybrid is unrecognizable and knocked unconscious, my eyes flicker with glee.

Grabbing a cloth to wipe the blood from my hands. "Give him human blood so he can heal," I command, tossing the cloth aside. "We'll resume once he regains consciousness."

Two of the guards move to follow my orders, returning with a bag of blood and a syringe, carefully injecting him with it.

"Sir, our blood supply is running low," one guard says. "We may need to kidnap more humans to replenish our stock."

Screwing up my face. "Very well," I respond. "We'll only heal the abomination once more after this."

The hybrid's body is already showing signs of improvement from the blood infusion.

"How long will it be until Akira comes to rescue him?" Chase asks.

"Lucas?" I turn to him and raise an eyebrow. "What's the status of Akira's arrival?"

"She'll be here soon," he assures us.

Nodding, I shift my gaze back to the hybrid. I wait for him to fully heal, and then I snap his fingers one by one, yet there is no reaction. He doesn't even move a muscle; he remains still.

"Give me the room!" I command. Everyone exits the cell, leaving me and the abomination alone. Pacing back and forth, he watches me with empty eyes.

"You're a strong little bastard, aren't you?" I mutter under my breath, trying to provoke a reaction.

Still, he remains stoic, refusing to give me satisfaction. *This vermin is mocking me!* Rage bubbles to the surface, and I clench my fists.

"None of you should have been created," I hiss, my voice dripping with venom. "You're an abomination that should never have existed."

The vermin's expression remains unchanged, and his voice is

calm and measured. "Neither should you. But here we are, existing together."

"I'm going to eradicate you and your entire kingdom," I growl. "The only reason you're still alive is because you're a pawn in a much larger game. Akira will walk right into my trap, and when she does, I'll be there to finish what I started."

With a mocking undertone, the creature laughs dryly.

"What's so funny?"

"Your plan is doomed to fail," the abomination spits out blood and chuckles.

Narrowing my eyes, unamused by his response. "Oh really? And why is that?"

His smirk widens. "Because you'll be waiting a long time for Akira to fall into your trap. She and I aren't together anymore. I broke her heart, so she won't be coming for me anytime soon."

My patience wears thin, and my fangs pierce into his arm. Releasing the pest, I throw him to the ground and speed out of the cell in seconds.

Grasping Lucas by the throat, I slam him against the wall, fury burning in my eyes.

"S—Sir?" he stammers beneath my tight grip.

"You told me that Akira would come for him!" I snarl through gritted teeth. "But she's not coming, is she?"

Lucas gasps for air and struggles to formulate a response. I let go of his throat, allowing him to breathe again, and he stumbles back, his hands reaching for his bruised neck.

"Speak!" I demand.

"Sir, she will. She's in love with him. I assure you she'll come for him."

"The abomination seems to think otherwise," I sneer, my anger boiling beneath the surface.

"Well, I know different," Lucas assures. "Akira told me herself she's still in love with him."

Narrowing my eyes at him. "You better be right. Otherwise, you'll suffer the consequences of your failure."

Lucas gulps and nods, sweat forming on his forehead. "I understand, Sir."

The next day...

"Sir, they're here!" Joel shouts in urgency.

"Prepare for war!" I bellow, my voice booming through the castle halls. "The Revolt is here!"

My soldiers immediately spring into action, donning their armor and grabbing their weapons.

BOOM!

We duck for cover as multiple bombs go off on the castle grounds.

"Here we go again," Chase murmurs.

Aika, my soldiers, and the witches are beside me, ready to defend our kingdom. We have locked the human slaves in a cell and bound them with a spell for safekeeping. And I have imprisoned Lucas in the dungeon because I hate him with every fiber of my being.

We surface from the cave to confront our enemy, emerging from the darkness, with our eyes locked on the approaching army.

Akira levitates with a sword in hand, along with the hybrid broad who fought alongside that blasted witch, Rosa.

"Where's Troy?" she demands, exhibiting a newfound confidence.

Who does she think she is?

"Child, mind your tongue," I warn from across the battlefield.

"The little brat thinks she can dominate us," Aika spits through gritted teeth.

"My daughter asked you a question, Abel, and she deserves an answer."

A male figure steps forward from the crowd, his voice commanding my attention. He sounds vaguely familiar, and as he approaches, his features become more evident. My eyes widen in recognition, and my mouth falls open in shock. *How could this be?*

"Jacobson?" Aika and I whisper in unison, disbelief coloring our voices.

"I've waited more than twenty years for this moment, Abel," Jacobson states, enjoying the look of surprise on our faces. "You thought you could kill me, but I've always been one step ahead of you."

He's been playing the long game, waiting for the perfect moment to strike. A surge of rage and adrenaline rushes through my veins, and I sprint toward my nemesis, gripping my sword tight. Jacobson meets me halfway, his own sword drawn and ready. His eyes burning with revulsion and purpose.

"Hello, *Brother*," I growl.

"We were never *brothers*," Jacobson shouts.

Our swords collide with a roaring crash, sending sparks and shockwaves into the air. Every clash of our blades resonates as loud as a thunderbolt, rumbling and vibrating. We are creating a thunderstorm of vengeance, each strike fueled by years of pent-up anger and resentment. Moving with grace and precision, he dodges and weaves his way through my attacks, each of us trying to gain the upper hand. Aiming my sword at his neck, I lunge forward, hoping to end this fight quickly. Shifting his head to the side, he dodges my attack.

Clever bastard!

Aiming to cleave my skull, he counters with a slash at my head. Blocking his strike, I raise my sword. We are equally matched. Looking to my left, Aika is charging toward the enemy. To my right, my soldiers are holding their ground, fighting fiercely.

One will become the victor, and it must be us.

Aika sprints over the abomination and snaps her neck with ease. A phoenix launches a fiery bolt toward the hybrid, and she raises. *What?*

Spinning my sword over my head, I meet Jacobson's sword with a resounding clash. Neither of us shows any sign of backing down. While glancing around the battlefield, I notice that The Revolts are grouped with phoenixes trailing their every move. There is another abomination: materializing weapons and hurling them to his allies.

"Ahh!" I shout, flipping my sword so the blade faces me and the hilt points towards Jacobson.

With a swift motion, I thrust my sword forward and hit him with force, sending him spiraling backward. I watch as the phoenix, apparently tasked to Jacobson, aids his rescue.

Every time we strike one of them down, a phoenix heals them.

A strike across my head causes me to stumble backward, momentarily disoriented. I regain my footing, and an abomination lunges towards me.

"I've always hated you," she snarls through gritted teeth.

Spinning around, I slice her throat in a matter of seconds, sending her carcass tumbling to the ground. Another phoenix appears by her side and heals her, resurrecting her back to life.

It's a never-ending cycle of destruction and revival, making it nearly impossible to gain the upper hand. I leap over a creature and toward Chase, who just finished breaking a hybrid's neck.

"What is it, Abel?" He pants, wiping the sweat off his forehead.

"We need reinforcement *now*. Where's Nico?"

"He's invisible somewhere on the battlefield, offering stealth support," Chase replies, slicing a shapeshifter in half with his sword.

"Nico, show yourself!" I demand, scouting the perimeter for any signs of him.

Nico appears on the other side of the field, near the hybrid broad that's levitating the werewolves and slamming them into one another.

"Go after the phoenixes," I command him.

"Abel, the phoenixes will resurrect after ten minutes," Chase advises.

"Yes, but they are the biggest threat right now. Everyone we kill is brought back to life," I explain. "Look around. They're all grouped with phoenixes."

Akira is a clever little brat.

"You're right," Chase acknowledges, scanning the battlefield. "We need to focus on taking out the phoenixes first to weaken their forces," he says, ripping the head off of a hybrid.

"Precisely," I respond and signal Nico to meet us.

He disappears and reappears beside me in an instant.

"Take my hand," I command him, extending my hand towards him. He grasps my hand, and we both become invisible. "We need to focus on the phoenixes."

He nods, and we join forces to slice through vampires, hybrids, and shapeshifters. We wait for the phoenixes to rush to their aid, strategically positioning ourselves to intercept them. Then, we break their necks and rip out the hearts of those they were reviving.

"Now they'll remain dead," I say with grim satisfaction.

"No," a familiar voice cries out.

Still invisible, I break her neck and rip out her heart in a swift motion.

"Sophia, no!" Akira cries out in horror, rushing towards the fallen figure. But it's too late.

Oh! That's who the vampire was! My lips twitch into a cruel smile as I revel in the taste of vengeance. *Splendid!*

"Now!" Akira orders, and a swarm of phoenixes fly above our heads, dropping potions that are turning my soldiers into futile creatures.

"What's happening?" Chase shouts.

"We must retreat!" Aika screams in my direction.

Not yet!

"Keep us invisible!" I instruct Nico. "We must go after Akira!"

We race through the chaos, avoiding the vessels of liquid falling from the sky, when suddenly, there are *three* Akira's levitating above us.

"Abel, where are you? We must retreat *now*!" Aika yells, then disappears at the speed of light.

Nico lets go of my hand and disappears as well.

"Retreat, retreat!" I circle my finger in the air, summoning my soldiers, who were untouched by the potions. Half of my kingdom is dead, and the other half are creatures rendered useless.

We take refuge in the cave to devise a Plan B and assess the situation.

"What are we going to do now?" Chase asks.

Turning to the witches. "Is there a spell you can conduct to turn my soldiers back into their original forms?"

"Yes," the head witch responds, "but we need time."

"Well, get to work! We don't have a moment to waste," I command, pacing back and forth.

When did Akira become so clever?

Paul enters the cave with a creature's arm over his shoulder.

"Who is that?" I raise an eyebrow.

"Cole," Paul sighs. "This potion bottle struck him." He shows me the shattered bottle in his hand.

"Let me see this," the blue-eyed witch says, taking the shattered bottle from Paul's hand and inspecting it.

"What is it?" Aika questions.

"This is an ancient potion," the head witch explains, his eyes narrowing as he studies the shards.

Furrowing my brow. "And what does that mean?"

The witch looks up from the shards, his expression grave. "It means that this potion is extremely rare and powerful. It's channeled from witches beyond the grave."

"Can you counteract it?" Chase asks.

"No," the head witch responds, shaking his head. "Once this potion is unleashed, magic cannot reverse its effects," he explains. "It is a force that cannot be tampered with or undone. It has to run its course."

My fury burns hotter with each word he speaks. "What use are you?" I spit back, grabbing the witch by his neck. "If you can't help us, then we have no need for you." I tighten my grip, feeling the witch struggle beneath my grasp.

"Abel, they're linked to you," Aika reminds me, her voice calm but firm.

Releasing my grip on his neck, I inhale and exhale.

"What do we do now?" I ask my wife.

Aika weaves her fingers with mine, her touch grounding me. "All magic has its limits. The spell will eventually wear off. We just have to wait for it to."

She addresses the witch, "Place a cloaking spell on the cave for the time being."

"The spell won't last long, but it should buy you enough time to figure out your next move," the witch replies.

"We only need the spell to last as long as their potion does. Until then, we must wait," Aika responds.

Once again, I'm a prisoner in my own home, or at least what's left of it.

CHAPTER 49: AKIRA

War!

"War is optional. War is essential. War is political. War is binding."

-KC

My vision has come to pass, and war is finally here. Abel and what's left of his kingdom have retreated, and my witches and I cannot break through the magical force field they have put up. Daisy, Amy, and I hold hands with the witches as they chant, but the invisible barrier is not budging.

I let go of their grasp and shake my hands, pacing back and forth. Daisy and Amy shapeshift back into themselves.

Tapping my foot repeatedly and grinding my teeth together. "How long until we find a way to break through?"

Monica sighs, "It takes time, Akira. Even with the magic from our ancestors, it will still require patience."

"The potion is not going to last much longer, and soon everyone will return to their original forms," I comment, gesturing toward half of Abel's kingdom, which is now a variety of different creatures.

"How about we conjure cages to hold them in? It might buy us some time until we figure out a more permanent solution." Niyla suggests.

"That could work," Monica responds, swaying her fingers in a circular motion. Cages materialize around the transformed creatures, trapping them within their confines.

"Can you cast a spell on the cages to make them impenetrable?" I ask, turning to Niyla.

"Yes," she nods, her eyes focused on the cages. She snaps her fingers and a shimmering barrier forms around each one. "These should hold them for now," she assures.

"Thank you," I say, and she nods.

The potion spell lasts for another twenty minutes before the creatures return to their original state. They shout and thrash against the cages.

"Help me!" A familiar voice cries out above the chaos.

I look up to see a terrified face pressed against the bars of one of the cages. *It's Sophia.*

My brows snap together, and I trade looks with Daisy, Shelly, and Cameron before we rush to Sophia's cage.

"Sophia, you're alive!" I shout, relief flooding through me.

Sophia nods, her eyes wide with fear.

"But how?" Shelly asks. "I saw your heart ripped from your chest."

"Shapeshifter!" Sophia replies.

We share gasps as we try to comprehend Sophia's explanation.

"Last minute, a shapeshifter saved me," she explains.

"It could have been me that was killed," she whispers to herself.

We were so close to losing Sophia forever. I press my forehead against hers.

"Don't scare me like that again, Lollipop," Daisy warns, wiping her teary eyes.

"Lollipop?" Shelly and I say in unison, sharing amused stares.

Daisy shrugs and explains, "It's her favorite candy, and it just stuck."

Sophia's cheeks shine a bright pink, and she cracks a small smile. "Can someone please get me out of here?"

"You love your nickname; don't deny it," Daisy teases her.

Chuckling at their banter, I call out to Jessica. "Hey Jess, can you let Sophia out?"

Jessica darts toward us, brows furrowed. "How are we certain this is Sophia and not a shapeshifter serving Abel?" she questions, eyeing Sophia suspiciously.

Daisy replies, "Trust me, Jess, it's her because only my Lollipop has that adorable blush when she's embarrassed."

"Kill me now," Amy groans, rolling her eyes. "Just let her out already."

My father approaches us with a crease between his brows, interrupting the conversation. "Amir is nowhere to be found. I haven't seen any of his followers either."

"Who is Amir?" I ask.

"He is a lead shapeshifter and a smug mastermind," my father explains. "He wouldn't miss the opportunity to face me in his true form if he knew I was alive."

Furrowing my brow, I try to process this new information. "So, Amir, is someone you have a history with?"

My father nods. "Yes, we have a long and complicated history."

Sophia coughs, directing our attention to her. "I don't mean to interrupt, but I would be much more useful outside of this cage than inside."

Nodding my head toward Jessica, she releases Sophia from the cage. She nods and grasps the cage bars. A gold shimmer glows around the bars, and the cage disintegrates.

Sophia stretches her limbs and sighs in relief. "Thank you," she says to Jessica, and Daisy and her share a passionate kiss.

Jessica returns to help Monica work on breaking through the barrier once more, and we turn away to give Sophia and Daisy some privacy. The rest of the caged supernatural creatures are shouting to be freed as well.

"What are we going to do with all of them?" Cameron asks, scanning the chaotic scene before us.

My gaze fixed on the captives, I observe the commotion. *I don't know.* Do we keep them locked up or ask them to join us in the fight against Abel? Who can we trust?

"Akira?" Shelly says, jolting me back to reality.

"I'm sorry," I say, snapping out of my thoughts, and they all look at me expectantly, waiting for a response.

Chewing on my bottom lip, I look at my father. "Dad?"

"Yes, Akira?" he replies.

"What do you think we should do with them?" I ask.

My father sighs, his brow furrowing in deep thought. "Akira, it's hard to say," he begins. "The werewolves cannot be trusted because they're loyal to Abel. The shapeshifters are not here, so we can't make a decision about them yet, but they could potentially be a threat as well. And Anju will handle the phoenixes and determine their loyalties."

"I'm bringing the phoenixes back to the island. They'll live out the rest of their existence behind bars for treason. Paul and Cole must be inside the cave with Abel because I don't see them on the field. Leave their fate for The Seekers to decide," she says.

My eyes widen at Anju's orders, and she smiles knowingly. "I'm the leader of the phoenixes, and these men and women betrayed me by following Abel's leadership." She points to every one of them. "With your permission, Queen Akira, I wish to take them back to the island and imprison them in cells."

"We're almost in!" Monica informs me of their progress in breaking through the force field.

Nodding at Monica's update, I turn my attention back to Anju. "Very well." I give a subtle bow of approval. "Take them back to the island and make sure you securely imprison them, but we need you back here as soon as possible. We have not won this war."

She nods. "I understand, Queen Akira. I'll make sure they're locked in prison and return to aid in the battle immediately," she assures me before gathering the traitors and leading them away.

"What about the vampires?" Cameron asks. "Can we trust them?"

We turn to face them. Some look worried and out of place

among the rest. "These have to be new vampires. Look at them—they seem unsure," I point out, studying their body language and expressions.

Cameron and I walk over to them, and some of them flinch when we are near, their eyes darting around.

"Leave them in the cages for now," I suggest. "We'll put each of them on trial before bringing them back to the island. The witches will deal with them accordingly."

"We're in!" Monica shouts, and we spring into action.

"Alert The Seekers," I say to my father.

He nods and disappears in a flash of lightning.

Queen Celine approaches me, pleading, "Please save my son, Akira. He's all I have left, and I cannot bear to lose him."

My gaze meets her tear-filled eyes. "I will do everything in my power to bring him back safely. You have my word. Now, please go back to the island. Your fight here is done."

She gives me a grateful nod and hurries back to the open portal. Although I'm the queen of all the kingdoms, I have great respect for Queen Celine and will continue to address her as such.

My eyes fill with tears as I repeat her plea in my head. *"Please save my son."*

I hope he is still alive.

When Anju and the phoenixes return moments after disappearing through the portal, we barge into the castle. Monica stays with the prisoners to interrogate them before sending them through the portal or leaving them behind for The Seekers.

The castle is unrecognizable from what I once knew. The walls are crumbling, and the air is heavy with smoke, and everything is out of place. Tears stream down my face.

This is my vision!

Abel emerges from behind the portrait of Aika with Troy. A sinister smile plays on his lips as he flings Troy to the floor. The man I love lies motionless, his eyes closed and his breath faint. Troy's fingers are twisted and mangled, his face is smeared with dirt and blood, and his clothes are torn and ragged. Clenching my fist, a wave of fury flows through my veins. Abel looks me directly in the eyes with twisted satisfaction as he kicks Troy's limp body aside. My heart is pounding, and I struggle to control the anger bubbling inside me. It takes every ounce of my strength to keep my soldiers from attacking. Abel is taunting me.

"Abel," I plead through choked sobs. "Let Troy go. *Please.*"

Abel laughs with malicious joy. His laughter ricochets through the empty halls of the castle, and my desperation grows as I watch Troy's frame on the cold stone floor.

With a trembling voice, I beg him once more to listen to me, but his heart is hardened, and he shows no mercy. Abel ignores me and orders one of his minions to fly me right into a brick wall that shatters on impact. Blood trickles down my forehead as I struggle to stay conscious, realizing that Abel's cruelty knows no bounds.

"Attack!" Shelly shouts, rallying our soldiers, and Abel rallies his own forces.

The people I love fight for their lives against my evil father. Innocents plunge to the ground, paralyzed by the pain, and their screams pierce through the air. Chaos and destruction unfold before my eyes. In the midst of the chaos, Felix rushes to Troy's side and evacuates him to safety while I regain my strength and join the battle.

"Take out the powerful ones first!" I command the witches, knowing that they are the key to Abel's strength.

The witches immediately heed my command, unleashing their magic upon Abel's forces.

In the corner of my eye, I notice a vampire disappearing and reappearing in different parts of the castle, swiftly taking down my soldiers with lightning-fast movements. Watching him, when he reappears again, I catch him by the throat and pin him to the floor. Just as I'm about to snap his neck, I pause.

"Please don't kill me," the vampire pleads. "I'm only following Abel's orders."

Contemplating the vampire's words, I release my grip slightly. "Take him to a cage!" I command Cameron.

Cameron nods and restrains the vampire, leading him away and returning in a flash. Just when I think the situation is under control, Aika snaps Cameron's neck from behind. Before she can finish him off, I intervene by kicking her with force and knocking her to the ground.

"Enough!" I shout.

She regains her footing and glares at me, her eyes filled with fury.

"I'm going to end you like I ended your mother," she seethes and charges at me with vengeance, knocking me back with a powerful blow.

Reclaiming my balance, I levitate off the ground, and she

jumps up, latches onto my leg, and pulls me back down.

"You can try all you want, but I won't let history repeat itself," I reply, flipping over her and tugging her head backward. She grips my arms to stop me from snapping her neck.

"You're strong," she gasps, her voice strained. "However, you little brat. I'm stronger!"

Aika grits her teeth and kicks the back of my leg. She frees her head from my grip and delivers a powerful kick to my chest, sending me sprawling out of the castle and into the dirt. I quickly recover, rolling to my feet. She's standing beside me in the blink of an eye, delivering punches, and this time, aiming for my face. With my forearm, I block her attack. Despite the pounding in my head, I refuse to let her relish in my pain. Unleashing a flurry of blows, she kicks me with lightning speed, each strike aimed at weakening my defenses.

Ducking and weaving, I counter her blows with quick jabs and well-timed kicks of my own.

"Soon, we will be victors, and we will eradicate your beloved hybrids," Aika taunts with malice in her voice.

Refusing to let her words shake me, I grit my teeth.

"It's been fun torturing your little prince," she continues, a wicked smile playing on her lips. "We fed him human blood to heal his injuries and did it all over again when he recovered," she laughs with sadistic pleasure.

Taking a deep breath, I channel my anger into my next attack. My father told me that Aika was the true villain and that Abel was a good man until he met her.

Aika's mockery fills my ears as I prepare to strike back.

A surge of rage boils inside me, and my hands glow with fiery red and orange energy. I delve my fingers into the earth beneath me, feeling the rough and gritty particles. Summoning the thick roots from deeper in the ground to the surface, I exhale slowly, concentrating on what I want my magic to do. The thicker roots whip through the air as the thinner ones appear, mingling mid-air. The roots lash out at Aika, jabbing her flesh with their sharp ends. She screams in pain, and blood spurts from her wounds. Her laughter from earlier still hunts me, and I let my powers consume me. Levitating, I push forward, releasing a last branch that pierces through her throat, silencing her screams.

The Seekers troop in with guns and arrows laced with sunlight and human blood, ready to finish her off. My kingdom scatters to the opposite side of Aika.

"Akira, quick! We need your blood to end her!" My father shouts, running towards me with a small vial in his hand.

"What will my blood do?" I observe the bottle.

"The Seekers believe that your blood has the power to heal or destroy," he explains.

Nodding in understanding, I take the vial from my father's hand. I bite into my wrist and let the blood drip into it, filling it with my essence and handing it to Ethan. The Seekers are firing arrows and bullets at Aika's limp body, ensuring she doesn't rise again. Ethan raises his hand, signaling for them to stop. He approaches Aika, holding the ball of sunlight in his hand. Aika tries to free herself from the branches that impale her body; her efforts are futile. Ethan mixes my blood with the glowing orb, creating a lethal weapon. One of my soldiers pries Aika's mouth open, and Ethan carefully places the ball of sunlight on her tongue, forcing her to swallow it. The ball travels down her throat and emits a burst of red and orange light that emanates from her skin and courses through her veins. The branch impaled into her throat explodes, and Aika's screams of agony fill the air as the sunlight engulfs her, searing through her flesh and bones.

Aika's screams attract Abel's attention, and he fights through the chaos to reach her side. Snapping necks and ripping out hearts with lightning speed, she explodes in a shower of ash and fire before he can get to her. The intense heat scorches his skin as he watches in horror as her body disintegrates. He falls to his knees and clutches his chest.

My father seizes this opportunity and spins around, wielding his sword at Abel, who counterattacks with his own sword, their blades clashing with a deafening sound.

"No, Dad! Stop!" I cry out, and they both pause for a moment, their eyes locking onto mine. My father lowers his sword, a flicker of uncertainty in his eyes, while Abel's grip on his sword tightens. "Let me handle Abel. It's my fight now."

My father looks torn, his gaze shifting between Abel and me, but ultimately, he nods and steps back, relinquishing the fight to me. Abel narrows his eyes, a smirk playing on his lips as he readies himself for my attack.

Taking a deep breath, I conjure my sword to my side and tighten my grip on the hilt. The weight of avenging those Abel caused so much pain to settles on my shoulders.

Everyone else on the battlefield turns their attention towards us, waiting to see the outcome of our confrontation.

Time freezes as our eyes lock in a tense stare of hatred and respect. Raising my sword above my head, it meets Abel's with a definite clang. The force of the impact sends a shockwave through my arms, but I stand my ground.

He flips over me with a graceful somersault and lands behind me, swinging his blade low and slicing my ankles. Biting my lip to suppress a yelp of pain, I regain my balance, refusing to give him satisfaction. Turning around, I aim for his head, but he dodges it easily with a swift duck. Slashing my arm with his sword, he draws blood. The gash is deep, and a stinging sensation washes over me. Gritting my teeth, I push through, launching a rapid series of strikes, aiming for any opening I can find in Abel's defenses. He effortlessly evades each of my attacks, his movements fluid and precise.

Abel smirks at my ineffective attempts to land a hit. "I thoroughly enjoyed torturing your little prince," he taunts. "And now it's your turn to suffer."

The man I once referred to as my father is standing before me, ready to kill me, his words cutting through me like a knife. I look around at the battlefield; my home is gone, reduced to rubble and ashes. They have destroyed everything I have known and loved, and now it's up to me to end this.

Taking a deep breath, I muster every ounce of strength and determination within me. With a newfound resolve, I let my power surge through my veins, fueling my every move. I conjure a storm and strike Abel with lightning bolts, his body convulsing with each powerful strike. Circling him like a whirlwind, I pierce his legs, arms, and torso with my sword, leaving deep lacerations and trails of blood in my wake. Gripping my sword in one hand and accessing my magic in the other, I hurl daggers into his skin that Roger is materializing for me. Abel plunges to the ground, his strength waning, and I aim my sword at his head, ready to deliver the final blow. The world seems to pause, waiting for my next move, as I contemplate ending Abel's life.

"Do it!" he roars.

The crowd watches in anticipation, their collective breath held, as I hesitate for a moment longer. Tears form in my eyes as I struggle with the weight of my decision.

"Finish me!" he shouts.

His words reverberate in my mind, reminding me of the countless lives he has taken. Yet, I can't do it as I stand there, sword in hand.

"Kill him!" Someone shouts from the crowd.

"Please don't. He is linked to us." A blonde-haired witch shouts.

Monica and the other witches work together to reverse the linking spell on Abel.

"It is done," Monica shouts.

Biting my lip, I wrestle with the conflicting emotions inside me. Pressing the blade firmly against his neck, drawing blood, I feel the cold steel against my trembling hand.

I *want* to kill him.

I *should* kill him.

But I *can't.*

Unable to go through with it, a sigh falls from Abel's lips. I lower my weapon, and my father recovers the sword from me. Niyla summons a cage around him, and a Seeker hands Jessica, a ball of sunlight, to weaken Abel further. She creates a force field surrounding Abel with the orb, ensuring he cannot escape. Maybe this is the best way to bring justice without resorting to murder.

Racing to the secluded area where Felix took Troy, my heart sinks as I see him sprawled out on the ground, barely conscious and covered in bruises. Kneeling beside him, I gently cradle his head in my hands. He looks up at me with tired eyes like he'd been holding on for dear life until he saw me.

"I love you," he whispers weakly.

Tears well up in my eyes as I hold back the overwhelming emotions threatening to consume me.

With a trembling voice, I whisper back, "I love you too, Troy."

He smiles faintly. "I'm sorry," he murmurs, his voice barely audible.

I plant soft kisses on his hands, chest, cheek, and then his lips.

"I'm sorry, too," I mumble, my heart breaking at the sight of his pain.

Troy closes his eyes, his body growing weaker by the second.

"No, no, no," I plead, my voice cracking with desperation. "Please don't leave me." I bury my face in his chest, sobbing uncontrollably. "Come back to me," I beg, clutching onto him tight.

Troy's grip on life slips away, his breath becoming shallow. Helplessness washes over me as I realize there is nothing more I can do.

My blood!

It can heal or destroy. I bite into my wrist and press it against Troy's lips, hoping that my blood will somehow revive him. As I watch, my blood seeps into his mouth.

Nothing happens.

His injuries are not healing.

"Anju!" I cry out in despair, tears streaming down my face.

She reaches for my trembling hand, gripping it with tears in her eyes.

"I'm so sorry," she says, "It's been longer than five minutes, and not possible for me to heal him."

Turning to my father, friends, and kingdom, tears welling up in my eyes, I am struck by the realization that there is nothing more that anyone can do.

"He can't be gone." My voice chokes with grief. "This is not how it's supposed to end."

The look of devastation on everyone's faces mirrors my anguish. Placing my hand over his heart, I let the magic within me flow through my fingertips, hoping for a miracle. Troy's body levitates, and his entire body glows with a golden light. His body descends slowly back to the ground, and I channel my magic into him again, desperately trying to revive him.

Filled with despair, I collapse onto him. My head lay on his chest, just like when we would hold each other in the early mornings or after we made love. Except...this time, there is no increased heartbeat or sexy smile. His lifeless form is here to greet me. Tears stream down my cheeks as memories of us flood my mind. All the things we can never do again. We are robbed of our future. Exhaling again, I place my hands over his chest, injecting him with my magic, aiming for his heart—red and orange light emanates from his chest. Planting soft kisses on his lips, I do it again and again until there is a sudden movement, which has me holding my breath.

Did I imagine it?

Hoping.

Praying.

His chest moves slightly.

My breath catches in my throat. *Is he breathing?*

Laying my head on his chest, I hear his heart starting to beat again.

He takes shallow breaths, and my heart beats faster.

He is alive!

"Troy?" I whisper, clutching him tighter.

He opens his eyes and weakly smiles at me, his voice barely a whisper. "I'm here," he says reassuringly.

Relief floods through me as I hear his voice. Our love and my magic brought him back from the brink of death.

Gazing into his eyes, I nudge him gently. "You scared me. Promise me you'll never do something like that again."

He reaches up and tucks my baby hair behind my ear. "I promise, my love," he murmurs. "Will you promise me something too?"

"Anything, Troy."

He takes a deep breath, his grip on my hand tightening. "Will you marry me?”

Everyone gasps, and so do I. “You’re asking me this now?”

“I couldn’t think of a better time,” he teases with a playful smile.

All eyes turn to me, waiting for my answer.

“Yes, Troy! A thousand times, yes!” I shout, kissing him on the lips as my kingdom erupts in cheers and applause.

The war is over. We defeated Abel and his army. And I am engaged to the love of my life!

Love Story

Four Months Later...

Troy's Point of View:

The day of my death was also the day I was reborn. It was a place of limbo where I had to confront my past actions and seek redemption. I desperately wanted to return to Akira to make amends for the pain I had caused her and confess my love for her.

She is the woman I am meant to be with, my soulmate. A bright light shone through the darkness of purgatory. It felt familiar, but my mind was conflicted about which way to go. Standing at the crossroads, torn between the light and the darkness, a soft voice whispered in my ear, urging me to follow my heart.

Akira is the love of my life and has been mine since the very first day I laid eyes on her. I got caught up in everything else going on, which caused me to make the biggest mistake. Those thirty days without her felt like an eternity, dragging me down into a dark abyss of despair. Drowning in sadness, I refused to let anyone see my weakness. Hiding my pain behind a mask of indifference and never admitting to her or anyone else how much I suffered. When Akira brought me back, I knew my life would never be the same without her. I proposed and had to make things right and never let her go again.

Thank the heavens, she said yes, and we are to be wed tomorrow. I picked out an 18k vanilla gold ring with brownstones engraved on it. The ring sparkles with a unique beauty, just like hers. And I cannot wait to see the look on her face when I slip it onto her finger.

We locked Abel away where he belongs and took care of all our enemies. Life is good! Although I miss my father and brother dearly, they would be proud if they were here. The kingdom is thriving under one rule, which would have never happened without Akira. Everyone on Abel's side suffered either murder or imprisonment at the hands of The Seekers.

Lucas, that repulsive vamp, serves the humans as their slave, and I couldn't be more satisfied with the justice served. Dawn and I are on good terms, and she has forgiven me for that kiss. And tonight, the guys are throwing me a bachelor party that I'm sure will be a night to remember. But most of all, I cannot wait to marry the love of my life tomorrow.

For my bachelor party, I'm going on a run with my best men, Felix and Kaden, and my groomsmen, Cameron and Roger, by

Lian Lake. We're indulging in a *friendly* little hybrid versus vampire race.

"Are you ready, Bro?" Cameron asks, barging into my chambers with a mischievous grin on his face.

Holding the brown velvet ring box, I nod. "I'm definitely ready for some *friendly* competition."

"Woah! Is that the ring?" Cameron lets out a whistle of admiration. "It's stunning, Bro. She's going to love it."

"Thanks, man. I really hope so." I reply, closing the box.

Cameron slaps me on the back playfully. "Now, are you ready to lose to some vampires?"

Pushing him back. "We'll see about that," I reply, raising an eyebrow. "I have a feeling you'll be the one losing tonight."

Cameron chuckles and shakes his head. "Don't get too confident, my friend."

We continue with our banter while heading out to meet up with the rest of the guys.

"How about we settle this once and for all," Kaden says when we arrive at the meeting spot, nudging Cameron with his elbow.

"Fine, but just know we're faster," Felix replies, smirking.

"And stronger," I add, flexing my muscles teasingly.

"Let's school them," Roger says, cracking his knuckles.

Felix, Roger, and I transform into wolves, and Kaden and Cameron exchange competitive looks at us, and on three, we race to Lian Lake.

The three of us sprint through the dense forest, paws pounding the earth with speed and agility. We dodge the trees and bushes, leaping over rocks and streams. Kaden and Cameron match our speed as they glide through the forest with seamless strides. Trying to gain an advantage over them, I howl. However, they are right on my tail. We are evenly matched; neither we nor they are willing to give up. We run for a few miles, pushing our limits and testing our endurance. We race until we reach the tip of Lian Lake, making it a stalemate.

"I told you we're faster!" Kaden brags, panting heavily.

Transforming back into a human. "We all made it here, Kaden. It's a tie," I point out, catching my breath.

"Nope, we're faster!" Cameron argues, grinning and wiping the sweat off his forehead.

Shaking my head, I chuckle. "Looks like we'll never settle this debate. We'll just have to agree to disagree."

Roger and Felix transform and join in the laughter. "It's always a competition with you guys," Roger remarks, nudging Kaden on the shoulder.

Felix chuckles. "Don't be sore losers, Cam and Kaden."

Cameron and Kaden exchange glances and we all share a laugh, settling down by the lake. Cameron starts a fire, and we share stories and jokes around the campfire. My mind drifts to memories of Claude and the adventures we had together. Feeling a pang of sadness, knowing he's no longer here with us, I exhale.

My little brother's memory will always linger in my heart, no matter how much time passes. He was my best friend, and I miss him every day. Being surrounded by friends and creating fresh memories helps ease the pain. And I have found happiness with Akira; I want nothing more than to marry her tomorrow.

Akira's Point of View:

Tomorrow, I'm marrying the love of my life.

We have been through so much together, and I couldn't be more excited to start this new chapter with Troy. My father is walking me down the aisle, which means the world to me. Shelly and Sophia are my maids of honor, and Daisy, Michelle, Amy, Niyla, Jessica, and Anju are my beautiful bridesmaids. They are planning a bachelorette party for me tonight to celebrate my last night of singlehood.

After the war, we locked Abel in a cage in the cave of his castle, and Jessica has been sustaining the ball of sunlight there that keeps him trapped. Some of the new vampires are flourishing in my kingdom, but unfortunately, we sentenced a few of them, like Chase, to the same fate as Abel. Amir and his shapeshifters still have made no contact, and The Seekers imprisoned most of the werewolves and phoenixes, including Paul and Cole. After I confronted Lucas and punched him in the face for betraying me, I dealt him a fair deal: he serves time in our kingdom, catering to every human need. Humans are welcome to become one of us on their own accord. They reside on Kiju Island, away from us, living out the rest of their days peacefully. Mr. Ryan Howard is the leader of the human-vampire group, and they live in the cabins by the Shaline Sea. My council and I reside in the castle on top of the Kian Mountains. All the supernatural creatures live amongst each other, and life is perfect!

Heading to Shelly's suite in the East Wing of our castle for the festivities, my heart is jumping with joy. Entering the room, I am greeted by a warm, soothing fragrance filling my senses. It is my favorite aroma, a blend of vanilla and lavender, that calms my nerves and relaxes my mind. The room is dimly lit by dozens of scented candles, creating a cozy atmosphere. *Wow, they have really gone all out.*

Shelly hands me a brown robe with 'bride' embroidered with gold thread on the back. "My queen," she smiles.

"Oh, stop it," I blush and wave her off, slipping the robe over my shoulders.

"Follow me," she says, leading me down a narrow, hidden hallway to a room filled with luxurious massage tables and a hot tub filled with rose petals floating on the surface. The soft music playing in the background adds to the serene ambiance. A few humans await us in white uniforms, and my eyes widen.

Shelly whispers. "They wanted to do it."

Nodding in approval, I smile. Everyone is adhering to my rules of the kingdom.

The rest of my bridal party arrives with games, bottles of wine, and animal blood. Excitement and laughter fill the air, and I can tell this is going to be a blast!

Laying back on the massage table, I feel the tension in my muscles already melting away. This is precisely what I needed before my big day.

"Who came up with this idea?" I wonder aloud while the brown-haired masseuse works his muscular hands over my lower back.

"We thought you could use some pampering before your wedding," Shelly replies with a smile.

"Well, it's a brilliant idea! Thanks to all of you, I can already feel the stress and nerves fading away."

Grinning from ear to ear, I feel the knots in my muscles loosen. Closing my eyes, I let the expert hands work their magic, transporting me further into blissful relaxation.

An hour of pure bliss passes too quickly and we get into the hot tub to enjoy each other's company while sipping on wine and animal blood. We laugh and gossip about cute couples in our friend group.

Daisy and Sophia are the sweetest pair, always stealing glances and holding hands whenever they think no one is looking. I love them together.

Amy and Cameron took me some time to get used to because Cam is my little brother, and sometimes Amy says inappropriate things about him that make me gag. However, they're happy, so I'm so glad for them.

Shelly and Felix are getting married in just a few months, and I can't wait to see them tie the knot.

Kaden has been giving Michelle the sweetest compliments lately, and it's clear something is blossoming between them.

Anju and Roger have a thing for one another, except they're keeping it low-key for now.

Niyla is still working through the untimely loss of Claude, and I noticed Jessica eyeing one of the newer vampires, Nico.

Shelly softly nudges me while everyone is engrossed in

conversation and laughter. "Did you think we would ever end up like this?" she asks with a wistful smile.

My brows snap together, and I cock my head to the side. "What do you mean?"

"In love!" she beams, her flaming red eyes sparkling.

Shaking my head. "Never in a million years did I imagine this," I laugh.

Shelly nods, her smile widening. "And with hybrids, no less!"

My heart swells at the unexpected love we found. "It's funny how life surprises us sometimes. If you asked me a year ago if I would marry a hybrid, I would have thought you were crazy."

"Yet, here we are, happier than ever," Shelly adds. "Love truly knows no boundaries, and I wouldn't change a thing."

Standing in the hot tub and squealing, "I'm getting married! I'm getting married!"

I'm marrying Troy Bishop tomorrow!

The excitement bubbles inside me, and I move in rhythm to the music playing in the background, singing at the top of my lungs. My girls join me in a chorus of laughter and cheers, matching my movements. Moments like these remind me of the incredible people I have in my life. I love them with my entire heart, and I wouldn't want to spend my bachelorette party any other way than with my girls.

Our wedding is being held in the ballroom of our castle; its majestic ambiance perfectly complements the elegance of our special day. Jace will officiate the ceremony, and the entire kingdom, including the humans, will be our guests.

My heart pounds with anticipation as I imagine Troy standing at the altar, waiting for me. Soft music fills the air, and my maid of honors walks down the aisle. Shelly is wearing a brown, half-strapped satin gown, while Sophia is wearing a brown satin gown with sleeves.

They both look absolutely gorgeous.

Shelly and Felix entwine their arms and walk toward the altar. Felix wears a sharp black tailored tux with a brown dress shirt.

Sophia follows arm in arm with Kaden, who wears the same attire as Felix and the rest of the groomsmen.

Next is Amy, wearing a strapless brown gown, and Cameron is by her side, looking dapper in his tux.

Cameron kisses me on the cheek. "Congratulations, Sis," he whispers before walking into the ballroom.

Daisy, Michelle, Niyla, Jessica, and Anju partner with Roger and follow behind, each wearing a brown gown with straps.

My father stands tall in his tailored black tux and brown satin button-up shirt. He embraces me.

"I love you so much, sweetheart. You look stunning," he says with a proud smile, kissing me on the cheek.

"I love you too, Dad," I reply, overwhelmed with emotion.

"Are you ready?" he asks, locking arms with me.

Taking a deep breath, I nod.

"As ready as I'll ever be," I say, trying to steady my racing heart.

He gives me a reassuring squeeze, and the doors to the ballroom swing open. Everyone stands up from their seats, their eyes fixed on us, and wedding music plays softly in the background. Stepping into the grand ballroom, I walk with slow, steady steps down the aisle, concentrating on placing one foot in front of the other. It's like I forgot how to walk, and I keep reminding myself to breathe and stay focused so I don't trip or lose my balance.

When Troy sees me approaching, his eyes mist over with tears of joy, and I gasp at the rush of emotions that flood my heart. He's wearing a tailored ivory tuxedo with a brown satin button-up shirt and a bowtie that complements his handsome features, and his gaze penetrates my skin, reaching into my core. Queen Celine is standing next to him, wearing a brown satin gown adorned with intricate lace patterns, with her hand over her heart. With every step I take forward, a surge of excitement and nerves builds up inside me as I approach the love of my life, waiting for me at the end of the aisle.

My wedding dress hugs my body, accentuating my every curve, and flares out into a beautiful train behind me. It's strapless with a subtle brown hue that matches my bouquet of earthy-toned flowers perfectly. The back of my dress is adorned with sparkling crystals that follow down my spine and extend to the hem of my train, catching the light with every movement I make.

"I give Akira away to you," my father says, placing my hands on my soon-to-be husband when we meet at the altar.

Looking into Troy's eyes, I see the same emotions reflected: love, excitement, and a hint of nervousness.

"Today, we gather here to celebrate the union of Akira and Troy in holy matrimony. Love is a beautiful thing, and it is evident in the way these two look at each other. May their journey together be filled with joy, laughter, and endless love," Jace announces. "The couple has written their own vows—you may proceed."

Troy takes a deep breath and squeezes my hands. "Akira, I never imagined marrying a vampire—I always hated them, although I'm half," he grins, and the crowd chuckles softly. "From the very first moment I saw you, I knew you were different. You exhibited such beauty, grace, and light that it was impossible not to fall in love with you. But most of all, I fell in love with your heart. You have shown kindness, compassion, and unwavering support like no other. You have shown me that love has no boundaries, and I will love you today, tomorrow, and for all the days to come. Thank you for choosing me."

He reaches into his pocket and pulls out a brown velvet box. Opening it, he reveals a gorgeous vanilla gold diamond ring. I cover my mouth in awe, my eyes welling up with tears.

Troy slips the ring onto my finger, and in the corner of my eye, I see Cameron pointing finger guns at us with a wide grin and wriggling his eyebrows. I giggle through my tears and admire the beautiful ring sparkling on my finger.

"Akira, your vows," Jace reminds me, breaking the momentary silence.

Clearing my throat, I gaze into Troy's eyes. "Troy Bishop, from the moment I met you, I knew my life would never be the same. I've romanticized finding a 'spark' with someone for what feels like a lifetime, and with you, I finally found it. Here we are, defying my expectations, as I never thought someone I was taught to hate would be my true love. It's funny how that happens, and it's like you were created specifically for me to love. You challenge me, support me, and love me unconditionally. I love you with every fiber of my being, and I cannot wait to spend forever with you."

Troy leans in and captures my lips in a sensual kiss in the heat of the moment.

Jace clears his throat, chuckling, "I didn't say kiss the bride *yet.*"

We break apart, sharing a sheepish smile, and the audience laughs along with us.

Jace shakes his head. "Rings?"

Felix steps forward with a chocolate wedding band, and Shelly presents a matching wedding band. Troy and I exchange rings, sealing our commitment to one another.

"I now pronounce you husband and wife," Jace announces with a wide grin.

The audience erupts into applause and cheers as Troy and I smile at each other.

Jace gestures for us to share our first kiss as a married couple. "*Now, you may kiss your bride.*"

Troy gently presses his lips against mine, sealing our vows with a passionate kiss, and the ballroom fills with joyous laughter and clapping. He kisses me, and sparks fly between us, melting me into his arms. Troy is the love of my life, and at this moment, I couldn't be happier to call him my husband. We stay locked in our embrace, savoring the sweetness of our first kiss as a married couple, hardly noticing the world.

Troy mumbles against my lips, "I love you so much, my beautiful wife."

Smiling against him, I whisper back. "I love you too, my spectacular husband."

He kisses me once more, and we break away, both of us wearing broad smiles on our faces.

Jace holds up my hand, entwined with Troy's. "Ladies and gentlemen, may I present to you Akira and Troy Bishop."

My husband and I walk hand in hand down the aisle while our kingdom rejoices.

Epilogue

Six weeks later...

The fate of Abel Ronin has been decided. Akira chose to spare his life because she didn't have the heart to kill the man she once called father. Death would be too easy of a punishment for the pain he caused her and so many others. He needs to face the consequences of his actions and live with the guilt that will haunt him for the rest of his days.

Everything has been going well since Troy and Akira's wedding. Still, I have unfinished business with Abel that I need to address. Felix was generous enough to get me in contact with the witch who brought Shelly's emotions back. She sent over a friend to conduct the spell in her place. The same spell the witch used on Shelly; I want the witch Laura to cast on Abel—because death is too easy for the likes of him. He must suffer and the weight of his actions every waking moment. Only then will justice truly be served, and perhaps, just maybe, I can find some closure and move on from this dark chapter in my life. He deserves to be tortured, and who other than myself is to be granted this? Abel took the love of my life from me. The only woman I have ever loved, and for that, he must pay the ultimate price.

Arriving at the cave underneath the fallen castle with Laura, my gaze meets Abel's. His eyes are vast when he sees me.

"Hello, Brother. Are you here to visit me?" Abel looks past me, his gaze fixed on Laura. "Or have you come to gloat that you have moved on already?" He chuckles. "And here I thought Serena was your beloved."

"I'm not here to gloat," I hiss through gritted teeth. "I came here to introduce you to my good friend Laura."

He looks from her to me and screws up his face. "Why? What makes you think I am interested in meeting any of your friends?"

"You see, my friend Laura has access to a spell that can let you see your beloved Aika again. And, here, I thought you would love to see your wife. I guess I was wrong." I sigh. "But if you're not interested, I suppose we can just leave and let you wallow in your loneliness."

Wrapping my arm around Laura, I laugh and proceed to exit the cave.

"Wait! I'm listening," he says, his interest piqued.

Turning back towards him, a sly smile plays on my lips. "Ah, so you are interested after all."

"Yes. Still, why should I trust you to do as you say?" He questions.

Laura disables the force field as I speed to his cage. Grasping Abel by the throat and pulling him close, my eyes locked with his. "You shouldn't," I reply coldly. "Now, Laura!" I command.

Laura chants in a foreign dialect, her blue-green eyes flashing with pleasure as red lights swirl around Abel.

"What are you doing?" he asks.

"Death is too good for you. Death is too easy. I want you to suffer the way I have for the past twenty-something years. You stole the love of my life from me, so you are plagued to watch your love, Aika, die over and over and over again."

His eyebrows snap together. "What do you mean?"

"You'll be stuck in a time loop for eternity, watching Aika repeatedly die, each time feeling the pain and loss as if it were the first. Enjoy your eternal torment, Abel," I beam with satisfaction.

"Wait, no, no, let's not be too hasty...Brother. Come on. Jacobson. Jacobson! Jacobson!"

"Goodbye, Abel," I say, turning away from him. "May your eternity be filled with the suffering you deserve."

He clutches the cage bars and presses his face against it, "Jacobson!" he shouts. "Jacobson! Jacobson! You cannot do this! Noooo!" His voice echoes, growing louder as it shifts to shouts of agony.

"The spell is working," Laura says, her auburn hair swaying back and forth.

A small smile forms on my lips. "Yes, it seems your spell is taking effect quite nicely," I reply.

Abel will spend the rest of his life reliving the death of his wife, Aika Ronin.

The fate only a man like him deserves.

The End.

Akira & Troy

Thank you for reading Akira and Troy's story.

If you enjoyed this, please consider leaving a review on Amazon, Bookbub, Goodreads, or anywhere you can. Reviews help other readers find good books!

Thank you. ♥

Amazon Link for review:
https://a.co/d/46rIxnQ

Goodreads Link for review:

https://www.goodreads.com/book/show/195716603-bright-a-forbidden-love-story

Thank you for purchasing this novel! I hope you have enjoyed my story as much as I enjoyed writing it.

Let's be friends!

I enjoy connecting with my readers and would love to hear from you.

Please find me on any of the social media platforms below.

Instagram: www.instagram.com/kcminspired_author

My Broadcasting Channel on Instagram:

https://ig.me/j/AbbtqGM3rQEE4wwD/

Facebook: www.facebook.com/kcmcmillianauthor

Join my Facebook Group:

https://www.facebook.com/groups/931639820833941/

TikTok: www.tiktok.com/@kcminspired_author

GR: www.goodreads.com/author/show/22481124.K_C_McMillian

- Seventeen Magic is Real Part I. novella is available now. You can scan the QR code to check it out.

- Earth Magic is Real Part II. Coming soon.
- The Forbidden Fruit
  Tales of the Remi Clan
  (The Nosis Series) 18+ and older (TBA)
- My Christmas Love: A Second Chance Romance Novella
  18+ and older (TBA)
- Fire & Ice
  The Toussaint Sisters (TBA)

Acknowledgments

I have learned a great deal from the book world and writing Bright's second edition. I would like to thank my ARC readers for their constructive criticism and honesty. Putting a story on paper took courage and determination. Drafting this book was extremely challenging since I have two children under five years old and a full-time job. Not to mention my mental health, but the words of encouragement from others helped me through this process.

To my husband, Troy McMillian, thank you for believing in me. Thank you for being the inspiration behind Troy Bishop's character.

I would like to thank my wonderful friend, Shalinie Rohit, for all the advice and encouraging words during the process. (Thank you so much for going through this process once again.) Thank you for being my second pair of eyes and for your insight. The friendship we have built over the years is appreciated. Thank you for being the inspiration behind my character "Shelly."

To Amy Sobel, girl, you are amazing! Thank you for your love and immeasurable support, from our venting sessions to your great advice. I cannot thank you enough. You are still sticking with me; it means so much to me. Thank you for inspiring my wonderful character, Amy Jun.

I love you all!

To my fantastic author friend Louise Davis, thank you so much for your kindness and helpful advice. I really don't know what I would have done without your assistance. Words aren't enough to express my gratitude.

Last, I would like to thank you for purchasing Bright, and I hope you have enjoyed reading my story as much as I loved writing it.

When Kiana "K.C." McMillian was a child, she would make up stories in her head and write them down. While attending high school, her favorite play was Romeo and Juliette, and she enjoyed reading it, but she sometimes fumbled over her words while reading in front of her classmates. And, of course, children can be cruel. Kiana didn't like being made fun of and lacked confidence in herself, and she felt that if she couldn't read in front of a crowd, then perhaps she wasn't good enough to write. She didn't think her stories would be well received and feared failing at something she loved. Kiana knew back then that she would one day want to share her imagination with others, but she wasn't sure about putting herself out there.

Fast forward twenty years later, after the death of her husband's grandmother on January 13th, 2022, she decided she wouldn't let the fear of failure hinder her from following her dreams. Before "Gran," as she and her husband called her, left this earth, she said, "I have lived my life, and I've done everything I

◆ 471 ◆

wanted to do; I'm ready." K.C. knew that if her life suddenly came to a tragic end, she wouldn't be satisfied. That statement inspired her, and she decided to follow her dream of becoming an author.